W9-BFP-927

COULD YOU SURVIVE

without food or water, light, power or transportation, while completely surrounded by deadly radiation?

Would you react with helpless, trembling paralysis? Or would you have the courage and ingenuity to invent a new way of life?

COULD YOU SURVIVE AN H-BOMB ATTACK
AS THE PEOPLE IN THIS NOVEL DO?

"Enthralling and vivid . . . we are made to live in the very presence of dreadful happenings and understand what a nuclear catastrophe would do to America."
—Chicago Tribune

Bantam Science Fiction
Ask your bookseller for the books you have missed

Alas, Babylon
by Pat Frank

*This low-priced Bantam Book
has been completely reset in a type face
designed for easy reading, and was printed
from new plates. It contains the complete
text of the original hard-cover edition.*
NOT ONE WORD HAS BEEN OMITTED.

RLI: $\dfrac{\text{VLM } 6.0}{\text{IL } 9\text{–}12}$

ALAS, BABYLON

*A Bantam Book / published by arrangement with
J. B. Lippincott Company*

PRINTING HISTORY
Lippincott edition published March 1959
2nd printing .... April 1959
3rd printing .... June 1959
Bantam edition / March 1960

2nd printing ..... March 1960	*6th printing ..... August 1961*
3rd printing ..... March 1960	*7th printing .... October 1961*
4th printing .... October 1960	*8th printing .... March 1962*
5th printing ... February 1961	*9th printing .... October 1962*
10th printing .... January 1963	

Bantam Pathfinder edition / May 1964

12th printing ...... June 1964	*22nd printing ...... June 1971*
13th printing ..... March 1965	*23rd printing . September 1971*
14th printing ... January 1966	*24th printing ... January 1972*
15th printing ... October 1966	*25th printing ...... July 1972*
16th printing ...... May 1967	*26th printing ..... August 1972*
17th printing . September 1968	*27th printing ... October 1972*
18th printing ..... April 1969	*28th printing ... January 1973*
19th printing .... August 1969	*29th printing ..... August 1974*
20th printing .. February 1970	*30th printing . November 1974*
21st printing ...... July 1970	*31st printing . September 1975*

New Bantam edition / August 1976

All rights reserved.
Copyright © 1959 by Pat Frank.
*This book may not be reproduced in whole or in part, by
mimeograph or any other means, without permission.
For information address: J. B. Lippincott Company,
E. Washington Square, Philadelphia, Pennsylvania 19105.*

ISBN 0-553-02923-1

Published simultaneously in the United States and Canada

*Bantam Books are published by Bantam Books, Inc. Its trade-
mark, consisting of the words "Bantam Books" and the por-
trayal of a bantam, is registered in the United States Patent
Office and in other countries. Marca Registrada. Bantam
Books, Inc., 666 Fifth Avenue, New York, New York 10019.*

PRINTED IN THE UNITED STATES OF AMERICA

FOREWORD

I have an acquaintance, a retired manufacturer, a practical man, who has recently become worried about international tensions, intercontinental missiles, H-bombs, and such.

One day, knowing that I had done some writing on military subjects, he asked: "What do you think would happen if the Russkies hit us when we weren't looking—you know, like Pearl Harbor?"

The subject was on my mind. I had recently returned from a magazine assignment at Offutt Field, Headquarters of the Strategic Air Command, several SAC operational bases, and the Missile Test Center on Cape Canaveral. More to the point, I had been discussing just such a possibility with several astute British staff officers. The British have lived under the shadow of nuclear-armed rockets longer than we. Also, they have a vivid memory of cities devastated from the skies, as have the Germans and Japanese.

A man who has been shaken by a two-ton blockbuster has a frame of reference. He can equate the impact of an H-bomb with his own experience, even though the H-bomb blast is a million times more powerful than the shock he endured. To someone who has never felt a bomb, bomb is only a word. An H-bomb's fireball is something you see on television. It is not something that incinerates you to a cinder in the thousandth part of a second. So the H-bomb is beyond the imagination of all but a few Americans, while the British, Germans, and Japanese can comprehend it, if vaguely. And only the Japanese have personal understanding of atomic heat and radiation.

It was a big question. I gave him a horseback opinion, which proved conservative compared with some of the official forecasts published later. I said, "Oh, I think they'd kill fifty or sixty million Americans—but I think we'd win the war."

He thought this over and said, "Wow! Fifty or sixty million dead! What a depression that would make!"

I doubt if he realized the exact nature and extent of the depression—which is why I am writing this book.

PAT FRANK

[1]

In Fort Repose, a river town in Central Florida, it was said that sending a message by Western Union was the same as broadcasting it over the combined networks. This was not entirely true. It was true that Florence Wechek, the manager, gossiped. Yet she judiciously classified the personal intelligence that flowed under her plump fingers, and maintained a prudent censorship over her tongue. The scandalous and the embarrassing she excised from her conversation. Sprightly, trivial, and harmless items she passed on to friends, thus enhancing her status and relieving the tedium of spinsterhood. If your sister was in trouble, and wired for money, the secret was safe with Florence Wechek. But if your sister bore a legitimate baby, its sex and weight would soon be known all over town.

Florence awoke at six-thirty, as always, on a Friday in early December. Heavy, stiff and graceless, she pushed herself out of bed and padded through the living room into the kitchen. She stumbled onto the back porch, opened the screen door a crack, and fumbled for the milk carton on the stoop. Not until she straightened did her china-blue eyes begin to discern movement in the hushed gray world around her. A jerky-tailed squirrel darted out on the longest limb of her grapefruit tree. Sir Percy, her enormous yellow cat, rose from his burlap couch behind the hot water heater, arched his back, stretched, and rubbed his shoulders on her flannel robe. The African lovebirds rhythmically swayed, heads pressed together, on the swing in their cage. She addressed the lovebirds: "Good morning, Anthony. Good morning, Cleo."

Their eyes, spectacularly ringed in white, as if

1

embedded in mint Life Savers, blinked at her. Anthony shook his green and yellow plumage and rasped a greeting. Cleo said nothing. Anthony was adventurous, Cleo timid. On occasion Anthony grew raucous and irascible and Florence released him into limitless freedom outside. But always, at dusk, Anthony waited in the Turk's-cap, or atop the frangipani, eager to fly home. So long as Cleo preferred comfortable and sheltered imprisonment, Anthony would remain a domesticated parrot. That's what they'd told her when she bought the birds in Miami a month before, and apparently it was true.

Florence carried their cage into the kitchen and shook fresh sunflower seed into their feeder. She filled Sir Percy's bowl with milk, and crumpled a bit of wafer for the goldfish in the bowl on the counter. She returned to the living room and fed the angelfish, mollies, guppies, and vivid neons in the aquarium. She noted that the two miniature catfish, useful scavengers, were active. She was checking the tank's temperature, and its electric filter and heater, when the percolator chuckled its call to breakfast. At seven, exactly, Florence switched on the television, turned the knob to Channel 8, Tampa, and sat down to her orange juice and eggs. Her morning routine was unvaried and efficient. The only bad parts of it were cooking for one and eating alone. Yet breakfast was not her loneliest meal, not with Anthony ogling and gabbling, the six fat goldfish dancing a dreamy oriental ballet on diaphanous fins, Sir Percy rubbing against her legs under the table, and her cheery friends on the morning show, hired, at great expense, to inform and entertain her.

As soon as she saw Dave's face, Florence could sense whether the news was going to be good or bad. On this morning Dave looked troubled, and sure enough, when he began to give the news, it was bad. The Russians had sent up another Sputnik, No. 23, and something sinister was going on in the Middle East. Sputnik No. 23 was the largest yet, according to the Smithsonian Institution, and was radioing continuous and elaborate coded signals. "There is reason to believe," Frank said, "that

Sputniks of this size are equipped to observe the terrain of the earth below."

Florence gathered her pink flannel robe closer to her neck. She glanced up, apprehensively, through the kitchen window. All she saw were hibiscus leaves dripping in the pre-dawn ground fog, and blank gray sky beyond. They had no right to put those Sputniks up there to spy on people. As if it were on his mind also, Frank continued:

"Senator Holler, of the Armed Services Committee, yesterday joined others of a Midwest bloc in demanding that the Air Force shoot down Sputniks capable of military espionage if they violate U.S. air space. The Kremlin has already had something to say about this. Any such action, the Kremlin says, will be regarded the same as an attack on a Soviet vessel or aircraft. The Kremlin pointed out that the United States has traditionally championed the doctrine of Freedom of the Seas. The same freedom, says the Soviet statement, applies to outer space."

The newsman paused, looked up, and half-smiled in wry amusement at this complexity. He turned a page on his clipboard.

"There is a new crisis in the Middle East. A report from Beirut, via Cairo, says that Syrian tanks of the most modern Russian design have crossed the Jordanian frontier. This is undoubtedly a threat to Israel. At the same time Damascus charges that Turkish troops are mobilizing. . . ."

Florence flipped to Channel 6, Orlando, and country music. She did not understand, and could not become interested in, the politics of the Middle East. Sputniks seemed a closer and more personal menace. Her best friend Alice Cooksey, the librarian, claimed to have seen a Sputnik one evening at twilight. If you could see it, then it could see you. She stared up through the window again. No Sputnik. She rinsed the dishes and returned to her bedroom.

As she wrestled with her girdle, Florence's thought gravitated to the equally prying behavior of Randy

Bragg. She adjusted the venetian blinds until she could peer out. He was at it again. There he was, brazenly immodest in checked red and black pajamas, sitting on his front steps, knees akimbo and binoculars pressed to his eyes. Although he was perhaps seventy-five yards distant, she was certain he stared directly at her, and could see through the tilted louvers. She ducked back against the bedroom wall, hands protecting her breasts.

Almost every evening for the past three weeks, and on a number of mornings, she had caught him at it. Sometimes he was on the piazza, as now, sometimes at a second-floor window, and sometimes high up on the captain's walk. Sometimes he swept the whole of River Road with his glasses, pretending an interest elsewhere, but more often he focused on her bungalow. Randolph Rowzee Bragg a Peeping Tom! It was shocking!

Long before Florence's mother moved south and built the brown-shingle bungalow, the Braggs had lived in the big house, ungainly and monolithic, with tall Victorian windows and bellying bays and broad brick chimneys. Once it had been the show place of River Road. Now, it appeared shabby and outmoded compared with the long, low, antiseptic citadels of glass, metal, and tinted block constructed by rich Northerners who for the past fifteen years had been "discovering" the Timucuan River. Still, the Bragg house was planked and paneled with native cypress, and encased in pine clapboard, hard as iron, that might last another hundred years. Its grove, at this season like a full green cloak flecked with gold, trailed all the way from back yard to river bank, a quarter mile. And she would say this for Randy, his grounds were well kept, bright with poinsettias and bougainvillea, hibiscus, camellias, gardenias, and flame vine. Florence had known Randolph's mother, Gertrude Bragg, well, and old Judge Bragg to speak to. She had watched Randolph graduate from bicycle to jalopy, vanish for a number of years in college and law school, reappear in a convertible, vanish again during the Korean War, and finally come home for good when Judge Bragg and Mrs. Bragg were taken in the same year. Now here was Randy, one of the best known and most eligible young men in Tumucuan County, even if he did run around with Pistolville girls and drink too much, a—what was it the French called it?—a *voyeur*. It was disgusting. The things that went on in small towns, people wouldn't believe. Florence faced the bureau mirror, wondering how much he had seen.

Many years ago a man had told her she looked something like Clara Bow. Thereafter, Florence wore her hair in bangs, and didn't worry too much about her chubby figure. The man, an imaginative idealist, had gone to England in 1940, joined the Commandos, and got himself killed. She retained only a vague and inexact memory of his caresses, but she could never forget how he had compared her to Clara Bow, a movie star. She could still see a resemblance, provided she sucked in her stomach and lifted her chin high to erase the fleshy creases in her neck—except her hair was no longer like Clara's. Her hair had thinned, and faded to mottled pink. She hurriedly sketched a Clara Bow pout on her lips, and finished dressing.

When she stepped out of the front door, Florence didn't know whether she should cut Randy dead or give him a piece of her mind. He was still there on the steps, the binoculars in his lap. He waved, grinned, and called across lawn and road, "Morning, Miss Florence." His black hair was tousled, his teeth white, and he looked boyish, handsome, and inoffensive.

"Good morning, Randy," Florence said. Because of the distance, she had to shout, so her voice was not formal and frigid, as she had intended.

"You look real pretty and chipper today," he yelled.

She walked to the carport, head averted as if avoiding a bad odor, her stiff carriage a reprimand, and did not answer. He really was nervy, sitting there in those vile pajamas, trying to sweet-talk her. All the way to town, she kept thinking of Randy. Who would ever guess that he was a deviate with a compulsion to watch women dress and undress? He ought to be arrested. But if she told the sheriff, or anybody, they would only laugh at her. Everybody knew that Randy dated lots of girls, and not all of them virgins. She herself had seen him take Rita Hernandez, that little Minorcan tart from Pistolville, into his house and, no doubt, up to his bedroom since the lights had gone on upstairs and off downstairs. And there had been others, recently a tall blonde who drove her own car, a new Imperial with Ohio plates, into the circular driveway and right up to the front steps as if she owned the place, and Randy. Nobody would believe that he found it necessary to absorb his sex at long range through optic nerves and binoculars. Yet it was strange that he had not married. It was strange that he lived alone in that wooden mausoleum. He even had his office in there, instead of in the Professional Building like the other lawyers. He was a hermit, and a snob, and a nigger-lover, and no better than a pervert. God knows what he did with those girls upstairs. Maybe all he did was make them take off their clothes and put them on again while he watched. She had heard of such things. And yet—

She couldn't make herself believe there was anything basically wrong with Randy. She had voted for him in the primaries and stood up for him at the meetings of the Frangipani Circle when those garden club biddies were pecking him to bits. After all, he was a Bragg, and a neighbor, and besides—

He obviously needed help and guidance. Randy's age, she knew, was thirty-two. Florence was forty-seven. Between people in their thirties and forties there wasn't too wide a gap. Perhaps all he needed, she decided, was a little understanding and tenderness from a mature woman.

Randy watched Florence's ten-year-old Chevy diminish and disappear down the tunnel of live oaks that arched River Road. He liked Florence. She might be a gossipy old maid but she was probably one of the few people on River Road who had voted for him. Now she was acting as if he were a stranger trying to cash a money order without credentials. He wondered why. Maybe she disapproved of Lib McGovern, who had been in and out of the house a good deal in the last few weeks.

What Florence needed, he guessed, was the one thing she was unlikely to get, a man. He rose, stretched, and glanced up at the bronze weathercock on the garage steeple. Its beak pointed resolutely northeast. He checked the large, reliable marine barometer and its twin thermometer alongside the front door. Pressure 30.17, up twenty points in twelve hours. Temperature sixty-two. It would be clear and warm and the bass might start hitting off the end of the dock. He whistled, and shouted, "Graf! Hey, Graf!" Leaves rustled under the azalea bed and a long nose came out, followed by an interminable length of dachshund. Graf, his red coat glistening and tail whipping, bounded up the steps, supple as a seal. "Come on, my short-legged friend," Randy said, and went inside, binoculars swinging from his neck, for his second cup of coffee, the cup with the bourbon in it.

Except for the library, lined with his father's law books, and the gameroom, Randy rarely used the first floor. He had converted one wing of the second floor into an apartment suitable in size to a bachelor, and to his own taste. His taste meant living with as little exertion and strain as possible. His wing contained an office, a living room, a combination bar and kitchen alcove, and bedroom and bath. The décor was haphazard, designed for his ease, not a guest's eye. Thus he slept in an outsize mahogany sleigh bed imported from New England by some remote ancestor, but it was equipped with foam rubber mattress and contour nylon sheets. When, in boredom, he wasted an evening preparing a full meal for himself, he ate from Staffordshire bearing the Bragg crest, and with silver from Paul Storr, and by candlelight; but he laid his place on the formica bar separating living room from efficient kitchen. Now he sat on a stool at this bar, half-filled a fat mug with steaming coffee, dropped two lumps of sugar into it, and laced it with an inch of bourbon. He sipped his mixture greedily. It warmed him, all the way down.

Randy didn't remember, exactly, when he had started taking a drink or two before breakfast. Dan Gunn, his

best friend and probably the best medic north of Miami,
said it was an unhealthy practice and the hallmark of an
alcoholic. Not that Dan had reprimanded him. Dan had
just advised him to be careful, and not let it become a
habit. Randy knew he wasn't an alcoholic because an
alcoholic craved liquor. He never craved it. He just
drank for pleasure and the most pleasurable of all
drinks was the first one on a crisp winter morning. Besides, when you took it with coffee that made it part of
breakfast, and therefore not so depraved. He guessed he
had started it during the campaign, when he had been
forced to load his stomach with fried mullet, hush pup-
pies, barbecued ribs dripping fat, chitlins, roasted oys-
ters gritty with sand, and to wash all down with warm
beer and raw rotgut. After such nights, only mellow
bourbon could clear his head and launch him on another day. Bourbon had buoyed him during the campaign, and now bourbon mercifully clouded its memory.
He could have beaten Porky Logan, certainly, except
for one small tactical error. Randy had been making his
first speech, at Pasco Creek, a cow town in the north
end of the county, when somebody shouted, "Hey,
Randy, where do y' stand on the Supreme Court?"

He had known this question must come, but he had
not framed the right kind of answer: the moderate
Southern quasi-liberal, semi-segregationist double-talk
that would have satisfied everybody except the palmetto
scrub woolhats, the loud-mouthed Kluxers and courthouse whittlers who would vote for Porky anyway, and
the Georgia and Alabama riffraff crowding the Minorcans for living space in the shanties and three-room
bungalows of Pistolville. The truth was that Randolph
Bragg himself was torn by the problem, recognizing its
dangers and complexities. He had certain convictions.
He had served in Korea and Japan and he knew that
the battle for Asia was being lost in counties like Timucuan. He also knew that Pasco Creek had no interest in
Asia. He believed integration should start in Florida,
but it must begin in the nursery schools and kindergar-
tens and would take a generation. This was all difficult
to explain, but he did voice his final conviction, ines-

capable because of his legal heritage and training, and the oaths he had taken as voter and soldier. He said: "I believe in the Constitution of the United States—all of it."

There had been snickers and snorts from the rim of the crowd, and his listeners, except for the reporters from Tampa, Orlando, and the county weekly, had drifted away. In later speeches, elsewhere, he attempted to explain his position, but it was hopeless. Behind his back he was called a fool and a traitor to his state and his race. Randolph Rowzee Bragg, whose great-grandfather had been a United States Senator, whose grandfather had been chosen by President Wilson to represent his country as Minister Plenipotentiary and Envoy Extraordinary in time of war, whose father had been elected, without opposition, to half a dozen offices, Randolph was beaten five-to-one in the Democratic primaries for nomination to the state legislature. It was worse than defeat. It was humiliation, and Randy knew he could never run for public office again. He refilled his mug, this time with more bourbon than coffee, and Missouri, his maid, shuffled in the hallway and knocked. He called, "Come in, Mizzoo."

Missouri opened the door, pushing a vacuum cleaner and carrying a pail filled with cans, bottles and rags. Missouri was the wife of Two-Tone Henry, neighbor as well as maid. She was six inches shorter than Two-Tone, who was just Randy's height, five-eleven, but Two-Tone claimed she outweighed him by a hundred pounds. If this was true, Missouri weighed around two-forty. But on this morning, it seemed to Randy that she had dwindled a bit. "You dieting, Mizzoo?" he said.

"No, sir, I'm not dietin'. I got nerves."

"Nerves!" Missouri had always seemed nerveless, solid, and placid as a broad, deeply rooted tree. "Two-Tone been giving you a bad time again?"

"No. Two-Tone been behavin'. He down on the dock fishin' right now. To tell you the truth, Mister Randy, it's Mrs. McGovern. She follow me around with white gloves."

Missouri worked two hours each morning for Randy,

and the rest of the day for the McGoverns, who lived
half a mile closer to town. The McGoverns were the W.
Foxworth McGoverns, the Central Tool and Plate
McGoverns, formerly of Cleveland, and the parents of
Lib McGovern, whose proper name was Elizabeth.
"What do you mean, Mizzoo?" Randy asked, fasci-
nated.

"After I dust, she follow me around with white gloves
to see has I dusted. I know I cleans clean, Mister
Randy."

"You sure do, Mizzoo."

Missouri plugged in the vacuum cleaner, started it,
and then shut it off. She had more on her mind. "That
ain't all. You been in that house, Mister Randy. You
ever seen so many ashtrays?"

"What's wrong with ashtrays?"

"She don't allow no ashes in 'em. That poor Mister
McGovern, he has to smoke his cigars outside. Then
there was that roach. Big roach in the silver drawer.
Mrs. McGovern opened that drawer yesterday and saw
that roach and screeched like she'd been hit by a scor-
pion. She made me go through every drawer in the
kitchen and dining room and put down fresh paper.
Was that roach sent me to Doctor Gunn yesterday. Mrs.
McGovern she can't 'bide bugs or little green lizards
and she won't go out of the house after dark for fear of
snakes. I don't think the McGoverns going to be with us
long, Mister Randy, because what's Florida except bugs
and lizards and snakes? I think they leave around May,
when bug season starts good. But Miss McGovern, she
won't want to leave. She stuck on you."

"What makes you think so?"

Missouri smiled. "Questions she asks. Like what you
eats for breakfast." Missouri glanced at the decanter on
the bar. "And who cooks for you. And does you have
other girls."

Randy changed the subject. "You say you went to
see Doctor Gunn. What'd he say?"

"Doctor says I'm a complicated case. He says I got
high blood, on account of I'm heavy. He says it's good
I'm losin' weight, because that lowers the high blood,

but frettin' about Mrs. McGovern white-glovin' me is the wrong way to do it. He says quit eatin' grits, eat greens. Quit pork, eat fish. And he gives me tranquil pills to take, one each day before I go to work for Mrs. McGovern."

"You do that, Mizzoo," Randy said, and, carrying his mug, walked out on to the screen upstairs porch overlooking grove and river. He then climbed the narrow ship's ladder that led to the captain's walk, a rectangle sixteen by eight feet, stoutly planked and railed, on the slate roof. Reputedly, this was the highest spot in Timucuan County. From it he could see all the riverfront estates, docks, and boats, and all of the town of Fort Repose, three miles downstream, held in a crook of sun-flecked silver where the Timucuan joined the broader St. Johns.

This was his town, or had been. In 1838, during the Seminole Wars, a Lieutenant Randolph Rowzee Peyton, USN, a Virginian, had been dispatched to this river junction with a force of eighteen Marines and two small brass cannon. Lieutenant Peyton journeyed south from Cow's Ford, its name patriotically changed to Jacksonville, by longboat. His orders from General Clinch were to throttle Indian communications on the rivers, thus protecting the flank of the troops moving down the east coast from St. Augustine. Lieutenant Peyton built a blockhouse of palm logs on the point, his guns covering the channel. In two years, except during one relief expedition overland to New Smyrna, he fought no battles or skirmishes. But he shot game and caught fish for the garrison pot, and studied botany and the culture of citrus. The balmy weather and idyllic life, described in a log now in a teak chest in Randy Bragg's office, inspired the Lieutenant to name his outpost Fort Repose.

When the wars subsided, the fort was decommissioned and Lieutenant Peyton was assigned to sea duty. Four years later he returned to Fort Repose with a wife, a daughter, and a grant from the government for one hundred acres. He had picked this precise spot for his homestead because it was the highest ground in the area, with a steep gradient to the river, ideal for planting the oranges just imported from Spain and the Far East. Peyton's original house had burned. The present house had been built by his son-in-law, the first Marcus Bragg, a native of Philadelphia and a lawyer eventually sent to the Senate. The captain's walk had been added for the aging Lieutenant Peyton, so that with his brass spyglass he could observe what happened at the junction of rivers.

Now the Bragg holdings had dwindled to thirty-six acres, but thirty were planted in prime citrus—navels, mandarins, Valencias, and Temples—all tended and sold in season by the county co-operative. Each year Randy received checks totaling eight to ten thousand dollars from the co-operative. Half went to his older brother, Mark, an Air Force colonel stationed at Offutt Field, Headquarters of the Strategic Air Command, near Omaha. With his share, plus dividends from a trust established by his father, and his occasional fees as an attorney, Randy lived comfortably. Since he drove a new car and paid his bills promptly, the tradespeople of Fort Repose thought him well-to-do. The rich newcomers classed him with the genteel poor.

Randy heard music below, and knew that Missouri had started his record player and therefore was waxing the floor. Missouri's method was to spread the wax, kick off her shoes, wrap her feet in rags, and then polish by dancing. This was probably as efficient, and certainly more fun, than using the electric waxer.

He dropped into a deck chair and focused his binoculars on Preacher Henry's place, looking for that damn bird in the hammock of pines, palmettos, and scrub oak. The Henrys had lived here as long as the Braggs, for the original Henry had come as slave and manservant to Lieutenant Peyton. Now the Henrys owned a four-acre enclave at the east boundary of the Bragg groves. Preacher Henry's father had bought it from Randolph's grandfather for fifty dollars an acre long before the first boom, when land was valued only for what it grew. Preacher was hitching his mule, Balaam—the last mule in Timucuan County so far as anyone knew—to the disk. In this month Preacher harrowed for his yam and corn planting, while his wife, Hannah, picked and sold tomatoes and put up kumquat preserves. He ought to go down and talk to Preacher about that damn bird, Randy thought. If anyone was likely to observe and recognize a Carolina parakeet floating around, it was Preacher, because Preacher knew all the birds and their calls and habits. He shifted his glasses to focus on the end of the Henrys' rickety dock. Two-Tone had five bamboo poles out. Two-Tone himself reclined on his side, head resting on his hand, so he could watch the corks without effort. Preacher's younger son, Malachai, who was Randy's yardman, and reliable as Two-Tone was no-account, was not about.

Randy heard the phone ringing in his office. The music stopped and he knew Missouri was answering. Presently she called from the piazza, "Mister Randy, it's for you. It's Western Union."

"Tell her I'll be right down," Randy said, lifted himself out of the deck chair, and backed down the ladder, wondering who would be sending him a telegram. It wasn't his birthday. If something important happened, people phoned. Unless—he remembered that the Air Force sent telegrams when a man was hurt, or killed. But it wouldn't be Mark, because for two years Mark had been flying a desk. Still, Mark would get in his flying time each month, if possible, for the extra pay.

He took the phone from Missouri's hand and braced himself. "Yes?" he said.

"I have a telegram, Randy—it's really a cable—from San Juan, Puerto Rico. It's signed by Mark. It's really very peculiar."

Randy let out his breath, relieved. If Mark had sent the message, then Mark was all right. A man can't pick his relatives, only his friends, but Mark had always been Randy's friend as well as brother. "What's the message say?"

"Well, I'll read it to you," Florence said, "and then if you want me to read it again I'll be glad to. It says, 'Urgent you meet me at Base Ops McCoy noon today. Helen and children flying to Orlando tonight. Alas, Babylon.'" Florence paused. "That's what it says, 'Alas,

Babylon.' Do you want me to repeat the whole thing for you, Randy?"

"No thanks."

"I wonder what 'Alas, Babylon' means? Isn't it out of the Bible?"

"I don't know. I guess so." He knew very well what it meant. He felt sick inside.

"There's something else, Randy."

"Yes?"

"Oh, it's nothing. I'll tell you about it next time I see you—and I hope not in those loud pajamas. Goodbye, Randy. You're sure you have the message?"

"I'm sure," he said, hung up and dropped into the swivel chair. Alas, Babylon was a private, a family signal. When they were boys, he and Mark used to sneak up to the back of the First Afro-Repose Baptist Church on Sunday nights to hear Preacher Henry calling down hell-fire and damnation on the sinners in the big cities. Preacher Henry always took his text out of the Revelation of St. John. It seemed that he ended every lurid verse with, "Alas, Babylon!" in a voice so resonant you could feel it, if you rested your fingertips gently on the warped pine boards of the church. Randy and Mark would crouch under the rear window, behind the pulpit, fascinated and wide-eyed, while Preacher Henry described the Babylonian revels, including fornication. Sometimes Preacher Henry made Babylon sound like Miami, and sometimes like Tampa, for he condemned not only fornication—he read the word right out of the Bible—but also horse racing and the dog tracks. Randy could hear him yet: "And I'm telling you right now, all wife-swappers, whisky-drinkers, and crap-shooters are going to get it! And all them who come out of those sin palaces on the beach, whether they be called hotels or motels, wearing minks and jewels and not much else, they's goin' to get it! And them fast-steppers in Cadillacs and yaller roadsters, they is going to get it! Just like it says here in the Good Book, that Great City that was clothed in fine linen, and purple, and scarlet, and decked with gold and precious stones and pearls, that

Great City was burned off the face of the earth in an hour. Just one hour Alas, Babylon!"

Either Preacher Henry was too old, or the Afro-Repose congregation had tired of his scolding and awful prophecies, for he no longer preached except on those Sundays when Afro-Repose's new minister, a light-skinned college graduate, was out of town. Randy and Mark never forgot Preacher Henry's thundering, and from it they borrowed their private synonym for disaster, real or comic, past or future. If one fell off the dock, or lost all his cash at poker, or failed to make time with a promising Pistolville piece, or announced that hurricane or freeze was on the way, the other commiserated with, "Alas, Babylon!"

But in this telegram it had very special and exact meaning. Mark had secured leave at Christmas season last year, and flown down with Helen and the two children, Ben Franklin and Peyton, for a week. On their last evening at Fort Repose, after the others were in bed, Mark and Randy had sat here, in this office, peering into the bourbon decanter and the deep anxieties of their hearts, trying to divine the future. Christmas had been a time of troubles, a time of confusions at home and tensions abroad, but in his whole life, Randy could recall no other sort of time. There had always been depression, or war, or threat of war.

Mark, who was in SAC Intelligence, had rolled the old-fashioned globe, three feet through, from its place in the window bay, so that the desk lamp shone on it. It was a globe purchased by their grandfather, the diplomat, before the First World War, so that the countries, some with unfamiliar names, seemed oddly scrambled. The continents and seas were the same, which was all that mattered. As Mark talked, his face became grave, almost gaunt, and his index finger traced great circle routes across the cracking surface—missile and bomber trajectories. He then drew a rough chart, with two lines that intersected. The line that continued upward after the intersection belonged to the Soviet Union, and the time of the intersection was right then.

"How did it happen?" Randy had asked. "Where did we slip?"

"It wasn't lack of money," Mark had replied. "It was state of mind. Chevrolet mentalities shying away from a space-ship world. Nations are like people. When they grow old and rich and fat they get conservative. They exhaust their energy trying to keep things the way they are—and that's against nature. Oh, the services were to blame too. Maybe even SAC. We designed the most beautiful bombers in the world, and built them by the thousands. We improved and modified them each year, like new model cars. We couldn't bear the thought that jet bombers themselves might be out of style. Right now we're in the position of the Federal Navy, with its wooden steam frigates, up against the Confederate iron-clad. It is a state of mind that money alone won't cure."

"What will?" Randy asked.

"Men. Men like John Ericsson to invent a *Monitor* to face the *Merrimac*. Bold men, audacious men, tenacious men. Impatient, odd-ball men like Rickover pounding desks for his atomic sub. Ruthless men who will fire the deadheads and ass-kissers. Rude men who will tell the unimaginative, business-as-usual, seven-carbon sons of bitches to go take a jump at a galloping goose. Young men because we've got to be a young country again. If we get that kind of men we may hack it—if the other side gives us time."

"Will they?"

Mark had spun the globe and shrugged. "I don't know. If I think the balloon is about to go up I'm going to send Helen and the kids down here. When a man dies, and his children die with him, then he is dead entirely, leaving nothing to show."

"Do you think they'd be safer here than in Omaha? After all, we've got the Jax Naval Air complex to the north of us, and Homestead and Miami to the south, and Eglin to the northwest, and MacDill and Tampa to the southwest, and the Missile Test Center on Canaveral to the east, and McCoy and Orlando right at the front door, only forty miles off. What about fallout?"

"There isn't any place that'll be absolutely safe. With

fallout and radiation, it'll be luck—the size of configuration of the weapons, altitude of the fireball, direction
of the wind. But I do know Helen and the children
won't have much chance in Omaha. SAC Headquarters
has got to be the enemy's number one target. I'll bet
they've programmed three five-megaton IC's for Offutt,
and since our house is eight miles from the base any
kind of near-miss does it—" Mark snapped his fingers—"like that. Not that I think it'll do the enemy any
good—command automatically shifts to other combat
control centers and anyway all our crews know their
targets. But they'll hit SAC Headquarters, hoping for
temporary paralysis. A little delay is all they'd need. I'll
have to be there, at Offutt, in the Hole, but the least a
man can do is give his children a chance to grow up,
and I think they'd have a better chance in Fort Repose
than Omaha. So if I see it's coming, and there is time,
I'll send Helen and the kids down here. And I'll try to
give you a warning, so you can get set for it."

"How?"

Mark smiled. "I won't call you up and say, 'Hey,
Randy, the Russians are about to attack us.' Phones
aren't secure, and I don't think my C-in-C, or the Air
Staff, would approve. But if you hear 'Alas, Babylon,'
you'll know that's it."

Randy had forgotten none of this talk. A week or so
later, thinking about Mark's words, Randy had decided
to go into politics. He would start in the state legislature, and in a few years be ready to run for Congress.
He'd be the kind of leader Mark wanted.

It hadn't worked out that way. He couldn't even beat
Porky Logan, a gross man whose vote could be bought
for fifty bucks, who bragged that he had not got beyond
the seventh grade but that he could get more new roads
and state money for Timucuan County than any half-
baked radical, undoubtedly backed by the burrheads
and the N.A.A.C.P., who didn't even know that the Supreme Court was controlled by Moscow. So Randy's fi-
asco had been inspired by that night, and now the night
bore something worse.

He wondered what Mark was doing in Puerto Rico,

and why his warning had come from there. It should have come from Washington or London or Omaha or Colorado Springs rather than San Juan. It was true that SAC had a big base, Ramey, in Puerto Rico, but—It was no use guessing. He'd know at noon. Of one thing he was certain, if Mark expected it to come, it would probably come. His brother was no alarmist. Randy sometimes allowed emotions to distort logic, Mark never did. Mark was capable of calculating odds, in war or poker, to the final decimal, which was why he was a Deputy Chief of Intelligence at SAC, and soon would have his star.

Randy knew there were a thousand things he should be doing, but he couldn't think of any of them. He became aware of a rhumba rhythm in the living room, and presently Missouri skated into view, feet bundled with waxing cloths, shoulders moving and hips bouncing with elephantine elegance, intent on her polishing. He yelled, "Missouri!"

"Yessir?" Her forward motion stopped, but her hips continued to wobble and feet shuffle.

"Quit that struttin' and make up the three bedrooms on the front. Colonel Bragg's family will be here tomorrow."

"Oh, ain't that nice! Just like last year."

"No, not like last year. The Colonel's not coming with them. Just Mrs. Bragg and Ben Franklin and Peyton."

Missouri peered through the door at him. "Mister Randy, you don't look good. Them telegrams are yellow death. You get bad news or something? Ain't nuthin' happen to Colonel Mark?"

"No. I'm driving over to McCoy to meet him at noon."

"Oh, that's good. How come the children up north get out of school so quick?"

"I don't know."

"I'll dust good, and make up the beds, and put towels and soaps in the bathrooms just like last year."

"Thanks, Mizzoo. That's fine."

"Caleb's going to be happy to see Ben Franklin,"

Missouri said. Caleb was Missouri's son, and just Ben's age, thirteen. Last year, Randy had let them take the boat out on the river, fishing, just as Randy, as a boy, had fished with Caleb's uncle, Malachai, except that twenty years ago the boat was a skiff, powered by muscle and oars, instead of a sleek Fiberglas job with a thirty-horse kicker.

Missouri gathered up her cleaning materials and left Randy alone with his nightmare. He shook his head, but he didn't wake up. The nightmare was real. Slowly, he forced his mind to function. Slowly, he forced himself to imagine the unimaginable. . . .

He must make a list of the things Helen and the children would need. He recalled that there was nothing stocked in the big kitchen downstairs, and little in the utility room except some steaks in the freezer and a few canned staples. My God, if there was going to be a war they'd need stocks of everything! He looked at his watch. He had yet to shave and dress, and he must allow an hour and a half for the drive to McCoy, ten miles south of Orlando, when you considered the main highways clogged with tourists, and Orlando's infuriating and hopeless traffic tangle on a sunny payday less than three weeks before Christmas. And there might be some delay at the McCoy gate. He decided to give himself two hours on the road.

Still, he could start the list, and there was one thing he should do right away. Ben Franklin drank a quart of milk a day and Peyton, his eleven-year-old sister, even more. He telephoned Golden Dew Dairy and revised his delivery order drastically upward. This was Randy's first act to meet the emergency, and it was to prove the least useful.

[2]

Randy left the house in time to see Missouri wedge herself under the wheel of the Henrys' Model-A Ford, an antique—so certified with a "Q" tag issued by the state—but kept in perfect running order by Malachai's mechanical ingenuity. "I haven't finished but I got to go now," she said. "Mrs. McGovern, she holds the clock on me. I'll be back tomorrow."

The Model-A, listing to port with Missouri's weight, bounced down the pebbled driveway. Randy got into his new Bonneville. It was a sweet car, a compromise between a sports job and a hardtop, long, low, very fast, and a lot of fun, even though its high-compression engine drank premium fuel in quantity.

At eleven, approaching Orlando on Route 50, he turned on the radio for the news. Turkey had appealed to the UN for an investigation of border penetrations by Syria. Syria charged Israel with planning a preventive war. Israel accused Egypt of sending snooper planes over its defenses. Egypt claimed its ships, bound from the Black Sea to Alexandria, were being delayed in the Straits, and charged Turkey with a breach of the Montreux Convention.

Russia accused Turkey and the United States of plotting to crush Syria, and warned France, Italy, Greece, and Spain that any nations harboring American bases would be involved in a general war, and erased from the earth.

The Secretary of State was somewhere over the Atlantic, bound for conferences in London.

The Soviet Ambassador to Washington had been recalled for consultation.

There were riots in France.

It all sounded bad, but familiar as an old, scratchy record. He had heard it all before, in almost the same words, back in '57 and '58. So why push the panic button? Mark could be wrong. He couldn't know, for certain, that the balloon was going up. Unless he knew something fresh, something that had not appeared in the newspapers, or been broadcast.

Shortly before noon Florence Wechek hung her "Back At One" sign on the office door and walked down Yulee Street to meet Alice Cooksey at the Pink Flamingo. Fridays, they always lunched together. Alice, tiny, drab in black and gray, an active, angry sparrow of a woman, arrived late. She hurried to Florence's table and said, "I'm sorry. I've just had a squabble with Kitty Offenhaus."

"Oh, dear!" Florence said. "Again?" Kitty was secretary of the PTA, past-president of the Frangipani Circle, treasurer of the Women's Club, and a member of the library board. Also, she was the wife of Luther "Bubba" Offenhaus, Chief Tail-Twister of the Lions Club, Vice President of the Chamber of Commerce, and Deputy Director of Civil Defense for the whole county. He owned the most properous business in town, the Offenhaus Mortuary, and a twin real estate development, Repose-in-Peace Park.

Alice lifted the menu. It fluttered. She set it down quickly and said, "Yes, again. I guess I'll have the tuna-fish salad."

"You should eat more, Alice," Florence said, noticing how white and pinched her friend's face looked. "What happened?"

"Kitty came in and said she'd heard rumors that we had books by Carl Rowan and Walter White. I told her the rumors were true, and did she want to borrow one?"

"What'd she say?" Florence put down her fork, no longer interested in her chicken patty.

"Said they were subversive and anti-South—she's a Daughter of the Confederacy—and ordered me to take them off the shelves. I told her that as long as I was librarian they would stay there. She said she was going to bring it before the board and if necessary take it up with Porky Logan. He's on the investigating committee in Tallahassee."

"Alice, you're going to lose your job!" Kitty Offenhaus was the most influential person in Fort Repose, with the exception of Edgar Quisenberry, who owned and ran the bank.

"I don't think so. I told her that if anything like that happened I'd call the *St. Petersburg Times* and *Tampa Tribune* and *Miami Herald* and they'd send reporters and photographers. I said, 'Kitty, can't you see your picture on the front page, and the headline—Undertaker's Wife Cremates Books?' "

This was the most fascinating news Florence had heard in weeks. "What happened then?"

"Nothing at all. If I may borrow an expression from one of my younger readers, she left in an eight-cylinder huff."

"You wouldn't really call the papers, would you?"

Alice spoke carefully, understanding fully that everything would soon be repeated. "I certainly would! But I don't think I'll have to. You see, publicity would hurt Bubba's business. One third of Bubba's customers are Negroes, and another third Yankees who come down here to live on their pensions and stay to die." She lifted her bright, fiercely blue eyes and added, as if repeating one of the Commandments: "Censorship and thought control can exist only in secrecy and darkness."

"And that was all?"

"That was all." Alice tried her salad. "What've you been doing, Florence?"

Florence could think of no adventure, or even any news culled from the wire, that could compete with telling off Kitty Offenhaus—except her experience with Randy Bragg. She had pledged herself not to say anything about Randy to anyone, but she could trust Alice, who was worldly-wise in spite of her appearance, and who might even, when younger, have encountered a Peeping Tom herself. So Florence told about Randy and his binoculars and how he had stared at her that morning. "It's almost unbelievable, isn't it?" she concluded.

"It is unbelievable," Alice said flatly.

"But I saw him at it!"

"I don't care. I know the Bragg boys. Even before you came here, Florence, I knew them. I knew Judge Bragg well, very well."

Florence remembered vague reports, many years back, of Alice Cooksey having gone with Judge Bragg before the judge married Gertrude. But that made no difference to what went on in the Bragg house now. "You'll have to admit that those Bragg boys are a little peculiar," Florence said. "You should have seen the cable Randy got from Mark this morning. Urgent they meet at McCoy today. Helen and the children flying to Orlando tonight—you know those children can't be out of school yet—and the last two words didn't make any sense at all. 'Alas, Babylon.' Isn't that crazy?"

"Those boys aren't crazy," Alice said. "They've always been bright boys. Full of hell, yes, but at least they could read, which is more then I can say for the children nowadays. Do you know that Randy read every history in the library before he was sixteen?"

"I don't think that has anything to do with his sex habits," Florence said. She leaned across the table and touched Alice's arm. "Alice, come out to my house tonight for the weekend. I want you to see for yourself."

"I can't. I keep the library open Saturdays. That's my only chance to get the young ones. Evenings and Sundays, they're paralyzed by TV."

"I'm open Saturday mornings, too, so we can drive in together. I'll pick you up when you're through tomorrow evening. It'll be a change for you, out in the country, away from that stuffy room."

Alice hesitated. It would be nice to visit with Florence, but she hated to accept favors she couldn't repay. She said, "Well, we'll see."

When Alice returned to the library, three old-timers, too old for shuffleboard or the Lawn Bowlers Club, were bent over the periodical table. Like mummies, she thought, partially unwrapped. One of the mummies leaned slowly over until his nose fell into the fold of *Cosmopolitan.* Alice walked over to the table and made certain he still breathed. She let him nap on, smiled at the other two, and darted into the reference room, with its towering, topheavy stacks. From the first stack, religious and spiritual works in steady demand, she brought down the King James Bible. She believed she would find the words in Revelation, and she did. She read two verses, lips moving, words murmuring in her throat:

And the kings of the earth, who have committed fornication and lived deliciously with her, shall bewail her, and lament for her, when they shall see the smoke of her burning,

Standing afar off for the fear of her torment, saying, Alas, alas, that great city Babylon, that mighty city! for in one hour is thy judgment come.

Alice put the Bible back on its shelf and walked, head down, to her cracked oak desk, like a schoolmarm's desk on a dais, in the main hallway. She sat there, staring at the green blotter, at the antiquated pen and the glass inkwell, at the wooden file filled with readers' cards, at the stack of publishers' spring lists. Alone of all the people in Fort Repose, Alice Cooksey knew Mark Bragg well enough, and had absorbed sufficient knowledge of the world's illness through the printed word, to understand that the books she had ordered from those spring lists might never be delivered. She had small fear of death, and of man none at all, but the formlessness of what was to come overwhelmed her. She always associated Babylon with New York, and she wished, now, that she lived on Manhattan, where one could die in a bright millisecond, without suffering, without risking the indignity of panic.

She picked up the telephone and called Florence. She would come out for the weekend, or even longer, if Florence was agreeable. When she set down the phone Alice felt steadier. If it came soon, she would have a friendly hand to hold. She would not be alone.

The Air Police sergeant at McCoy's main gate questioned Randy, and then allowed him to call Lieutenant Colonel Paul Hart, a squadron commander, and friend of Mark's. Hart had been to Fort Repose to fish for bass, first as Mark's guest, and later, on several occasions, as a guest of Randy, so he was something more than an acquaintance. Randy said he had had a wire from Mark to meet him at noon, and Hart said, "He whistled through here yesterday. Didn't expect him back so soon. Anyway, drive to Base Ops. We'll go out on the line and meet him together. Let me talk to the Air Police. I'll clear you through."

Driving through the base, Randy sensed a change since his last visit, the year before. Physically, McCoy looked the same. It felt different. The Air Police questioning had been sharper, and more serious. That wasn't the difference. He realized something was missing; and then he had it. Where were all the people? McCoy seemed almost deserted, with less activity, and fewer men and fewer cars than a year ago. He saw no other civilians. He saw no women, not even around the clubs and the BX. The most congested area on the base was the steps and lawn in front of the alert barracks opposite wing headquarters, where standby crewmen, rigid and stiff in pressure suits, talked and smoked. Trucks, tail gates down, were backed to the curb. Drivers slouched over their wheels as if they had been there a long time.

He drove onto Base Operations and parked close to the flight-line fence. Last year he had seen B-47's, tankers, and fat transports stretching their wings, tip to tip, the length of the line—miles. Now, their numbers had dwindled. He counted fewer than twenty B-47's, and guessed that the wing was in Africa or Spain or England on ninety-day foreign duty. But this could not be so, because Paul Hart, winner of bombing and navigation trophies, a Select Crew Aircraft Commander, would have led the flight.

Hart, a stocky, bandy-legged man with punched-in nose, a fighter's chin, and an easy grin, met him at the door of Operations. "Hi, Randy," he said. "Just checked the board. Mark will touch down in eight minutes. How's the fishing?"

"It's been lousy." He looked up at the wind sock. "But it'll get better if this high sticks around and the wind holds from the east. What's he flying?"

"He's not flying anything. He's riding soft and plush in a C-One-thirty-five—that's the transport version of our new jet tanker—with a lot of Offutt brass. Other brass, that is. I hear he gets his star soon. Only promotion I'll ever get is to a B-Five-eight."

"Penalty for being a hot pilot," Randy said. "What's going on around here? Looks like a ghost town. You boys shutting up shop?"

"You haven't heard about SAC's interim dispersal?"

"Vaguely, yes, on some of the commentaries."

"Well, we're not shouting about it. We try to keep half the wing off this base, because where we're standing right now is a primary target. We farm out our planes to fighter fields and Navy fields and even commercial airports. And we try to keep ten percent of the wing airborne at all times, and if you look down there in front of the jumbo hangar you'll see four standby Fortysevens, bombed up and ready to go. Damn expensive way to run an air force."

Randy looked. They were there, wings drooping with full tanks, bound to earth by slender umbilical cords, the starter cables. "I didn't mean the planes so much as the people," Randy said. "Where's everybody?"

"Oh, that." Hart frowned, as if deciding how much could be said and what words to use. "The papers know about it but they aren't printing it," he said finally, "and the people around Orlando must know about it by now so it can't be any great secret. We've been on sort of a modified alert for four or five weeks. Maybe I should call it a creeping evacuation. We've cleared the area of all civilian and nonessential personnel, and we're encouraging everybody to move their families out of the blast zone. You see, Randy, we can't expect three to six hours' warning any more. If we're lucky, we might get fifteen minutes."

Randy nodded. He noticed long red missiles slung

under the wings of the standby B-47's. He recognized them, from the newspaper photographs, as the Rascal, an air-to-ground H-bomb carrier. "Is that red baby much help?" he asked.

"That red baby," Hart said, "is what we call the crew-saver. The Russkies are no dopes. They'll try to stop us with missiles air-to-air and ground-to-air, beam-riders, heat-seekers, sound-finders, and, for all I know, smellers. It'll be no milk run but with the Rascal—and some other gadgets—we don't have to write ourselves off as a kamikaze corps. We won't have to penetrate their inner defense zones. We can lay off target and let that red baby fly. It knows where to go. Do you know what?"

"What?"

Paul Hart's smile had vanished, and he looked older, and when he spoke it was gravely. "When the whistle blows, I'll have a better chance if I'm in my aircraft, headed for target, than if I'm sitting at home with my feet propped up, drinking a Scotch, and Martha rubbing the kinks out of my neck—and our little place on the lake is five miles from here. So I'm a man of peace. I wish Martha and the kids lived in Fort Repose."

Randy heard the low whine of jet engines at fractional power and saw a cigar-shaped C-135 line up with the runway in its swoop downward. Presently it wheeled into a taxi strip and braked in front of Operations. A flag, three white stars on a blue field, popped out of the cockpit, indicating that a lieutenant general was aboard, and alerting McCoy to provide the courtesies due such rank.

The three-star general was first down the ramp, his pink-cheeked aide scurrying about his heels like an anxious puppy. Mark was last off. Randy waved and caught his eye and Mark waved back but did not smile. Coming down the ramp and across the concrete, knees bare in tropical uniform, Mark looked like a slightly larger edition of Randy, an inch taller, a shade broader. At thirty feet they looked like twins, with the same jet hair, white teeth behind mobile lips, quizzical eyes set deep, the same rakish walk and swing of shoulders, cleft in

chin and emphatic nose with a bony bump on the
bridge. At three feet, fine, deep lines showed around
Mark's eyes and mouth, gray appeared in his black
thicket, his jaw thrust out an extra half-inch, his face
was leaner. At three feet, they were entirely different,
and it was apparent Mark was the older, harder, and
probably wiser man.

Mark put one hand on Hart's shoulder and the other
on Randy's, and walked them toward the building.
"Paul," he told Hart, "you better get with General Heycock. He's hungry and when he gets hungry he gets
fierce. How about helping his aide dig up some transport and get him over to the O Club? We're only here
to gas up. Takeoff is in fifty minutes."

Hart looked up and saw three blue Air Force sedans
swing up the driveway. "There's the General's transport
right there," he said, and then, realizing that Mark had
tactfully implied he wanted to be alone with his brother,
added, "But I'll go along to the O Club, and get the
mess officer on the ball." He shook hands and said,
"See you, Mark, next time around."

"Sure," Mark said. He turned to Randy. "Where's
your car? I've got a lot to say and not much time to say
it. We can talk in the car. But first let's get some candy,
or something, inside Ops. We didn't load any flight
lunches at Ramey."

The front seat of the Bonneville was like a sunny,
comfortable private office. Randy asked the essential
question first: "What time do Helen and the children
get in?"

Mark brought a notebook out of his hip pocket.
"Three-thirty tomorrow morning, local time, at Orlando
Municipal. Carmody—he's Wing Commander at Ramey
—has a friend in the Eastern office in San Juan.
He ramrodded it through for me. The plane leaves
Omaha at seven-ten tonight. One change, in Chicago."

"Isn't that a little rough on Helen and the kids?"

"They can sleep all the way from Chicago to Orlando. It'll be just as tough on you, meeting them. The
important thing is I got the reservation. This time of
year, it took some doing."

"What's the great rush?" Randy demanded. "What the hell's going on?"

"Contain yourself, son," Mark said. "I'm going to give you a complete briefing."

"Have you told Helen yet?"

"I sent her a cable from San Juan. Just told her I'd made reservations for tonight. She'll understand." He squinted at the gaudy dials and gleaming knobs on the dash. "Some buggy you've got here, Randy. Won't be worth a damn to you. About Helen, she and I thrashed all this out long ago, but she won't like it. Not at all will she like it, now that the time has come. But I'll have her on that plane if I have to truss her up and send her air freight."

Randy said nothing. He simply tapped the car clock, a reminder.

"Okay," Mark said, "I'll brief you. First strategic, then tactical." He pushed a peanut-butter cracker into his mouth, found his pen, and began to sketch in his notebook. He drew a rough map, the Mediterranean.

Mark doesn't cerebrate until he has a pen in his hand, Randy thought, and can see a map. Probably makes him feel comfortable, like he's holding a pointer in the SAC War Room.

"The key is the Med," Mark said. "For three hundred years the Russians have tried to pry open the Straits and debouch into the Mediterranean. Peter the Great, Catherine the Great, Czar Alexander, they all tried it. Now, more than ever, control of the Med means control of the world."

Randy nodded. Conquerors knew or sensed this. Caesar had done it, Xerxes, Napoleon, and Hitler failed. "If Xerxes had won at Salamis," he said, "we'd all be speaking Persian—but that was a long time pre-Sputnik, and pre-ICBM. I thought the fight, now, was for control of space. Who controls space controls the world."

Mark smiled. "It can also happen just the other way around. We—by we I mean the NATO coalition—aren't going to be allowed time to catch up with them in operational IC's, much less control space. Now don't argue with me. We have their War Plan."

Randy took a deep breath and sat up straight.

"For the first time Russia has bridgeheads in the Mediterranean—here, here, and here—" Mark drew ovals on the map. "They have a fleet in the Med as powerful as ours when you match their submarine strength against our carriers. They have Turkey ringed on three sides, and if they could upset the Turkish government, and force capitulation of the Bosporus and Dardanelles, they would have won the war without fighting. The Med would be theirs, Africa cut off from Europe, NATO outflanked on the south, and one by one all our allies—except England—would fall into their laps or declare themselves neutral. SAC's bases in Africa and Spain would be untenable and melt away. NATO would fold up, and the IR sites we're planning never be finished."

"That was their gambit in 'fifty-seven, wasn't it?" Randy asked.

"You have a good memory, Randy, and that's a good simile. The Russians are great chess players. They rarely make the same mistake twice. Now, today, they're making moves. It's the same gambit—but with a tremendous difference. In 'fifty-seven, when it looked like they were going to make another Korea out of Turkey, we warned the Kremlin that there'd be no sanctuary inside Russia. They took a look at the board and resigned the game. Then in 'fifty-eight, after the Iraq king was assassinated, we grabbed the initiative and landed Marines in Lebanon. We got there fustest. They saw that we were ready, and could not be surprised. They were caught off balance, and didn't dare move. This time it's different. They're ready to go through with it, because the odds have changed."

"How can you know this?"

"Remember reading about the Russian General who came over, in Berlin? An air general, a shrewd character, a human being. He brought us their War Plan, in his head. This time, they're not resigning the game.

They'd still like to win the war without a war, but if we make any military countermove, we're going to receive it."

For a moment, they were both silent. On the other side of the flight-line fence, three ground-crewmen were throwing a baseball. Two were pitching, an older sergeant, built like Yogi Berra, catching. The plate was a yellow parachute pack. The ball whirred and plopped sharply into mitt. "That tall boy has a lot of stuff," Randy said. Again, he felt he moved in the miasma of a dream. Something was wrong. Either Mark shouldn't be talking like this, or those airmen shouldn't be throwing a baseball out there in the warm sunlight. When he lit a cigarette, his fingers were trembling again.

"Have a bad night, Randy?"

"Not particularly. I'm having a bad day."

"I'm afraid it's going to get worse. Here's the tactical part. They know that the only way they can do it is knock off our nuclear capability with one blow—or at least cripple us so badly that they can accept what retaliatory power we have left. They don't mind losing ten or twenty million people, so long as they sweep the board, because people, per se, are only pawns, and expendable. So their plan—it was no surprise to us—calls for a T.O.T. on a worldwide scale. You get it?"

"Sure. Time-on-target. You don't fire everything at the same instant. You shoot it so it all arrives on target at the same instant."

Mark glanced at his watch, and then looked up at the big jet transport, still loading fuel through four hoses from the underground tanks. "That's right. It won't be Zero Hour, it'll be Zero Minute. They'll use no planes in the first wave, only missiles. They plan to kill every base and missile site in Europe and Africa and the U.K. with their T-2 and T-3 IR's. They plan to kill every base on this continent, and in the Pacific, with their IC's, plus missiles launched from subs. Then they use SUSAC—that's what we call their Strategic Air Force—to mop up."

"Can they get away with it?"

"Three years ago they couldn't. Three years hence,

when we have our own ICBM batteries emplaced, a big fleet of missile-toting subs, and Nike-Zeus and some other stuff perfected, they couldn't. But right now we're in what we call 'the gap.' Theoretically, they figure they can do it. I'm pretty sure they can't—we may have some surprises for them—but that's not the point. Point is, if they *think* they can get away with it, then we have lost."

"I don't understand."

"LeMay says the only way a general can win a modern war is not fight one. Our whole *raison d'être* was deterrent force. When you don't deter them any longer, you lose. I think we lost some time ago, because the last five Sputniks have been reconnaisance satellites. They've been mapping us, with infrared and transitor television, measuring us for the Sunday punch."

Randy felt angry. He felt cheated. "Why hasn't anybody—everybody been told about this?"

Mark shrugged. "You know how it is—everything that comes in is stamped secret or top secret or cosmic or something and the only people who dare declassify anything are the big wheels right at the top, and the people at the top hold conferences and somebody says, 'Now, let's not be hasty. Let's not alarm the public.' So everything stays secret or cosmic. Personally, I think everybody ought to be digging or evacuating right this minute. Maybe if the other side knew we were digging, if they knew that we knew, they wouldn't try to get away with it."

"You really think it's that close?" Randy said. "Why?"

"Two reasons. First, when I left Puerto Rico this morning Navy was trying to track three skunks—unidentified submarines—in the Caribbean, and one in the Gulf."

"Four subs doesn't sound like enough force to cause a big flap," Randy said.

"Four subs is a lot of subs when there shouldn't be any," Mark said. "It's like shaking a haystack and having four needles pop out at your feet. Chances are that haystack is stiff with needles." He rubbed his hand across his eyes, as if the glare hurt, and when he spoke again his voice was strained. "They've got so blasted many! CIA thinks six hundred, Navy guesses maybe seven-fifty. And they don't need launchers any more. Just dump the bird, or pop it out while still submerged. The ocean itself is a perfectly good launching pad."

Randy said, "And the other reason?"

"Because I'm on my way back to Offutt. We flew down yesterday on a pretty important job—figure out a way to disperse the wing on Ramey. There aren't enough fields in Puerto Rico and anyway the island is rugged and not big enough. We'd just started our staff study when we got a zippo—that's an operational priority message—to come home. And two thirds of the Ramey wing was scrambled with flyaway kits for—another place. I made my decision right then. I just had time to arrange Helen's reservation and send the cables."

Mark spoke more of the Russian General, with whom he had talked at length, and whom apparently he liked. "He isn't a traitor, either to his country or to civilization. He came over in desperation, hoping that somehow we could stop those power-crazed bastards at the top. He doesn't think their War Plan will work any more than I do. Too much chance for human or mechanical error." Mark used phrases like "maximum capability," and "calculated risk," and "acceptance of any casualties except important people," and "decentralization of industry and control, announced as an economic measure, but actually military."

Randy listened, fascinated, until he saw three blue sedans turn a corner near wing headquarters. "Here comes your party," he said. "Anything else I ought to know?"

Mark brushed cracker crumbs and slivers of chocolate from his shirt front. "Yes. Also, there's something I have to give you." He found a green slip of paper in his wallet and handed it to Randy. "Made out to you," he said.

Randy unfolded the check. It was for five thousand. "What am I supposed to do with this?" he asked.

"Cash it—today if you can. Don't deposit it, cash it!

It's a reserve for Helen and Ben Franklin and Peyton. Buy stuff with it. I don't know what to tell you to buy. You'll think of what you'll need as you go along."

"I did start a list, this morning."

Mark seemed pleased. "That's fine. Show's you're looking ahead. I don't know whether money will help Helen or not, but cash in hand, in Fort Repose, will be better than an account in an Omaha bank."

Randy kept on looking at the check, feeling uncomfortable. "But suppose nothing happens? Suppose—"

"Spend some of it on a case of good liquor," Mark said. "Then if nothing happens we'll have a wonderful, expensive toot together, and you can laugh at me. I won't care."

Randy slipped the check into his pocket. "Can I tip off anybody else? There are a few people—"

"You've got a girl?"

"I don't know whether she's my girl or not. I've been trying to find out. You don't know her. New people from Cleveland. Her family built on River Road."

Mark hesitated. "I don't see any objection. It is something Civil Defense should have done weeks— months ago. Use your own judgment. Be discreet."

Randy noticed that the jet transport's wings were clear of hoses. He saw the three blue sedans pull up at Operations. He saw Lieutenant General Heycock get out of the first car. He felt Mark's hand on his shoulder, and braced himself for the words he knew must come.

Mark spoke very quietly. "You'll take care of Helen?"

"Certainly."

"I won't say be a good father to the children. They love you and they think you're swell and you couldn't be anything but a good father to them. But I will say this, be kind to Helen. She's—" Mark was having trouble with his voice.

Randy tried to help him out. "She's a wonderful, beautiful gal, and you don't have to worry. Anyway, don't sound so final. You're not dead yet."

"She's—more," Mark said. "She's my right arm. We've been married fourteen years and about half that time I've been up in the air or out of the country and I've never once worried about Helen. And she never had to worry about me. In fourteen years I never slept with another woman. I never even kissed another woman, not really, not even when I had duty in Tokyo or Manila or Hongkong, and she was half a world away. She was all the woman I ever needed. She was like this: Back when I was a captain and we were moving from rented apartment to rented apartment every year or so, I got a terrific offer from Boeing. She knew what I wanted. I didn't have to tell her. She said, 'I want you to stay in SAC. I think you should. I think you ought to be a general and you're going to be a general.' There's an old saying that anyone can make colonel on his own, but it takes a wife to make a general. I guess there wasn't quite enough time, but had there been time, she would've had her star."

Randy saw Lieutenant General Heycock walk from the Operations building toward the plane. "It's time, Mark," he said.

They got out of the car and walked quickly toward the gate, and Mark swung an arm around Randy's shoulders. "What I mean is, she has tremendous energy and courage. If you let her, she'll give you the same kind of loyalty she gave me. Let her, Randy. She's all woman and that's what she's made for."

"Stop worrying," Randy said. He didn't quite understand and he didn't know what else to say.

Heycock's aide fidgeted at the end of the ramp. "Everybody's in, Colonel," he said. "The General was looking for you at lunch. The General wondered what happened to you. He was most anxious—"

"I'll see the General as soon as we're airborne," Mark said sharply.

The aide retreated two steps up the ramp, then waited stubbornly.

They shook hands. Mark said, "Better try to catch a nap this evening."

"I will. When I get home shall I call Helen and tell her you're on the way?"

"No. Not much use. This aircraft cruises at five-fifty.

By the time you get back to Fort Repose, we'll be west of the Mississippi." He glanced down at his bare knees. "Looks like I'll have to change into a real uniform on the aircraft. I'd look awfully funny in Omaha."

"So long, Mark."

Without raising his head, Mark said, "Goodbye, Randy," turned away, and climbed the ramp.

Randy walked away from the transport, got into his car, and drove slowly through the base. At the main gate he surrendered his visitor's pass. He turned into a lonely lane outside the base, near the village of Pinecastle, and stopped the car in a spot shielded by cabbage palms. When he was sure no one watched, and no car approached from either direction, he leaned his head on the wheel. He swallowed a sob and closed his eyes to forbid the tears.

He heard wind rustle the palms, and the chirp of cardinals in the brush. He became aware that the clock on the dash, blurred, was staring at him. The clock said he had just time to make the bank before closing, if he pushed hard and had luck getting through Orlando traffic. He started the engine, backed out of the lane into the highway, and let the car run. He knew he should not have spared time for tears, and would not, ever again.

[3]

Edgar Quisenberry, president of the bank, never lost sight of his position and responsibilities as sole representative of the national financial community in Fort Repose. A monolithic structure of Indiana limestone built by his father in 1920, the bank stood like a gray fortress at the corner of Yulee and St. Johns. First National had weathered the collapse of the 1926 land boom, had been unshaken by the market crash of 'twenty-nine and the depression that followed. "The only person who ever succeeded in closing First National," Edgar often boasted, "was Franklin D. Roosevelt, in 'thirty-three, and he had to shut down every other bank in the country to do it. It'll never happen again, because we'll never have another s.o.b. like him."

Edgar, at forty-five, had grown to look something like his bank, squat, solid, and forbidding. He was the only man in Fort Repose who always wore a vest, and he never wore sports clothes, even on the golf links. Each year, when he attended the branch Federal Reserve convention in Atlanta, two new suits were tailored, one double-breasted blue, one pin-stripe gray, both designed to minimize, or at least dignify, what he called "my corporation."

First National employed two vice presidents, a cashier, an assistant cashier, and four tellers, but it was a one-man bank. You could put it in at any window, but before you took it out on loan, or cashed an out-of-town check, you had to see Edgar. All Edgar's loans were based on Character, and Character was based on cash balance, worth of unencumbered real estate, ownership of bonds and blue-chip stocks. Since Edgar was the only person in town who could, and did, maintain a mental index of all these variables, he considered himself the sole accurate judge of Character. It was said you could gauge a grove owner's crop by the way Edgar greeted him on Yulee Street. If Edgar shook his hand and chatted, then the man had just received a big price for his fruit. If Edgar spoke, cracked his face, and waved, the man was reasonably prosperous. If Edgar nodded but did not speak, nemotodes were in the citrus roots. If Edgar didn't see him, his grove had been destroyed in a freeze.

When Randolph Bragg burst into the bank at Four minutes to three, Edgar pretended not to see him. His antipathy for Randy was more deeply rooted than if he had been a bankrupt. Bending over a desk as if examining a trust document, Edgar watched Randy scribble his name on the back of a check, smile at Mrs. Estes, the senior teller, and skid the check through the window. Randy's manner, dress, and attitude all seemed an affront. Randy had no respect for institutions, persons, or even money. He would come bouncing in like this, at the last minute, and demand service as casually as if The Bank were a soda fountain. He was a lazy, insolent odd-ball, with dangerous political ideas, who never made any effort to invest or save. Twice in the past few years he had overdrawn his account. People called the Braggs "old family." Well, so were the Minorcans old family—older, the descendants of Mediterranean islanders who had settled on the coast centuries ago. The Minorcans were shiftless no-goods and the Braggs no better. Edgar disliked Randy for all these, and another, secret reason.

Edgar saw Mrs. Estes open her cash drawer, hesitate, and speak to Randy. He saw Randy shrug. Mrs. Estes stepped out of the cage and Edgar knew she was going to ask him to okay the check. When she reached his side he purposely ignored her for a moment, to let Randy know that The Bank considered him of little importance. Mrs. Estes said, "Will you initial this, please, Mr. Quisenberry?"

Edgar held the check in both hands and at a distance, examining it through the bottom lens of his bifocals, as if it smelled of forgery. Five thousand, signed by Mark Bragg. If Randy irritated Edgar, Mark infuriated him. Mark Bragg invariably and openly called him by his school nickname, Fisheye. He was glad that Mark was in the Air Force and rarely in town. "Ask that young man to come here," he told Mrs. Estes. Perhaps now he would have the opportunity to repay Judge Bragg for the humiliation of the poker game.

Five years before, Edgar had been invited to sit in the regular Saturday night pot-limit game at the St. Johns Country Club in San Marco, county seat and largest town of Timucuan. He had sat opposite Judge Bragg, a spare, straight, older man. Except for a small checking account, the Judge banked and did his business in Orlando and Tallahassee, so Edgar knew him hardly at all.

Edgar prided himself on his cagey poker. The idea was to win, wasn't it? Judge Bragg played an open, swashbuckling game, as if he enjoyed it. On occasion he bluffed, Edgar deduced, but he seemed to be lucky so it was difficult to tell whether he was bluffing or not. In the third hour a big pot came along—more than a thousand dollars. Edgar had opened with three aces and not bettered with his two-card draw, and the Judge had also drawn two cards. After the draw, Edgar bet a hundred and the men who had taken only one card dropped out and that left it up to the judge. The judge promptly raised the size of the pot. Edgar hesitated, looked into the Judge's amused dark eyes, and folded. As the Judge embraced and drew in the hill of chips, Edgar reached across the table and exposed his hand—three sevens and nothing else. Judge Brag had said, very quietly, "Don't ever touch my cards again, you son of a bitch. If you do, I'll break a chair over your head."

The five others in the game had waited for Edgar to do or say something, but Edgar only tried to laugh it off. At midnight, the Judge cashed in his chips and said, "See you all next Saturday night—if this tub of rancid lard isn't here. He's a bore and a boor and he forgets to ante." That was the first and last time Edgar played at the St. Johns Club. He had never forgotten it.

Randy walked into the bank's office enclosure, wondering why Edgar wanted to see him. Edgar knew perfectly well that Mark's check was okay. "What's the trouble, Edgar?" he asked.

"Isn't it a little late to bring in a big check like this, and ask us for cash?"

The clock said 3:04. "It wasn't late when I came in," Randy said. He noticed other customers still in the bank—Eli Blaustein, who owned Tropical Clothing; Pete Hernandez, Rita's older brother and manager of Ajax Super-Market; Jerry Kling, from the Standard station; Florence Wechek, with her Western Union checks and receipts. It was their custom to hurry to the bank just at three.

"It's all right for business people to make deposits after closing hour, but I think we ought to have more time to handle an item like this," Edgar said.

Randy noticed that Florence, finished at the teller's window, had wandered within hearing. Florence didn't miss much. "How much time do you need to cash a check for five thousand?" he asked. He was sure his face was reddening. He told himself he must not lose his temper.

"That isn't the point," Edgar said. "The point is that your brother doesn't have an account here."

"You don't doubt that my brother's check is good, do you?" Randy was relieved to find that his voice, instead of rising, sounded lower and steadier.

"Now, I didn't say that. But it wouldn't be good banking procedure for me to hand you five thousand dollars and wait four or five days for it to clear all the way from Omaha."

"I endorsed it, didn't I?" Randy loosened his shoulders and flexed his toes and fingers and looked intently at Edgar's face. It would squash, like a potato.

"I doubt that your account would cover it."

Randy's account stood below four hundred. This had been little to worry about, with his citrus checks due on the first of the year. Now, considering Mark's urgency, it was dangerously low. He decided to probe Edgar's weakness. He said, "Penny-wise, pound-foolish, that's you, Edgar. You could have been in on a very good thing. Give me back the check. I'll cash it in San Marco or Orlando in the morning."

Edgar realized he might have made an error. It was most unusual for anyone to want five thousand in cash. It indicated some sort of a quick, profitable deal. He should have found out why the cash was needed. "Now, let's not be in a rush," he said.

Randy held out his hand. "Give me the check."

"Well, if I knew exactly why you had to have all this cash in such a hurry I might be able to make an exception to banking rules."

"Come on. I don't have time to waste."

Edgar's pale, protruding eyes shifted to Florence, frankly listening, and Eli Blaustein hovering nearby, interested. "Come into my office, Randolph," he said.

After Randy had the cash, in hundreds, twenties and tens, he said, "Now I'll tell you why I wanted it, Edgar. Mark asked me to make a bet for him."

"Oh, the races!" Edgar said. "I very rarely play the races, but I know Mark wouldn't be risking that much money unless he had a sure thing. Running in Miami, tomorrow, I supopse?"

"No. Not the races. Mark is simply betting that checks won't be worth anything, very shortly, but cash will. Good afternoon, Fish-eye." He left the office and sauntered across the lobby. As Mrs. Estes unlocked the bank door she squeezed his arm and whispered, "Good for you!"

Edgar rocked in his chair, furious. It wasn't a reason. It was a riddle. He repeated Randy's words. They made no sense at all, unless Mark expected some big cataclysm, like all the banks closing, and of course that was ridiculous. Whatever happened, the country's financial structure was sound. Edgar reached a conclusion. He had been tricked and bluffed again. The Braggs were scoundrels, all of them.

Randy's first stop was Ajax Super-Market. It really wasn't a super-market, as it claimed. Fort Repose's population was 3,422, according to the State Census, and this included Pistolville and the Negro district. The Chamber of Commerce claimed five thousand, but the Chamber admitted counting the winter residents of Riverside Inn, and people who technically were outside the town limits, like those who lived on River Road. So Fort Repose had not attracted the big chain stores. Still, Ajax imitated the super-markets, inasmuch as you wheeled an aluminum cart around and served yourself, and Ajax sold the same brands at about the same prices.

Randy hated grocery shopping. None of the elaborate surveys, and studies in depth of the buying habits of Americans had a classification for Randolph Bragg. Usually he grabbed a cart and sprinted for the meat counter, where he dropped a written order. Then he raced up and down the aisles, snatching cans and bottles and boxes and cartons from shelves and freezers apparently at random, running down small children and bumping old ladies and apologizing, until his final lap brought him past the meat counter again. The butchers had learned to give his order priority, for if his meat wasn't cut he didn't stop, simply made a violent U-turn and barreled off for the door. When the checker rang up his bill Randy looked at his watch. His record for a full basket was three minutes and forty-six seconds, portal to portal.

But on this day it was entirely different, because of the length of his list to which he had been adding, the quantities, and the Friday afternoon shopping rush. After he'd filled three carts, and the meat order had already been carried to the car, he was still only halfway down the list, but physically and emotionally exhausted. His toes were mashed, and he had been shoved, buffeted, butted in the ribs, and rammed in the groin. His legs trembled, his hands shook, and a tic had developed in his left eye. Waiting in the check-out line, maneuvering two topheavy carts before one behind, he cursed man's scientific devilishness in inventing H-bombs and super-markets, cursed Mark, and swore he would rather starve than endure this again.

At last he reached the counter. Pete Hernandez, act-

ing as checker, gaped. "Good God, Randy!" he said.
"What're you going to do, feed a regiment?" Until the
year before, Pete had always called him "Mr. Bragg,"
but after Randy's first date with Pete's sister their rela-
tionship naturally had changed.

"Mark's wife and children are coming to stay with
me a while," he explained.

"'What's she got—a football team?"

"Kids eat a lot," Randy said. Pete was skinny,
chicken-breasted, his chin undershot and his nails dirty,
completely unlike Rita except for black eyes and olive
skin.

Pete began to play the cash register with two fingers
while the car boy, awed, filled the big sacks. Randy was
aware that seven or eight women, lined up behind him,
counted his purchases, fascinated. He heard one whisper, "Fifteen cans of coffee—fifteen!" The line grew,
and he was conscious of a steady, complaining murmur.
Unaccountably, he felt guilty. He felt that he ought to
face these women and shout, "All of you! All of you
buy everything you can!" It wouldn't do any good.
They would be certain he was mad.

Pete pulled down the total and announced it loudly:
"Three hundred and fourteen dollars and eighty cents,
Randy! Gees, that's our record!"

From habit, Randy looked at his watch. One hour
and six minutes. That, too, was a record. He paid in
cash, grabbed an armful of bags, nodded for Pete's car
boy to follow, and fled.

He stopped at Bill Cullen's bar, short-order grill,
package store, and fish camp, just outside the town limits. There was space for two cases in the front seat, so
he'd lay in his whisky supply. Bill and his wife, a straw-
haired woman usually groggy and thick-tongued with
spiked wine, operated all this business in a two-room
shack joined to a covered wharf, its pilings leaning and
roof askew, in a cove on the Timucuan. The odors of
fried eggs, dead minnows, gasoline and kerosene
fumes, decaying gar and catfish heads, stale beer and
spilt wine oozed across land and water.

Ordinarily, Randy bought his bourbon two or three

bottles at a time. On this day, he bought a case and a half, cleaning out Bill's supply of his brand. He recalled that Helen, when she drank at all, preferred Scotch. He bought six fifths of Scotch.

Bill, inquisitive, said, "Planning a big barbecue or party or something, Randy? You figure you'll try politics again?"

Randy found it almost impossible to lie. His father had beaten him only once in his life, when he was ten, but it had been a truly terrible beating. He had lied, and the Judge had gone upstairs and returned with his heaviest razor strop. He had grabbed Randy by the neck and bent him across the billiard table, and implanted the virtue of truth through the seat of his pants, and on bare hide, until he screamed in terror and pain. Then Randy was ordered to his room, supperless and in disgrace. Hours later, the Judge knocked and came in and gently turned him over in the bed. The Judge spoke quietly. Lying was the worst crime, the indispensable accomplice of all others, and would always bring the worst punishment. "I can forgive anything except a lie." Randy believed him, and while he could no longer remember the lie he had told, he never forgot the punishment. Unconsciously, his right hand rubbed his buttocks as he thought up an answer for Bill Cullen.

"I'm having visitors," Randy said, "and Christmas is coming." This was the truth, if not the whole truth. He couldn't risk saying more to Bill. Bill's nickname was Bigmouth and his lying not limited to the size of yesterday's catch. Bigmouth Bill could spark a panic.

When he turned into the driveway, Randy saw Malachai Henry using a scuffle hoe in the camellia beds screening the garage. "Malachai!" he called. "How about helping me get this stuff into the house?"

Malachai hurried over. His eyes, widening, took in the cartons, bags, and cases filling the trunk and piled on the seats. "All this going up to your apartment, sir?"

"No. It goes into the kitchen and utility room. Mrs. Bragg and the children are flying in from Omaha tomorrow."

As they unloaded, Randy considered the Henrys.

They were a special problem. They were black and they were poor but in many ways closer to him than any family in Fort Repose. They owned their own land and ran their own lives, but in a sense they were his wards. They could not be abandoned or the truth withheld from them. He couldn't explain Mark's warning to Missouri. She wouldn't understand. If he told Preacher, all Preacher would do was lift up his face, raise his arms, and intone, "Hallelujah! The Lord's will be done!" If he told Two-Tone, Two-Tone would consider it an excuse to get drunk and stay that way. But he could, with confidence, tell Malachai.

With the meat packed in the freezer and everything else stacked in cupboards and closets Randy said, "Come on up to my office, Malachai, and I'll give you your money." He paid Malachai twenty-five dollars a week for twenty hours. Malachai picked his own days to mow, rake, fertilize, and trim, days when he had no fruit picking, repairing, or better paying yard jobs elsewhere. Randy knew he was never short-timed, and Malachai knew he could always count on that twenty-five a week.

Malachai's face was expressionless, but Randy sensed his apprehension. Malachai never before had been asked upstairs to receive his pay. In the office, Randy dropped into the high-backed, leather-covered swivel chair that had come from his father's chambers. Malachai stood, uncertain. "Sit down," Randy said. Malachai picked the least comfortable straight chair and sat down, not presuming to lean back.

Randy brought out his wallet and looked up at the portrait of his bald-headed grandfather, Woodrow Wilson's diplomat, with the saying for which he was known stamped in faded gold on the discolored frame: "Small nations, when treated as equals, become the firmest of allies."

It was difficult. From the days when they fished and hunted together, he had always felt close to Malachai. They could still work in the grove, side by side, and discuss as equals the weather and the citrus and the fishing but never any longer share any personal, any important matters. They could not talk politics or women or finances. It was strange, since Malachai was much like Sam Perkins. He had as much native intelligence as Sam, the same intuitive courtesy, and they were the same size, weighing perhaps 180, and the same color, cordovan-brown. Randy and Sam Perkins had been lieutenants in a company of the 7th (Custer) Regiment of the First Cav. Together, Randy and Sam had dug in on the banks of the Han and Chongchon, and faced the same bugle-heralded human wave charge at Unsan, and covered each other's platoons in advance and retreat. They had slept side by side in the same bunker, eaten from the same mess tins, drunk from the same bottle, flown to Tokyo on R. and R. together and together bellied up to the bar of the Imperial Hotel. They had (if it were learned in Fort Repose he would be ostracized) even gone to a junior-officer-grade geisha house together and been greeted with equal hospitality and favors. So it was a strange thing that he could not speak to Malachai, whom he had known since he could speak at all, as he had to Sam Perkins in Korea. It was strange that a Negro could be an officer and a gentleman and an equal below Parallel Thirty-eight, but not below the Mason-Dixon Line. It was strange, but this was not the time for social introspection. His job was to tell Malachai to brace and prepare himself and his family.

Randy took two tens and a five from his wallet and shoved them across the desk. "That's for the week."

"Thank you, sir," Malachai said, folding the bills and tucking them into the breast pocket of his checked shirt.

Perhaps the difference was that Malachai had not been an officer, like Sam Perkins, Randy thought. Malachai had been in service for four years, but in the Air Defense Command, a tech sergeant babying jet engines. Perhaps it was their use of the language. Sam spoke crisp upstate-New York-Cornell English, but when Malachai talked you didn't have to see him to know he was black. "Malachai," Randy said, "I want to ask you a serious question."

"Yes, sir."

"What would you say if I told you I have very good

information—about as good as you can get—that before long a war is coming?"

"Wouldn't surprise me one bit."

The answer surprised Randy. His swivel chair banged upright. "What makes you say that?"

Malachai smiled, pleased with Randy's reaction. "Well, sir, I keep up with things. I read all I can. I read all the news magazines and all the out-of-state papers I can get hold of and some service journals and lots of other stuff."

"You do? You don't subscribe to them all, do you?"

Malachai tried to control his grin. "Some I get from you, Mister Randy. You finish a magazine and throw it away and Missouri finds it and brings it home in her tote bag. And every day she collects the Cleveland papers and the business magazines from Mrs. McGovern's. Mondays I work for Admiral Hazzard. He saves *The New York Times* and the Washington papers for me and the Naval Institute *Proceedings* and technical magazines. And I listen to all the commentators."

"How do you find the time?" Randy had never realized that Malachai read anything except the *San Marco Sun* ("It Shines for Timucuan County").

"Well, sir, there's not much for a single, non-drinkin' man to do around Fort Repose, week nights. So I read and I listen. I know things ain't good, and the way I figure is that if people keep piling up bombs and rockets, higher and higher and higher, someday somebody's going to set one off. Then blooey!"

"More than one," Randy said, "and soon—maybe very soon. That's what my brother believes and that's why he's sending Mrs. Bragg and the children down here. You'd better get set for it, Malachai. That's what I'm doing."

Malachai's smile was gone entirely. "Mister Randy, I've thought about it a lot, but there's not a doggone thing we can do about it. We just have to sit here and wait for it. There's not much we can lay up—" he patted his breast pocket. "This twenty-five dollars, with what Missouri brings home this evening, is it. Fast as we make it, it goes. Of course, we don't need much and we've got one thing hardly anybody else has got."

"What's that?"

"Water. Running water. Artestian water that can't be contaminated. You all only use it in the sprinkling system because it smells funny, some say like rotten eggs. But that sulphur water ain't bad. You gets to like it."

Until that moment, Randy hadn't thought of water at all. His grandfather, in a year of freakish drought, at great cost had drilled nearly a thousand feet to find the artesian layer and irrigate the grove. And his grandfather had allowed the Henrys to tap the main pipe, so the Henrys had a perpetual flow of free water, although it was hard with dissolved minerals and Randy hated to taste it out of the sprinkler heads in grove and garden, even on a hot summer day.

"I'm afraid I'd never get used to it," he said. He counted out two hundred dollars in twenties and thrust the money across the desk. "This is for an emergency. Buy what you need."

The new notes felt slippery in Malachai's fingers. "I don't know when I can pay this back."

"Don't worry about it. I'm not asking you to pay it back."

Malachai folded the bills. "Thank you, sir."

"See you next week, Malachai."

Malachai left and Randy mixed a drink. You turned a tap and lo, water came forth, sweet, soft water without odor, pumped from some sub-surface pool by a silent, faithful servant, a small electric motor. Every family on River Road, except the Henrys, obtained its water in the same way, each with its own pump and well. More important than anything he had listed was water, free of dangerous bacilli, unpolluted by poisons human, chemical, or radioactive. Pure water was essential to his civilization, accepted like pure air. In the big cities, where even a near miss would rupture reservoirs, demolish aqueducts, and smash mains, it would be hell without water. Big cities would become traps deadly as deserts or jungles. Randy began to consider how little he really knew of the fundamentals of survival. Helen, he guessed, would know a good deal more. It was a required subject in the education of Air Force wives. He decided to talk to Bubba Offenhaus, who ran Civil Defense in Fort Repose. Bubba must have pamphlets, or something, that he could study.

Downstairs Graf began to bark, an insistent, belligerent alarm announcing a strange car in the driveway. Randy went to the head of the stairs, shouted, "Shut up, Graf!" and waited to see who would knock.

Nobody knocked but the door opened and Randy saw Elizabeth McGovern in the front hall, bending over Graf, her face curtained by shoulder-length blond hair. She stroked Graf's hackles until his tail wigwagged a friendly signal. Then she looked up and called, "You decent, Randy?"

One day she would barge in like this and he would be indecent. She bewildered him. She was brash, unpredictable, and sometimes uncomfortably outspoken. "Come on up, Lib," he said. Like the Henrys, she was a special problem.

All through the summer and early fall Randy had watched the McGoverns' house and dock go up, while landscapers spotted palms in orderly rows, laid down turf, and planted flower pots and shrubbery. On a sultry October afternoon, trolling for bass in the channel, he had seen a pair of faultlessly curved and tapered legs incongruously stretched toward the sky from the McGovern dock. Since she was lying on the canvas-covered planking, heels propped up on a post, the legs were all that could be seen from water level. He turned the prow toward shore to discover whose body was attached to these remarkable and unfamiliar legs. When his boat was almost under the dock he'd spoken, "Hello, legs."

"You may call me Lib," she'd said. "You're Randy Bragg, aren't you? I've sort of been expecting you'd call."

When they'd become something more than friends, although less than lovers, he'd accused her of luring him with her lovely legs. Lib had laughed and said, "I didn't know, then, that you were a leg man but I'm glad you are. Most American males have a fixation about the mammary gland. A symptom of momism, I think. Legs are for men's pleasure, breasts for babies'. Oh, that's really sour grapes. I only said it because I know my legs are my only real asset. I'm flat and I'm not pretty." Technically, she was accurate. She was no classic beauty when you considered each feature individually. She was only beautiful in complete design, in the way she moved and was put together.

She came up the stairs and curled a bare arm around his neck and kissed him, a brief kiss, a greeting. "I've been trying to get you on the phone all day," she said. "I've been thinking and I've reached an important conclusion. Where've you been?"

"My brother stopped at McCoy, flying back to Omaha. I had to meet him." He led her into the living room. "Drink?"

"Ginger ale, if you have it." She sat on a stool at the bar, one knee raised and clasped between her hands. She wore a sleeveless, turquoise linen blouse, doeskin shorts, and moccasins.

He tumbled ice into a glass and poured ginger ale and said, "What's this important conclusion?"

"You'll get mad. It's about you."

"Okay, I'll get mad."

"I think you ought to go to New York or Chicago or San Francisco or any city with character and vitality. You should go to work. This place is no good for you, Randy. The air is like soup and the people are like noodles. You're vegetating. I don't want a vegetable. I want a man."

He was instantly angry, and then he told himself that for a number of reasons, including the fact that her diagnosis was probably the truth, it was silly to be angry. He said, "If I went away and left you here, wouldn't you turn into a noodle?"

"I've thought it all out. As soon as you get a job, I'll follow you. If you want, we can live together for a while. If it's good, we can get married."

He examined her face. Her mouth, usually agile and humorous, was drawn into a taut, colorless line. Her eyes, which reflected her moods as the river reflected the sky, were gray and opaque. Under the soft tan painted by winter's sun her skin was pale. She was serious. She meant it. "Too late," he said.

"What do you mean, 'too late'?"

Yesterday, there might have been sense and logic to her estimate, and he might have accepted this challenge, invitation, and proposal. But since morning, they had lived in diverging worlds. It was necessary that he lead her down into his world, yet not too abruptly, lest sight and apprehension of the future imperil her capacity to think clearly and act intelligently. "My sister-in-law and her two children are coming to stay with me," he began. "They get in tonight—in the morning, really. Three thirty."

"Fine," she said. "Meet them, turn the house over to them, and then pick yourself a city—a nice, big, live city. They can have this place all to themselves and while they're here you won't have to worry about the house. How long are they staying?"

"I don't know," Randy said. Maybe forever, he almost added, but didn't.

"It won't matter, really, will it? When they leave you can rent the house. If they leave soon you ought to get a good price for it for the rest of the season. What's your sister-in-law like?"

"I haven't told you the reason they're coming." He reached out and covered her hands. Her fingers, long, round, strong, matched her throat. Her nails were tinted copper, and carefully groomed. He tried to frame the right words. "My brother believes—"

Graf, lying near Randy's stool, rolled to his feet, hair bristling like a razorback pig, tail and ears at attention, and then raced into the hallway and down the stairs, barking wildly.

"That's the loudest dog I've ever met!" Lib said. "What's eating him now?"

"He's got radar ears. Nothing can get close to the house without him knowing." Randy went downstairs. It was Dan Gunn at the door. An angular, towering man, sad-faced and saturnine, wearing heavy-framed glasses, awkward in movement and sparing of speech, he stepped into the hallway, not bothering to glance at Graf. Dan said, "You got a woman upstairs, Randy? I know you have because her car is in the driveway." He removed his pipe from his mouth and almost smiled. "I'd like to talk to her. About her mother. Her father, too."

"Go on up to the apartment, Dan," Randy said. "I'll just wander around in the yard." He guessed that Dan had just come from a professional visit to the McGoverns. Lib's mother had diabetes. He didn't know what her father had, but if Dan was going to discuss family illnesses with Lib, he would politely vanish.

"I don't think Elizabeth will mind if you sit in on this," Dan said. "Practically one of the family by now, aren't you?"

Going upstairs Randy decided that Dan, too, should know of Mark's warning. If anybody ought to know, it was a doctor. And at the same time Randy realized he had not included drugs in his list, and the medicine cabinet held little except aspirin, nasal sprays, and mouthwash. With two children coming, he should've planned better than that. Anyway, Dan was the man to tell him what to get, and write the prescriptions.

Randy mixed Dan a drink and said, "Our medic is here to see you, Lib, not me. When he's finished talking, I've got something to say to both of you."

Dan looked at him oddly. "Sounds like you're about to make a pronouncement."

"I am. But you go first."

"It's nothing urgent or terribly important. I was just making the placebo circuit and dropped in to see Elizabeth's mother."

"The what?" Lib asked. Randy had heard Dan use the phrase before.

"Placebo, or psychosomatic circuit—the middle-aged retirees and geriatrics who have nothing to do but get lonely and worry about their health. The only person they can call who can't avoid visiting them is their doctor. So they call me and I let them bend my ear with symptoms. I give them sugar pills or tranquilizers—one seems about as good as the other. I tell them they're going to live. This makes them happy. I don't know why."

At thirty-five, Dan was a souring idealist. After medical school in Boston he'd started practice in a Vermont town and in his free hours slaved at post-graduate studies in epidemiology. His target had been the teeming continents and the great plagues—malaria, typhus, cholera, typhoid, dysentery—and he was angling for a World Health Organization or Point Four appointment. Then he'd married. His wife—Randy did not know her name because Dan never uttered it—apparently had been extravagant, a nympho, a one-drink alcoholic, and a compulsive gambler. She'd recoiled at the thought of living in Equatorial Africa or a delta village in India, and pestered him to set up practice in New York or Los Angeles, where the big money was. When Dan refused, she took to spending weekends in New York, an easy pickup at her favorite bar in the Fifties. So he'd been a gentleman and let her go to Reno and get the divorce. When her luck ran out she returned East, filed suit for alimony, and the judge had given her everything she'd asked. Now she lived in Los Angeles and each week shovelled the alimony into bingo games or pari-mutuel machines, and Dan's career was ended before it had begun. A World Health or Point Four salary would barely pay her alimony and leave nothing for him, and a doctor can't skip, except into the medical shadowland of criminal practice. He had come to Florida because the state was growing and his practice and fees would be larger and he thought he'd eventually accumulate enough money to offer her a cash settlement and suture the financial hemorrhage.

In Fort Repose, Dan shared the one-story Medical Arts Building with an older man, Dr. Bloomfield, and two dentists. He lived frugally in a two-room suite in the Riverside Inn, where he acted as house physician for the aging guests during the winter season. His gross income had doubled. While he delivered babies for Pistolville and Negro families for $25, he balanced this with ten-dollar house calls on the placebo circuit. In a single two-hour sweep up River Road, handing out place-bos and tranquilizers, he often netted $100. It did him no good. He discovered he was inexorably squeezed between alimony and taxes. Taxes rose with income and the escalator clause in his alimony order took effect. Once, he and Randy figured out that if his gross rose to more than $50,000 a year he would have to go into bankruptcy. Dan could imagine no combination of circumstances that would allow him to amass enough capital to buy off his former wife and set him free to fight the plagues. So he was a bitter man, but, Randy believed, a kind man, perhaps even a great one.

Lib said, "You don't consider our house a stop on the placebo circuit, do you?"

"No," Dan said, "and yes. Your mother does have diabetes." He paused, to let her understand that was not all that was wrong. "She called me today. She was very much upset. She wondered whether she could change from insulin to the new oral drug. You've been giving her her insulin shot every morning, haven't you?"

"Yes," Lib said. "She can't bear to stick herself and she won't let my father do it. She says he's too rough. Says Dad jabs her like he enjoys it."

This was something Randy hadn't known before.

Dan said, "She wants me to get her oranise because she says you're talking about leaving her."

Lib said, "Yes, I do intend to leave. I'm going to leave when Randy leaves."

Randy started to speak, but checked himself. He could wait a moment.

Dan wiped his glasses. His face dropped unhappily. "I don't know about experimenting," he said. "Your mother is balanced at seventy units of insulin a day. A pretty solid shot. I don't want to take her off insulin. She'll have to learn to use the hypodermic herself. Now, let's move on to your father."

"My father! Nothing's wrong with Dad, is there?"

"Maybe nothing. Maybe everything. He's turning into a zombie, Elizabeth. Doesn't he have any hobbies? Can't he start a new business? He's only sixty-one and, except for a little hypertension, in good shape physically. But he is dying faster than he should. The better a man is at business, the worse in retirement. One day he's running a big corporation and the next day he isn't allowed to run anything, even his own home. He wishes himself dead, and he dies."

Lib had been listening intently. She said, "It's even harder on Dad. You see, he didn't retire by choice. He was fired. Oh, we all call it retirement, and he gets his pension, but the board eased him out—he lost a quiet little proxy fight—and now he doesn't think he is of any use to anyone at all."

"I felt," Dan said, "it was something like that." He was silent a moment. "I'd like to help him. I think he's worth saving."

Now Randy knew it was time to speak. "When you came in, Dan, I was about to tell Lib what Mark told me today, out at McCoy. He is afraid—he is sure—that we are on the verge of war. That's why Helen and the children are being sent down here. Mark thinks the Russians are already staged for it."

Randy watched them. Comprehension seemed to come first to Elizabeth. She said, softly, "Oh, God!" Her fingers locked in her lap and grew white.

Dan's head shook, a negative tremor. He looked at the decanter and Randy's half-empty glass on the bar. "You haven't been drinking, have you, Randy?"

"First today—since breakfast."

"I didn't think you'd been drinking. I was just hoping." Dan's massive head, with the coarse, wiry, reddish hair at the temples, bent forward as if his neck could no longer support it. "I guess that makes everything hypothetical," he said. "How soon?"

"Mark doesn't know and I can't even guess. Today—tomorrow—next week—next month—you name it."

Lib looked at her watch. "News at six," she said. A portable radio no larger than a highball glass stood at the end of the bar. She turned it on.

Randy kept the portable tuned to WSMF (Wonderful San Marco, Florida) the biggest station in the county. The dance music faded and the voice of Happy Hedrix, the disk jockey, said:

"Well, all of you frozen felines, I've got to take the needle out of the groove for five minutes so the cubes—a cube is a square anyway you look at him, hah, hah—can get hip with what cooks around the sphere. So let's start in with the weather. It's sixty-nine outside our studios right now and the forecast for Central Florida is fair and mild with light to moderate east winds tomorrow, and no frost danger through Tuesday. That's good fishing weather, folks, and to prove it here's a story from Tavares, over in Lake County, Jonas Corkle, of Hyannis, Nebraska, today caught a thirteen pound, four-ounce bigmouth in Lake Dora to take the lead in Lake County's Winter Bass Tournament. He used a black eel bait. A UP item from Washington says the Navy has ordered preventive action against unidentified jet planes which have been shadowing the Sixth Fleet in the Eastern Mediterranean. At Tropical Park today, Bald Eagle won the Coral Handicap by three lengths, paying eleven-sixty. Careless Lady was second and Rumpus third. Now, turning to news of Wall Street, stocks closed mixed, with missiles up and railroads off, in moderate trading. The Dow-Jones averages . . ."

Lib turned off Happy Hendrix. She said, "What's it mean?"

Randy shrugged. "That business in the Mediterranean? It's happened before. I guess that's one of the dangerous things about it. We get shockproof. We've been conditioned. Standing on the brink of war has become our normal posture." He turned to Dan. "I think we should lay in some drugs—an emergency kit. How about prescribing for war, Doctor?"

Dan fumbled in his jacket pocket and brought out a pad. He moved slowly and seemed very tired. "I'll give you both some," he said, starting to write. "Stuff you can use yourselves without my help. And for your mother, Elizabeth, extra bottles of insulin. Also, I'll order some oranise from a drug house in Orlando. Local pharmacy doesn't carry it yet."

"I thought you'd decided not to experiment with it on Mother?" Lib said.

"Insulin," Dan said, continuing to write, "requires refrigeration."

Dan dropped the prescriptions on the bar. "Good night," he said. "I'm delivering a baby at the clinic at seven. Caesarian section. Life goes on. At least that's what I'm going to believe until proved otherwise." He rose and shambled out of the room.

Lib walked around the counter. "Hold me," she said.

Randy held her, crushed her, strangely without any passion except fear for her. Usually he had only to feel her body, or brush his lips across her hair and smell what she called "my courting perfume" to become aroused. Now his arms were completely encircling and completely protective. All he asked was that she live and he live and that things remain the same.

She kept rolling her smooth head against his throat. She was saying no to it. She was willing and praying the clock to stand still, as Randy was; but, as Mark had said, this was against nature.

She raised her head and gently pushed herself away and said, "Thanks, Randy. I get strength from you. Did you know that? Now tell me, what should I do?"

"You'd better drive back to your house and speak with your mother and father."

"I don't think they'll believe it. They don't pay much attention to the international situation and Mother doesn't ever like to talk about anything unpleasant."

"They probably won't believe it. After all, they don't know Mark. Put it up to your father, as a business proposition. Tell him it's like taking out insurance. Anyway, be sure and get Dan's prescriptions filled."

"I'll get the medicines tomorrow," she said. "Food isn't a problem. Our cupboard isn't exactly bare. What are you going to do, Randy? Hadn't you better get some rest if you have to be at the airport at three-thirty?"

"I'll try." He took her into his arms again and kissed her, this time not feeling protective at all, and she responded, her fears contained.

They left the house as the distended red run dropped into the river where it joined the wide St. Johns. She got into the car. He touched her lips again. "If you need me, call."

"Don't worry. I will. See you tomorrow, Randy."
"Yes, tomorrow."

Now at this hour, when the cirrus clouds stretched like crimson ribbons high across the southwest sky, in such a hush that not even a playful eddy dared stir moss or palm fronds, the day died in calm and in beauty. This was Randy's hour, this and dawn, time of stillness and of peace.

His eye was attracted by movement in a clump of Turk's-cap across the road, and then again, he saw the damn bird. There could be little doubt of it. Even at this distance, without binoculars, he could distinguish the white-rimmed eyes. Moving very slowly and in silence, drifting from bush to bush, he crossed the lawn.

If he could cross the road and Florence Wechek's front yard without frightening it, he might make a positive identification.

Florence and Alice Cooksey watched him. Florence had been observing him from behind the bedroom blinds while he talked with the McGovern girl, and kissed her goodbye, a disgusting public exhibition. She had watched him stand in the driveway, hands on hips, alone and, for a long time, motionless. Then incredulously, she had seen him bend over and stealthily move toward her, and she had called Alice. "There he is!" she said triumphantly. "I told you so. Come and see for yourself. He's a Peeping Tom, all right!"

Alice, peering through the louvers, said, "I think he's stalking something."

"Yes, me."

They watched while he crossed the road, placing his feet carefully as a heron feeding on minnows in the shallows. "The sneak!" Florence said.

He reached Florence's lawn and for a moment hid behind a clump of boxwood. "He's going around the side of the house," Florence said. "I think we can watch better from the dining room." She ran into the dining room, Alice following.

Bent almost double, he advanced from the boxwood toward the Turk's-cap. Suddenly he straightened, threw an imaginary hat to the ground, and Florence heard him say distinctly, "Oh, Goddam!" At the same time she heard Anthony shaking the cage on the back porch. Anthony had come home for the night. Then she heard Randy on the back porch. Anthony squawked. Randy swore, and shouted, "Hey, Florence!"

She opened the kitchen door and said, "Now look here, Randolph Bragg, I'm not having any more of your prowling around the house and staring at me while I'm dressing. You ought to be ashamed!"

Randy, mouth open, astonished, stared at the two birds, Anthony on the outside of the cage, Cleo fluttering within. He said, "Is that your bird?" He pointed at Anthony.

"Certainly it's my bird."

"What kind of a bird is it?"

"Why he's an African lovebird, of course."

Randy shook his head. "I'm a dope. I thought he was a Carolina parakeet. You know, the Carolina parakeet is, or was, our only native parrot. A specimen hasn't been identified since 1925. They're supposed to be extinct. If that isn't one, I'm willing to admit they are."

"Is that why you've been spying on me? I saw you at it this morning, with glasses."

"I haven't been spying on you, Florence. I've been spying on that fake Carolina parakeet." He noticed Alice Cooksey standing behind Florence, smiling. Alice was one of his favorite people. He really ought to tell Alice about Mark, and what Mark predicted. Ought to tell Florence as well, but Florence still looked upset and angry. He said, "Now, Florence, cool off. I've got something important to tell you."

"Bird watcher!" Florence shrieked. She slammed the kitchen door in his face and fled into the house.

Randy put his hands in his pockets and strolled home. The world was real crazy. He'd talk to Florence and Alice in the morning, after Florence settled down.

In his kitchen, Randy made himself a cannibal sandwich. Lib considered his habit of eating raw ground round, smeared with horseradish and mustard and pressed between slices of rye bread, barbarous. He'd explained it was simply a bachelor's meal, quick and lazy, and anyway he liked it.

He trotted downstairs and examined the purchases lined on shelves and stacked in closets. Some of it was pretty exotic stuff for an emergency. Perhaps he should make up a small kit of delicacies. If the worst happened, this would be their iron rations for a desperate time. If nothing happened, it would all keep. He selected a jar of English beef tea, a sealed package of bouillon cubes, a jar of Swiss chocolates and a sealed tin of hardcandies, a canned Italian cheese and a few other small items. He placed them all in a small carton, wrapped the carton in foil, and took it up to the apartment. The teak chest in the office was a fine place to hide it and forget it. He rummaged through the chest, rearranging old legal documents, abstracts, bundles of letters, a packet of Confederate currency, peeling photograph albums. Lieutenant Peyton's log and a half-dozen baby books—all family memorabilia judged not valuable enough to warrant space in a safe deposit vault but too valuable to throw away—and made space for the iron rations at the bottom.

At seven o'clock he listened to the news. There was nothing startling. He flopped down on a studio couch, picked up a magazine, and started to read an article captioned, "Next Stop—Mars." Presently the words danced in front of his eyes, and he slept.

When it was seven Friday evening in Fort Repose, it was two o'clock Saturday morning in the Eastern Mediterranean, where Task Group 6.7 turned toward the north and headed for the narrow seas between Cyprus and Syria. The shape of the task group was a giant oval, its periphery marked by the wakes of destroyers and guided-missile frigates and cruisers. The center of Task Group 6.7, and the reason for its existence, was the U.S.S. *Saratoga,* a mobile nuclear striking base. In *Saratoga*'s Combat Information Center two officers watched a bright blip on the big radar repeater. It winked on and off, like a tiny green eye opening and closing. Interrogated by a "friend or foe" radar impulse, it had not replied. It was hostile. For thirty-six hours, ever since passing Malta, *Saratoga* had been shadowed. This blip was the latest shadower.

One of the officers said, "No use sending up a night fighter. That bogy is too fast. But an F-11-F could catch him. So we'll let him hang around, let him close in. Maybe he'll come close enough for a missle shot from *Canberra*. If not, we'll launch F-11-F's at first light."

The other officer, an older man, a senior captain, frowned. He disliked risking his ship in an area of restricted maneuver while under enemy observation. He always thought of the Mediterranean as a sack, anyway, and they were approaching the bottom of it. He said, "All right. But be damn sure we chase him out of radar range before we enter the Gulf of Iskenderun."

[4]

Helen Bragg's battle was over, and she had lost. The tickets were in her handbag. Their luggage— Mark had made them pack almost all the clothes they owned and paid an outrageous sum for the extra weight—was piled on the baggage cart already wheeled outside on the concrete, fine snow settling on it. She had lost, and yet fifteen minutes before plane time she still protested, not in the hope that Mark would change his mind. It was simply that she felt miserable and guilty. She said, "I still don't think I ought to go. I feel like a deserter."

The stood together in the terminal lobby, a tiny island oblivious to the human eddies around them. Her gloved hand held to his arm, her cheek was pressed tightly against his shoulder. He pressed her hand and said, "Don't be silly. Anybody with any sense gets out of a primary target area at a time like this. You aren't the first to leave, and you won't be the last."

"That doesn't make it right and it isn't right. My place is here with you."

He pulled her around to face him, so that her upturned mouth was inches from his own. "That's just it. You can't stay with me. If and when it comes I'll be in the Hole, protected by fifty feet of concrete and steel and good earth. That's where my place is and that's where you can't be. You'd be somewhere on the surface exposed. If you could come down into the Hole with me, then you could stay, darling."

This was something he had not said before, a fact she had not considered. Somehow it made her feel a bit better, yet she continued to argue, although dispiritedly. "Still, I think my job is here."

His fingers banded her arm and when he spoke his voice was flat, a direct order. "Your job is to survive because if you don't the children won't survive. That is your job. There is no other. You understand that, Helen?"

On the other side of the draughty terminal Ben Franklin and Peyton buzzed around the newsstand, each with a dollar to spend on candy, gum, and magazines. They knew only that they were getting out of school a week early, and were spending Christmas vacation in Florida. That's all Helen had told them, and in the excitement of packing, and greeting their father, and then packing more bags, there had been no questions. Helen said, "I understand." Her head dropped against Mark's chest. "If this business blows over you'll let us come right home, won't you?"

"Sure."

"You promise?"

"Certainly I promise."

"Maybe we could be home before the next school term."

"Don't count on it, darling. But I'll call you every day, and as soon as I think it's safe I'll give you the word."

The loudspeaker announced Flight 714 for Chicago, connecting with flights east and south.

The children ran over to them. Peyton carried a quiver and bow slung over her shoulder. Ben Franklin a cased spinning rod, his Christmas present from Randy the year before.

Mark shepherded them outside, and toward Gate 3. He lifted Peyton off the ground and held her a moment and kissed her, disarranging her red knitted cap. "My hair!" she said, laughing, and he put her down.

He noticed other passengers filtering through the gate. He drew Ben Franklin aside. He said, "Behave yourself, son."

Ben looked up at him, his brown eyes troubled. When he spoke, his voice was intentionally low. "This is an evacuation, isn't it, Dad?"

"Yes." It was Mark's policy never to utter an untruth when replying to a question from the children.

"I knew it as soon as I got home from school. Usually Mother gets all excited and happy about traveling. Not today. She hated to pack. So I knew it."

"I hate to send you away but it's necessary." Looking at Ben Franklin was like looking at a snapshot of himself in an old album. "You'll have to be the man of the family for a while."

"Don't worry about us. We'll be okay in Fort Repose. I'm worried about you." The boy's eyes were filling. Ben Franklin was a child of the atomic age, and knowledgeable.

"I'll be all right in the Hole."

"Not if . . . Anyway, Dad, you don't have to worry about us," he repeated.

Then it was time. Mark walked them to the gate, Peyton's glove in his left hand, Ben Franklin's in his right. Helen turned and he kissed her once and said, "Goodbye, darling. I'll phone you tomorrow afternoon. I've got the duty tonight and I'll probably sleep all morning but I'll call as soon as I get up."

She managed to say, "Tomorrow."

He watched them walk to the plane, a small procession, and out of his life.

At nine o'clock Randy awoke, aware of a half-dozen problems accumulated in his subconscious. The problem of transportation he had neglected entirely. He certainly ought to have a reserve of gas and oil. Half his grocery list remained to be purchased. He had not filled Dan Gunn's prescriptions. He had yet to visit Bubba Offenhaus and collect Civil Defense pamphlets. He went into his bathroom, turned on the lights, and washed the sleep out of his eyes. Lights! What would happen if the lights went out? Several boxes of candles, two old-fashioned kerosene lamps, and three flashlights were cached in the sideboard downstairs, a provision against hurricane season. He had a flashlight in his bedroom and another in the car. He added candles, kerosene, and flashlight batteries to his list. Everything, except the gasoline, would have to wait until tomorrow anyway. With Helen to help him fill in the gaps, it would be easy to lay in all the essentials Saturday.

He changed his clothes, shivering. The nights were getting cooler. Downstairs the thermometer read sixty-one and he turned up the thermostat. The Bragg house had no cellar—they were rare in Central Florida—but it did have a furnace room and was efficiently heated by oil. Oil! He doubted that he'd have to worry about oil. The fuel tank had been filled in November and thus far the winter had been mild.

In the garage Randy found two empty five-gallon gasoline cans. He put them in the car trunk and drove to town.

Jerry Kling's station was still open, but Jerry had already turned off his neon sign and was checking the cash register. Jerry filled the tank, and the two extra cans, and as an afterthought Randy asked for a gallon of kerosene and five extra quarts of oil.

Driving back on River Road, Randy slowed when he reached the McGoverns'. All the lights were on in the McGoverns' house. He turned into the driveway. It was ten-thirty. It was not necessary that he leave for the Orlando airport until two A.M.

It was near dawn in the Eastern Mediterranean when *Saratoga,* working up speed in narrowing waters between Cyprus and Lebanon, catapulted four F-11-F Tigers, the fastest fighters in its complement. By then, the reconnaissance jet that had shadowed Task Group 6.7 through the darkness hours had vanished from the radar screens. The Admiral's staff was convinced another would take its place, as on the previous morning, but this day the snooper would receive a surprise. Task Group 6.7's primary mission was to take station in Iskenderun Gulf and give heart to the Turks, who were under heavy political and propaganda pressure. The force's security would be endangered if its perilously tight formation, in this confined area, was observed.

Quite often the flood of history is undammed or diverted by the character and actions of one man. In this case the man was not an official in Washington, or the Admiral commanding Task Group 6.7, or even the Captain or Air Group Commander of *Saratoga*. The man was Ensign James Cobb, nicknamed Peewee, the youngest and smallest pilot in Fighter Squadron 44.

Ensign Cobb was assigned Combat Air Patrol duty on this Saturday morning simply because it was his turn. He was scarcely five feet, six inches tall, weighted 124, and looked younger than his twenty-three years. Under a flat-top haircut, his read head appeared knobby and outsized. His face was pinched, and mottled with freckles. In the presence of girls, he was shy to the point of panic. In the wonderful ports of Naples, Nice, and Istanbul, he distinguished himself as the only pilot in Fighting Forty-Four who never found reason to request a night's liberty ashore.

When he climbed into the cockpit of his aircraft, Peewee Cobb's whole character changed. The instant his hands and feet were on the controls, he became as large and fast as his supersonic fighter, and as powerful as its armament. As compensation for outer physical deficiencies, he was gifted with superb reactions and eyesight. He was rated superior in rocketry and gunnery. He got a fierce thrill in pushing his F-11-F through the mach, and to the limit of its capability. He could outfly anybody in the squadron, including the Lieutenant Commander who led it, and who had once said, "Peewee may be a mouse aboard ship, but he's a tiger in a Tiger. If I sent him up with orders to shoot down the moon, he'd try."

Now, for the first time, Peewee Cobb was flying CAP under wartime conditions, in a fighter armed with live rockets and with orders to intercept and destroy a snooper if it appeared. Climbing steadily in the darkness, he prayed that if the bogy came back, it would attempt to penetrate his sector. If it did, nobody would laugh at his size, his squeaky voice, his face, or his ineffectual awkwardness with women, ever again.

Peewee Cobb had been given a code name, Sunflower Four, and instructions to orbit over an area of sea off Haifa, astern of Task Group 6.7. If the hostile reconnaissance jet came in from a base in Egypt or Albania, he would be in a position to intercept. His fighter was armed with Sidewinders, ingenious, single-minded rockets, heat-seekers. A Sidewinder's nose was sensitive to infra-red rays from any heat source. Peewee had fired two in practice. They not only had destroyed the targets, but had unerringly vanished up the tail pipes of the drones.

At thirty thousand feet, Peewee judged he was on station and called for a radar fix. The missile-cruiser *Canberra,* closest ship in the formation, confirmed his position. As he circled, the sky in the southeast grew light. When the sun touched his wingtips, the sea was still dark below. Then gradually, the shape and color of sea and earth became plain. He felt entirely alone and apart from this transformation, as if he watched from a separate planet. He checked his map. Far to the east he picked out Mount Carmel, and a river, and beyond were the hills of Megiddo, also called Armageddon. He continued to orbit.

His earphones crackled and he acknowledged *Saratoga*. The fighter controller's voice said, "Sunflower Four, we have a bogy. He is at angels twenty-five, his speed five hundred knots. Your intercept course is thirty degrees. Go get him!"

So the snooper was already north of him and racing up the coast, hoping to hang on to the flank of the task group and observe it by radar from a position close to friendly Syrian territory. Peewee took his heading and pushed his throttle up to ninety-nine percent power. He slid through the mach with a slight, thrilling tremor. Every fifteen or twenty seconds he made minute alterations in course in response to directions from *Saratoga,* which was holding both planes on its screens.

Then he saw it, flicker of sun on metal, diving at great speed.

He pushed the Tiger's nose over and followed, reporting, "I am closing target." He touched the switch that armed his rockets, and another calling for manual fire, singly.

The chase had carried him down to nine thousand

feet and the bogy was still losing altitude. It was a two-engined jet, an IL-33, Peewee believed, and remarkably fast at this low level. There was no doubt the bogy knew he was on its tail, for reconnaissance aircraft would be well equipped with radar. His speed held steady at mach 1.5, but his rate of closure slowed.

Far ahead Peewee saw the Syrian port of Latakia, reputedly built into an important Red submarine base. Within a few seconds he would be within Syrian territorial waters, and a few more would carry him over the port itself.

At this point Peewee should have dropped the chase, for they had been strictly warned, in the briefing, against violating anyone's borders. He hung on. In another five seconds—

The bogy jinked violently to the right, heading for the port and its anti-aircraft and rocket batteries and perhaps the sanctuary of an airfield in the brown hills and dunes beyond.

Peewee turned the F-11-F inside him, instantly shortening the range.

He pushed the firing button.

The Sidewinder, leaving a thin pencil mark of smoke, rushed out ahead.

For an instant the Sidewinder seemed to be following the flight of the bogy beautifully, and Peewee waited for it to merge into the tail pipe of one of the jet engines. Then the Sidewinder seemed to waver in its course.

Peewee believed, although he could not be certain, that the bogy had cut its engines and was in a steep glide. Following the Sidewinder, Peewee lost sight of the bogy.

The Sidewinder darted downward, toward the dock area of Latakia.

It seemed to be chasing a train.

That crazy roccket, Peewee thought.

There was an orange flash and an enormous ball of brown smoke and black bits of debris rushing up to meet him. Peewee kicked his rudder hard and climbed away from it, compressed within his G-suit and momentarily losing his vision. Then the shock wave kicked him in the rear and he was out over the Mediterranean again. He was asking for a vector back to his ship when another flash reflected on his instrument panel. He banked to look back, and saw a black cloud, red flames at its base, rising from Latakia.

Fifteen minutes later Ensign Cobb, freckles standing out on his white face like painted splotches, was standing in Admiral's Country of *Saratoga* trying to explain what had happened.

Randy Bragg pulled up in the rear driveway of the McGovern house, wondering whether he should go in. He was not exactly popular with the elder McGoverns, which was why Lib visited him more often than he visited her.

Whenever he entered the McGovern home, Randy felt as if he were stepping into an enormous department-store window. The entire front of the house, facing the Timucuan, was plate glass clamped between thin stainless steel supports, and every piece of furniture appeared unused, as if a price tag and warranty would be found tied to one of the legs. Lavinia McGovern herself had thought up the basic plan, collaborated with the architect, and supervised the construction. The architect, pleading a hotel commission in Miami, had returned part of his fee and absented himself from Fort Repose before the foundation was laid.

On his first visit, Randy had not endeared himself to Lavinia. She took him on what she called "the grand tour," proudly showing off the multiple heat pumps insuring constant year-round temperature; the magnificent kitchen with electronic ovens and broilers operated from a central control panel; the cunning round holes in the ceiling which sprayed gentle light on dining-room table, bar, bridge table, and strategically located abstract statuary; the television screens faired into the walls of bedrooms, living room, dining room, and even kitchen; and the master bathroom's free form tub, which extended through the wall and into a tiny, shielding garden. There were no fireplaces, which she called "soot-producers," or bookshelves, which were "dust catchers." All was new, modern, and functional. "When we came down here," Lavinia said, "we got rid of everything in Shaker Heights and started fresh, bright, and new. See how I've brought the river right to our feet?" She indicated the expanse of glass. "What do you think of it?"

Randy tried to be at once tactful and truthful. "It reminds me of an illustration out of *Modern Living,* but—"

"But?" Lavinia inquired, nervously.

Randy, feeling he was being helpful, pointed out that in the summer months the sun's direct rays would pour through the glass walls, and that the afternoon heat would become unbearable no matter how large and efficient the air-conditioning system. "I'm afraid that in summer you'll have to shutter that whole southwest side of the house," he said.

"Is there anything else you think is wrong?" Lavinia asked, her voice dangerously sweet.

"Well, yes. That indoor-outdoor bath is charming and original, but come spring it'll be a freeway for moccasins and water snakes. On cool nights they'll plop in and swim or crawl right into the house."

At this point Lavinia had squealed and clutched at her throat as it suffocating, and her husband and daughter had half-carried her to the bedroom. The next day plumbers and masons remodeled the sunken tub, eliminating the outdoor feature. Later, Lib explained that her mother dreaded snakes, and had been solely responsible for the design of the house. Randy never felt comfortable in Lavinia's presence thereafter. And Lavinia, while attempting to be gracious, sometimes became pale and grew faint when he appeared.

Randy's relations with Bill McGovern were little better. On occasion, after a few extra drinks, he disagreed with Mr. McGovern on matters political, social, and economic. Since Bill for many years had been president of a manufacturing concern employing six thousand people, few of whom ever disagreed with him about anything, he had been affronted and angry. He considered Randy an insolent young loafer, an example of decadence in what once might have been a good family, and a sadly scrambled egghead, and had so informed his daughter.

So Randy, sitting in his car, hesitated. He was certain to be coolly received. Lib didn't expect to see him until the next day, but he had a hunch she needed him now. He guessed a considerable argument was going on inside. Lib would be verbally overpowered by her father, and Mark's warning go unheeded. Randy got out of his car.

Lib opened the north door before he could ring. "I thought I heard a car in the drive," she said. "I'm glad it's you. I've got troubles."

Bill McGovern was standing in the living room, wrapped in an ankle-length white bathrobe, smiling as if nothing were funny. Lavinia McGovern, her eyes swollen and pink against pallid skin, lay back on a chaise. She held a hankerchief to her nose. Bill was bald, square shouldered, and rather tall. His nose was beaked and his chin prominent and strong. In his toga of toweling, and with feet encased in leather sandals, he looked like an angry Caesar. "So here comes our local Paul Revere," he greeted Randy. "What are you trying to do, frighten my wife and daughter to death?"

Randy regretted having come in, but now that he was in he saw no point in being anything less than frank. "Mr. McGovern," he said—ordinarily he addressed Lib's father as Bill—"you aren't as bright as I thought. If I gave you a hot tip, from a good source, on the market, you would listen. This is somewhat more important than the market. I thought I was doing you a favor." He turned to leave.

Lib touched his arm. "Please, Randy, don't go!"

"Elizabeth,"—when her parents were present he always called her Elizabeth—"I'll leave things the way they are. If you need me, call."

Lavinia began to sniffle, audibly. In a worried voice Bill said, "Now don't rush off half-cocked, Randy. I'm sorry if I was rude. There are certain things you don't understand."

"Like what?" Randy asked.

Bill's voice was conciliatory. "Just sit down and I'll explain."

Randy continued to stand.

"Now I'm twice as old as you are," Bill said, "and I think I know more about what goes on in this world. After all, I know quite a few big men—the biggest. All these war scares are concocted by the Pentagon—no offense meant to your brother—to get more appropriations, and give more handouts to Europe, and jack up taxes. It's all part of the damnable inflationary pattern that's designed to cheat people on pensions and with fixed incomes and so forth. Now I know your brother thinks he's doing the right thing, and I appreciate your telling Elizabeth. But chances are your brother's been taken in too."

"Have you been listening to the news for the past few days?"

"Yes. Oh, I'll admit it looks bad in the Mideast but that doesn't scare me. We might have a little brushfire war, like Korea, sure. But no atomic war. Nobody's going to use atomic bombs, just like nobody used gas in the last war."

"You'll guarantee that, eh, Bill?"

Bill locked his hands behind his back. "I can't guarantee it, of course, but only the other day I was talking to Mr. Offenhaus. You must know him. Runs Civil Defense here. Well, he isn't worried. Says the only real danger we face is being overrun by people swarming out of Orlando and Tampa. He doesn't even think there's much chance of that. Fort Repose isn't on any main highway. But he does say we'll have to watch out for the dinges. Keep 'em under control."

"Please, Bill!" Lavinia said. "Say darkies!"

"Darkies, hell! The dinges are liable to panic and start looting. Oh, the local niggers, like Daisy, our cook and Missouri, the cleaning woman, may be all right. Mr. Offenhaus was talking about the migrant labor, the orange pickers and so forth. So if Mr. Offenhaus isn't worried, then I'm not worried. Mr. Offenhaus strikes me as a pretty solid businessman."

Randy knew that Bubba Offenhaus had been picked

to head Civil Defense because he owned the only two
ambulances, which with the addition of black scroll-
work doubled as hearses, in Fort Repose. "Did you talk
to him about fallout?" he asked.

"Well, no, I didn't," Bill said. "Mr. Offenhaus said
they sent him some booklets from Washington but he's
not passing them around because they're too gruesome.
Says why worry about something you can't see, feel,
hear, or smell? Says it's just as bad to frighten people to
death as kill them with radiation, and I must say that I
agree with him."

Lavinia said, "If it came I suppose we'd have rationing like last time and all kinds of shortages. Bill, don't
you think we ought—no, I won't think of it. Please, let's
not talk about it any more. It's horrid." She dabbed at
her eyes and tried to smile. "Randolph, when your
sister-in-law comes won't you bring her over for dinner?
Afterwards, we could play bridge. Perhaps you'd like to
play a rubber now? I know you're going to stay up to
meet the plane, and I'm too overwrought to sleep."

"I'm sure Helen will be delighted to come to dinner,"
Randy said. "As for bridge, I'll take a rain check. I still
have some things to do at home. Good night, Lavinia.
Sorry I upset you."

Lib came out to the car with him. "Didn't get very
far, did I?" he said.

"You started Dad thinking. That's far."

Overhead he heard multi-engined jets. On that night
there was three quarters of the moon. He looked up,
and seeing nothing, knew the jets were military aircraft,
too high for their running lights to show against the
bright sky. On any night, if you listened for a while, you
could hear the B-52's and 47's and 58's, but on this
night there seemed to be more of them.

"Where are they from?" Lib asked. "Where are they
going?"

"I guess they're from McCoy and MacDill and Eglin
and Homestead," Randy said, "and I don't think they're
going anywhere much. They're just stooging around up
there because they're safer up there than on the ground.

When you can hear them floating around like that, high, you know you're all right."

"I see," Lib said. For the second time, he kissed her good night.

When he reached home it was almost midnight. He made coffee and, yawning, turned on the radio and tuned an Orlando station for the late network news. The first bulletin jerked him wide awake:

"From Washington—The official Arab radio, in a broadcast from Damascus, claims that American carrier planes are conducting a violent bombing attack on the harbor of Latakia. This news broke in Washington just a few minutes ago. There has been no reaction from the Pentagon, which at this hour of night is lightly staffed. However, it is reported that high Navy and Defense Department officials are being summoned into emergency conference. We will give you more on this as we receive it from our Washington newsroom. Here is the text of the official Arab broadcast: 'At about six-thirty o'clock this morning'—please remember that it is morning in the Eastern Mediterranean, which is seven hours ahead of American Eastern Standard Time—'low-flying jet aircraft, of the type used on United States aircraft carriers and bearing United States insignia, brutally and without warning bombed the harbor area of Latakia. It is reported that civilian casualties are high and that many buildings are in flames.' That was the text of the Arab broadcast and that is all the hard news we have at the moment. Latakia is the most important Syrian harbor. Within the last few years it has been heavily fortified, and there has been extensive construction of submarine pens under the direction of Russian technicians. It is generally regarded as one of the most powerful anti-Western naval bases in the Mediterranean. It is known that units of the United States Sixth Fleet are now in the Eastern Mediterranean, and that these units have been shadowed by fast, unidentified aircraft. . . ."

The network announcer went on to other news, and Randy's phone rang.

He picked it up, irritated. It was Bill McGovern. "Did you hear the news?" Bill asked.

"Yes. I'm trying to get more of it."

"What do you think?"

"I don't think anything, yet. I want to hear our side of it."

"Sounds to me like we're starting a small preventive war," Bill said.

"I don't believe that for an instant," Randy said. "You don't prevent a war by starting one."

"Well, we'll see who's right in the morning."

Mark Bragg missed the first news flash on Latakia. At that moment he was straightening up the house before driving to Offutt to assume direction of Intelligence analysis in the Hole. He had been recalled from the Puerto Rico mission because SAC's Commander in Chief, General Hawker, felt that in this newest crisis senior members of his Operations and Intelligence staffs should maintain a round-the-clock watch. An attack is rarely planned to conform to a victim's five-day, forty-hour week so Hawker divided his most experienced officers into three shifts covering the whole day. As SAC's third-ranking Intelligence officer, junior to the A-2 and his deputy, both brigadiers, Colonel Bragg naturally drew the most onerous hours—midnight to 0800.

At eleven P.M., Omaha time, while the Damascus broadcast was being repeated around the world, Mark was in the children's rooms, feeling like an intruder. It was the silence that discomforted him. He found himself tiptoeing, listening for the missing sounds. The house was still as northern woods in winter, when all the creatures are gone.

Ben Franklin's room looked as if it had been ransacked by a band of monkeys rather than that a thirteen-year-old boy had packed. Mark closed dresser drawers and picked up ties, clothes-hangers, and shoes and socks, never in pairs. He supposed all boys were like that. Peyton's room looked no different than if this had been an ordinary day, as if she had been invited to a slumber party at the home of a friend and would return in the morning. Her bedspread was uncreased, and the furry toy animal that held her pajamas rested pre-

cisely in its center, as always. She had forgotten it. Her
doll collection, carefully propped up on a tier of
shelves, formed a silent audience to his silent inspection.
Peyton hadn't asked to take her dolls to Florida. Perhaps she was outgrowing dolls. Or perhaps she didn't
realize, when she left them, that it might be forever. Her
desk was neat, pencils aligned as if at squads right,
schoolbooks stacked in a pyramid. He picked up the
books and took them downstairs. He would mail them
from Offutt in the morning, after he was off duty. Peyton was a tidy and thoughtful little girl, in looks and
temperament much like her mother. He loved her. He
loved them both. They had been very satisfactory children. The house was intolerably quiet. In the whole
house the only sound was the ticking of clocks.

Driving toward Offutt, and his job, Mark felt better.
When he turned into the four-lane highway that ran
south to the base he saw that it was eleven-thirty and
flipped on the car radio. It was then that he heard the
Arab charge that Latakia had been bombed by American planes and, in addition, a rather strange statement
from Washington. "A Navy Department spokesman,"
the newscaster said, "denies that there has been any in-
tentional attack on the Syrian coast."

Mark stepped down on the accelerator and watched
the speedometer needle pass seventy-five. On a turn the
back wheels weaved. Ice. He forced himself to concentrate on his driving. Soon he would know everything
that was known in the Hole, which meant everything
that was known to American Intelligence, and the
world-wide news networks, everywhere. Meanwhile it
was pointless to guess, or end up in a ditch, a useless
casualty with no Purple Heart.

Twelve minutes later Mark entered the War Room,
fifty feet underground. Blinking in the brilliant but
shadowless artificial sunlight, he glanced at the map
panels. Nothing startling. He walked on to the offices of
A-2, Intelligence. In the inner office Dutch Klein, Deputy A-2 and a buck general in his early forties, waited
for his relief. An electric coffee maker steamed on
Dutch's desk. Two ashtrays were filled with crushed

cigarette butts. Dutch had been busy. Dutch said, "I guess you've heard the news."

"I caught it on the radio. It's not true, is it?"

"It's fantastic!" Dutch touched a sheaf of pink flimsies, decoded priority messages, on his desk. "Two hours ago Sixth Fleet scrambled fighters to intercept a jet snooper. An ensign from *Saratoga*—an ensign, mind you—sighted the bogy and chased him all the way up the Levant. He closed at Latakia and fired a bird. Whether it was human error or an erratic rocket isn't clear. Anyway, everything blew." Dutch, a muscular, keg-shaped man with round, rubbery face, groaned and sank back into his chair.

Automatically the fortifications of the port area of Latakia came into focus in Mark's mind. "Large stores of conventional mines, torpedoes, and ammo," he said. "They usually have four to eight subs in the new pens and a couple of cruisers and escort vessels in the harbor." He hesitated, thinking of something else, worse. "The fire and blast could have cooked off nuclear weapons, if they were in combat configuration. That could well be. What do you make of it?"

"Worst foul-up on record," Dutch said. "Glad it's the Navy and not us."

"I mean, how do you think the Russians will react?" Mark asked the question not because he thought Dutch could give him the answer, but as a catalyst to his own imagination. Intelligence wasn't Dutch's primary interest. On the way up to two stars and command of an air division, Dutch had been forced to assimilate two years of staff, part of his education. To Mark, the Intelligence job, with all its political and psychological facets, was a career in itself. He had a feel for it, the capacity to stir a headful of unrelated facts until they congealed into a pattern arrowing the future.

Dutch said, "Maybe it'll throw them off balance."

"It might upset their timetable," Mark agreed, "but I'm afraid they're all set. It might just give the Kremlin a *casus belli,* an excuse."

Dutch lifted himself out of the chair. "I leave it with you. The C in C was here until a few minutes ago. He said he had to get some sleep because it might get even hairier tomorrow. If there are any important political developments you're to call him. Operations will handle the alert status, as usual."

For thirty minutes Mark concentrated on the pile of flimsies, the latest intelligence from NATO, Smyrna, Naples, the Philippines, Eastern Sea Frontier, and the summaries from Air Defense Command and the CIA. When he was abreast of the situation he crossed the War Room to Operations Control.

The Senior Controller on duty was Ace Atkins, a former fighter pilot, like Mark an eagle colonel. He was called Ace because he had been one, in two wars. Because of proven courage and absolute coolness, he was at the desk now occupied, with the red phone a few inches from his fingers. One code word into Ace's red phone would cock SAC's two thousand bombers and start the countdown at the missile sites. It would take another word, either spoken by General Hawker or with his authority, to launch the force.

Ace, slight and wiry, looked up and said, "Welcome to Bedlam!" The Control Room, separated from the War Room by heavy glass, was utterly quiet.

Mark said, "I'm worried. I wish Washington would come forth with a complete statement. As things stand now, most of the world will believe we attacked Latakia deliberately."

"Why don't the Navy information people give out?"

"They want to. They've got a release ready. But they're low echelon and you know Washington."

"Not very well."

"I know it well," Mark said, "and I think I can pretty well guess what's happening. Everybody wants to put his chop on it because it's so important but for the same reason nobody wants to take the responsibility. The Navy PIO probably called an Assistant Secretary, and the Assistant Secretary called the Secretary and the Secretary probably called the Secretary of Defense. By that time the Information Agency and State Department were involved. By now more and more people are getting up and they are calling more and more people."

Mark looked at the clocks, above the War Room maps, telling the time in all zones from Omsk to Guam. "It's two A.M. in Washington now. As each man gives his okay to the release it turns out that somebody else has to be consulted. Eventually they'll have the Secretary of State out of bed and then the White House press secretary. Maybe he'll wake up the President. Until that happens, I don't think there'll be any full statement."

Ace said, "My God! That sounds awful."

"It is, but what worries me most is Moscow."

"What's Moscow saying?"

"Not a word. Not a whisper. Usually Radio Moscow would be screaming bloody murder. That's what worries me. As long as people keep talking, they're not fighting. When Moscow quits talking, I'm afraid they're acting." Mark borrowed a cigarette and lit it. "I think the chances are about sixty-forty," he said, "that they've started their countdown."

Ace's fingers stroked the red phone. "Well," he said, "we're as ready as we ever will be. Fourteen percent of the force is airborne now and another seventeen percent on standby. I'm prepared to hold that ratio until we're relieved at 0800. How's that sound to you, Mark?"

As always, the responsibility to act lay with A-3. Mark Bragg, as A-2, could only advise. He said, "That's a pretty big effort. You can't keep the whole force in the air and on standby all the time. I know that, and yet—" He stretched. "I'll trot back to my cave and see what else comes in. I'll check with you in an hour."

On his desk, Mark found copies of three more urgent dispatches. One, from the Air attaché in Ankara, reported Russian aerial reconnaissance over the Azerbaijan frontier. Another, from the Navy Department, gave a submarine-sighting two hundred miles off Seattle, definitely a skunk. The third, received by the State Department from London in the highest secret classification, said Downing Street had authorized the RAF to arm intermediate range missiles, including the Thor, with nuclear warheads.

In an hour Helen's plane would touch down in Orlando. In two hours, if the plane was on time, Helen and the children would be in an area of comparative safety. Mark prayed that for the next two hours, at least, nothing more would happen. He held fast to the thought, so long as there was no war, there was always a chance for peace. As the minutes and hours eroded away, and no word came from Moscow, he became more and more certain that a massive strike had been ordered. He diagnosed this negative intelligence as more ominous than almost anything that could have happened, and determined to awaken General Hawker if it persisted.

At three-thirty in the morning Randolph Bragg waited in Orlando's air terminal for Helen's flight. With only a few night coaches scheduled in from New York, plus the non-stop from Chicago, the building was almost empty except for sweepers and scrubwomen. When he saw a plane's landing lights, Randy walked outside to the gate. On the other side of the field, near the military hangars used by Air-Sea Rescue Command, he saw the silhouettes of six B-47's, part of the wing from McCoy, he deduced, using this field in accordance with a dispersal plan. The military hangars and Operations building were bright with light, which at this hour was not usual.

The big transport came in for its landing, approached on the taxi strip, pivoted to a halt before him, and cut its engines. He saw that only a few people were getting off. Most would be going on to Miami. He saw Peyton and Ben Franklin come down the steps, Ben incongruously wearing an overcoat, Peyton carrying a bow, a quiver of arrows over her shoulder. Then he saw Helen and she waved and he ran out to meet them.

Randy rumpled Ben Franklin's hair. The children were both owl-eyed and tired. He leaned over, kissed Peyton, and relieved her of the bow slung over her shoulder. Helen said, "She's been watching Robin Hood. She thinks she's Maid Marion."

Helen was wearing a long cashmere coat and carrying a fur cape over her arm. She appeared fresh, as if starting rather than completing a journey. She was slight—Mark sometimes referred to her as "my pocket Venus—" yet Randy was never aware of that except when he saw her completely relaxed. At all other times her body seemed to obey the physical law that kinetic energy increases mass. Her abundant vitality she somehow communicated to others, so that when Helen was present everyone's blood flowed a little faster, as Randy's did now. She tiptoed to kiss him and said, "I feel like ten kinds of a fool, Randy."

He said, "Don't be silly."

They walked toward the terminal. She presented him with a sheaf of baggage checks. "Mark made me take everything. We're going to be an awful nuisance. Also, I feel like a coward."

"You won't when you hear what's just happened in the Med."

Ben Franklin turned, suddenly awake, and said, "What happened in the Med, Randy?"

Randy looked at Helen, inquiringly. She said, "It's all right. Both of them know all about it. I didn't realize it until we were on the plane. Children are precocious these days, aren't they? They learn the facts of life before you have a chance to explain anything."

While they waited for the luggage, Randy spoke of the news. They listened gravely. Ben Franklin alone commented. "Sounds like the kickoff. I guess Dad knew what he was doing."

Nothing more was said about it for a time.

Randy felt relieved when the suburbs of Orlando were behind them and, with traffic thin at this hour, he was holding to a steady seventy. He thought his apprehension illogical. Why should he be upset by the remark of a thirteen-year-old boy? When he was sure the children slept in the back seat, he said, "They take it calmly, almost as a matter of course, don't they?"

"Yes," Helen said. "You see, all their lives, ever since they've known anything, they've lived under the shadow of war—atomic war. For them the abnormal has become normal. All their lives they have heard nothing else, and they expect it."

"They're conditioned," Randy said. "A child of the

nineteenth century would quickly go mad with fear, I think, in the world of today. It must have been pretty wonderful to have lived in the years, say, between 1870 and 1914, when peace was the normal condition and people really were appalled at the idea of war, and believed there'd never be a big one. A big one was impossible, they used to say. It would cost too much. It would disrupt world trade and bankrupt everybody. Even after the first World War people didn't accept war as normal. They had to call it The War to End War or we wouldn't have fought it. Helen, what has become of us?"

Helen, busy tuning the car radio, trying to bring in fresh news, said, "You're a bit of an idealist, aren't you, Randy?"

"I suppose so. It's been an expensive luxury. Maybe one day I'll get conditioned. I'll accept things, like the children."

Helen said, "Listen!" She had brought in a Miami station, and the announcer was saying the station was remaining on the air through the night to give news of the new crisis.

"Now we have a bulletin from Washington," he said: "The Navy Department has finally released a full statement on the Latakia incident. Early today a Navy carrier-based fighter fired a single air-to-air rocket at an unidentified jet plane which had been shadowing units of the Sixth Fleet. This rocket exploded in the harbor area of Latakia. The Navy calls it a regrettable mechanical error. It is possible that this rocket struck an ammunition train and started a chain explosion, the statement admits. The Navy categorically denies any deliberate bombardment. We will bring you further bulletins as they are received."

The Miami station began to broadcast a medley of second World War patriotic songs which Randy remembered from boyhood. One was "Praise the Lord and Pass the Ammuniton." It sounded tinny and in poor taste, but Miami's entertainment was usually in poor taste.

Randy said, "Do you believe it? Is it possible?"

Helen didn't answer. She was staring straight ahead,

as if hypnotized by the headlights' beam, and her lips were moving. He realized that her mind was far away. She had not heard him.

Randy had them all in their rooms, and asleep, by five-thirty. He had carried all their luggage, eleven bags, upstairs.

He went to his own apartment and collapsed on the studio couch in the living room. Graf jumped up and snuggled under his arm. Almost at once, without bothering to loosen his belt or remove his shoes, Randy slept.

It was 0500 at Offutt Field, with dawn still more than two hours distant, when General Hawker, unbidden, returned to the Hole. The General followed in the tradition of Vandenberg, Norstad, and LeMay. He had received his fourth star while still in his forties, and now, at fifty, considered it part of his job that he remain slim and in excellent physical condition. Once warfare, except among the untutored savages, had been fought during the daylight hours. This had changed during the twentieth century until now rockets and aircraft recognized neither darkness nor bad weather, and were handicapped neither by oceans nor mountains nor distance. Now, the critical factor in warfare was time, measured in minutes or seconds. Hawker had adjusted his life to this condition. In the past week he had not slept more than four hours at a stretch. He had trained himself to catnap in his office for ten- or twenty-minute periods, after which he felt remarkably refreshed.

The engineers who designed the Hole had arranged that the Commander in Chief's Command Post be on a glass-enclosed balcony, from which he could see all the War Room maps, and all the activity on the floor below, and be surrounded by his staff.

In this moment it wasn't operating like that at all. Hawker had his feet up on the desk in the Control Room. He was drinking black coffee from a green dimestore mug, and rapidly reading through a stack of the more important operational and intelligence dispatches.

Occasionally, the General fired a question at one or the other of his two colonels, Atkins and Bragg.

An A-2 staff sergeant came into the room with two pink flimsies and handed them to Mark Bragg. The General looked up, inquiringly.

Mark said, "From the Eastern Sea Frontier. Patrol planes on the Argentina-Bermuda axis report three unidentified contacts. These skunks are headed for the Atlantic coast."

"Sounds bad, doesn't it?"

"I think this one sounds worse," Mark said. "All news service and diplomatic communications between Moscow and the United States have been inoperative for the last hour. This comes from USIA. The news agencies have been calling their Moscow correspondents. All the Moscow operators will say is, 'Sorry. I am unable to complete the call.' "

"And there's been no reaction to Latakia from Moscow at all?"

"None, sir. Not a whisper."

The General shook his head, slowly, frowning, lines appearing and deepening around mouth and eyes, his whole face undergoing a transformation, growing older, as if in a few seconds all the strain and fatigue of weeks, months, years had accumulated and were marking his face and bowing his shoulders.

Hawker said, "This is the witching hour, you know. This is the bad one. Their submarines have had a whole night to run in on the coast if that's what they're doing. We're in darkness. They'll soon be in daylight. Dawn is the bad time. What time does it start to get light in New York and Washington?"

"Sunrise on the seaboard is seven-ten Eastern Standard," Ace Atkins said. Washington's clock read 6:41.

Mark Bragg's mind raced ahead, If an attack came, they could count on no more than fifteen minutes' warning. If they used every one of those minutes with maximum efficiency, retaliation could be decisive. But Mark feared a minute, or even two, might be lost in necessary communication with Washington. He made a bold proposal. "May I suggest, sir, that we ask for the release of our weapons?"

This was the one mandatory, essential act that must precede the terrible decision to use the weapons. Under the law, the President of the United States "owned" the nuclear bombs and missile warheads. General Hawker was entrusted with their custody only. Before SAC could use the weapons, the permission of the President— or his survivor in a line of succession—must be secured. If an attack were underway, that permission would come almost, but not quite, instantly.

The General seemed a little startled. "Don't you think we can wait, Mark?"

"Yes, sir, we can wait, but if we get it out of the way, it could save us a minute, maybe two. The danger, and the necessity of not having a communications' snafu, must be just as apparent in the Pentagon, or the White House, or wherever the President is, as it is here."

"What do you think, Ace?" Hawker asked.

"I'd like to have it behind us, sir."

The General picked up one of the four phones on Atkins' desk, the phone connecting directly with the Pentagon Command Post. In this CP, day and night, was a general officer of the Air Force. This duty officer was never out of communication with the President, the Secretary of Defense, and the Chairman of the Joint Chiefs of Staff.

The General spoke briefly into the phone and then waited, keeping it pressed against his ear. Mark's eyes followed the red second hand on the desk clock. This was an interesting experiment. The General said, "Yes, John, this is Bob Hawker. I want the release of my weapons." Mark knew that "John" was Chairman of the Joint Chiefs. "Yes, I'll hold," the General said. The seconds raced away. The General said, "Thank you, John. It is now eleven forty-four, Zulu. You will confirm by teletype? Goodbye, John."

The General reached across the desk and wrote in Ace Atkins' log: "Weapons released to SAC at 11:44, Zulu." The Operations log was kept in Greenwich Time.

Mark said, "I timed it. One minute and thirty-five seconds."

"I hope we don't need it," Hawker said, "but I'm glad to have it." The worry lines became less conspicuous around his mouth and eyes. His back and shoulders straightened. Now that the responsibility was his, with complications and entanglements minimized, he accepted it with confidence. His manner said that if it came he would fight it from here, and by God win it, as much as it could be won.

The General poured himself another cup of coffee. Ace Atkins told the General, "With your permission, I'm going to scramble fifty percent of all our tankers at Bluie West One, Thule, Limestone, and Castle. They'd be sitting ducks for missiles from subs. They're right under the gun. They wouldn't get fifteen minutes." The General nodded. Ace flipped two keys on the intercom and dictated an order.

Beside Ace's desk, a tape recorder steadily turned, monitoring phone calls and conversations. The General glanced at it and said, "Do you realize that everything said in this room is being recorded for posterity?"

They all smiled. On all the clocks another minute flipped.

The direct line from NORAD, North American Air Defense, in Colorado Springs, buzzed. Ace picked it up, said, "Atkins, SAC Operations," listened, said, "Roger. I repeat. Object, may be missile, fired from Soviet base, Anadyr Peninsular."

The emergency priority teletype machine from NORAD began to clatter.

It's only one, Mark thought. It could be a meteor. It could be a Sputnik. It could be anything.

The NORAD line buzzed again. Ace answered and repeated the flash, as before, for the General and the tape recorder. "DEW Line high sensitivity radar now has four objects on its screens. Speed and trajectory indicates they are ballistic missiles. Presque Isle and Homestead report missiles coming in from sea. We are skipping the yellow. This is your red alert."

The General gave an order.

Mark rose and said, "I think I'd better get back to my desk."

The General nodded and smiled thinly. He said, "Thanks for the ninety-five seconds."

[5]

At first Randy thought someone was shaking the couch. Graf, nestled under his arm, whined and slipped to the floor. Randy opened his eyes and elevated himself on his elbow. He felt stiff and grimy from sleeping in his clothes. Except for the daschund, tail and ears at attention, the room was empty. Again the couch shook. The world outside still slept, but he discerned movement in the room. His fishing rods, hanging by their tips from a length of pegboard, inexplicably swayed in rhythm. He had heard such phenomena accompanied earthquakes, but there had never been an earthquake in Florida. Graf lifted his nose and howled.

Then the sound came, a long, deep, powerful rumble increasing in crescendo until the windows rattled, cups danced in their saucers, and the bar glasses rubbed rims and tinkled in terror. The sound slowly ebbed, then boomed to a fiercer climax, closer.

Randy found himself on his feet, throat dry, heart pounding. This was not the season for thunder, nor were storms forecast. Nor was this thunder. He stepped out onto the upstairs porch. To his left, in the east, an orange glow heralded the sun. In the south, across the Timucuan and beyond the horizon, a similar glow slowly faded. His sense refused to accept a sun rising and a sun setting. For perhaps a minute the spectacle numbed reaction.

What had jolted Randy from sleep—he would not learn all the facts for a long, a very long time after— were two nuclear explosions, both in the megaton range, the warheads of missiles lobbed in by submarines. The first obliterated the SAC base at Homestead, and incidentally sank and returned to the sea a considerable area of Florida's tip. Ground Zero of the second missile was Miami's International Airport, not far from the heart of the city. Randy's couch had been shaken by shock waves transmitted through the earth, which travel faster than through the air, so he had been awake when the blast and sound arrived a little later. Gazing at the glow to the south, Randy was witnessing, from a distance of almost two hundred miles, the incineration of a million people.

The screen door banged open. Ben Franklin and Peyton, barefoot and in flannel pajamas, burst out onto the porch. Helen followed. The sight of war's roseate birthmark on the sky choked back their words. Helen grabbed Randy's arm tightly in both hands, as if she had stumbled. Finally, she spoke. "So soon?" It was a moan, not a question.

"I'm afraid it's here," Randy said, his mind churning among all the possibilities, including their own dangers, seeking a clue as to what to do, what to do first.

Helen was wearing a flowered kimono and straw slippers, booty from one of Mark's inspection trips to the Far East. Her chestnut hair was disheveled, her eyes, a deep and stirring blue, round in apprehension. She seemed very slight, in need of protection, and hardly older than her daughter. She was, at this moment, less composed than the children.

Ben Franklin, staring to the south, said, "I don't see any mushroom cloud. Don't they always have a mushroom cloud?"

"The explosions were very far off," Randy said. "Probably a lot of haze, or other clouds, between us and the mushrooms. What we see is a reflection in the sky. It's dying, now. It was much brighter when I first came out here."

"I see," Ben Franklin said, satisfied. "What do you think they clobbered? I'd guess Homestead and the Boca Chica Navy base at Key West."

Randy shook his head. "I don't see how we could get rocked from that distance. Maybe they hit Palm Beach and Miami. Maybe they missed and pitched two into the Glades."

"Maybe," Ben said, not as if he believed they had missed.

It was so quiet. It was wrongly quiet. They ought to hear sirens, or something. All Randy heard was a mockingbird tuning up for his morning aria.

Helen released her grip on his arm. Thoughts seemed to parallel his, she said, "I haven't heard any planes. I don't hear any now. Shouldn't we hear fighters, or something?"

"I don't know," Randy said.

Ben Franklin said, "I heard 'em. That's what first woke me. I heard jets—they sounded like B-Forty-sevens—climbing. Traveling that way." He showed them with a sweep of his arm. "That's southwest to northeast, isn't it?"

"That's right," Randy said, and at that instant he heard another aircraft, whining under full power, following the same path. They all listened. "That one will be from MacDill," Randy decided, "heading across."

Before its sound faded they heard another, and then a third.

They all pressed close to the porch screen, looking up.

High up there, where it was already sunlight, they saw silver arrows speeding and three white contrails boldly slashed across morning's washed blue sky.

Ben Franklin whispered, "Go, baby, go!"

Terror departed Helen's eyes. "Could we go up on the captain's walk?" she said. "I want to watch them. They're mine, you know."

Ben and Peyton sprinted for the ladder.

"No!" Randy said. "Wait!"

Ben stopped instantly. Peyton ran on. Her mother said, "Peyton! That was an order!"

Peyton, her hand on the ladder, went no further. She said, "Shucks."

"You might as well start learning to obey your uncle Randy, just as you obey your father, right now!"

Peyton said, "Why can't we go up on the roof?"

Randy had spoken instinctively. He found it difficult to put his objection into words. "I think it's too exposed," he said. "I think we all ought to be underground right now, but there isn't any cellar and it's too late to start digging."

Ben Franklin said, "You're right, Randy. If they laid an egg close, we could get flash burns. Then there's radiation." The boy looked at the weathercock on the garage steeple. "Wind's from the east, so we won't get any fallout, anyway not now. But suppose they hit Patrick? We're almost exactly west of Patrick, aren't we? Patrick could cook us."

"Where did you learn all that stuff about fallout?" Randy asked.

"I thought everybody knew it." Ben frowned. "I don't think they'll hit Patrick. It's a test center, not an operational base. Patrick can't hurt them, but MacDill and McCoy, they can't hurt them. And, brother, they will!"

Randy, Helen, and Ben Franklin were facing the east, where the missile test pads on Cape Canaveral lay, and where the fat red sun now showed itself above the horizon. Peyton, nose pressed against the screen, was still trying to follow the contrails of the B-47's. A stark white flash enveloped their world. Randy felt the heat on his neck. Peyton cried out and covered her face with her hands. In the southwest, in the direction of Tampa, St. Petersburg, and Sarasota, another unnatural sun was born, much larger and infinitely fiercer than the sun in the east.

Automatically, as a good platoon leader should, Randy looked at his watch and marked the minute and second in his memory. This time he would know the point of impact exactly, using the flash-and-sound system learned in Korea.

A thick red pillar erected itself in the southwest, its base the unnatural sun.

The top of the pillar billowed outward. This time, the mushroom was there.

There was no sound at all except Peyton's whimpering. Her fists were pressed into her eyes.

A bird plunged against the screen and dropped to earth, trailed by drifting feathers.

Within the pillar and the cloud, fantastic colors played. Red changed to orange, glowed white, became red again. Green and purple ropes twisted upward through the pillar and spread tentacles through the cloud.

The gaudy mushroom enlarged with incredible speed, angry, poisonous, malignant. It grew until the mushroom's rim looked like the leading edge of an approaching weather front, black, purple, orange, green, a cancerous man-created line squall.

They shrank from it.

Peyton screamed, "I can't see! I can't see, Mommy. Mommy, where are you?" Her eyes were wide, her face tear-stained and mottled. Arms outstretched, she was moving across the porch with tiny, stiff, uncertain steps.

Randy scooped her into his arms. She seemed weightless. Helen opened the door and he rushed into the living room. Talking to her, saying, "Easy, Peyton, honey! Easy! Stop rubbing your eyes. Keep your eyes closed." He stretched the child out on the couch.

Helen was at his side, a wet towel in her hands. She laid the towel over her daughter's eyes. "This will make you feel better, baby."

"Mommy?"

"Yes." This was the first time, since she was six, that Peyton had used Mommy instead of Mother.

"All I can see is a big white ball. I can see it with my eyes closed. It hurts me, Mommy, right through my head."

"Sure, just like a big flashlight bulb. Lie still, Peyton, you're going to be all right." Now, with fear for her child's sight supplanting all other fears, Helen steadied. Again she was composed, able, efficient, and she knew the moment of panic would not return. She told Randy, calmly, "Hadn't you better call Dan Gunn?"

"Of course." Randy hurried into his office. Dan had two phones in his suite in the Riverside Inn. Randy dialed the private number. It was busy. He dialed Riverside Inn. Again, he heard the impersonal busy-beep. The inn had a switchboard. All its lines shouldn't be busy. He tried the clinic building, although he knew it was most unlikely that Dan, or anybody, would be there at this hour. It was busy. He dialed operator. The same beep sounded in his ear. Once again, Randy tried Dan's private number. The infuriating beep persisted. He gave up and announced, "I'll have to drive into town and bring Dan out here."

At that moment the ground-conducted shock wave rocked the house.

Peyton cried out, in her sightless terror. Helen pressed her down on the couch, murmuring reassuring mother words. Randy noticed that Ben Franklin was missing from the room.

The blast and sound wave covered them, submerging all other sound and feeling. Again the kitchenware and glasses and china danced. A delicate vase of Viennese crystal crumpled into powder and shards on the mantle. The glass protecting a meticulous and vivid still life, a water color by Lee Adams, shattered in its frame with a loud report.

Randy looked at his watch, marked the time, and did the flash-and-sound arithmetic in his head.

Helen, watching him while soothing Peyton's tense body with her fingers, watching and understanding, said, "What was it?"

"That was MacDill," Randy said. "Six minutes and fifteen seconds. That means seventy-five miles, just right for MacDill."

"MacDill means Tampa," Helen said.

"And St. Petersburg. You'll be all right until I get back?"

"We'll be all right."

Randy banged into Ben Franklin on the stairs. "Where've you been?"

"Opening up the windows and doors downstairs. Just made it. Not a window broke."

"Smart boy. Now you go on up and help your mother take care of Peyton. I'm going for the Doctor."

"Randy—"

"Yes?"

"I'm going to fill up all the pails and sinks and tubs

with water. That's what you're supposed to do, you know."

"I didn't know." Randy put his hand on Ben's shoulder. "But if that's what you're supposed to do, go ahead and do it."

Randy ran outside in time to see the Golden Dew Dairy truck career past on River Road, headed for Fort Repose. The milkman was always a little late with his Saturday deliveries, since orders were heavier than on weekdays. He must have barely begun his route when the first blasts illuminated the sky in the south. Now he was racing home to his wife and children.

As Randy reached his car he heard the undulating tocsin of the siren atop Fort Repose's firehouse. A little redundant, he thought. Still, there was no sound quite like a siren wailing its air-raid alarm to spur people to constructive action—or paralyze them in fear.

Randy caught and passed the milk truck before the turn in the road. A minute later he saw a big, new sedan overturned in the ditch, wheels still spinning. He slowed, and saw that the sedan's front end was telescoped, its windshield shredded; that it bore New York plates. On the shoulder of the road lay a woman, arms outstretched, one bare leg grotesquely twisted under her back. Pallid flesh showed under blue and yellow checked shorts. Her upturned face was a red smear and he judged she was dead.

In this second Randy made an important decision. Yesterday, he would have stopped instantly. There would have been no question about it. When there was an accident, and someone was hurt, a man stopped. But yesterday was a past period in history, with laws and rules archaic as ancient Rome's. Today the rules had changed, just as Roman law gave way to atavistic barbarism as the empire fell to Hun and Goth. Today a man saved himself and his family and to hell with everyone else. Already millions must be dead and other millions maimed, or doomed by radiation, for if the enemy was hitting Florida, they would hardly skip SAC bases and missile sites in more densely populated areas. Certainly they would not spare Washington and

New York, the command posts and communication center of the whole nation. And the war was less than a half hour old. So one stranger on the roadside meant nothing, particularly with a blinded child, his blood kin, dependent on his mission. With the use of the hydrogen bomb, the Christian era was dead, and with it must die the tradition of the Good Samaritan.

And yet Randy stopped. He touched the power brakes and burned rubber, swearing, and thinking himself soft and stupid. He backed, got out of the car, and examined the wreck. The woman was dead, her neck broken. She had been traveling alone. Examining tire marks and a shattered cabbage palm, he deduced she was driving at high speed when the explosion at Mac-Dill—he could see an orange patch in the southwest, probably fire storms consuming Tampa and St. Petersburg—unnerved or blinded her. She had swerved, hit the tree, and catapulted through the windshield. In the car were several pigskin bags, locks burst by the impact, and a pocketbook. He touched nothing. He would report the wreck to a road patrolman or deputy sheriff, if he could find one and when there was time.

Randy drove on, although at reduced speed, for sight of a fatal accident always compels temporary caution. The incident was important only because it was self-revelatory. Randy knew he would have to play by the old rules. He could not shuck his code, or sneak out of his era.

With respite for anxiety about what went on beyond his own sight and hearing, he clicked on his radio, tuned to a Conelrad frequency, 640, and turned it up to maximum power.

All he heard was a distant and incoherent babble.

He tried the other frequency, 1240. He heard a steady hum, and then the familiar voice of Happy Hedrix, the disk jockey on WSMF, in San Marco. "This is a Civil Defense broadcast. Listen carefully, because we are only allowed to broadcast for thirty seconds, after which there will be two minutes of silence. An AP dispatch from Jacksonville says that a Red Alert was declared about thirty minutes ago. Another dispatch from

Jacksonville says it is believed the country is under attack. Since that time, there has been disruption of communications between Jacksonville and the north." Happy's voice, usually so glib, was shaky and halting, and he seemed to have difficulty reading, "Obey the orders of your local Civil Defense Director. Do not use the telephone except for emergencies. You will receive further instructions later. This station will return to the air in two minutes."

Randy tuned in 640 again. Again, he heard many voices, far away and indistinguishable. He knew that under the Conelrad system all stations were required to operate at low power. He surmised that he was hearing a broadcast from Orlando or Ocala, but with interference from stations in other nearby cities, perhaps Daytona, or Leesburg and Eustis, not far off in Lake County. With every station confined to two frequencies, and limited to low-power operation, the confusion was understandable.

A year before, Mark had warned him that the Conelrad system was tricky, and might not work at all. Mark had said, further, that the enemy was not dependent on radio homing devices to find the targets. "Conelrad," Mark had said, "is as obsolete as the B-two-nine. Neither missiles nor jets equipped with modern radar and inertial guidance would think of homing on a radio beam. In the first phase, Conelrad is going to be next to useless, I'm afraid, except for local instructions. The news you get will be only as fresh and accurate as the news that comes in on the teletypes in your local stations. That news flows from the national news agencies. When their teletype circuits go out of business—which will happen immediately when the big cities blow—everything will be screwed up. You're not likely to find out anything until Phase Two—that's the mopping-up stage when the first attack is over. In Phase Two the government will use clear channel stations to tell you what's happening."

Mark apparently had been right about the inadequacy of Conelrad, as about all else. He wondered whether Mark was also right in his prediction that Offutt and the Hole would be one of the primary targets. Randy wondered whether Mark still lived, and how long it would be before he found out.

On the edge of town he began to encounter traffic, heavier than usual and extraordinarily erratic. People were tensed over their wheels like racing drivers, even while moving at normal speeds, mouths set, eyes fixed, each intent on a personal crisis. Some obeyed the stop signs. Other cars progressed as if no hand were at the wheel.

A dozen cars were lined up at Jerry Kling's service station, blocking the sidewalk. Jerry was standing beside one of his pumps, filling a tank, and at the same time listening to three men, all gesticulating, all obviously demanding priority service. One of the men had a billfold in his hand and was waving money before Jerry's eyes.

Randy skirted Marines Park, a green triangular area, its walks lined with tall palms, its apex lapped by the waters of both Timucuan and St. Johns. Here, at the junction of the rivers, Lieutenant Randolph Rowzee Peyton had erected the original Fort Repose. The fort's palm logs long ago had disintegrated, but relics remained, two small brass cannon. They were now mounted in concrete, and flanked the bandstand. Usually, on a bright Saturday morning, the tennis courts were occupied and the pre-breakfast lawn bowlers and shuffle boarders active. But today the park was deserted except for two youths slumped on a bench.

He turned north on Yulee Street, and, three blocks further, into the driveway of Riverside Inn, which with its grounds occupied a block facing the St. Johns. The Riverside Inn catered to a vanishing race of hotel dwellers—widows, widowers, and elderly couples, supported by trusts, annuities, and dividends, spending their summers in New England or the Poconos, and each November migrating to Florida with the coots and mallards.

Randy parked and went into the inn. Its ordered regimen had exploded with the first missile.

The guests were milling around in the lobby like first-class passengers on a liner that has struck an iceberg, and that they suspect may founder at any moment. Some swarmed around the bellboys and assistant manager, babbling questions and demands. "I've been waiting in the dining room for fifteen minutes and I can't seem to find a single waitress. . . . Are you sure you can't get me a reservation on the Champion that leaves Orlando for New York tomorrow? . . . I'd like to know what's wrong with the phone service? If my daughter doesn't hear from me, she'll be frantic. . . . The television in my room isn't working. All television is off the air? Gracious, this really must be serious! . . . I've been a guest at this hotel for twenty-two seasons and this is the first time I've ever asked for anything special. . . . Is there any reason the hotel station wagon can't take us to Tampa? . . . Please don't think me timid, but I would like to know the location of a shelter. . . . It was that damned Roosevelt, at Yalta. . . . Do you think plane schedules will be interrupted for long? . . . You mean to say that your cooks have all cravenly left for their homes? I never heard of such a thing! They ought to be arrested. How, then, are we going to eat? . . . My husband slipped in the shower. I can't seem to get him up. . . ."

A retired major general, in full-dress uniform and displaying all his ribbons, burst out of the elevator. "Attention!" he cried. "Attention, everybody! Let's have order here. You will all please be quiet. There is no cause for alarm!"

Nobody heeded him.

A bowlegged man, in Bermuda shorts and a bright red cap, a golf bag slung over one shoulder, and carrying two suitcases, bulled his way toward the entrance. He was followed by a woman wearing a fur coat over pajamas. She also was weighted with a golf bag, and held a jewel box under one arm and a make-up kit under the other. These two had a sanctuary, and a means of getting there, or so they believed. For most of the others, there was no place to go. They were rootless people. If the Riverside Inn sank, they must go down with the ship.

Dan Gunn's suite was on the second floor. Randy ignored the elevator and took the stairs two at a time.

Dan's rooms were empty, and his doctor's bag missing. He was probably out on an emergency call, or at the clinic in the Medical Arts Building. Randy tried Dan's private phone. There was no dial tone, only sounds like static. He lifted the room telephone. The hotel switchboard failed to answer.

Randy heard voices in the hall, high-pitched and angry. He threw open the door.

Feet apart and braced a thin, sallow woman, very pregnant, leaned against the wall. Her bony arms supported her abdomen, and she was sniffling. In the center of the hallway two men argued. The taller man was Jennings, manager of the Riverside Inn. The other man was John Garcia, a Minorcan fishing guide. Randy recognized the woman as Garcia's wife.

Jennings was saying, "She can't have her baby here in the hotel. There's too much confusion here already. You people will have to get out!"

Garcia, an undersized man with face browned and shrunken by wind and sun, stepped back. His hand went to his hip pocket and he brought out a short, curved pruning knife, suitable for cutting lines, or slitting the bellies of perch and bass.

Randy stepped between them. "Put that thing up, John," he told Garcia. "I'll get the Doctor." He turned on Jennings. "Where's Doctor Gunn?"

"He's busy," Jennings said. "He's very busy with one of our guests. A heart case. Tell these people to go to his clinic and wait."

"Where is he?"

"It doesn't matter. These people are trespassing."

Randy's left hand grasped Jennings' lapels. He slapped Jennings savagely across the face. He did this without any conscious thought except that it was necessary to slap the hysteria out of Jennings in order to locate Dan Gunn. He said, "Where is he?"

Jennings' knees buckled and Randy pinned him against the wall. "Let go! You're choking me! Gunn is in two forty-four."

Randy relaxed his grip. The left side of Jennings'
face was flaming red and blood trickled from the corner
of his mouth. Randy was astonished. This was the first
time in his adult years that he had struck anyone, so far
as he recalled, except one snarling North Korean line-
crosser. Jennings backed away, mumbling that he would
call the police, and disappeared down the stairs.

Randy told Garcia, "Take your wife in there. She can
lie down on the bed. I'll get Doctor Gunn."

Randy went down the hall and entered Room 244
without bothering to knock. It was a single room. On
the bed lay a mound of gray flesh, a corpulent man past
middle age, dead. Randy felt no sense of surprise or
shock whatsoever. He had become a familiar of sudden
death in Korea. This familiarity had left him, as a foreign language is quickly forgotten once you leave the
country where it is spoken. Now it returned, as a foreign tongue is swiftly reacquired in its native land.

Dan Gunn came out of the bathroom, drying his
hands.

"You've got more trouble waiting in your room,"
Randy said. "A woman's having a baby, or about to.
Garcia's wife."

Dan dropped his towel across the foot of the bed and
pulled the sheet over the corpse. "Everybody who was
going to have a coronary just had one," he said, "and I
suppose that every woman who was due to have a baby
in the next two months is having one now. What's your
trouble, Randy?"

"Peyton's blind. You remember her from last year,
don't you? Helen's little girl—not so little—eleven. I
know you're swamped, Dan, but—"

Dan raised his immensely long, hairy arms and cried
out, "Oh, God! Why? Why to that child?"

He looked and sounded like a rebellious Old Testa-
ment prophet. He looked and sounded half-mad. The
worst thing that Randy could imagine, at that moment,
was that Dan Gunn should lose his mental equilibrium.
Randy said, "God had nothing to do with it. This was
strictly man-made. The one that dropped on MacDill,

or somewhere in the Tampa area. Peyton was looking right at it when it blew."

"Oh, the foul, life-destroying, child-destroying bastards! Those evil men, those evil and callous men! God damn them!" He used the expression as a true and awful curse, and then Dan's arms drooped, his anger spent. He visibly shook off the madness. He said, "Sounds like a retina flash burn. To the human eye it's what overexposure is to film. Her eyes can recover from that."

He looked down at the form on the bed. "Not much I can do for cardiacs. This was the third, right here in the hotel. Maybe the other two will live, for a while. It's fear that kills 'em, and the worst fear is that they'll have a shock and not be able to reach the doctor. I pity all the other cardiacs around here, with the phones out. I pity them, but I can't help them. You don't have to worry so much with women having babies. They'll have them whether I'm there or not, and chances are that both mother and baby will do all right." He grasped Randy's elbow. "Now let's take a look at the Garcia woman, and then I'll see about Peyton." They left the room, and its lonely dead.

Marie Garcia said her pains were coming at four- or five-minute intervals. Dan said, "It'll be much better if you can have the baby at home. It'll be easier for me, too. This hotel is no place to be having a baby. Do you think you can make it?"

Marie looked at her husband and nodded. Garcia said, "You'll follow us, Doc?"

"I'll be right behind you," Dan promised. He helped Marie to her feet. Leaning on John Garcia, she left, her lips compressed, awaiting the next clamp of pain, but her fear gone.

Dan went into his bathroom and came out with a small bottle. "Eyedrops," he said. "Once every three hours." He dug into his bag and handed Randy a pillbox. "Sedative. One every four hours. And give her a couple of aspirins as soon as you get home. She stays in a dark room. Better yet, put a dark cloth over her eyes. As long as she knows she can't see, she won't strain her eyes trying. And it won't frighten her so much. It's frightening to open your eyes and not see."

"You're coming out, aren't you?" Randy asked.

"Certainly. As soon as I can. I have to deliver this baby, and I have to check in at the clinic—God knows what's waiting for me there—and I have to see Bloomfield. Somehow we have to coordinate what little we'll be able to do. But soon as I can, I'll be out to see Peyton. There really isn't anything more I can do for her than you can do right now. And Randy—"

"Yes?"

"Did you get those prescriptions filled?"

"No. I never had time."

"Don't worry about it. I'll handle it for you. I'll bring the stuff out when I come."

They left the hotel together. A gibbering woman, reddish wig astray on her head like an ill-fitting beret, clawed at Dan's arm. He shook himself loose. She dove for his medicine bag. He snatched it away and ran.

Outside, they parted. Randy drove through town. Traffic was piling up. Those stores that opened early on Saturdays were crowded, and groups waited in front of others, and on the steps of the bank. There was as yet no disorder. It was a shopping rush, as on Christmas Eve. At the corner of Yulee and St. Johns he saw Cappy Foracre, the Fort Repose Chief of Police, directing traffic. He stopped and yelled, "Cappy, there's a woman dead in a wreck out on River Road."

"That's outside the town limits," Cappy shouted. "Nothing I can do about it. I've got plenty of trouble right here."

Randy drove on, tuning his radio to the Conelrad frequencies, scouting for news. As before, the 640 channel brought only an incoherent jumble of distant voices, but Happy Hedrix was still broadcasting over WSMF, from San Marco, on 1240, although, obeying the Conelrad rules, he never mentioned the call sign. The AP ticker from Jacksonville told of a sea and air battle off the coast. The Governor had issued a pronouncement from Tallahassee—all target cities were to be evacuated at once. The cities named included Orlando and Jacksonville. There was no mention of Miami or Tampa.

Randy wondered why the evacuation order originated in Tallahassee, instead of from a Civil Defense headquarters. Of the national situation, there was no word at all. Up to now, it sounded as if Florida were fighting the war alone. More than anything, Randy wanted news—real news. What had happened? What had happened everywhere? Was the war lost? If it was still being fought who was winning?

On River Road he passed a dozen convicts, white men, clad in their blue denim with the white stripe down the trouser leg. They were straggling toward Fort Repose. Two of the convicts carried shotguns. Another had a pistol strapped to his waist. This was wrong. Road gang guards, not convicts, should be carrying the weapons. But the guards were missing. It wasn't difficult to guess what had happened. The guards, some of them, were dour and sadistic men, skilled in unusual and degrading punishments. It was likely that any breakdown in government and authority would begin with a revolt of prisoners against road gang guards. There was a convict camp between Fort Repose and Pasco Creek. Randy guessed that these prisoners were being transported, by truck, to their work area, when the nuclear attack came. With realization, rebellion, and perhaps murder of the guards, had been almost instantaneous.

He passed the wrecked car. The woman's body still lay on the roadside. The luggage had been looted. Dresses, shoes, and lingerie littered the grassy shoulder. A pink-silk pajama top fluttered from a palmetto, a forlorn flag to mark the end of a vacation.

As Randy reached his home, Florence Wechek's Chevy bounced out of her driveway. He yelled, "Hey, Florence!"

Florence stopped. Alice Cooksey was in the car with her.

"Where are you going?" Randy asked.

"To work," Florence said. "I'm late."

"Don't you know what's happened?"

"Certainly I know. That's why it's very important I open up the office. People will have all sorts of messages. This is an emergency, Randy."

"It sure is," Randy said. "On the way to town you'll see some convicts. They're armed. Don't stop."

Florence said, "I'll be careful." Alice smiled and waved. They drove on.

On Friday night, Florence and Alice had split a bottle of sherry, an unaccustomed dissipation, and stayed up long past midnight, exchanging confidences, opinions, and gossip. As a result, Florence had neglected to set her alarm, and they had overslept. The explosions far to the south had shaken them awake, but it was not until some time later, when they had seen the glow in the sky, that Alice had thought to turn on the radio, and they first realized what was happening.

Immediately, Florence wanted to start for the office. Having no close relatives, and approaching an age beyond which she could not reasonably hope for a proposal of marriage, and when even speculative second looks from rakish or lonely widowers had grown rare, her whole life centered in the office. Western Union didn't expect her to open the wire until eight, but she was usually a bit early. Afternoons, she dreaded the relentless downsweep of the hour hand, which at five guillotined her day. After five, nothing awaited her except lovebirds, tropical fish, and vicarious journeys back to more romantic centuries via historical novels. In the office she was part of a busy and exciting world, a necessary communicating link in affairs of great importance to others. On this day of crisis, she could be the most important person in Fort Repose.

Yet she allowed Alice to persuade her not to start at once. For such a wisp of a woman, Alice seemed remarkably brave and cool. Alice pointed out that Florence had better eat breakfast, because she'd need her strength and it might be many hours before she'd have an opportunity to eat again. And Alice had volunteered to go to town with her, although Florence had insisted it

wasn't necessary. "Who's going to do any reading today?" she asked. "Why bother with the library?"

"Maybe a good many people will be reading," Alice
said, "once they find out that Civil Defense pamphlets
are stocked in the library. Not that it's likely to be much
help to them now, but perhaps it'll help some. Bubba
Offenhaus claimed they were taking up too much space
in his office. So I offered to store them."

"You were farsighted."

"Do you think so? When two ships are on a collision
course, and the men at the wheel inflexibly hold to that
course, there is going to be a collision. You don't have
to be farsighted to see that."

And Alice had suggested that it would be wise for
them to use their time and resources to buy provisions
while they were in town. "Canned goods would be best,
I think," she said, "because if the lights go out, refrigeration goes too."

"Why should the lights go out?" Florence asked.

"Because Fort Repose's power comes from Orlando."

Florence didn't quite understand this reasoning. Nevertheless, she followed Alice's advice, listing certain essentials they would need and filling pails and bathtub
with water before they left.

Florence and Alice passed the dead woman and pillaged wreck on the way to town. It frightened them.
But, when far ahead Florence saw the procession of
convicts, and two of them, one armed, stepped into the
middle of the road to wave her down, she stamped on
the accelerator. The car quivered at a speed she never
in her life had dared before. At the last second the two
men jumped to safety and the others shook their fists,
their mouths working but their curses unheard. Florence didn't slow until she reached Marines Park. She
dropped Alice at the library. She parked behind Western Union, which occupied a twenty-foot frontage in a
one-story block of stores on Yulee Street. Her fingers
were trembling and her legs felt numb. It was several
seconds before her heart stopped jumping, and she
found sufficient courage to enter her office. Fourteen

or fifteen men and women, some of them strangers, swarmed in behind her. "Just a minute! Just a minute!" Florence said, and barricaded herself behind the protection of the counter.

This was the first morning in years that she had been late, and so, on this of all mornings, waiting at the door would be more customers than she might customarily expect in a whole day. In addition, on Saturdays, Gaylord, her Negro messenger boy, was off. His bicycle stood in the back of the office. "Now you will all have to wait," she said, "while I open the circuit."

Fort Repose was one of a dozen small towns on a local circuit originating in Jacksonville and terminating in Tampa. Florence switched on her teleprinter and announced: "THIS IS FR RETURNING TO SERVICE."

Instantly the machine chattered back at her from JX, which was Jacksonville: "YOU ARE LIMITED TO ACCEPTING AND TRANSMITTING OFFICIAL DEFENSE EMERGENCY MESSAGES ONLY UNTIL FURTHER NOTICE. NO MESSAGES ACCEPTED FOR POINTS NORTH OF JACKSONVILLE."

Florence acknowledged and inquired of Jacksonville: "ANY INCOMERS?"

JX said curtly: "NO. FYI TAMPA IS OUT. JX EVACUATION ORDERED BUT WE STICKING UNTIL CIVIL DEFENSE FOLDS UP HERE."

Florence turned to her customers behind the counter, started to speak, and was battered by demands: "I was expecting a money order from Chattanooga this morning. Where is it? . . . I want you to get this off for New York right away. . . . Can I send a cable from here? My husband is in London and thinks I'm in Miami and I'm not in Miami at all. What is the name of this place? . . . This is a very important message. I tried to phone my broker but all the lines are tied up. It's a sell order and I want you to get it right out. I'll make it worth your while. . . . I can't even telephone Mount Dora. Can I send a telegram to Mount Dora from here? . . . If I wire Chicago for money, how soon do you think before I'll get an answer? . . ."

Florence raised her hands. "Please be quiet— That's better. I'm sorry, but I can't take anything except official defense emergency messages. Anyway, nothing is going through north of Jacksonville."

She watched the transformation in their faces. They had been grim, determined, irritated. Suddenly, they were only frightened. The woman whose husband was in London murmured, "Nothing north of Jacksonville? Why, that's awful. Do you think . . ."

"I've just told you all I know," Florence said. "I'm sorry. I can't take any messages. And nothing has come in, nothing for anybody." She pitied them. "Come back in a few hours. Maybe things will be better."

At a quarter to nine Edgar Quisenberry, the president of the bank, stepped into the Western Union office. His face was pink and shaven, he was dressed in a new blue suit, white handkerchief peeping from the breast pocket, and he wore a correct dark blue tie. His manner was brisk, confident, and businesslike, which was the way a banker should behave in time of crisis. In his hand he carried a telegram, already typed up at the bank. "Good morning, Miss Wechek," he said, and smiled.

Florence was surprised. The bank was her best customer, and yet she rarely saw Edgar Quisenberry, in person, and she never before had seen him smile. "Good morning, Mr. Quisenberry," she said.

"Really can't say there's anything good about it," Edgar said. "Reminds me of Pearl Harbor Day. That bunch in Washington have been caught napping again. I'd like you to send this message for me—" he slid it across the counter—"the telephone seems to be out of order, temporarily, or I would have called."

She picked up the telegram. It was addressed to the Atlanta branch of the Federal Reserve Bank, and it read: "URGENTLY NEED DIRECTIVE ON HOW TO HANDLE CURRENT SITUATION."

Florence said, "I've just received orders not to accept anything but official defense emergency messages, Mr. Quisenberry."

Edgar's smile disappeared. "There isn't anything more official than the Federal Reserve Bank, Miss Wechek."

"Well, now I don't know about that, Mr. Quisenberry."

"You'd better know, Miss Wechek. Not only is this message official, but in a defense emergency there isn't anything more important than maintaining the financial integrity of the community. You will get this message off right away, Miss Wechek." He looked up at the clock. "It is now thirteen to nine. I'm going to ask for a report on exactly how quickly this is delivered."

Florence was flustered. She knew Edgar Quisenberry could make a great deal of trouble for her. However, Atlanta was far north of Jacksonville. She said, "We don't have any communication with any points north of Jacksonville, Mr. Quisenberry."

"That's ridiculous!"

"I'm sorry, Mr. Quisenberry."

"Very well." Edgar snatched the telegraph blank from the counter and revised the address. "There. Send it to the Jacksonville sub-branch."

Hesitating, Florence took the message and said, "I'll see if they'll accept it, Mr. Quisenberry."

"They'd better. I'll wait."

She sat down at the teleprinter called in JX, and typed: "I HAVE MESSAGE FOR JX SUB-BRANCH OF FEDERAL RESERVE. SENDER IS EDGAR QUISENBERRY, PRESIDENT OF FIRST NATIONAL BANK. WILL YOU TAKE IT?"

JX replied: "IS IT AN OFFICIAL DEF . . ."

Florence blinked. For an instant it seemed that someone had flashed mirrored sunlight into her eyes. At the same instant, the message from JX stopped. "That's funny," she said. "Did you see anything, Mr. Quisenberry?"

"Nothing but a little flash of light. Where did it come from?"

The teleprinter chattered again. "PK TO CIRCUIT. BIG EXPLOSION IN DIRECTION JX. WE CAN SEE MUSHROOM CLOUD." PK meant Palatka, a small town on the St. Johns south of Jacksonville.

Florence rose and walked to the counter with Edgar's message. "I'm very sorry, Mr. Quisenberry," she said, "but I can't send this. Jacksonville doesn't seem to be there any more."

Fort Repose's financial structure crumbled in a day.

During the winter season the First National was open on Saturday mornings from nine until noon, and Edgar saw no reason why a war should interfere with banking hours. Like almost everyone else, he was awakened by the rumble of the first distant explosions, and he felt a thrill of fear when the siren on the firehouse let loose. He urged his wife, Henrietta, to make breakfast at once while he tried to put through a long distance call to Atlanta. When his phone made strange noises, and the operator would not respond, he listened to the scanty, thirty-second local news broadcasts. Hearing nothing that sounded immediately alarming for Fort Repose, he reminded Henrietta that nothing drastic had occurred after Pearl Harbor. On the Monday after Pearl Harbor there had been no runs, and no panic. Nevertheless, he could not force himself to finish his bacon and eggs. He left for the bank fifteen minutes earlier than usual.

But at the bank nothing was right. The phones weren't working there, either, and at eight-thirty, when his staff should have reported for work, half his people hadn't shown up. At about the same time he noticed a line of depositors forming at the front entrance, and it was this that made him decide to send a wire to Federal Reserve. He had never received any instructions on what to do in an emergency of this kind, and, as a matter of fact, had never even considered it.

Western Union's failure to send his telegram worried Edgar somewhat, but he told himself that it was impossible that the enemy could have bombed all these big cities at once. It was probably some sort of mechanical trouble that would be cleared up before long, just as repairmen would soon have the Fort Repose phone system back in working order.

When the bank's doors opened at nine the people seemed orderly enough. It was true that everyone was withdrawing cash, and nobody making deposits. Edgar wasn't overly worried. There was almost a quarter million cash on hand, a far higher ratio of cash than regulations required, but consistent with his conservative principles.

In ten minutes Edgar's optimism dwindled. Mrs. Estes, his senior teller, turned over her cage to the bookkeeper and entered his office. "Mr. Quisenberry," she said, "these aren't ordinary withdrawals. These people are taking out everything—savings accounts and all."

"No reason for that," Edgar snapped. "They ought to know the bank is sound."

"May I suggest that we limit withdrawals? Let them take out enough so that each family can buy what's necessary in the emergency. In that way we can stay open until noon, and there won't be any panic. It'll protect the merchants, too."

Edgar was incensed by her effrontery, practically amounting to insubordination. "When you are president of this bank," he said, "then it will be up to you to make such decisions. But let me tell you something, Mrs. Estes. The only way to stop a run on a bank is to shovel out the cash. As soon as you do that, people regain confidence and the run stops."

"It's entirely different today, Mr. Quisenberry. Don't you see that? You have to assume some sort of leadership or there's going to be a panic."

"Mrs. Estes, will you please return to your cage. I'll run the bank."

This was Edgar's first, and perhaps his vital error.

Corrigan, the mailman, came in and dropped a packet of letters on the secretarial desk. Edgar was heartened to see Corrigan. The good old U.S. government still functioned. "Neither rain nor snow nor dark of night," Edgar said, smiling.

"This is my last delivery," Corrigan said. "Planes and trains aren't running, and the truck didn't come in from Orlando this morning. This batch is from last night. We can accept outgoing mail but we don't guarantee when it will go out, if ever."

Corrigan left and wedged himself into a queue before one of the teller windows.

Paralysis of the United States mail was more of a shock to Edgar Quisenberry than anything that had occurred thus far. At last, he confessed to himself the impossible reality of the day. Realization did not come all at once. It could not, for his mind refused to assimilate it. He attempted to accept the probability that the Treasury in Washington, Wall Street, and Federal Reserve banks everywhere, all were now radioactive ash. No longer any clearinghouses or correspondent banks. He was sickened by the realization that a great part of his own assets—that is, the assets of his bank—were no longer assets at all. Of what use were Treasury bonds and notes when there was no Treasury? What good were the municipal bonds of Tampa, Jacksonville, and Miami when there were no municipalities? Who would straighten all this out, and how, and when? Who would tell him? Who would know? With all communications out, he could not even confer with fellow bankers in San Marco. He began to sweat. He took out his fountain pen and began jotting down figures on a scratch pad. If he could just get everything down in figures, they ought to balance. They always had.

Edgar's cashier came into the office and said, "We're not cashing any out-of-town checks, are we, Mr. Quisenberry?"

"Certainly not! How can we cash out-of-town checks when we don't know whether a town's still there?" Edgar flinched, remembering that only yesterday he had cashed a big check for Randolph Bragg on an Omaha bank. Certainly Omaha, right in the center of the country, ought to be safe. Edgar had never given much thought to all the talk about rockets and missiles and such. He always prided himself on keeping his feet firmly on the ground, and examining the facts in a hardheaded, practical manner. And the facts, as he had publicly stated, were that Russia intended to defeat the United States by scaring us into an inflationary, socialistic depression, and not by tossing missiles at us. The country was basically sound and the Russians would never attack a basically sound country. And yet they had attacked, and if they could hit Florida they could hit Omaha—or anywhere.

His cashier, Mr. Pennyngton, a thin man with a veined nose and nervous stomach, a man given to fretting over detail, clasped his hands tightly together as if to prevent his fingers from flying off into space. He asked another question, haltingly: "Mr. Quisenberry, what about travelers checks? Do we cash those?"

"No sir! Travelers checks are usually redeemed in New York, and between me and you, I don't think there'll be much left of New York."

"And what about government savings bonds, sir? There are some people in line who want to cash in their bonds."

Edgar hesitated. To refuse to cash government savings bonds was fiduciary sacrilege so awful that the possibility never before had entered his head. Yet here he was, faced with it. "No," he decided, "we don't cash any bonds. Tell those individuals that we won't cash any bonds until we find out where the government stands, or if."

The news that First National was refusing to honor travelers checks and government bonds spread through Fort Repose's tiny business section in a few minutes. The merchants, grocers, druggists, the proprietors of specialty shops and filling stations, deduced that if travelers checks and government bonds were worthless, then all checks would soon be worthless. Since opening their doors that morning, all sales records had been smashed. Everybody was buying everything, which to the shopkeepers was exhilarating as well as frightening. Most of them, from the first, had been cautious, refusing to accept out-of-town checks, except, of course, payroll and annuity and government pension checks, which everyone assumed were always as good as cash. When the bank acted, their first reaction was to regard all paper except currency as probably worthless.

Their next reaction was to race to the bank and attempt to convert their suddenly suspect paper assets into currency.

Looking out through the office door, Edgar watched the queues in the lobby, hoping they would shorten. Instead, they lengthened. He called Mr. Pennyngton and together they checked the cash position. Incredibly, in a single hour it had been reduced to $145,000. If continued at this rate, the bank would be stripped of currency by eleven-thirty, and Edgar guessed that the rate of withdrawals would only increase.

Edgar Quisenberry made his decision. He went into the four tellers' cages and, one by one, removed the cash drawers and carried them into the vault. He then closed and locked the vault. He walked back to the lobby, stepped up on a chair, and raised his hands. "Quiet please," he said.

At that moment, there were perhaps sixty people in the queues. They had been murmuring. They were silent.

"For the benefit of all depositors, I have been forced to order that the bank be temporarily closed," Edgar said.

They were all looking up at him. He was relieved to see Cappy Foracre, the Chief of Police, and another officer, turning people away from the door. Apparently, they had sensed there might be trouble. Yet Edgar saw no menace in the faces below. They looked confused and uncomprehending, dumb and ineffectual as cattle barred from the barn at nightfall. He said, "This temporary closing has been ordered by the government as an emergency measure." It was only a white lie. He was quite sure that had he been able to get in touch with Federal Reserve, this is the course that would have been advised.

His depositors continued to stare at him, as if expecting something more. He said, "I can assure you that your savings are safe. Remember, all deposits up to ten thousand dollars are insured by the government. The bank is sound and will be reopened as soon as the emergency is over. Thank you."

He stepped down and returned to his office, careful to maintain a businesslike and dignified attitude. The people trickled out. He kept his staff busy until past noon balancing books and accounts. When all was in order, he advanced each employee a week's salary, in cash, and informed them that he would get in touch with them when they were needed. When all had left, and he was entirely alone, he felt relieved. He had saved the bank. His position was still liquid. Dollars were good, and the bank still had dollars. Since he was the bank, and the bank was his, this meant that he possessed the ready cash to survive personally any forseeable period of economic chaos.

Edgar's calculations were not correct. He had forgotten the implacable law of scarcity.

Like most small towns, Fort Repose's food and drug supply was dependent upon daily or thrice weekly deliveries from warehouses in the larger cities. Each day tank trucks replenished its filling stations. For all other merchandise, it was dependent upon shipments by mail, express, and highway freight, from jobbers and manufacturers elsewhere. With the Red Alert, all these services halted entirely and at once. Like thousands of other towns and villages not directly seared by war. Fort Repose became an island. From that moment, its inhabitants would have to subsist on whatever was already within its boundaries, plus what they might scrounge from the countryside.

Provisions and supplies melted from the shelves. Gasoline drained steadily from the pumps. Closing of the First National failed to inhibit the buying rush. Before closing, the bank had injected an extra $100,000 in cash into the economy, unevenly distributed. And strangers appeared, eager to trade what was in their wallets for necessities of the moment and the future.

The people of Fort Repose had no way of knowing it, but establishments on the arterial highways leading down both coasts, and crisscrossing between the large cities, had swiftly been stripped of everything. From the time of the Red Alert, the highways had been jammed with carloads of refugees, seeking asylum they knew not where. The mushroom cloud over Miami emptied Hollywood and Fort Lauderdale. The tourists instinctively headed north on Route 1 and A1A, as frightened birds

seek the nest. By nightfall, they would be stopped outside the radioactive shambles of Jacksonville. Some fled
westward toward Tampa, to discover that Tampa had
exploded in their face. The evacuation of Jacksonville,
partially accomplished before missiles sought out the
Navy Air complex, sent some of its people toward Savannah and Atlanta. Neither city existed. Others sped
south, toward Orlando, to meet the evacuees from Orlando rushing toward the holocaust in Jacksonville.
When the authorities in Tallahassee suspected that the
fallout from Jacksonville, carried by the east wind,
would blanket the state capital, they ordered evacuation. Some from Tallahassee drove south on Route 27,
toward Tampa, unaware that Tampa was no longer
there.

This chaos did not result from a breakdown in Civil
Defense. It was simply that Civil Defense, as a realistic
buffer against thermonuclear war, did not exist. Evacuation zones for entire cities had never been publicly announced, out of fear of "spreading alarm." Only the
families of military personnel knew what to do, and
where to go and assemble. Military secrecy forbade radio identification of those cities already destroyed, since
this might be information for the enemy.

In Florida alone several hundred thousand families
were on the move, few with provisions for more than
one day and some with nothing at all except a car and
money. So of necessity they were voracious and all-
consuming as army ants. The roadside shops, restaurants, filling stations, bars, and juice stands along the
four-lane highways were denuded of stocks, or put out a
sign claiming so. Only the souvenir shacks, with their
useless pink flamingos and tinted shells, were not
picked clean. This is why strangers, swinging off these
barren highways, invaded Fort Repose and other little
towns off the main traffic streams.

Those people in Fort Repose who remembered rationing from the second World War also remembered
what goods had been in short supply, back in 'forty-two
and 'forty-three, and bought accordingly. There were
runs on tires, coffee, sugar, cigarettes, butter, the choic-

er cuts of beef, and nylon stockings. Some proprietors, realizing that these items were vanishing, instituted their own rationing systems.

The more thoughtful wives bought portable radios and extra batteries, candles, kerosene lanterns, matches, lighter fluid and flints, first-aid kits, and quantities of soap and toilet paper.

When news spread that armed convicts, escaped from road gangs, had been seen near the town, Beck's Hardware sold out of rifles, shotguns, pistols, and very nearly out of ammunition.

By afternoon the cash registers of Fort Repose were choked with currency, but many shelves and counters were bare and others nearly so. By afternoon the law of scarcity had condemned the dollar to degradation and contempt. Within a few more days the dollar, in Fort Repose, would be banished entirely as a medium of exchange, at least for the duration.

Sitting alone in his office, Edgar Quisenberry was aware of none of these facts, nor could his imagination anticipate the dollar's fall, any more than he could have imagined the dissolution of the Treasury and the Federal Reserve System in the space of a single hour. Methodically, he read through the last batch of mail. There was nothing of any great importance, except heartening items in the Kiplinger Letter, predicting another increase in FHA mortgage rates, and better retail business in the South during the Christmas season. Also, from Detroit there was notice of a ten-percent stock dividend in automobile shares in his personal portfolio. He'd certainly got in on the ground floor of that one, he thought. He hoped nothing happened to Detroit, but he had a disquieting feeling that something would, or had.

At two o'clock, as always on Saturdays, he left the bank, first setting the time lock on the vault for eight-thirty Monday morning. His car was a black Cadillac, three years old. He recalled that during the last big war automobile production had halted. He decided that on Monday, or perhaps this very afternoon, he would drive to San Marco and see what sort of a trade he could make on a new Caddy. Henrietta would be pleased, and it would be a hedge against long disruption of the economy.

When he started the engine he saw that his gas was low, and on the way home stopped at Jerry Kling's service station. He was surprised that there was no line of cars waiting, as there had been early that morning. Then he saw the big cardboard sign with its emphatic red lettering: SORRY. NO MORE GAS.

Edgar honked and Jerry came out of the station, looking worn and limp. "Yes, Mr. Quisenberry?" Jerry said.

"That's just to keep away tourists and floaters and such, isn't it?" Edgar said.

"No, sir. I'm not only out of gas. I'm out of tires, spark plugs, batteries, thirty-weight oil, vulcanizing kits, drinks and candy, and low on everything else."

"I've got to have gas. I'm just about out."

"I should've put up that sign an hour after I opened. You know what, Mr. Quisenberry? I sold plumb out of tires before I got to thinking I needed new tires myself. I just let myself be charmed by that bell on the cash register. What a damn fool! I've got nothing but money."

"I don't know that I can get home," Edgar said.

"I think we'll all be walking pretty soon, Mr. Quisenberry." Jerry sighed. "I'll tell you what I'll do. You're an old customer. I've got a drum stashed away in the stockroom. I'll let you have three gallons. Back that thing up by the ramp, so nobody'll see."

When he had his three gallons, Edgar brought out his wallet and said, "How much?"

Jerry laughed and raised his hands in a gesture of repugnance. "Keep it! I don't want money. What the hell's money good for? You can't drive it and you can't eat it and it won't even fix a flat."

Edgar drove on slowly, hunched over the wheel. He knew, vaguely, that in the second World War the Greek drachma and Hungarian pengo had become utterly worthless. And in the War of the Revolution the shilling of the Continental Congress hadn't been worth, in the British phrase, a Continental damn. But nothing like this had ever happened to the dollar. If the dollar was worthless, everything was worthless. There was a phrase he had heard a number of times, "the end of civilization as we know it." Now he knew what the phrase meant. It meant the end of money.

When Edgar reached home Henrietta's car was gone. He found a note in the salver on the hall table. It read:

1:30.

EDGAR—tried to get you all morning but the phone is still out of order. The radio doesn't say much but I am frightened. Nevertheless, I am off to do the grocery shopping. I hope the stores aren't crowded. I do think that henceforth I will shop on Tuesdays or Wednesdays instead of Saturdays.

Hadn't we better have both cars filled with gas? There may be a shortage. You remember how it was last time, with those silly A and B ration cards.

You didn't leave any money when you rushed off this morning, but I can always cash checks. It may be hard for a while, but life goes on.

HENRIETTA

Edgar went up to the master bedroom and sat on the edge of the bed. What a fool she was. Life goes on, she said. How could life go on with no Federal Reserve, no Treasury, no Wall Street, no bonds, no banks?

Henrietta didn't understand it at all. How could life go on if dollars were worthless? How could anybody live without dollars, or credit, or both? She didn't understand that the Bank had become only a heap of stone filled with worthless paper, so his credit would be no better than anybody's credit. If dollars were worthless then there was nothing they could buy. You couldn't even buy a ticket, say, to South America, and even if you could how would you get to an airport? Grocery shopping, indeed! How would they shop a week, or a month from now?

Henrietta was a fool. This was the end. Civilization was ended. Of one thing, Edgar was certain. He would not be crushed with the mob. He had been a banker all his life and that was the way he was going to die, a banker. He would not allow himself to be humiliated. He would not be reduced to begging gasoline or food, and be dragged down to the level of a probationary teller. He thought of all the notes outstanding that now would never be paid, and how his debtors must be chuckling. He scorned the improvident, and now the improvident would be just as good as the careful, the sound, the thrifty. Well, let them try to go on without dollars. He would not accept such a world.

He found the old, nickel-plated revolver, purchased by his father many years before, in the top drawer of his bureau. Edgar had never fired it. The bullets were green with mold and the hammer rusted. He put it to his temple, wondering whether it would work. It did.

[6]

Always before, important events and dates had been marked in memory with definite labels, not only such days as Thanksgiving, New Year's, and Lincoln's Birthday, but Pearl Harbor Day, D-Day, VE-Day, VJ-Day, Income Tax Day. This December Saturday, ever after, was known simply as The Day. That was sufficient. Everybody remembered exactly what they did and saw and said on The Day. People unconsciously were inclined to split time into two new periods, before The Day, and after The Day. Thus a man might say, "Before The Day I was an automobile dealer. Now I operate a trotline for catfish." Or a mother might boast, "Oh, yes, Oscar passed his college boards. Of course that was before The Day." Or a younger mother say, "Hope was born after The Day, I wonder about her teeth."

This semantic device was not entirely original. Several generations of Southerners had referred to before and after "The War" without being required to explain what war. It seemed incongruous to call The Day a war—Russo-American, East-West, or World War III—because the war, really was all over in a single day. Furthermore, nobody in the Western Hemisphere ever saw the face of a human enemy. Very few actually saw an enemy aircraft or submarine, and missiles appeared only on the most sensitive radar screens. Most of those who died in North America saw nothing at all, since they died in bed, in a millisecond slipping from sleep into deeper darkness. So the struggle was not against a human enemy, or for victory. The struggle, for those who survived The Day, was to survive the next.

This truth was not quickly or easily assimilated by

Randy Bragg, although he was better prepared for it than most. It was totally outside his experience and without precedent in history.

On The Day itself, whatever else he might be doing, he was never beyond sound of a radio, awaiting the news that ought to accompany war—news of victories or defeats, mobilization, proclamations, declarations, a message from the President, words of leadership, steadfastness and unity. Altogether, there were seven radios in the house. All of them were kept turned on except the clock-radio in Peyton's room where the child, her eyes lubricated and bandaged, slept with the help of Dan Gunn's sedatives.

Even when he ran up or down stairs, or discovered imperative duties outside, Randy carried his tiny transistor portable. Twice he left the grounds, once on a buying mission to town, again briefly to visit the McGoverns. The picture window on the river side of the McGovern home had been cracked by concussion, and this, rather than the more terrifying and deadly implications of The Day, had had a traumatic effect on Lavinia. She had been fed sleeping pills and put to bed. Lib and her father were functioning well, even bravely. Randy was relieved. He could not escape his primary duty, which was to his own family, his brother's wife and children. He could not devote his mind and energy to the protection of two houses at once.

Until midafternoon, Randy heard only the quavery and uninformative thirty-second broadcasts from WSMF.

Now he was downstairs, in the dining room with Helen. She had been making an inventory of necessities in the house, discovering a surprising number of items she considered essential, war or no war, which Randy had entirely forgotten. He was eating steak and vegetables—Helen, disapproving of his cannibal sandwiches, had insisted on cooking for him—and washing it down with orange juice. Leaning back in the scarred, massive captain's chair he relaxed for the first time since dawn. A weariness flowed upward from his throbbing legs. He had slept only two or three hours in the past thirty-six, and he knew that when he finished eating the fatigue would seep through his whole body, and it would be necessary to sleep again. Across the circular, waxed teak table, looking fresh and competent, Helen sipped a Scotch and checked what she called her "must" list. "One of us," she was saying, "has got to make another trip to town. I have to have detergent for the dishwasher and washing machine, soap powder, paper napkins, toilet paper. We ought to have more candles and I wish I could get my hand on some more old-fashioned kerosene lamps. And, Randy, what about ammunition? I don't like to sound scary, but—"

The radio, in an interval of silence between the local Conelrad broadcasts, suddenly squealed with an alien and powerful carrier wave. Then they heard a new voice. "This is your national Civil Defense Headquarters. . . ."

The front legs of Randy's chair hit the floor. He was wide awake again. The voice was familiar, the voice of a network newscaster, not one of the best known New York or Washington correspondents, but still recognizable, a strong and welcome voice connecting them with the world beyond the borders of Timucuan County. It continued:

"All local Conelrad stations will please leave the air now, and whenever they hear this signal. This is an emergency clear channel network. If the signal strength is erratic, do not change stations. It is because the signal is rotated between a number of transmitters in order to prevent bombing by enemy aircraft. The next voice you hear will be that of the Acting Chief Executive of the United States, Mrs. Josephine Vanbruuker-Brown—"

Randy couldn't believe it. Mrs. Vanbruuker-Brown was Secretary of Health, Education and Welfare in the President's Cabinet, or had been until this day.

Then they heard her Radcliffe-Boston voice. It was Mrs. Vanbruuker-Brown, all right. She said:

"Fellow countrymen. As all of you know by now, at dawn this morning this country, and our allies in the free world, were attacked without warning with thermonuclear and atomic weapons. Many of our great cities have been destroyed. Others have been contaminated, and their evacuation ordered. The toll of innocent lives taken on this new and darker day of infamy cannot as yet even be estimated."

These first sentences had been clearly and bravely spoken. Now her voice faltered, as if she found it difficult to say what it was now necessary to say. "The very fact that I speak to you as the Chief Executive of the nation must tell you much."

They heard her sob. "No President," Helen whispered.

"No Washington," Randy said. "I guess she was out of Washington, at home, or speaking somewhere, and wherever she lives—"

Randy hushed. Mrs. Vanbruuker-Brown was talking again:

"Our reprisal was swift, and, from the reports that have reached this command post, effective. The enemy has received terrible punishment. Several hundred of his missile and air bases, from the Chukchi Peninsula to the Baltic, and from Vladivostok to the Black Sea, have certainly been destroyed. The Navy has sunk or damaged at least a hundred submarines in North American waters.

"The United States has been badly hurt, but is by no means defeated.

"The battle goes on. Our reprisals continue.

"However, further enemy attacks must be expected. There is reason to believe that enemy air forces have not as yet been fully committed. We must be prepared to withstand heavy blows.

"As Chief Executive of the United States, and Commander in Chief of the Armed Forces, I hereby declare a state of unlimited national emergency until such time as new elections are held, and Congress reconvenes.

"In the devastated areas, and in those other areas where normal functions of government cannot be carried out, I hereby declare martial law, to be administered by the

Army. I appoint Lieutenant General George Hunneker
Army Chief of Staff, and Director of Martial Law in the
Zone of the Interior, which means within the forty-nine
states.

"There have been grave dislocations of communications,
of industrial, economic, and financial functions. I declare,
effective at this moment, a moratorium on the payment of
all debts, rents, taxes, interest, mortgages, insurance claims
and premiums, and all and any other financial obligations
for the duration of the emergency.

"From time to time, God willing, I will use these facilities to bring you further information, as it is received, and
to issue further decrees as they become necessary. I call
upon you to obey the orders of your local Civil Defense
directors, state and municipal authorities, and of the military. Do not panic.

"Some of you may have guessed how it happens that I,
the head of the most junior of government departments and
a woman, have been forced to assume the duties and responsibilities of Chief Executive on this, the most terrible
day in our history.

"One of the first targets of the enemy was Washington.

"So far as we have been able to discover at this hour,
neither the President nor the Vice President, nor any other
Cabinet member, nor the leaders of House or Senate survived. It appears certain that only a small percentage of the
members of the Congress escaped. I survive only by
chance, because this morning I was in another city, on an
inspection tour. I am now in a military command post of
relative safety. I have designated this command post Civil
Defense Headquarters, as well as temporary seat of government."

Mrs. Vanbruuker-Brown coughed and choked, re-
covered herself and continued: "With a sick heart, but
the resolution to lead the nation to victory and peace, I
leave you for the time being."

The radio hummed for a second, the carrier wave cut
off, and then there was silence.

Randy said, "It's about what I expected, but it's awful to hear it."

"Still," Helen said, "there is a government."

"I guess that's some comfort. I wonder what's left. I mean, what cities are left."

Helen looked up at Randy. She looked at him, and through him, and far away. Her hands came together on the table, and her fingers interwined; when she spoke it was in a soft, almost inaudible voice, as if her thoughts were so fragile that they would be shattered by more than a whisper. "Do you think—is it possible—that the military command post she spoke of could be Offutt Field? Do you think she might be down in what we call the Hole, at SAC Headquarters? If she is at SAC, you know what that means, don't you?"

"It could mean that Mark is okay. But Helen—"

"Yes?"

Randy didn't think it likely that Mrs. Vanbruuker-Brown was speaking from Omaha. The odds were against it. There were many headquarters, and the first one the enemy would try to destroy, after Washington itself, was SAC. Mark had feared this, and so did he. He said, "I don't think we should count on it."

"I'm not counting on it. I'm just praying. If Mark is—alive—how long do you think it'll be before we hear from him?"

"I can't even guess. But I do know who can make an educated guess. Admiral Hazzard. He lives on the other side of the Henrys' place. He listens to short wave and keeps up with everything that goes on. He served a tour in ONI, and later was on the Intelligence staff of the Joint Chiefs—I think that was his last duty before they retired him. So if anybody around here should know what's happening then old Sam Hazzard should know."

"Can we see him?"

"Of course we can see him. Any time we want. It's only a quarter mile. But we can't leave Peyton alone and I don't have any idea what time Dan Gunn will get here." His arms felt wooden, and detached, and his head too heavy for his neck. His chin drooped on his chest. "And I'm so blasted tired, Helen. I feel that if I don't get a couple of hours of real sleep I'll go off my rocker. If I don't get some rest I won't be much good from here in, and God knows what'll happen tonight."

Helen said, "I'm sorry, Randy. Of course you're groggy. Go on up stairs and get some sleep. I'm going to drive to town. There's so much stuff we've just got to have."

"Suppose Peyton calls? I'll never wake up."

"Ben Franklin will be here. I'll tell him to wake you up if anything serious happens."

"Okay. Be careful. Don't stop for anybody on the way to town." Randy went upstairs, each step an effort. It was true, he thought, that women had more stamina than men.

Randy decided not actually to take off his clothes and get into bed because once he got under the covers he would never get up. Instead, he took off his shoes and dropped down on the couch in the living room. He stared at the gunrack on the opposite wall. Until very recent years guns had been an important part of living on the Timucuan. Randy guessed they might become important again. He had quite an arsenal. There was the long, old-fashioned 30-40 Krag fitted with sporting sights; the carbine he had carried in Korea, dismantled, and smuggled home; two .22 rifles, one equipped with a scope; a twelve-gauge automatic, and a light, beautifully balanced twenty-gauge double-barreled shotgun. In the drawer of his bedside table was a .45 automatic and a .22 target pistol hung in a holster in his closet.

Ammo. He had more than he would ever need for the big rifle, the carbine, and the shotguns. But he had only a couple of boxes of .22's, and he guessed that the .22's might be the most useful weapons he owned, if economic chaos lasted for a long time, a meat shortage developed, and it became necessary to hunt small game. He rose and went into the hallway and shouted down at the stairwell, "Helen!"

"Yes?" She was at the front door.

"If you get a chance drop in at Beck's Hardware and buy some twenty-two caliber long-rifle hollow points."

"Just a second. I'll write it down on my list. Twenty-two long-rifle hollow points. How many?"

"Ten boxes, if they have them."

Helen said, "I'll try. Now, Randy, get some sleep."

Back on the couch, he closed his eyes, thinking of guns, and hunting. In his father's youth, this section of Florida had been a hunter's paradise, with quail, dove, duck, and deer in plenty, and even black bear and a rare panther. Now the quail were scattered and often scarce. Three coveys roamed the grove, and the hammock behind the Henrys' place. Randy had not shot quail for twelve years. When visitors noticed his gunrack and asked about quail shooting, he always laughed and. said, "Those guns are to shoot people who try to shoot my quail." The quail were more than pets. They were friends, and wonderful to watch, parading across lawn and road in the early morning.

Only the ducks were now truly plentiful in this area, and they were protected by Federal law. Once in a while he shot a rattlesnake in the grove, or a moccasin near the dock. And that was all he shot. Still, there were rabbits and squirrels, and so the .22 ammo might come in handy. A long time ago—he could not have been more than fourteen or fifteen—he remembered hunting deer with his father, and shooting his first deer with buckshot from the double-twenty. His first, and his last, for the deer had not died instantly, and had seemed small and piteous, twitching in the palmetto scrub, until his father had dispatched it with his pistol. He could still see it, and the round, bright red spots on the green fronds. He shivered, and he slept.

Randy awoke in darkness. Graf was barking, and he heard voices downstairs. He turned on a light. It was nine-thirty. He had slept almost four hours. He felt refreshed, and good for whatever might come through the night. He was putting on his shoes when the door opened and Helen came into his apartment, followed by Ben Franklin and Dan Gunn.

"I was just going to wake you up," Helen said. "Dan is going in to look at Peyton."

Dan's eyes were hollowed, and his face carved with fissues of exhaustion. Randy said, "Have you eaten anything today, Dan?"

"I don't know. I don't think so."

Helen said, "You'll eat, Doctor, right after you've seen Peyton. Do you want me to go in with you?"

"You and Randy can both come in with me. But don't say anything. Let me do the talking."

They went into the child's room. Randy flicked on the overhead light. "Not that one," Dan said. "I want a dim light at first." He turned on a lamp on the dressing table.

Peyton's hands crept out from under the sheet and touched the bandages over her eyes. "Hello," she said, her voice small and frightened.

"Hello, dear," Helen said. "Doctor Gunn is here to see you. You remember Doctor Gunn from last year, don't you?"

"Oh, yes. Hello, Doctor."

Dan said, "Peyton, I'm going to take the bandage off your eyes. Don't be surprised if you don't see anything. There isn't much light in the room."

Randy found he was holding his breath. Dan removed the bandage, saying, "Now, don't rub your eyes."

Peyton tried to open her eyes. She said, "They're stuck. They feel all gooey."

"Sure," Dan said. He moistened cotton in a borax mixture and wiped Peyton's eyes gently. "That better?"

Peyton blinked. "Hey, I can see! Well, sort of. Everything looks milky." Helen moved and Peyton said, "Isn't that you, Mother?"

"Yes. That's me."

"Your face looks like a balloon but I could tell it was you."

Dan smiled at Randy and nodded. She was going to be all right.

He rummaged in his bag and brought out a small kit, a bottle, and applicator, a tube. He said, "Peyton, you can stop worrying now. You're not going to be blind. In perhaps a week, you'll be able to see fine. But until then you've got to rest your eyes and we've got to treat them. This is going to sting a little."

He held her eyelids open and, his huge hands sure and gentle, applied drops, and an ointment. "Butyn sulphate," he said. "This is really outside my line, but I remembered that butyn sulphate was what Air-Sea Rescue used for rescued fliers. After floating around in a raft for two or three days, the glare would blind them just as Peyton was blinded. It fixed them up, and it ought to fix her up."

Dan turned to Helen. "Did you see how I did it?"

"I was watching."

"I'll try to get out here at least once a day, but if I don't make it, you'll have to do it yourself."

"I won't have any trouble. Peyton's quite brave."

Peyton said, "Mommy, I'm not. I'm not brave at all. I'm scared all the time. Have you heard from Dad, yet? Do you think Dad's all right?"

"I'm sure he's all right, dear," Helen said. "But we can't expect to hear right away. All the phones are out, and I suppose the telegraph too."

"I'm hungry, Mother."

Helen said, "I'll bring something right up."

They turned off the light. Helen went downstairs. Dan Gunn came into Randy's rooms. He took off his wrinkled jacket and dropped it on a chair and said, "Now I can use a drink."

Randy mixed a double bourbon. Dan drank half of it in a gulp and said, surprised, "Aren't you drinking, Randy?"

"No. Don't feel like I want one."

"That's the first good news I've heard all day. I've already treated two fellows who've drunk themselves insensible since morning. You could've been the third."

"Could I?"

"Well, not quite. You react to crisis in the right way. You remember what Toynbee says? His theory of challenge and response applies not only to nations, but to individuals. Some nations and some people melt in the heat of crisis and come apart like fat in the pan. Others meet the challenge and harden. I think you're going to harden."

"I'm really not a very hard guy," Randy said, looking across the room at his guns and thinking, oddly, of the young buck he'd shot when a boy, and how he'd never been able to shoot a deer since that day. To change the subject he said, "You must've had a pretty harrowing day."

Dan drank the second half of his bourbon and water. "I have had such a day as I didn't think it was possible to have. Seven cardiacs are dead and a couple more will go before morning. Three miscarriages and one of the women died. I don't know what killed her. I'd put down 'fright' on the death certificate if I had time to make out death certificates. Three suicides—one of them was Edgar Quisenberry."

Randy said, "Edgar—why?"

Dan frowned. "Hard to say. He still had as much as anybody else, or more. He wasn't organically ill. I'll refer to Toynbee again. Inability to cope with a sudden change in the environment. He swam in a sea of money, and when money was transmuted back into paper he was left gasping and confused, and he died. You've read the history of the 'twenty-nine crash, haven't you?"

"Yes."

"Dozens of people killed themselves for the same reason. They created and lived in an environment of paper profits, and when paper returned to paper they had to kill themselves, not realizing that their environment was unnatural and artificial. But it wasn't the adults that got me down, Randy, it was the babies. Give me another drink, a small one."

Randy poured another.

"Eight babies today, three of them preemies. I've got the preemies in San Marco hospital. I don't know whether they'll make it or not. The hospital's a mess. Cots end to end on every corridor. A good many of them are accident cases, a few gunshot wounds. And all this, mind you, with only three casualties caused directly by the war—three cases of radiation poisoning."

"Radiation?" Randy said. "Around here?" Suddenly the word had a new and immediate connotation. It was now a sinister word of lingering death, like cancer.

"No. Refugees from Tallahassee. They drove through pretty heavy fallout, I guess. We estimate at the hospital that they received fifty to a hundred roentgens. Anyway, a pretty hefty dose, but not fatal."

"Are we getting any radiation, do you think?"

Dan considered. "Some, undoubtedly. But I don't think a dangerous dose. There isn't a Geiger in town, but there is a dosimeter in the San Marco hospital and I guess we're getting what San Marco gets. Most of the radioactive particles decay pretty fast, you know. Not cesium or strontium 90 or cobalt or carbon 14. Those will always be with us."

"Lucky east wind," Randy said, and then was surprised at his words. The danger of radiation was still there, and might increase. Long before this day scientists had been worried about tests of nuclear weapons, even when conducted in uninhabited areas under rigid controls. Now the danger obviously was infinitely greater, but since there were other and more immediate dangers—dangers that you could see, feel, and hear—radiation had become secondary. He wasn't thinking of its effect upon future generations. He was concerned with the present. He wasn't exercised over the fallout blanketing Tallahassee from the attack on Jacksonville. He was worried about Fort Repose. He suspected that this was a necessary mental adjustment to aid self-preservation. The exhausted swimmer, struggling to reach shore, isn't worried about starving to death afterwards.

When Helen called, they sat down to a dinner table that, under the circumstances, seemed incongruous. The meal was only soup, salad, and sandwiches, but Helen had laid the table as meticulously as if Dan Gunn had agreed to stay for a late supper on an ordinary evening. When Ben Franklin sat down Helen said, "Did you wash your hands?"

"No, ma'am."

"Well, do so."

And Ben disappeared and returned with his hands washed and hair combed. They listened to the radio as they ate, hearing only the local broadcasts from San Marco at two-minute intervals. Their ears had become dulled to the repetitive, unimportant announcements and warnings, as those who live on the seashore fail to hear the sea. But any fresh news, or break in the routine, instantly alerted and silenced them.

Several times they heard a brief bulletin: "County Civil Defense authorities warn everyone not to drink fresh milk which may have been exposed to fallout. Canned milk, or milk delivered this morning prior to the attack, can be presumed safe."

Dan Gunn explained that this precaution was probably a little premature. It was designed primarily for the protection of children. Strontium 90, probably the most dangerous of all fallout materials, collected in calcium. It caused bone cancer and leukemia. "In a week or so it can be a real hazard," he said. "It can't be a hazard yet, because the cows haven't had time to ingest strontium 90 in their fodder. Still, the quicker these dangers are broadcast, the more people will be aware of them."

Helen asked, "What happens to babies?"

"Evaporated or condensed canned milk is the answer—while it lasts. After that, it's mother's milk."

"That will be old-fashioned, won't it?"

Dan nodded and smiled. "But the mothers will have to be careful of what they eat." He looked down at the lettuce. "For instance, no greens, or lettuce, if your garden has received fallout. Trouble is, you won't know, really, whether your ground, or your food, is safe or not. Not without a Geiger counter. We'll all have to live as best we can, from day to day."

Ben Franklin looked up at the ceiling, listening. He said, "Listen!"

The others heard it, very faintly.

"A jet," Ben said. "A fighter, I think."

The sound faded away. Randy discovered he had been holding his breath. He said, "I guess it's still going on."

Helen laid her salad fork on the plate. She had eaten very little. She said, "I have to know what's happening—I just have to. Can't we go over to see your retired admiral tonight, Randy?"

"Sure, we can see him. But what about Peyton? We can't leave her alone."

Helen looked at Ben Franklin and Ben said, "Is this what I'm going to be—a professional baby-sitter?"

Dan Gunn rose. "I've got to get back to town. I've got to check in at the clinic and then I've got to get some sleep."

"Why don't you stay here for the night, Dan?" Randy said.

"I can't. They're expecting me at the clinic. And Randy, I brought the emergency kit for you." He turned to Helen. "It was a wonderful supper. Thanks. I was so hungry I was weak. I didn't realize it."

Randy walked him to his car. Dan said, "That poor girl."

"Peyton?"

"No. Helen. Uncertainty is the worst. She'd be better off if she knew Mark was dead. See you tomorrow, Randy."

"Yes. Tomorrow." He walked back to the house and paused on the porch to look at the thermometer and barometer. The barometer was steady, very high. Temperature was down to fifty-five. It would get colder tonight. It might go to forty before morning. From across the river, far off, he heard a string of shots. In this stillness, at night, and across water, the sound of shots carried for miles. He could not tell from whence the sound came, or guess why, but the shots reminded him of a nervous sentry on post cutting loose with his carbine. It sounded like a carbine, or an automatic pistol.

He walked into the house, head down, and went up to his bedroom and pulled on a sweater. He called Ben Franklin to the living room and Ben came in, his mother following. "Ben," Randy said, "ever shoot a pistol?"

"Only once, on the range at Offutt."

"What about a rifle?"

"I've shot a twenty-two. I'm pretty good with a twenty-two."

"Okay," Randy said, "I'm going to give you what you're good at."

He walked to the gunrack. The Mossberg was fitted with a sixpower scope, and a scope was not good for snap shooting, and hard to use at night. He took down the Remington pump, a weapon with open sights, a present from his father on his thirteenth birthday. He handed it to Ben.

The boy took it, pleased, worked the action and peered into the chamber.

"It's not loaded now," Randy said, "but from now on every gun in this house is going to be loaded. I hope we never have to use them but if we do there probably won't be any time to load up."

Helen said, "I forgot to tell you, Randy. I couldn't get ten boxes of the ammunition you wanted but I did get three. They're somewhere in the kitchen. I'll find them later."

"Thanks," Randy said. He took a package of cartridges out of his ammunition case and handed it to Ben. "You load up your gun, Ben," he said. "It's yours now. Never point it at a man unless you intend to shoot him, and never shoot unless you mean to kill. You understand that?"

Ben's eyes were round and his face sober. "Yes, sir."

"Okay, Ben. You can baby-sit now. We should be back in an hour."

When Rear Admiral Hazzard retired he embarked upon what he liked to call "my second life." He and his wife had prepared carefully for retirement. They had wanted an orange grove to supplement his pension and a body of water upon which he could look and in which he could fish. While still a four-striper he had located this spot on the Timucuan, and bought it for a surprisingly reasonable sum. The real estate agent had carefully explained that the low price included "niggers for neighbors," meaning the Henrys. At the same time the agent had grumbled at the Braggs, who had allowed the Henrys to buy water-front property in the first place, thereby lowering values along the entire river, or so he said.

The Hazzards first had planted a grove. A few years later they built a comfortable six-room rambler and started landscaping the grounds. Thereafter they lived in the house one month each year, when Sam took his annual leave, trying it and wearing it until it fitted perfectly.

On his sixty-second birthday Sam Hazzard retired, to the relief of a number of his fellow admirals. There were rivalries within, as well as between, the armed services. In the Navy, the rivalry had once been between the battleship and carrier admirals. When it became a rivalry between atomic subs and super-carriers, Hazzard had outspokenly favored the submarines. Since he once had commanded a carrier task force, and never had been a submariner, the carrier admirals regarded his stand as just short of treason. Worse, for years he had claimed that Russia's most dangerous threat was the terrible combination of submarines equipped with missiles armed with nuclear warheads. Such a theory, if unchallenged, would force the Navy to spend a greater part of its energy and money on anti-submarine warfare. Since this, *per se,* was defense, and since the Navy's whole tradition was to take the offensive, Hazzard spent his final years of duty conning a desk.

Two days after his retirement his wife died, so she never really lived in the house on the Timucuan, and she never physically shared his second life. Yet often she seemed close, when he trimmed a shrub she had planted, or when in the evenings he sat alone on the patio, and reached to touch the arm of the chair at his side.

The Admiral discovered there were not enough hours in the day to do all the things that were necessary, and that he wanted to do. There was the citrus, the grounds, experiments with exotic varieties of bananas and papaya, discreet essays to be written for the United States Naval Institute *Proceedings* and not-so-discreet articles for magazines of general circulation. Sam Hazzard found that the Henrys were extraordinarily convenient neighbors. Malachai tended the grounds and helped design and build the dock. Two-Tone, when in the mood—broke and sober—worked in the grove. The Henry women cleaned, and did his laundry. Preacher Henry was the Admiral's private fishing guide, which meant that the Admiral consistently caught more and bigger bass than anyone on the Timucuan, and possibly in all of Central Florida.

But Sam Hazzard's principal hobby was listening to shortwave radio. He was not a ham operator. He had no transmitter. He listened. He did not chatter. He monitored the military frequencies and the foreign broadcasts and, with his enormous background of military and political knowledge, he kept pace with the world outside Fort Repose. Sometimes, perhaps, he was a bit ahead of everyone.

It was ten to eleven when Randy knocked on Admiral Hazzard's door. It opened immediately. The Admiral was a taut, neatly made man who had weighed 133 when he boxed for the Academy and who weighed 133 now. He was dressed in a white turtleneck sweater, flannels, and boat shoes. A halo of cottony hair encircled his sunburned bald spot. Otherwise, he was not saintly. His nose had been flattened in some long-forgotten brawl in Port Said or Marseilles. His gray eyes, canopied by heavy white brows, were red-rimmed, and angry. For the Admiral, this had been a day of frustration, helplessness, and hatred—hatred for the unimaginative, purblind, selfish fools who had not believed him, and frustration because on this day of supreme danger and need, his lifetime of training and experience was not and could not be put to use. The Admiral said, "I saw your headlights coming down the road. Come in." He squinted at Helen.

"My sister-in-law, Helen Bragg," Randy said.

"An evil day to receive a beautiful woman," the Admiral said, his voice surprisingly mild and mannered to issue from such a pugnacious face. "Come on in to my Combat Plot, and listen to the war, if such a massacre can be called a war."

He led them to his den. A heavily planked workbench ran along the wall under the windows overlooking the river. On this bench was a large, black, professional-looking shortwave receiver, a steaming coffee-maker, notebooks and pencils. The radio screeched with power, static, interference, and occasional words in the almost unintelligible language of conflict.

On two other walls, cork-covered, were pinned maps—the polar projection and the Eurasian land mass on one wall, a military map of the United States on the other.

A hoarse voice broke through the static: "This is Adelaide Six-Five-One. I am sitting on a skunk at Alpha Romeo Poppa Four. Skunk at Alpha Romeo Poppa Four."

A different voice replied immediately: "Adelaide Six-Five-One, this is Adelaide. Hold one."

There was silence for a moment, and then the second voice continued: "Adelaide Six-Five-One—Adelaide. Have relayed your message to Hector. He is busy but will be free in ten to fifteen minutes. Squat on that skunk and wait for Hector."

"Adelaide from Adelaide Six-Five-One. Charley."

Helen sat down. For the first time that day, she was showing fatigue. The Admiral said, "Coffee?"

"I'd love a cup," she said.

Randy said, "Sam, what was that on the radio? Part of the war?"

The Admiral poured coffee before he replied. "A big part of it, for us. Right now I'm tuned to a Navy and Air Force ASW frequency in the five megacycle band."

"ASW?"

"Anti-submarine warfare. I'll interpret. A Navy super-Connie with a saucer radome has located a skunk—an enemy submarine—at coordinates Alpha Romeo Poppa Four. I happen to know that's about three hundred miles off Norfolk. The radar picket has called home base—Adelaide—and Adelaide is sending Hector to knock off the skunk. Hector is one of our killer subs. But Hector is presently engaged. When he is free, he will communicate directly with Adelaide Six-Five-One. The plane will give Hector a course and when he is in range Hector will cut loose with a homing torpedo and that will be the end of the skunk. We hope."

"Who's winning?" Randy asked, aware that it was a ridiculous question.

"Who's winning? Nobody's winning. Cities are dying and ships are sinking and aircraft is going in, but nobody's winning."

Helen asked the question she had come to ask. "Did you hear Mrs. Vanbruuker-Brown on the radio a while ago?"

"Yes."

"Where do you think she was speaking from?"

The Admiral walked across the room and looked at the map of the United States. It was covered with acetate overlay and ten or twelve cities were ringed with red-crayon goose eggs, in the way that a unit position is marked on an infantry map. The Admiral scratched the white stubble on his chin and said, "I think Denver. Hunneker, the three-star she named Chief of Staff, was Army representative on NORAD, in Colorado Springs. Chances are that he was in Denver this morning, or she was in Colorado Springs, when the word came through that Washington had been atomized."

Helen set down her coffee cup. Her fingers trembled. "You're sure that she couldn't have been in Omaha?"

"Omaha!" said the Admiral. "That's the last place she'd be speaking from! You notice that whenever I've heard a broadcast, of any kind, that allowed me to identify a city, I ringed it on the map. I've heard no amateurs talking from Omaha, and I haven't heard SAC since the attack. Ordinarily, I can pick up SAC right away. They're always talking on their single side band transmitters to bases out of the country. Their call sign was 'Big Fence.' I haven't heard 'Big Fence' all day on any frequency. And the enemy hates and fears SAC, more, even, than they fear the Navy, I'll admit. Scratch Omaha."

Sam Hazzard noticed the effect of his words on Helen's expression; he recalled that Randy's brother, her husband, was an Air Force colonel, and he sensed that he had been tactless. "Your husband isn't in Omaha, is he, Mrs. Bragg?"

"It's our home."

"I'm terribly sorry that I said anything."

A tear was quivering on her cheek. Her first, Randy thought. He felt embarrassed for Sam.

Helen said, "There's nothing to be sorry about, Admiral. Mark expected Omaha would be hit, and so did I. That's why I'm here, with the children. But even if Omaha is gone, Mark may still be there, and all right. He had the duty this morning. He was in the Hole."

"Oh, yes," the Admiral said. "The Hole. I've never been in it, but I've heard about it. A tremendous shelter, very deep. He may be perfectly safe. I sincerely hope so."

"I'm afraid not," Helen said, "since you haven't heard any SAC signals."

"They may have shifted communications or changed code names." The Admiral looked at his maps. "Besides, I'm only guessing. I'm just playing games with myself, trying to G-two a war with no action reports or intelligence. I do this because I haven't anything else to do. I just scramble around and move pins and make marks on the maps and try to keep myself from thinking about Sam, Junior. He's a lieutenant JG with Sixth Fleet in the Med, if Sixth Fleet is still in the Med. I don't think it is. For the Russkies, it must have been like shooting frogs in a puddle." He turned to Helen again, "We inhabit the same purgatory, Mrs. Bragg, the dark level of not knowing."

Randy asked a question. "What are the Russians saying? Can you still get Radio Moscow?"

"I get a station that calls itself Radio Moscow in the twenty-five meter band. But it isn't Moscow. All the voices on the English-language broadcasts are different so we can be pretty certain Moscow isn't there any more. However, the Russian leaders all seem to be alive and well, and they issue the kind of statements you'd expect. The very fact that they are alive indicates that they took shelter before it started. They probably aren't anywhere close to a target area."

"Couldn't the President have escaped?"

"He probably had fifteen minutes' warning. He could

have been in a helicopter and away. But in that fifteen minutes he had to make the big decisions, and so my guess is that he deliberately chose to stay in Washington, either at his desk in the White House, or in the Pentagon Command Post. It was the same for the Joint Chiefs, and probably for the Secretarys of Defense and State. As to the other Cabinet members, they probably received it in their sleep, or were just getting up. Do you want to hear something strange?" The Admiral changed the wave length on his receiver. He said, "Now listen."

All Randy heard was static.

"You didn't hear anything, did you?" the Admiral said. "Right now, on this band, you ought to be hearing the BBC, Paris, and Bonn. I haven't heard any of them all day. They must've truly clobbered England."

"Then you do think we're finished?" Randy said.

"Not at all. SAC may have been able to launch up to fifty percent of its aircraft, counting the planes they always have airborne. And remember that the Navy does have a few missile submarines and the carriers must've got in some licks. Also, I'm pretty sure they weren't able to take out all our SAC bases, including the auxiliaries. For all I know, the enemy may be finished."

"Doesn't exactly hearten me."

The lights went out in the room, the radio died, and at the same time the world outside was illuminated, as at midday. At that instant Randy faced the window and he would always retain, like a color photograph printed on his brain, what he saw—a red fox frozen against the Admiral's green lawn. It was the first fox he had seen in years.

The white flashed back into a red ball in the southeast. They all knew what it was. It was Orlando, or McCoy Base or both. It was the power supply for Timucuan County.

Thus the lights went out, and in that moment civilization in Fort Repose retreated a hundred years.

So ended The Day.

[7]

When nuclear fireballs crisped Orlando and the power plants serving Timucuan County, refrigeration stopped, along with electric cooking. The oil furnaces, sparked by electricity, died. All radios were useless unless battery powered or in automobiles. Washing machines, dryers, dishwashers, fryers, toasters, roasters, vacuum cleaners, shavers, heaters, beaters—all stopped. So did the electric clocks, vibrating chairs, electric blankets, irons for pressing clothes, curlers for hair.

The electric pumps stopped, and when the pumps stopped the water stopped and when the water stopped the bathrooms ceased functioning.

Not until the second day after The Day did Randy Bragg fully understand and accept the results of the loss of electricity. Temporary loss of power was nothing new in Fort Repose. Often, during the equinoctial storms, poles and trees came down and power lines were severed. This condition rarely lasted for more than a day, for the repair trucks were out as soon as the wind abated and the roads became passable.

It was hard to realize that this time the power plants themselves were gone. There could be no doubt of it. On Sunday and Sunday night a number of survivors from Orlando's suburbs drove through Fort Repose, foraging for food and gasoline. They could not be positive of what had happened, except that the area of destruction extended for eight miles from Orlando airport, encompassing College Park and Rollins College, and another explosion had centered on McCoy Air Force Base. The Orlando Conelrad stations had warned of an air raid just before the explosions, so it was presumed that this attack had not come from submarine-based missiles or ICBM's, but from bombers.

Randy did not hear Mrs. Vanbruuker-Brown again, or any further hard news or instructions on the clear channel stations on Sunday or Monday. He did hear WSMF announcing that it would be on the air only two minutes each hour thereafter, since it was operating on auxiliary power. He knew that the hospital in San Marco possessed an auxiliary diesel generator. He concluded that this source of power was being tapped, each hour on the hour, to operate the radio station.

Each hour the county Conelrad station repeated warnings—boil all drinking water, do not drink fresh milk, do not use the telephone, and, in the Sunday morning hours after the destruction of Orlando, warnings to take shelter and guard against fallout and radiation. There had been no milk deliveries and the telephones hadn't worked since the first mushroom sprouted in the south; nor were there any actual shelters in Fort Repose. All Sunday, Randy insisted that Helen and the children stay in the house. He knew that any shelter, even a slate roof, insulation, walls and roof, was better than none. There was no time to dig. The time to dig had been before The Day. After Orlando, digging seemed wasted effort. Anyway, there were so many other things to do, each minor crisis demanding instant attention. While radiation was a danger, it could not be felt or seen, and therefore other dangers, and even annoyances, seemed more imperative.

At two o'clock Monday afternoon Helen was in Randy's apartment, and they were listening to the hourly Conelrad broadcast, when Ben Franklin marched in and announced, "We're just about out of water."

"That's impossible!" Randy said.

"It's Peyton's fault," said Ben Franklin. "Every time she goes to the john she has to flush it. The tub in our bathroom is empty, and she's been dipping water out of mother's bathtub too."

Randy looked at Helen. This was a mother's problem.

"Peyton's a fastidious little girl," Helen said. "After all, one of the first things a child learns is always to flush the john. What're we going to do?"

Randy said, "For now, Ben Franklin and I will drive down to the dock and fill up what washtubs and buckets we have out of the river. You can't drink river water without boiling it but it'll be okay for the toilets. And from now on Peyton—all of us—can't afford to be so fastidious. We'll flush the toilets only twice a day. Then I guess we'll have to dig latrines out in the grove because I can't haul water from the river forever. Matter of gasoline."

Randy looked out on the grove, noticing a thin powder of dust on the leaves. There had been a long dry spell. The fine, clear, crisp days with low humidity were wonderful for people but bad for the orange crop. He would have to turn on the sprinklers in the grove. . . .

He slammed his fist on the bar counter and shouted, "I'm a damn fool! We've got all the water we want!"

"Where?" Helen asked.

"Right out there!" Randy waved his arms. "Artesian water, unlimited!"

"But that's in the grove, isn't it?"

"I'm sure we can pipe it into the house. After all, that's the same water the Henrys use every day. I think there are some big wrenches in the garage and Malachai will know how to do it. Come on, Ben, let's go over to the Henrys'."

Randy and the boy walked down the old gravel and clay road that led from the garage through the grove and to the river. Randy's navels had been picked, but the Valencias were still on the trees. They would not be picked this year. Matching strides with Randy, Ben Franklin said, "I just thought of something."

"Yes?"

"I don't have to go to school any more."

"What makes you think you don't have to go to school? As soon as things get back to normal you're going to school, young feller. Want to grow up to be an ignoramus?"

Ben Franklin scuffed a pebble, looked up sideways at Randy, and grinned. "What school?"

"Why, the school in Fort Repose, of course, until you can go back to Omaha, or wherever your father is stationed."

Ben stopped. "Just a minute, Randy. I'm not fooling myself. Nobody's going back to Omaha, maybe ever. And I don't think I'll ever see Dad again. The Hole wasn't safe, you know. Maybe you think so. I know Mother does. But I'm not fooling myself, Randy, and don't you try to fool me."

Randy put his hands on the boy's shoulders and looked into his face, measuring the depth of courage behind the brown eyes, finding it at least as deep as his own. "Okay, son," he said, "I'll level with you. I'll level with you, and don't you ever do anything less with me. I think Mark has had it. I think you're the man of the family from now on."

"That's what Dad said."

"Did he? Well, you're a man who still has to go to school. I don't know where, or when, or how. But as soon as school reopens in Fort Repose, or anywhere around, you go. You may have to walk."

"Golly, Randy, walk! It's three miles to town."

"Your grandfather used to walk to school in Fort Repose. When he was your age there weren't any school busses. When he couldn't hitch a ride in a buggy, or one of the early automobiles, he walked." Randy put his arm around the boy's shoulder. "Let's get going. I guess we'll both have to learn to walk again."

They walked down to the dock, and then followed a trail that led through the dense hammock to the Henrys' cleared land.

The Henrys' house was divided into four sections, representing four distinct periods in their fortunes and history. The oldest section had originally been a one-room log cabin. It was the only surviving structure of what had once been the slave quarters, and Randy recalled that his grandfather had always referred to the Henrys' place as "the quarters." In recent years the cabin had been jacked up and a concrete foundation

laid under the stout cypress logs. The logs, originally
chinked with red clay, were bound together with white-
washed mortar. It was now the Henrys' living room.

Late in the nineteenth century a two-room pine shack
had been added to the cabin. In the 'twenties another
room, and a bath, more soundly constructed, had been
tacked on. In the 'forties, after Two-Tone's marriage to
Missouri, the house had been enlarged by a bedroom
and a new kitchen, built with concrete block. It was a
comfortable hodgepodge, its ugliness concealed under a
patina of flame vine, bougainvillea, and hibiscus. A
neat green bib of St. Augustine grass fell from the
screened porch to the river bank and dock. In the back
yard was a chicken coop and wired runs, a pig pen, and
an ancient barn of unpainted cypress leaning wearily
against a scabrous chinaberry tree. The barn housed
Balaam, the mule, the Model-A, and a hutch of white
rabbits.

Fifty yards up the slope Preacher Henry and Balaam
solemnly disked the land, moving silently and evenly, as
if they perfectly understood each other. Caleb lay flat
on his belly on the end of the dock, peering into the
shadowed waters behind a piling, jigging a worm for
bream. Two-Tone sat on the screened porch, rocking
languidly and lifting a can of beer to his lips. From the
kitchen came a woman's deep, rich voice, singing a spiritual. That would be Missouri, washing the dishes. Hot,
black smoke from burning pine knots issued from both
brick chimneys. It seemed a peaceful home, in time of
peace.

Ben Franklin yelled, "Hey, Caleb!"

Caleb's face bobbed up. "Hi, Ben," he called. "Come
on out."

"What're you catching?"

"Ain't catchin,' just jiggin'."

Randy said, "You can go out on the dock if you
want, Ben, but I'll probably need your help in a while."

Ben looked surprised. "Me? You'll need my help?"

"Yep," Randy said. "A man of the house has to do a
man's work."

Preacher Henry dropped his reins, yelled, "Ho!" and

Balaam stopped. Preacher walked across the dusty field, to be planted in corn in February, to meet Randy. Malachai came out of the barn. He had been under the Model-A. Two-Tone stopped rocking, put down his can of beer, and left the porch. Inside, Missouri stopped singing.

Randy walked toward the back door and the Henrys converged on him, their faces apprehensive. Malachai said, "Hello, Mister Randy. Hope everything's all right."

"About as right as they could be, considering. Everything okay here?"

"Just like always. How's the little girl? Missouri told me she was about blinded."

"Peyton's better. She can see now and in a few days she'll be allowed outside again. No permanent injury."

"The Lord be merciful!" said Preacher Henry. "The Lord has spared us, for the now. I knew it was a-comin', for it was all set down, Alas, Babylon!" Preacher's eyes rolled upward. Preacher was big-framed, like Malachai, but now the muscles had shrunk around his bones, and age and troubles deeply wrinkled and darkened his face.

Randy addressed his words to Preacher, because Preacher was the father and head of the household. "We don't have water in our house. I want to take up some pipe out of the grove and hook it on to the artesian system."

"Yes, sir, Mister Randy! I'll drop my diskin' right now and help."

"No, you stick with the disking, Preacher. I thought maybe Malachai and Two-Tone could help."

Two-Tone, who was called Two-Tone because the right side of his face was two shades lighter than the left side, looked stricken. "You mean now?" Two-Tone said.

Malachai grinned. "You heard the man, Two-Tone. He means now."

The three men, with Ben Franklin and Caleb helping, required two hours to lift the pipes and connect the artesian line with the water system in the pumphouse.

It was the hardest work Randy remembered since climbing and digging in Korea. The palm of his right hand was blistered from the pipe wrench, and a swatch of skin flapped loose. He was exhausted and wet with sweat despite the chill of evening. He was grateful when Malachai offered to carry the tools back to the garage. He said, "Thanks, Malachai. You know that two hundred bucks I loaned you?"

"Yes, sir."

"Just consider the debt canceled."

They both grinned.

Randy and Ben Franklin went back into the house. Randy turned on the tap in the kitchen sink. It gurgled, coughed, sputtered, and then spurted water.

"Isn't it beautiful!" Helen said.

Randy washed the grime from his hands, the water stinging the broken blisters. He filled a glass. The artesian water still smelled like rotten eggs. He gulped it. It tasted wonderful.

Just after dawn on the third day after The Day a helicopter floated over Fort Repose and then turned toward the upper reaches of the Timucuan. Randy and Helen, hearing it, ran up to the captain's walk on the roof. It passed close overhead, and they distinguished the Air Force insignia.

This was also the day of disastrous overabundance.

That morning, when Helen apprehensively opened the freezer, she found several hundred pounds of choice and carefully wrapped meat floating in a noxious sea of melted ice cream and liquified butter. As any housewife would do under the circumstances, she wept.

This disaster was perfectly predictable, Randy realized. He had been a fool. Instead of buying fresh meat, he should have bought canned meats by the case. If there was one thing he certainly should have forseen, it was the loss of electricity. Even had Orlando escaped, the electricity would have died within a few weeks or months. Electricity was created by burning fuel oil in the Orlando plants. When the oil ran out, it could not be replenished during the chaos of war. There was no longer a rail system, or rail centers, nor were tankers plying the coasts on missions of civilian supply. It was Sam Hazzard's guess that few major seaports had escaped. After the first wave of missiles from the submarines, they could still be taken out by atomic torpedoes, atomic mines, or bombs or missiles from aircraft. It was Sam Hazzard's guess that what had been the great ports were now great, water-filled craters. Even those sections of the country which escaped destruction entirely would not long have lights. Their power would last only as long as fuel stocks on hand.

They stared into the freezer, Helen sniffling, Randy numb, Ben Franklin fascinated. Ben dipped his finger into a pool of liquid chocolate and licked it. "Still tastes good but it isn't even cool," he said. "All that ice cream! I could've been eating ice cream all yesterday; Peyton, too."

Helen stopped sniffling. "The meat won't spoil for another twenty-four hours. I'm going to salvage what I can."

"How?" Randy asked.

"Boil it, salt it, preserve it, pickle it. I've got a dozen Mason jars in the closet. There may be more around somewhere. Perhaps you can get some downtown, Randy."

"Town and back means a half-gallon of gas," Randy said.

"It's worth it, if you can just find a few. And we'll need more salt."

"Okay, I'll give it a try. Maybe I can find jars at the hardware store, if Beck is still keeping it open."

Helen reached into the freezer and lifted out two steaks, six-pounders two inches thick. She brought out two more steaks, even thicker. "Steaks, steaks, steaks. Everywhere steaks. How many steaks can Graf eat tonight? How does Graf like his steaks, charcoal-broiled?"

Graf, lying in the doorway between kitchen and utility room, ears cocked and alert at sound of his name, sniffed the wonderful odor of ripening meat in quantity.

"He likes 'em and I like 'em," Randy said, "and we've got a few sacks of charcoal in the garage. So let's have a party. A steak party to end all steak parties. Literally, that is. We'll have the Henrys, and the McGoverns."

"I've always believed in mixing crowds at my parties," Helen said. "But what about mixing colors?"

"It'll be all right. I'll ask Florence Wechek and Alice Cooksey and Sam Hazzard too. And Dan Gunn, if I can find him. And I'll scrounge around for more charcoal. It'll be a relief from cooking in the fireplace."

"Don't forget the salt," Helen said. "We're going to need a lot to save this meat."

On this, the third day after The Day, the character of Fort Repose had changed. Every building still stood, no brick had been displaced, yet all was altered, especially the people.

Earlier, Randy had noticed that some of the plate-glass store windows had cracked under the shock waves from Tampa and Orlando. Now the windows of a number of stores were shattered entirely, and glass littered the sidewalks. From alleyways came the sour smell of uncollected garbage.

Most of the parking spaces on Yulee and St. Johns incongruously were occupied, but the cars themselves were empty, and several had been stripped of wheels.

There was no commerce. There were few people. Altogether, Randy saw only four or five cars in motion. Those who were not out of gas hoarded what remained in their tanks against graver emergencies to come.

The pedestrians he saw seemed apprehensive, hurrying along on missions private and vital, shoulders hunched, eyes directed dead ahead. There were no women on the streets, and the men did not walk in pairs, but alone and warily. Randy saw several acquaintances who must have recognized his car. Not one smiled or waved.

Four young men, strangers, idled in front of the drugstore. The store's windows were broken, but Randy saw the grim, unhappy face of Old Man Hockstatler, the druggist, at the door. He was staring at the young men, and they were elaborately ignoring him. They were waiting for something, Randy felt. They were waiting like vultures. They were outwaiting Old Man Hockstatler.

Randy pulled into the parking lot alongside Ajax Super-Market. It appeared to be empty. The front door was closed and locked but Randy stepped through a smashed window. The interior looked as if it had been stripped and looted. All that remained of the stock, he noticed immediately, were fixtures, dishes, and plastics on the home-hardware shelves. Significantly nobody had bothered to buy or take electric cords, fuses, or light bulbs. As for food, there seemed to be none left.

Randy tried to remember where the salt counter had been, but salt was something one bought without thought, like razor blades or toothpaste, not bothering about it until it was needed. He thought of razor blades. He was low on them. Finally he examined the guidance signs hanging over the empty shelves. He saw, "Salt, Flour, Grits, Sugar," over a wall to his left. The space where these commodities should have been was bare. Not a single bag of salt remained.

As Randy turned to leave he heard a noise, wood scraping on concrete, in the stockroom in the rear of the store. He opened the stockroom door and found himself looking into the muzzle of a small, shiny revolver. Behind the gun was the skinny, olive-colored face of Pete Hernandez. Pete lowered the gun and jammed it into a hip pocket. "Gees, Randy," he said, "I thought it was some goddam goon come back to clean out the rest of the joint."

"All I wanted was some salt."

"Salt? You out of salt already?"

"No. We want to salt down some meat. We thought we could save part of the meat in the freezer." Randy saw a grocery truck drawn up to the loading platform behind the store. It was half-filled with cases, and Pete had been pushing other cases down the ramp. So Pete had saved something. "What happened here?" Randy asked.

"We'd sold out of just about everything by closing time yesterday. When I tried to close up they wouldn't leave. They wouldn't pay, neither. They started hollerin' and laughin' and grabbin'. I locked myself in back here and that's how come I've got a little something left." Pete winked. "Bet I can get some price for these canned beans in a couple of weeks."

Randy sensed that Pete, perhaps because he had never had much of it, still coveted money. He said, "I'll give you a price for salt right now."

Pete's eyes flicked sideways. There was a cart in the corner. It was filled with sacks—sugar and salt. Pete said, "I've hardly got enough salt to keep things goin' at home. We're in the same boat you are, you know. Freezer full of meat. Maybe Rita will be saltin' meat down too."

Randy brought out his wallet. Pete looked at it. Pete looked greedy. Randy said, "What'll you take for two ten-pound sacks of salt?"

"I ain't got much salt left."

"I'll give you ten dollars a pound for salt."

"That's two hundred dollars. Bein' it's you, okay."

Randy gave him four fifties.

Pete felt the bills. "Ten bucks a pound for salt!" he said. "Ain't that something!"

Randy cradled the sacks under each arm. "Better go out the back way," Pete said. "Don't tell nobody where you got it. And Randy—"

"Yes?"

"Rita wonders when you're coming to see her. She's all the time talking about you. When Rita latches on to a guy she don't let go in a hurry. You know Rita."

Randy rejected the easy evasion of excuses. One of the things he hadn't liked about Rita was her possessiveness, and another was her brother. He was irritated because he had placed himself in the position of being forced to discuss personal matters with Pete. He said, "Rita and I are through."

"That's not what Rita says. Rita says that other girl—that Yankee blonde—won't look so good to you now. Rita says this war's going to level people as well as cities."

Randy knew it was purposeless to talk about Rita, or

anything, with Pete Hernandez. He said, "So long, Pete," and left the market.

Beck's Hardware was still open, and Mr. Beck, looking tired and bewildered, presided over rows of empty shelves. On The Day itself everything that could be immediately useful, from flashlights and batteries to candles and kerosene lanterns, had vanished. In the continuing buying panic, almost everything else had disappeared. "Only reason I'm still here," Mr. Beck explained, "is because I've been coming here every weekday for twenty-two years and I don't know what else to do."

In the warehouse Beck found a dusty carton of Mason jars. "People don't go in much for home canning nowadays," Beck said. "I'd just about forgotten these."

"How much?" Randy asked.

Beck shook his head. "Nothing. That safe is full up to the top with money. That's all I've got left—money. Ain't that funny—nothing but money?" Mr. Beck laughed. "Know what, I could retire."

Randy drove on to the Medical Arts Building. Here, he had expected to find activity. He found none, but he did see Dan Gunn's car in the parking lot.

There were reddish brown stains on the sidewalk and the green concrete steps. The glass in the front door was shattered and the door itself swung open. The waiting room was ominously empty. There was no one at the reception desk. Randy possessed a country dweller's keen sense of smell. Now he smelled many alarming odors—disinfectant, ether, spilled drugs, spilled blood, stale urine. He called, "Dan! Hey, Dan!"

"I'm back here. Who's that?" Dan's voice emerged muffled after echoing through a corridor.

"It's me—Randy."

"Come on back. I'm in my office."

In the corridor's gloom Randy stumbled over a pair of feet, and he stepped back, shivering. A body lay athwart the doorway of the examination room, legs in the corridor, torso in the room, face up, arms outstretched. The face was half blown away, but when put together with the uniform, it was recognizable as Cappy Foracre, Fort Repose's Chief of Police.

Randy hurried on. A fireproof door hung crazily from one hinge. It had been axed open. Behind the door was the laboratory and drug storage. The smell of chemicals that came from the laboratory was choking and overpowering. Within, Randy glimpsed a hillock of smashed jars and bottles. The clinic had been wrecked, insanely and deliberately.

He was relieved to find Dan Gunn standing in his office. Dan's face was more deeply shadowed with fatigue and a two-day growth of beard, his shirt was torn, and he looked dirty, but he apparently was unhurt. Two medical bags were open on his desk. He was examining and sorting vials and bottles. Randy said, "What happened?"

"A carload of addicts—hopheads—came through last night. About three this morning, rather. Jim Bloomfield was here, sleeping on the couch in his office. We'd split up the duty. He took one night, I took the next. You see, with no phones people don't know what else to do except rush to the clinic in an emergency. Anyway, the addicts—there were six of them, all armed—came in and woke Jim up. They wanted a fix. Poor old Jim was something of a puritan. If he'd given them a fix he might've got rid of them."

Dan picked up a hypodermic syringe and slowly squeezed the plunger with his tremendous fingers. "I'd have given 'em a fix all right—three grains of morphine and that would've finished them." Dan dropped the syringe into one of the bags and shook his head. "That probably wouldn't have been smart either. Three grains would kill a normal man but it wouldn't faze an addict. Anyway, Jim told them to go to hell. They beat him up. They emptied these bags and found what they were after. That wasn't enough. They took the fire ax and broke into the lab and drug storage. They cleaned us out of narcotics—everything, not only morphine but all the barbiturates and sodium amytal and pentothal and stimulants like benzedrine and dexedrine. What they didn't take they smashed."

"What about Cappy Foracre?" Randy asked.

"Some woman came in and heard the commotion and ran out and got Cappy. He was sleeping in the fire-house. Cappy and Bert Anders—you know, that kid assistant—came screaming over here. Literally screaming, with their siren going, the darn fools. So the hopheads were set for them. There was a battle. More like a fire fight, an ambush, I guess. Cappy caught a shotgun load in the face. Anders got one in the belly. Cappy was dead when I got here, about fifteen minutes later."

"And old Doc Bloomfield?" Randy asked.

Dan swayed and rested his palms on the desk. His head bent. When he spoke it was in a monotone. "I drove Anders and Jim Bloomfield to the hospital in San Marco. I couldn't operate here, you see. No anesthesia. Couldn't even sterilize my instruments. Everything septic. Young Anders was dead when I got there. Jim was still alive. I thought he was going to be all right. Beaten up, maybe a rib or two caved in, maybe concussion. Still, he was able to tell me, quite coherently, what had happened. Then he slipped away from me. I don't know why. He had lived a long time and after this thing happened maybe he didn't want to live any longer. Maybe he didn't want to belong to the human race any more. He resigned. He died."

Randy said, "The bastards! Where did they come from? Where did they go?"

Dan Gunn shivered. The night had been chilly and it had warmed only slightly during the day and of course there was no heat in the building. He shook his head and slowly straightened, like a great storm-beset ship that has been wallowing in the trough of the sea but will not founder. "Where did they come from?" he said, slipping on his coat. "Maybe they broke out of a state hospital. But more likely they were hoods from St. Louis or Chicago driving to Miami or Tampa for the season. Probably they were addicts as well as pushers. The war caught them between sources of supply. So by last night they were wild for junk, and the quickest way to get it was to detour to some little town like this and raid the clinic. As to where they're going, I don't care so long as it's far from here."

Randy resolved never again to leave the house unless he was armed. "You should carry a gun, Dan. I am, from now on."

Dan said, "No! No, I'm not going to carry a gun. I've spent too many years learning how to save lives to start shooting people now. I'm not worried about punishment for the addicts. They carry a built-in torture chamber. Eventually—I'd say within a few weeks—no matter how many people they kill they'll find no drugs. After this big jag they're bound to have withdrawal sickness. They will die, horribly I hope."

Dan closed the two bags. "So ends the clinic in Fort Repose. Can you give me a lift to the hotel, Randy? I think my gas tank is dry."

"I'll take you to your hotel only so you can pack," Randy said. "On River Road, we've got food, and good water, and wood fireplaces. At the hotel you don't have any of those things." He picked up one of the bags. "Now don't argue with me, Dan. Don't start talking about your duty. Without food and water and heat you can't do anything. You can't even sterilize a scalpel. You won't have strength enough to take care of anybody. You can't even take care of yourself."

When they entered the hotel Randy smelled it at once, but not until they reached the second floor did he positively identify the odor. Like songs, odors are catalysts of memory. Smelling the odors of the Riverside Inn, Randy recalled the sickly, pungent stench of the honey carts with their loads of human manure for the fields of Korea. Randy spoke of this to Dan, and Dan said, "I've tried to make them dig latrines in the garden. They won't do it. They have deluded themselves into believing that lights, water, maids, telephone, dining-room service, and transportation will all come back in a day or two. Most of them have little hoards of canned foods, cookies, and candies. They eat it in their rooms, alone. Every morning they wake up saying that things will be back to normal by nightfall, and every night they fall into bed thinking that normalcy will be restored by morning. It's been too big a jolt for these poor people. They can't face reality."

Dan had been talking as he packed. As they left the hotel, laden with bags and books, Randy said, "What's going to happen to them?"

"I don't know. There's bound to be a great deal of sickness. I can't prevent it because they won't pay any attention to me. I can't stop an epidemic if it comes. I don't know what's going to happen to them."

Dan moved into the house on River Road that day. Thereafter he slept in the sleigh bed, the only bed in the house that could comfortably accommodate his frame, in Randy's apartment, while Randy occupied the couch in the living room.

That night, afterwards, was remembered as "the night of the steak orgy." Yet it was not for the rich taste of meat well hung that Randy remembered the night. He and the Admiral and Bill McGovern cooked the steaks outside, and then brought them into the living room. Fat wood burned in the big fireplace and a kettle steamed on hot bricks. At a few minutes before ten Randy clicked on his transistor radio, and they all listened. Lib McGovern was sitting on the rug next to him, her shoulder touching his arm. The room was warm, and comfortable, and somehow safe.

They heard the hum of a carrier wave, and then the voice of an announcer from the clear channel station somewhere deep in the heart of the country. "This is your Civil Defense Headquarters. I have an important announcement. Listen carefully. It will not be repeated again tonight. It will be repeated, circumstances permitting, at eleven o'clock tomorrow morning."

Randy felt Lib's long fingers circle his forearm, and grasp tight. Around the group before the fire, all the faces were anxious, the white faces in the front row, the Negro faces, eyes white and large, behind.

"A preliminary aerial survey of the country has been completed. By order of the Acting Chief Executive, Mrs. Vanbruuker-Brown, certain areas have been declared Contaminated Zones. It is forbidden for people to enter these zones. It is forbidden to bring any material of any kind, particularly metal or metal containers, out of these zones.

"Persons leaving the Contaminated Zones must first be examined at check points now being established. The location of these check points will be announced over your local Conelrad stations.

"The Contaminated Zones are:

"The New England States."

Sam Hazzard, sitting in a prim cherry-wood rocker which, like Sam, had originated in New England, drew in his breath.

The newscaster continued:

"All of New York State south of the line Ticonderoga-Sacketts Harbor.

"The state of Pennsylvania, New Jersey, Delaware, and Maryland.

"The District of Columbia.

"Ohio east of the line Sandusky-Chillicothe. Also in Ohio, the city of Columbus and its suburbs.

"In Michigan, Detroit and Dearborn and an area of fifty-mile radius from these cities. Also in Michigan, the cities of Flint and Grand Rapids.

"In Virginia, the entire Potomac River Basin. The cities of Richmond and Norfolk and their suburbs.

"In South Carolina, the port of Charleston and all territory within a thirty-mile radius of Charleston.

"In Georgia, the cities of Atlanta, Savannah, Augusta and their suburbs.

"The state of Florida."

Randy felt angry and insulted. He shifted his weight and started to get to his feet. "Not the whole state!" he said, at the same time realizing his protest was completely irrational.

"Sh-h!" Lib said, and pulled him back to the rug.

The voice went on, ticking off Mobile and Birmingham, New Orleans and Lake Charles.

It moved into Texas, obliterating Fort Worth and Dallas, and everything within a fifty-mile radius of these two cities, and Abilene, Houston, and Corpus Christi.

It moved northward again:

"In Arkansas, Little Rock and its suburbs, plus an area of forty miles to the west of Little Rock."

Missouri, who through the whole evening had said nothing except in answer to questions, now said something. "How come they hit Little Rock?"

The Admiral said, "There's a big SAC base in Little Rock, or was."

The voice moved up to Oak Ridge, in Tennessee, and then spoke of Chicago, and everything around Chicago in northern Indiana, and crept up the western shore of Lake Michigan to Milwaukee, and Milwaukee's suburbs. Inexorably, it uttered the names of Kansas City, Wichita, and Topeka.

The voice continued:

"In Nebraska, Lincoln. Also in Nebraska, Omaha and all the territory within a fifty-mile radius of Omaha."

There goes all hope of Mark, Randy thought. More than one missile for Omaha. Probably three, as Mark had expected. From the moment of the double dawn on The Day, he had known it was probable. Now he must accept it as almost certain. He looked across the circle, at three faces in the firelight. Peyton's face was half-hidden against her mother's breast. Helen's face bent down, and her arms were around Peyton's shoulders. Ben Franklin stared into the fire, his chin straight. Randy could see the tear path down Helen's face, and the unshed tears in Ben's eyes.

The announcements went on, the voice calling out portions of states, and cities—Seattle, Hanford, San Francisco, all the southern California coast, Helena, Cheyenne—but Randy only half-heard them. All he could hear, distinctly, were the sharp sobs out of Peyton's throat.

Randy's heart went out to them but he said nothing.

What was there to say? How do you say to a little girl that you are sorry she no longer has a father?

Close to his side Lib stirred and spoke, two words only, to Helen. "I'm sorry." Randy had noticed, that evening, a tenseness between Helen and Lib. Nothing was said, and yet there was a watchfulness, a hostility, between them. So he was glad that Lib had spoken. He wanted them to like each other. He was puzzled that they didn't.

Then it was over. The radio stilled. More than ever, Randy felt cut off and isolated. Florida was a prohibited zone, and Fort Repose a tiny, isolated sector within that zone. He could appreciate why the whole state had been designated a contaminated area. There were so many bases, so many targets which had been hit, with resulting contamination. They had been extraordinarily fortunate in Fort Repose. The wind had favored them. They had received only a residue of fallout from Tampa and Orlando, and none at all from Miami and Jacksonville. Even a reasonably clean weapon on Patrick would have rained radioactive particles on Fort Repose, but the enemy had not bothered to hit Patrick.

Standing on the other side of the room, Preacher Henry had been listening, but he did not fully understand the designation of contaminated zones or comprehend the implications. He did feel and understand the shock and grief the broadcast brought to the Braggs, and he sensed it was time for him to leave. He nudged Malachai, touched Two-Tone's rump with his toe, caught the attention of Hannah and Missouri, and said, with dignity, "We be going now. I thank you, Mister Randy, for a real fine steak dinner. I hopes we can sometime repay it."

Randy rose to his feet and said, "Good night, Preacher. It was good to have you all."

On the fourth day after The Day, Randy, Malachai, and Two-Tone extended the artesian water system to the houses of Admiral Hazzard and Florence Wechek. Stretching pipe across the grove to the Admiral's house was simple, but to provide water for Florence Wechek and Alice Cooksey it was necessary to dig through the macadam of River Road with picks.

On the night of the sixth day the Riverside Inn burned. With no water in the hydrants, and the hotel's sprinkler system inoperative, the fire department was all but helpless. Only a few reserve firemen showed up, and only one pumper was got into action, using river water. It was a puny effort, and far too late. The old, resinous wooden structure was burning brightly before the first stream touched the walls. Soon the heat drove the firemen away. A few minutes thereafter the last scream was heard from the third floor.

Dan had been summoned an hour later, and Randy had driven him into town. By then, there was nothing to do except care for the survivors. They were few. Some of these died of smoke poisoning or fear—it was hard to diagnose—within a few hours. The burned were taken to San Marco in Bubba Offenhaus' hearse-ambulances. The uninjured were lodged in the Fort Repose school. There was no heat in the school, or food, or water. It was simply shelter, less comfortable than the hotel, and within a few days more squalid.

Dan Gunn suspected that the fire had started in a room where the guests were using canned heat in an attempt to boil water. Or perhaps someone had built a makeshift wood stove. It was, Dan said, inevitable.

On the ninth day after The Day, Lavinia McGovern died. This, too, had been inevitable ever since the lights went out and refrigeration ceased. Since Lavinia McGovern suffered from diabetes, insulin had kept her alive. Without refrigeration, insulin deteriorated rapidly. Not only Lavinia, but all diabetics in Fort Repose, dependent upon insulin, died at about the same period as the drug lost its potency.

Randy and Dan had done their best to save her. They had driven to San Marco hoping to find refrigerated insulin, or the new oral drug, at the hospital.

It was eighteen miles to San Marco. Even driving at the most economical speed in his heavily horsepowered car, Randy estimated that the trip would consume three gallons of gasoline. He estimated he had only five gallons remaining in his tank, plus a five-gallon can in reserve.

Randy made a difficult decision. By then, the Bragg home was linked to the houses of Admiral Hazzard, Florence Wechek, and the Henrys not only by an arterial system of pipes fed by nature's pressure, but by other common needs. The Henrys' Model-A was neither beautiful nor comfortable but its engine was twice as thrifty as Randy's rakish sports hardtop. Sam Hazzard's car gulped gasoline as fast as Randy's. Dan's was empty. The Model-A was even more economical than Florence's old Chevy. Randy decided that henceforth the Model-A would furnish community transportation. So it was in the Model-A that Randy and Dan made the trip to San Marco.

The trip was a failure. The hospital no longer possessed insulin or substitutes for insulin. Like the pharmacies, the hospital had purchased its supplies in small quantities, and was dependent on weekly or bi-weekly deliveries from jobbers in the large cities. Its insulin had already gone to meet the demand in its own community. Further, the hospital's auxiliary generator was operated only during the evening hours, for emergency operations, and for a few minutes each hour on the hour to supply power for WSMF. It was necessary to conserve fuel, and unless the generator ran continuously it was inadequate for refrigeration.

Bouncing back to Fort Repose in the Model-A, Dan grumbled, "The place we should have built up stockpiles was out in the country, like Timucuan County. Stockpiles weren't going to be of much use in the cities because after The Day there weren't going to be any cities left. But where were the stockpiles? In the cities, of course. It was easier."

So Lavinia McGovern, after forty-eight hours in coma, died.

Alice Cooksey was at her bedside after midnight on the ninth day, when Lavinia died. Lavinia's husband and daughter, both exhausted from the effort to keep the house in some sort of order, slept. Alice did not awaken them, or anybody, until morning. She kept vigil alone, dozing on a chaise. Nothing could help Lavina, but everybody needed sleep.

Alice brought the news to the Bragg house in the morning. A fire blazed in the dining room, which smelled pleasantly of bacon and coffee. Randy, Helen, the children, and Dan Gunn were at breakfast—a breakfast exactly like one they would have eaten ten days before, with one important exception. There was orange juice, freshly squeezed, fresh eggs from the Henrys' yard, bacon, coffee. There was no toast, because there was no bread. Randy already was beginning to miss bread, and he wondered why he had not thought to buy flour. By the time Helen had put flour on their list the shelves were bare of it. He suspected that the older housewives of Fort Repose, remembering a time when people baked their own bread instead of buying it packaged, sliced, with vitamins re-injected, had cleaned the stores out of flour on The Day. He resolved, when he could, to trade for flour. It would be June before they could look forward to corn bread from Preacher Henry's crop.

Alice had bicycled from the McGovern house. Before she closed the Western Union office, Florence Wechek had salvaged the messenger's bicycle. It was a valuable possession. Now that all their remaining gasoline was pooled to operate one car, the bicycle was primary transportation for Alice and Florence. Alice was for the first time in her life dressed in slacks, a necessity for bicycling. She accepted coffee and told of Lavinia's death. Bill McGovern and Elizabeth, she said, were taking it well, but they didn't know what to do with the body. They needed help with the burial.

"I'll go to see Bubba Offenhaus right away," Dan said, "and try to arrange for burial. I've got to talk to Bubba anyway. I can't seem to impress upon him the importance of burying the dead as quickly as possible. He suddenly seems to hate his profession."

"That's not like Bubba," Alice Cooksey said. "Bubba always bragged that he was the most efficient undertaker in Florida. He used to say, 'When the retireds started coming to Fort Repose, they found a mortuary with all modern conveniences.' "

"That's the trouble," Dan said. "Bubba abhors unorthodox funerals. He almost wept when I insisted that the poor devils who died in the fire be buried at once in a single grave. We had to use a bulldozer, you know. Bubba claims Repose-in-Peace Park is ruined for good."

Randy had been silent since Alice brought the news. Now he spoke, as if he had been holding silent debate with himself, and had finally reached a conclusion. "They'll have to live here."

Helen set down her coffee cup. "Who'll have to live here?"

"We'll have to ask Lib and Bill McGovern to stay with us."

"But we don't have room! And how will we feed them?"

Randy was puzzled and disturbed. He had never thought of Helen as a selfish woman, and yet obviously she didn't want the McGoverns. "We really have plenty of room," he said. "There's still an empty bedroom upstairs. Bill can have it, and Lib can sleep with you."

"With me?"

He could see that Helen was angry. "Well, you have twin beds in your room, Helen. But if you seriously object, Bill can sleep in my apartment—there's an extra couch—and Lib can have the room."

"After all, it's your house," Helen said.

"As a matter of fact, Helen, the house is half Mark's, which makes it half yours. So the decision is yours as well as mine. Lib and Bill have no water and no heat and not much food left because almost all their food reserve was in their freezer. They don't even have a fireplace. They've been cooking and boiling water on a charcoal grill in the Florida room."

Helen shrugged and said, "Well, I guess you'll have to ask them. Elizabeth can sleep with me. But I hope it isn't a permanent arrangement. After all, our food supply is limited."

"It is limited," Randy said, "and it's going to get worse. Whether the McGoverns are here or not, we're all going to have to scrounge for food pretty quick."

Dan rose and said, "I'd better get going."

Randy followed him. He had cultivated the habit of leaving his .45 automatic on the hall table and pocketing it as he left the house, as a man would put on his hat. Since he never wore a hat, and never before had carried a gun except in the Army, he still had to make a conscious effort to remember.

When they were in the car Randy said, "That was a strange way for Helen to behave. Don't know what's eating her."

"Not at all strange," Dan said. "Just human. She's jealous."

"That's ridiculous!"

"No. Helen is a fiercely protective woman—protective of her children. With Mark gone, you and the house are her security and the children's security. She doesn't want to share you and your protection. Matter of self-preservation, not infatuation."

"I see," Randy said, "or at least I think I see."

They drove up to the front of the McGovern house. Randy said, "It's pointless for both of us to go in. Nothing you can do here. While you get Bubba Offenhaus, I'll tell them they're going to move and get them going."

"Right," Dan said. "Economy of effort and forces. Always a good rule of war."

Randy walked to the house, wondering a bit about himself. Without being conscious of it, he had begun to give orders in the past few days. Even to the Admiral he had given orders. He had assumed leadership in the tiny community bound together by the water pipes leading from the artesian well. Since no one had seemed to resent it, he guessed it had been the proper thing to do. It was like—well, it wasn't the same, but it was something like commanding a platoon. When you had the responsibility you also had the right to command.

The McGovern house was damp and it was chilly. It retained the cold of night. Lib, wearing corduroy jodhpurs and a heavy blue turtleneck sweater, greeted him at the door. She said, "I heard the jalopy and I knew it was you. Thanks for coming, Randy."

She held out her hands to him and he kissed her. Her hands felt cold and when he looked down at them he saw that her fingernails, always so carefully kept, were broken and crusted with dirt. Still she was dry-eyed and calm. Whatever tears she had had for her mother were already shed. Randy said, "Alice told us. We're all terribly sorry, darling." He knew it sounded insincere, and it was. With so many dead—so many friends for whom he had as yet not had time even for thought—the death of one woman, whom he did not admire overmuch and with whom he had never been and could not be close, was a triviality. With perhaps half the country's population dead, death itself, unless it took someone close and dear, was trivial.

She said, "Come on in and talk to Dad. He's worried about how we're going to bury her."

"We're arranging that," Randy said, and followed her into the house.

Bill McGovern sat in the living room, staring out on the river. He had not bothered to dress, or shave. Over his pajamas and robe he had pulled a topcoat. Randy turned to Lib. "Have either of you had any breakfast?"

She shook her head, no.

Bill spoke without turning his head. "Hello, Randy. I'm not much of a success, am I, in time of crisis? I can't feed my daughter, or myself, or even bury my wife. I wish I had enough guts to swim out into the channel and sink."

"That can't help Lavinia and wouldn't help Elizabeth, or anybody. You and Lib are going to live with me. Things will be better."

"Randy, I'm not going to impose myself on you. I might as well face it. I'm finished. You know, I'm over sixty. And do you know what the worst thing is? Central Tool and Plate. I spent my whole life building it up. What is it now? Chances are, just a mess of twisted and burned metal. Junk. So there goes my life and what good am I? I can't start over. Central Tool and Plate is junk and I'm junk."

Randy stepped over and stood between Bill and the cracked window, so as to look into his face. "You might as well stop feeling sorry for yourself," he said. "You're going to have to start over. Either that or die. You have to face it."

Lib touched her father's shoulder. "Come on, Dad."

Bill didn't move, or reply.

Randy felt anger inside him. "You want to know what good you are? That means what good you are to somebody else, not to yourself, doesn't it? If you're no good to anybody else I guess you'd better take the long swim. You know something about machinery, don't you?"

McGovern pushed himself in his chair. "I know as much about machine tools as any man in America."

"I didn't say machine tools. I said machinery. Batteries, gasoline engines, simple stuff like that."

"I didn't start at Central Tool as president, or board chairman. I started in the shop, working with my hands. Sure, I know about machinery."

"That's fine. You can help Malachai and Admiral Hazzard. We've taken the batteries out of my car, and the admiral's car, and hooked them on to the Admiral's shortwave set so we can find out what cooks around the world. Only it doesn't work right—something's wrong with the circuit—and the batteries are fading and I don't know how we can charge 'em."

"Very simple," said Bill. "Power takeoff from the Model-A. It'll work so long as you have gas."

"Fine," Randy said. "That's your first job, Bill, helping Malachai."

"Malachai? Isn't he the brother of our cleaning woman, Missouri? Your yardman?"

"That's him. First-class mechanic."

Bill McGovern smiled. "So I'll be mechanic, second class?"

"That's right."

Bill rose. "All right. It's a deal. I'll dress, and then—" He stopped. "Oh, Lord, I forgot. Poor Lavinia.

Randy, what am I going to do about her—" he hesitated as if the word were crude but he could find no other—"body?"

"We're attending to that," Randy said. "Dan Gunn has gone up to get Bubba Offenhaus. I hope Bubba will handle the burial. Meanwhile, I think you and Lib better start packing. We'll have to make three or four trips, I guess. How much gas have you got in your car?"

Lib said, "A couple of gallons, I think."

"That'll be enough to make the move, and you won't need the car after that. We can use the battery for Sam Hazzard's short-wave set."

While they packed, Randy prowled the house searching for useful items. In a kitchen cupboard he discovered an old, pitted iron pot of tremendous capacity, and, forgetting the presence of death in the house, whooped with delight.

Lib raced into the kitchen, demanding a reason for the shouting. He hefted the pot. "I'll bet it'll hold two gallons," he said. "What a find!"

"It's just an old pot Mother bought when we were in New England one summer. An antique. She thought it would look wonderful with a plant. It looked awful."

"It'll look beautiful hanging in the dining-room fireplace," Randy said, "filled with stew."

The old pot was the most useful object—indeed it was one of the few useful objects—he found in the McGovern house.

Twenty minutes later Dan Gunn returned, alone and worried. "Bubba Offenhaus," he said, "can't help us. Bubba would like to bury himself. He's got dysentery. Running at both ends. He and Kitty were certain it was radiation poisoning. Symptoms are pretty much alike, you know. Both of them were in panic. He'll get over it in a few days, but that's not helping us now."

Randy said, "So what do we do?"

Dan looked at Bill McGovern, fully dressed now but still unwashed and unshaven, for there was no water in the house except a jug, for drinking, that Randy had brought to them the day before. Dan said, "I think that's up to you to decide, Bill."

"What is there to decide?" Bill asked.

"Whether to bury your wife here or in the cemetery. You don't have a plot in Repose-in-Peace but I'm sure Bubba won't mind. Anyway, there's nothing he can do about it, and you can settle with him later."

Bill McGovern turned to his daughter. "What do you say, Elizabeth?"

"Well, of course I think Mother deserves a proper funeral in a cemetery. It seems like the least we can do for her. And yet—" She turned to Randy. "You don't agree, do you, Randy?"

Randy was glad that she asked. Intervening in this private and personal matter was brutal but necessary. "No, I don't agree. It's six miles to the cemetery. We'd have to make the trip in two cars because of the—because of Lavinia. That's twenty-four miles' worth of gasoline, round trip, and we can't afford it. We will have to bury Lavinia here, on the grounds."

"But how—" Lib began.

"Where do you keep the shovels, Bill?"

"There's a tool shed back of the garage."

While handing a shovel to Dan, and selecting one for himself, Randy examined the other tools. There was a new ax. It would be very useful. There were pitchforks, edgers, a scythe, a wheelbarrow. He would bring Malachai over before dark and they would divvy up the McGovern tools. In everything he did, now, he found he looked into the needs of the future.

Between house and river, a crescent-shaped azalea bed flanked the west border of the McGovern property. The bitter-blue grass had been carefully tended, and the bed was shaded from afternoon's hot sun by a live oak older than Fort Repose. Looking around, Randy could find no spot more suitable for a grave. He stepped off six feet and marked a rectangle within the crescent. He and Dan began to dig.

After a few minutes Randy removed his sweater. This was no easy job. Dan stopped and inspected his plans. He said, "I'm getting ditchdigger's hands. Very bad for a surgeon." They continued to dig, steadily, until it was awkward working from the surface. Randy stepped into the deepening grave. They had made a discovery. A grave designed to accommodate one person must be dug by one person alone.

When Randy paused, winded, Bill McGovern stepped down and took the shovel, saying, "I'll spell you."

From above, Lib watched. Presently she said, "That's enough for you, Dad. Remember the blood pressure. I don't want to lose you too." She stepped into the hole and relieved him of the shovel. After he climbed out, panting and white-faced, she thrust the shovel savagely into the sand. As she dug, her stature increased in Randy's eyes. She was like a fine sword, slender and flexible, but steel; a woman of courage. It was not gentlemanly, but Randy allowed her to dig, recognizing that physical effort was an outlet for her emotions. When her pace slowed he dropped into the hole and took the shovel. "That's enough. Dan and I will finish. You and your father had better go back to the house and get on with your packing."

"You don't want us to help you carry her out, do you?"

"I think it would be better if you didn't."

Dan reached down and lifted her out of the hole.

When the grave was finished, they wrapped Lavinia's emaciated body in her bedsheets, Her coffin was an electric blanket and her hearse a wheelbarrow. They lowered her into the five-foot hole and packed in the sand and loam afterwards, leaving an insignificant mound. Randy knew that when spring came the mound would flatten with the rains, the grass would swiftly cover it, and by June it would have disappeared entirely.

Randy called the McGoverns. There was no service, no spoken word. They all stood silent for a moment and then Bill McGovern said, "We don't even have a wooden marker for her, or a sliver of stone, do we?"

"We could take something out of the house," Randy suggested, "a statue or a vase or something."

"It isn't necessary," Lib said. "The house is my mother's monument."

This of course was true. They turned from the grave and back to their work.

That evening Bill McGovern, with some eagerness, walked to the Henrys' house and talked to Malachai. Together they went along the river bank to Sam Hazzard's house and conferred with him on a plan for supplying power for the Admiral's short-wave receiver.

Dan Gunn drove to Fort Repose to visit the homeless, some of them sick or burned, lodged in the school.

Randy and Lib McGovern sat alone on the front porch steps, Lib's elbows on her knees, her chin supported by her hands, Randy's arms encircling her shoulders. She was speaking of her mother. "I'm sure she never really comprehended what happened on The Day, or ever could. Perhaps I am only rationalizing, but I think her death was an act of mercy."

Randy heard someone running up the driveway and then he saw the figure and recognized Ben Franklin. "Ben!" he called. "What's the matter?"

Ben stopped, out of breath, and said, "Something's happened at Miss Wechek's!"

Randy rose, ready to get his pistol. "What happened?"

"I don't know. I was just walking by her house and I heard somebody scream. I think Miss Wechek. Then I heard her crying."

Randy said, "We'd better take a look, Lib. You stay here, Ben."

Yellow candlelight shone from Florence's kitchen. They went to the back door. Florence was wailing and Randy entered without bothering to knock.

As he opened the screen door green and yellow feathers fluttered around his feet. Florence's head rested on her arms on the kitchen table. She was dressed in a quilted, rose-hued robe. Alice Cooksey was with her, coaxing water to a boil on a Sterno kit. Randy said, "What seems to be the trouble?"

Florence raised her head. Her untidy pink hair was moist and stringy. Her eyes were swollen. "Sir Percy ate Anthony!" she said. She began to sob.

"She's had a terrible day," said Alice Cooksey. "I'm trying to make tea. She'll be better after she's had tea."

"What all happened?" Randy asked.

"It really began yesterday," Alice said. "When we woke up yesterday morning the angelfish were dead. You know how cold it was night before last, and of course without electricity there's no heat for the aquarium. And this morning all the mollies and neons were dead. As a matter of fact nothing's alive in the tank except the miniature catfish and a few guppies. And then, this evening—"

"Sir Percy," Florence interrupted, "a murderer!"

"Hush, dear," Alice said. "The water will be boiling in a moment." She turned to Randy. "Florence really shouldn't blame Sir Percy. After all, there's been no milk for him, and very little of anything else. As a matter of fact, we haven't seen Sir Percy in three or four days—I suppose he was out hunting for himself—but a few minutes ago when Anthony flew home Sir Percy was on the porch."

"Ambushed poor Anthony," Florence said. "Actually ambushed him. Killed him and ate him right there on the porch. Poor Cleo."

"Where's Sir Percy now?" Randy asked.

"He's gone again," Alice said. "He'd better not come back."

Randy was thoughtful. Hunting cats would be a problem. And what would happen to dogs? He still had a few cans of dog food for Graf, but he could foresee a time when humans might look upon dog food as a delicacy. He said aloud, but speaking to himself rather than the others, "Survival of the fittest."

"What do you mean?" Lib said.

"The strong survive. The frail die. The exotic fish die because the aquarium isn't heated. The common guppy lives. So does the tough catfish. The house cat turns hunter and eats the pet bird. If he didn't, he'd starve. That's the way it is and that's the way it's going to be."

Florence had stopped crying. "You mean, with humans? You mean, we humans are going to have to turn savage, like Sir Percy? Well, I can't do it. I don't want to live in that kind of a world, Randy."

"You'll live, Florence," Randy said.

Walking back to his own house, Randy said, "Florence is a guppy, a nice, drab little guppy. That's why she'll survive."

"What about you and me?" Lib said.

"We're going to have to be tough. We're going to have to be catfish."

[8]

On a morning in April, four months after The Day, Randy Bragg awoke and watched a shaft of sunlight creep down the wall. At the foot of the couch, Graf squirmed and then wormed his way upward under the blanket. During the January cold spell Randy had discovered a new use for Graf. The dachshund made a most satisfactory footwarmer, mobile, automatic, and operating on a minimum of fuel which he would consume anyway. Randy flung off the blanket and swung his feet to the floor. He was hungry. He was always hungry. No matter how much he ate the night before, he was always starving in the morning. He never had enough fats, or sweets, or starches, and the greater part of each day was usually spent in physical effort of one kind or another. Downstairs, Helen and Lib would be preparing breakfast. Before Randy ate he would shower and shave. These were painful luxuries, almost his only remnant of routine from before The Day.

Randy walked to the bar-counter and began to sharpen his razor. The razor was a six-inch hunting knife. He honed its edges vigorously on a whetstone and then stropped it on a belt nailed to the wall. A clean, smooth, painless shave was one of the things he missed, but not what he missed most.

He missed music. It had been a long time since he had heard music. The record player and his collection of LP's of course were useless without electricity. Music was no longer broadcast, anywhere. Anyway, his second and last set of batteries for the transistor radio was losing strength. Very soon, they would have neither flashlights nor any means of receiving radio except through the Admiral's short wave. WSMF in San Marco was no longer operating. Something had happened to the diesel supplying the hospital and the radio station and it was impossible to find spare parts. This was the word that had come from San Marco, eighteen miles away. It had required two days for the word to reach Fort Repose.

He missed cigarettes, but not so much. Dan Gunn still had a few pounds of tobacco, and had lent him a pipe. Randy found more pleasure in a pipe after each meal, and one before bedtime, than he had ever found in a whole carton of cigarettes. With tobacco so limited, each pipe was a luxury, relaxing and wonderful.

He missed whiskey not at all. Since The Day, he had drunk hardly anything, nor found need for it. He no longer regarded whiskey as a drink. Whiskey was Dan Gunn's emergency anesthetic. Whiskey, what was left of his supply, was for medical use, and for trading.

He missed his morning coffee most. It had been, he calculated, six or seven weeks since he had tasted coffee. Coffee was more precious than gasoline, or even whiskey. Tobacco could be grown, and doubtless was being grown in a strip all the way from northwest Florida to Kentucky, Maryland and Virginia in the rural areas still habitable. Whiskey you could make, given the proper equipment and ingredients. But coffee came from South America.

Randy tested his knife on a bit of paper. It was as sharp as he could ever make it. He went into the bathroom and showered. The cold water no longer chilled him as it had through January and February. He was inured to it. Soap he used sparingly. The house reserve was down to three cakes.

He dried and stepped on the scales. One fifty-two. This was exactly what he had weighed at eighteen, as a freshman at the University. Even after three months on the line in Korea, he had dropped only to one fifty-six. He had lost an average of a pound a week for the past sixteen weeks, but now, he noted, his weight loss was slower. He had held one fifty-two for the past three days. He was leaner and harder, and, truthfully, felt better than before The Day.

There was a knock on the living-room door. That

would be Peyton. He slipped on his shorts and said, "Come in."

Peyton came in, carefully balancing the tiny pot of steaming water allotted for his morning shave. She set the pot before him on the counter as if it were a crystal bowl filled with flowers. "There," she said. "Can I watch you shave this morning, Randy?"

The sight of Peyton enriched Randy's mornings. She was brash and buoyant, bobbing like a brightly colored cork in the maelstrom, unsinkable and unafraid. "Why do you like to watch me shave?" he asked.

"Because you make such funny faces in the mirror. You should see yourself."

"I do."

"No, you don't really see yourself. All you watch is the knife, as if you're afraid of cutting your throat."

Dan Gunn came out of the bedroom, dressed in levis and a blue checked sports shirt. Until The Day, Dan had used an electric razor. Now, rather than learn to shave with a knife or whatever was available, he did not shave at all. His beard had bloomed thick and flaming red. He looked like a Klondike sourdough or Paul Bunyan transplanted to the semi-tropics. On those rare days when his beard was freshly trimmed and he dressed formally in white shirt and a tie, he looked like a physician, outsized 1890 model.

"You can't watch today," Randy told the child. "I want to talk to Doctor Gunn." He poured his hot water into the basin and returned the pot to Peyton. Peyton smiled at Dan and left.

Randy soaped and soaked his face. "Did you know that Einstein never used shaving soap?" he said. "Einstein just used plain soap like this. Einstein was a smart man and what was good enough for Einstein is good enough for me." He scraped at his beard, winced, and said, "Einstein must have had an awfully good razor. Einstein must've used a fresh blade every morning. I'll bet Einstein never shaved with a hunting knife."

Dan said, "I had an awful dream last night. Dreamed I'd forgotten to pay my income tax and was behind in my alimony and the Treasury agents and a couple of deputy sheriffs were chasing me around the courthouse with shotguns. They finally cornered me. They were arguing about whether to send me to the Federal pen or state prison. I tried to sneak out. I think they shot me. Anyway, I woke up, shaking. All I could think of was that I really hadn't paid my income tax, or alimony either. What day is it, anyway?"

"I don't know what day it is but I know the date. April fourteenth."

Dan smiled through the red beard. "My subconscious must be a watchdog. Income tax day tomorrow. And we don't have to file a return, Randy. No tax. No alimony. Let us count our blessings. Never thought I'd see the day."

"No coffee," Randy said. "I would gladly pay my tax tomorrow for a pound of coffee. Dan, if you drive to town today I want to go with you. I want to trade for coffee."

Dan had evolved a barter system for his services. He charged a gallon of gas, if the patient had it, for house calls. Most families had somehow managed to obtain and conserve a few gallons of gasoline. It was their link with a mobile past, insurance of mobility in some emergency of the future. Sickness and injury were emergencies for which they would gladly dip into their liquid reserve. Dan made little profit. Perhaps half his patients were able and willing to pay with gasoline. Still, he managed to keep the Model-A's tank nearly full, and on his rounds he was continuously charging batteries. Bill McGovern had instituted a system of rotating the batteries in the car. In turn, the charged batteries powered Admiral Hazzard's short-wave receiver. Not only was the car transport for Randy's water-linked enclave of families, it was necessary to maintain their ear to the world outside. Not that the world, any longer, said much.

Dan said, "Sure, Randy, but it's going to take all morning. I've got a bad situation in town."

"What's the trouble?"

From downstairs they heard Helen's voice, "Breakkast!"

"Tell you later," Dan said.

Randy was last to reach the dining room. There was a tall glass of orange juice at his place, and a big pitcher of juice in the center of the table. Whatever else they might lack, there was always citrus. Yet even orange juice would eventually disappear. In late June or early July they would squeeze the last of the Valencias and use the last grapefruit. From then until the new crop of early oranges ripened in October, citrus would be absent from their diet.

He saw that this morning there was a single boiled egg and small portion of broiled fish left over from the night before. "Where's my other boiled egg?" he said.

"Malachai only brought over eight eggs this morning," Helen said. "The Henrys have been losing chickens."

"What do you mean, losing them?"

"They're being stolen."

Randy put down his juice. Citrus, fish, and eggs were their staples. A drop in the egg supply was serious. "I'll bet it's an inside job," he said. "I'll bet that no-good Two-Tone has been swapping hens for liquor."

Lib spoke. "Malachai thinks it's wild cats—that is, house cats that have gone wild."

"That's not the worst of it," Helen said. "One of the Henrys' pigs is missing. They heard it squeal, just once. Preacher thinks a wolf took it. Preacher says he found a wolf track."

"No wolves in Florida," Randy said. "No four-legged wolves." The loss of hens was serious, but the loss of pigs disastrous. The Henry sow had produced a farrow that in a few weeks would add real meat to everybody's diet. Even now they weighed twelve to fifteen pounds. Each evening, all food scraps from the Bragg, Wechek, and Hazzard households were carried to the Henry place to help feed the pigs and chickens. Every day, Randy had to argue with Helen and Lib to save scraps for Graf. Randy was conscious that the Henrys supplied more than their own share of food for the benefit of all. When Preacher's corn crop ripened in June, the disparity would be even greater. And it had been Two-Tone, of all people, who had suggested that they grow sugar cane and then had explored the river banks in the Henrys' leaky, flat-bottomed skiff until he had found wild cane. He had sprigged, planted, and cultivated it. Because of the Henrys, they could all look forward, one day, to a breakfast of corn bread, cane syrup, and bacon. He was sure they would find a way to convert the corn to meal, even if they had to grind it between flagstones. "I don't think we're doing enough for the Henrys," Randy said. "We'll have to give them more help."

"What kind of help?" Bill McGovern asked.

"At the moment, help them guard the food supply. Keep away the prowlers—cats, wolves, humans, or whatever."

"Can't the Henrys do it themselves?" Helen asked. "Don't they have a gun?"

"They've got a gun—an old, beat-up single barrel twelve gauge—but they don't have time. You can't expect Preacher and Malachai to work as hard as they do every day and then sit up all night. And I wouldn't trust Two-Tone. He'd just sleep. Do I hear volunteers?"

"Me!" said Ben Franklin.

Randy's first impulse was to say no, that this wasn't a job for a thirteen-year-old boy. Yet Ben was eating as much as a man, or more, and he would have to do a man's work. "I thought you and Caleb were chopping firewood today?"

"I can chop wood and stand watch too."

"Better let me take it the first night," said Bill McGovern. "I wouldn't want to see anything happen to those pigs." Bill was thinner, as they all were, and yet it seemed that he had dropped years as well as weight. With his fork he touched a bit of fish at the edge of his plate. "You know, for years I looked forward to my vacation in the bass country. That's why I built a house on the Timucuan when I retired. But now I can hardly look a bass in the face. I want meat—real red meat."

Randy made his decision. "All right, Bill, you can take the watch tonight, and we'll rotate thereafter. I'm sure the Admiral will take a night too."

"Do I get a night?" Ben Franklin asked. His eyes were pleading.

"You get a night, Ben. I'll make up a schedule and post it on the bulletin board." A bulletin board in the hallway, with assignment of duties, had become a necessity. In this new life there was no leisure. If everybody worked as hard as he could until sundown every day, then everybody could eat, although not well. Each day brought a crisis of one kind or another. They faced shortages of the most trivial but necessary items. Who would have had the foresight to buy a supply of needles and thread? Florence Wechek owned a beautiful new sewing machine, electric and useless of course. Florence, Helen, and Hannah Henry did the sewing for Randy's community. Yesterday Florence had broken a needle and had come to Randy, close to tears, as if it were a major disaster, as indeed it was. And everybody had unthinkingly squandered matches, so that now there were no matches. He still had five lighter flints and one small can of lighter fluid. Luckily, his old Army lighter would burn gasoline, but flints were priceless and impossible to find. Within a few months it might be necessary to keep the dining-room fire going day and night in spite of unwelcome heat and added labor. Nor would their supply of wood last forever. They would have to scout farther and farther afield for usable timber. Hauling it would become a major problem. When Dan could no longer collect his gasoline fees and the tank in the Model-A finally ran dry their life was bound to change drastically, and for the worse.

Staring down at his plate, he thought of all this.

Lib said, "Randy, finish your fish. And you'd better drink another glass of orange juice. You'll be hungry before lunch, if Helen and I can put a lunch together."

"I hate orange juice!" Randy said, and poured himself another glass.

Dan drove. Randy sat beside him. It was warm, and Randy was comfortable in shorts, boat shoes, and a pullover shirt. He carried his pistol holstered at his hip. The pistol had become a weightless part of him now. He had dry-fired it a thousand times until it felt good in his hand, and even used it to kill a rattlesnake in the grove and two moccasins on the dock. Shooting snakes was a waste of ammunition but he was now confident of the pistol's accuracy and the steadiness of his hand. In Randy's lap, encased in a paper bag, was the bottle of Scotch he hoped to trade for coffee. They smoked their morning pipes. Randy said, "Dan, what's this bad situation in town?"

"I haven't said anything about it," Dan said, "because I can't get to the bottom of it and I didn't want to frighten anybody. I've got three serious cases of radiation poisoning."

"Oh, God!" Randy said, not an exclamation but a prayer. This was the sword that had been hanging over all of them. If a man kept busy enough, if his troubles and problems were immediate and numerous, if he was always hungry, then he could for a time wall off this thing, forget for a time that he lived in what had officially been designated a contaminated zone. He could forget the insidious, the invisible, the implacable enemy, but not forever.

"This is very strange," Dan said. "I can't believe it's caused by delayed fallout. If it were, I'd have three hundred cases, not three. This is more like a radium or X-ray burn. All of them have burned hands in addition to the usual symptoms—nausea, headache, diarrhea, hair falling out."

"When did it start?" Randy asked.

"Porky Logan was the first man hit. His sister caught me at the school three weeks ago and begged me to look at him."

"Wasn't Porky somewhere in the southern part of the state on The Day? Couldn't he have picked up radiation then?"

"Porky was perfectly all right when he got back here and since then he hasn't received any more exposure than the rest of us. And the other two have not left Fort Repose. Porky's a mess. Every time I see him he's drunk. But the radiation is killing him faster than the liquor."

"Who else is sick?"

"Bigmouth Bill Cullen—we'll stop at his fish camp on the way to town—and Pete Hernandez."

"It couldn't be sort of an epidemic, could it?" Randy asked.

"No, it couldn't. Radiation's not a germ or a virus. You can eat or drink radioactive matter, like strontium 90 in milk. It can fall on you in rain. It can sift down on you in dust, or in particles you can't see on a day that seems perfectly clear. You can track it into the house on your shoes, or pick it up by handling any metal or inorganic matter that has been exposed. But you can't catch it by kissing a girl, unless, of course, she has gold teeth."

At the bend of River Road they caught up with Alice Cooksey riding Florence's Western Union bicycle. Alone of all the people in Fort Repose, Alice continued with her regular work. Every morning she left the Wechek house at seven. Often, ignoring the unpredictable dangers of the road, she did not return until dark. Since The Day, the demand for her services had multiplied. They slowed when they overtook her, shouted a greeting, and waved. She waved back and pedaled on, a small, brave, and busy figure.

Watching the car chuff past, Alice reminded herself that this evening she must bring back new books for Ben Franklin and Peyton. It was a surprise, and a delight, to see children devour books. Without ever knowing it, they were receiving an education. Alice would never admit it aloud, but for the first time in her thirty, years as librarian of Fort Repose she felt fulfilled, even important.

It had not been easy or remunerative to persist as librarian in Fort Repose. She recalled how every year for eight years the town council had turned down her annual request for air conditioning. An expensive frill, they'd said. But without air conditioning, how could a library compete? Drugstores, bars, restaurants, movies, the St. Johns Country Club in San Marco, the lobby of the Riverside Inn, theaters and most homes, were air conditioned. You couldn't expect people to sit in a hot

library during the humid Florida summer, which began
in April and didn't end until October, when they could
be sitting in an air-conditioned living room coolly and
painlessly absorbing visual pablum on television. Alice
had installed a Coke machine and begged old electric
fans but it had been a losing battle.

In thirty years her book budget had been raised ten
percent, but the cost of books had doubled. Her magazine budget was unchanged, but the cost of magazines
had tripled. So while Fort Repose grew in population,
book borrowings dwindled. There had been so many
new distractions, drive-in theaters, dashing off to
springs and beaches over the weekends, the mass hypnosis of the young every evening, and finally the craze
for boating and water-skiing. Now all this was ended.
All entertainment, all amusements, all escape, all information again centered in the library. The fact that the
library had no air conditioning made no difference now.
There were not enough chairs to accommodate her
readers. They sat on the front steps, in the windows, on
the floor with backs against walls or stacks. They read
everything, even the classics. And the children came to
her, when they were free of their chores, and she guided
them. And there was useful research to do. Randy and
Doctor Gunn didn't know it, but as a result of her research they might eat better thereafter. It was strange,
she thought, pedaling steadily, that it should require a
holocaust to make her own life worth living.

At the town limits, Dan turned into Bill Cullen's fish
camp, café, and bar. The grounds were more dilapi-
dated and filthier than ever. The liquor shelves were
bare. The counters in the boathouse tackle shop were
empty. Not a plug, fly, or hook remained. Bigmouth
Bill had been cleaned out months before. His wife,
straw-haired and barrel-shaped, stepped out of the living quarters. Randy sniffed. She didn't smell of spiked
wine this day. She simply smelled sour. Alone of all the
people he had seen, she had gained weight since The
Day. Randy guessed that she had cached sacks of grits

and had been living on grits and fried fish. She said, "He's in here, Doc."

Dan didn't go in immediately. "Does he seem any better?" he asked.

"He's worse. His hands is leakin' pus."

"How do you feel? You haven't had any of his symptoms, have you?"

"Me? I don't feel no different. I've felt worse." She giggled, showing her rotting teeth. "You ever had a hangover, Doc? That's when I've felt worse. Right now I wish I felt worse so I could take a drink and feel better. You get it, Doc?" She came closer to Dan and lowered her voice. "He ain't goin' to die, is he?"

"I don't know."

"The old tightwad better not die on me now. He's not leavin' me nuthin', Doc. He don't even own this place free and clear. He ain't never even made no will. He's holdin' out on me, Doc. I can tell. He had six cases stashed away after The Day. Claims he sold all six to Porky Logan. But he don't show me no money. You know what, Doc? I think he's got that six cases hid!"

Dan brushed past her and they entered the shack. Bill Cullen lay on a sagging iron bed, a stained sheet pulled up to his bare waist. In the bad light filtering through the venetian shade over the single window, he was at first unrecognizable to Randy. He was wasted, his eyes sunken, his eyeballs yellow. Tufts of hair were gone from one side of his head, exposing reddish scalp. His hands, resting across his stomach, were swollen, blackened, and cracked. He croaked, "Hello, Doc." He saw Randy and said, "I'll be damned—Randy."

The stench was too much for Randy. He gagged, said, "Hello, Bill," and backed out. He leaned over the dock railing, coughing and choking, until he could breathe deeply of the sweet wind from the river. When Dan came out they walked silently back to the car together. All Dan said was, "She was right. He's worse. I'll swear he's had a fresh dose of radiation since I saw him last."

They drove on to Marines Park. The park had become the barter center of Fort Repose. Dan said, "Do you want to go on with me to the schoolhouse?"

"No, thanks," Randy said. He was glad he wasn't a doctor. A doctor required special courage that Randy felt he did not possess.

"I'll pick you up here in an hour. Then I'll see Hernandez and Logan and then home."

"Okay." Randy got out of the car.

"Don't swap for less than two pounds. Scotch is darn near as scarce as coffee."

"I'll make the best deal I can," Randy promised. Dan drove off.

Randy tucked the bottle under his arm and walked toward the bandstand, an octagon-shaped wooden structure, its platform elevated three feet above what had once been turf smooth as a gold green, now unkempt, infiltrated with weeds and booby-trapped with sandspurs. A dozen men, legs dangling, sat on the platform and steps. Others moved about, the alert, humorless smile of the trader on their faces. Three bony horses were tethered to the bandstand railing. Like Randy, some of the men carried holsters at their belts. A few shotguns and an old-fashioned Winchester leaned against the planking. The armed men had come in from the countryside, a risk.

A third of the traders in Marines Park, on this day, were Negroes. The economics of disaster placed a penalty upon prejudice. The laws of hunger and survival could not be evaded, and honored no color line. A back-yard hen raised by a Negro tasted just as good as the gamecocks of Carleton Hawes, the well-to-do realtor who was a vice president of the county White Citizens Council, and there was more meat on it. Randy saw Hawes, a brace of chickens dangling from his belt, drink water, presumably boiled, from a Negro's jug. There were two drinking fountains in Marines Park, one marked "White Only," the other "Colored Only." Since neither worked, the signs were meaningless.

Hawes saw Randy, wiped his mouth, and called, "Hey, Randy."

"Hello, Carleton."

"What're you trading?"

"A bottle of Scotch."

Hawes' eyes fixed on the paper bag and he moved closer to Randy, cautious as a pointer blundered upon quail. Randy recalled from Saturday nights at the St. Johns Club that Scotch was Hawes' drink. "What's your asking price?" Hawes asked.

"Two pounds of coffee."

"I'll swap you these two birds. Both young hens. See how plump they are? Better eating you'll never have."

Randy laughed.

"Being it's you, I'll tell you what I'll do. I've got eggs at home. I'll throw in a couple of dozen eggs. Have 'em here tomorrow. On my word. If you don't believe me, you can take the birds now, as a binder."

"The asking price," Randy said, "is also the selling price. Two pounds of coffee. Any brand will do."

Hawes sighed. "Who's got coffee? It's been three months since I've had a drink of Scotch. Let me look at the bottle, will you?"

Randy showed him the label and moved on to the bandstand.

The square pillars supporting the roof had become a substitute for the county weekly's want-ad section and the radio station announcements. Randy read the notices, some in longhand, some hand printed, a few typewritten, pinned to the timbers.

WILL SWAP—*Late model Cadillac Coupe de Ville, radio, heater, air-conditioned, battery run down but undamaged, for two good 28-inch bicycle tires and pump.*

DESPERATELY NEED *evaporated milk, rubber nipple and six safety pins. Look over our house and make your own deal.*

HAVE SMALL CANNED HAM, *want large kettle, Encyclopaedia Britannica, box 12-gauge No. 7 shells, and toothpaste.*

Randy closed his eyes. He could taste that ham. He had an extra kettle, the encyclopedia, the shells, and toothpaste. But he also had prospects of fresh ham if

they could preserve the Henrys' young pigs from ma-
rauders, wolves or whatever. Anyway, it was too big a
price to pay for a small ham.

WANTED—*Three 2/0 fishhooks in exchange for expen-*
sive fly rod, reel, assorted lures.

Randy chuckled. Sports fishing no longer existed.
There were only meat fishermen now.

WILL TRADE 50-*HP Outboard motor, complete*
set power tools, cashmere raglan topcoat for half pound
of tobacco and ax.

Randy saw a notice that was different:

EASTER SERVICES

An interdenominational Easter Sunrise Service will be
held in Marines Park on Sunday, April 17th. All citizens of
Fort Repose, of whatever faith, are invited to attend.
Signed,
Rev. John Carlin, First Methodist Church
Rev. M. F. Kenny, Church of St. Paul's
Rev. Fred Born, Timucuan Baptist Church
Rev. Noble Watts, Afro-Repose Baptist Church

The name of the Rector of St. Thomas Episcopal
Church, where there had always been a Bragg pew, was
missing. Dr. Lucius Somerville, a gentle, white-haired
man, a boyhood companion of Judge Bragg, had been
in Jacksonville on the morning of The Day and therefore would not return to his parish.

Randy wasn't much of a churchgoer. He had contributed to the church regularly, but not of his time or himself. Now, reading this notice, he felt an unexpected
thrill. Since The Day, he had lived in the imperative
present, not daring to plan beyond the next meal or the
next day. This bit of paper tacked on peeling white
paint abruptly enlarged his perspective, as if, stumbling
through a black tunnel, he saw, or thought he saw, a
chink of light. If Man retained faith in God, he might

also retain faith in Man. He remembered words which for four months he had not heard, read, or uttered, the most beautiful words in the language—faith and hope. He had missed these words as he had missed other things. If possible, he would go to the service. Sunday, the seventeenth. Today was the fourteenth, and therefore Thursday.

He stepped up on the platform. The men lounging there, some of them acquaintances, some strangers, were estimating the shape of bulk of the sack he held, like a football, under his arm. Dour, bearded, hair unshorn or ludicrously cropped, they looked like ghost-town characters in a Western movie, except they were not so well fed as Hollywood extras, and their clothing, flowered sports shirts, shorts, or slacks, plaid or straw-peaked caps, was incongruous. John Garcia, the Minorcan fishing guide, asked the orthodox opening question, "What're you trading, Randy?"

"A fifth of Scotch—twelve years old—the best."

Garcia whistled. "You must be hard up. What're you askin'?"

"Two pounds of coffee."

Several of the men on the platform shifted their position. One snickered. None spoke. Randy realized that these men had no coffee, either for trading or drinking. No matter how well stocked their kitchens might once have been, or what they had purchased or pillaged on The Day and in the chaotic period immediately after, four months had exhausted everything. Randy's community was far more fortunate with the bearing groves, fish loyally taking bait, the industrious Henrys and their barnyard, and some small game—squirrels, rabbits, and an occasional possum.

John Garcia was trading two strings of fish, a four-pound catfish and small bass on one, warmouth perch and bream on the other. Garcia's brown and weathered skin had shriveled on his slight frame until he seemed only bones loosely wrapped in dried leather. The sun was getting warm. With his toe Garcia nudged his fish into the shadow. "Wouldn't trade for fish, would you, Randy?" he asked, smiling.

"Fish we've got," Randy said.

"You River Road people do all right by yourselves, don't you?" a stranger said. "If you got Scotch likker, you got everythin'. Us, we ain't got nuthin'." The stranger was trading a saw, two chisels, and a bag of nails. Randy guessed he was an itinerant carpenter settled in Pistolville.

Randy ignored him and asked Marines Park's inevitable second question, "What do you hear?"

Old Man Hockstatler, who was trading small tins of aspirins and tranquilizers, salvage from his looted pharmacy, said, "I hear the Russians are asking that we surrender."

"No, no, you got that all wrong," said Eli Blaustein. "Mrs. Vanbruuker-Brown demanded that the Russians surrender. They said no and then they said we should be the ones to surrender."

"Where did you hear that?" Randy asked.

"My wife got it from a woman whose husband's battery set still works," Blaustein said. Blaustein was trading work pants and a pair of white oxfords and he was asking canned corn beef or cheese. Randy knew that as the sun got higher John Garcia's asking price for his fish would drop lower. At the same time Blaustein's hunger would grow, or he would be thinking of his protein-starved family. Before the fish were tainted, there would be a meeting of minds. John Garcia would have a new pair of work pants and Blaustein would have food.

"What I would like to know," said Old Man Hockstatler, "is who won the war? Nobody ever tells you. This war I don't understand at all. It isn't like World Wars One or Two or any other wars I ever heard of. Sometimes I think the Russians must've won. Otherwise things would be getting back to normal. Then I think no, we won. If we hadn't won the Russians would still be bombing us, or they would invade. But since The Day I've never seen any planes at all."

"I have," said Garcia. "I've seen 'em while I was fishing for cats at night. No, that ain't exactly right. I've heard 'em. I heard one two nights ago."

"Whose?" Blaustein asked.

Garcia shrugged. "Beats me."

This discussion, Randy knew, would continue through the day. The question of who won the war, or if the war still continued, who was winning, had replaced the weather as an inexhaustible subject for speculation. Each day you could hear new rumors, usually baseless and always garbled. You could hear that Russian landing craft were lined up on Daytona Beach or that Martian saucers were unloading relief supplies in Pensacola. Randy believed nothing except what he himself heard or saw, or those sparse hard grains of fact sifted from the air waves by Sam Hazzard. Randy had been leaning on the bandstand railing. He straightened, stretched, and said, "Guess I'll circulate around and look for somebody who's holding coffee."

John Garcia said, "You coming to the Easter service, Randy?"

"Hope so. Hope to come and bring the family." As he stepped from the bandstand he looked again at the two useless drinking fountains. There was something important about them that he could not recall. This was irritating, as when the name of an old friend capriciously vanishes from memory. The drinking fountains made his mind itch.

He saw Jim Hickey, the beekeeper, a picnic basket under his long, outstretched legs, relaxed on a bench. Before The Day Jim had rented his hives to grove owners pollinating young trees. Before The Day, Jim's honey was a secondary source of income; "gravy," he called it. Now, honey was liquid gold, and beeswax, with which candles could be dipped, another valuable item of barter. Jim Hickey, who was Mark's age, had learned beekeeping at the College of Agriculture in Gainesville. It would never make him rich, he had been warned, and until The Day it hadn't. Now he was regarded as a fortunate man, rich in highly desirable commodities endlessly produced by tens of thousands of happy and willing slaves. "What are you trading?" he greeted Randy.

"A bottle of Scotch. Are you holding coffee?"

"No. I've been trying to trade for coffee myself. Can't find any. All I hold is honey." He lifted the lid of the picnic basket. "Lovely stuff, isn't it?"

It was lovely. Randy thought of Ben Franklin and Peyton, whose need and desire for sweets could not be wholly supplied by the sugar content of citrus. It would be weeks before Two-Tone's cane crop matured. Randy wondered whether he was being selfish, trading for coffee. It was true that he would share the coffee with the other adults on River Road, but the children didn't drink it. There were no calories or vitamins in coffee and it was of no use to them. He forced himself to be judicial. When you examined the facts judicially, and asked which would provide the greatest good for the greatest number, there could be only one answer. Coffee would furnish only temporary and personal gratification. He said, "Jim, maybe I could be persuaded to trade for honey."

"I'm sorry, Randy. We're Adventists. We don't drink whiskey or trade in it."

This contingency Randy had never imagined. Half-aloud he said, "Well, I tried."

"I suppose you wanted the honey for Mark's children," Hickey said.

"Yes. I did."

Hickey reached into the basket and brought out two square, honey-packed combs. "I wouldn't like to see Mark's kids go without," he said. "Here. I'd give you more except my supply is 'way down. There's something wrong with my bees this spring. Half my broods are foul, full of dead pupae and larvae. At first I thought it was what we call sacbrood, or queen failure. I've been to the library, reading up on it, and now I wonder whether it couldn't be radiation. We must've had fallout on The Day—after all, the whole state is a contaminated zone—and maybe it affected some of my queens and drones. I don't know what to do about it. It isn't something they taught us at the University."

Randy removed the bottle from his paper bag, locked it under his arm, and replaced it with the honeycombs. He was overwhelmed. He knew that Mark and Hickey had been in the same grade in primary school, but they had never been close friends. Hickey was no more than an acquaintance. He lived in a neat, sea-green, five-room concrete block house far out on the road to Pasco Creek. Randy, before The Day, rarely saw him, and then only to wave a greeting. Randy said, "Jim, this is the nicest, most generous thing I can remember. I just hope I can repay you some way, some day."

"Forget it," Hickey said. "Children need honey. My kids have it every meal."

Randy heard the Model-A's horn, raucous as an angry goose, and saw it pull up to the curb. Walking to the car, he noticed that it was a clear and beautiful spring day, a better day than yesterday. The spores of kindness, as well as faith, survived in this acid soil.

Randy climbed into the car and showed the honey to Dan and explained how it had been given to him. "The world changes," Dan said. "People don't. I still have one old biddy in the schoolhouse who prunes and trims the camellias, and weeds the beds. They aren't her camellias and nobody gives a damn about flowers any more, except her. She loves flowers and it doesn't matter where she is or what happens she's going to take care of 'em. This same old lady—Mrs. Satterborough, she's been spending her winters at the Riverside Inn for years—she picks up the telephone in the principal's office every morning and dials Western Union. She thinks that one day the phone will be working just fine and that she'll get off a telegram to her daughter. She's certain of it. Her daughter lives in Indiana."

"I don't understand how those old people stay alive," Randy said. He knew that Dan brought them oranges by the bushel, and Randy sent them fish whenever there was a surplus catch.

"Most of them didn't. Death can be merciful, especially for the old and sick. I was about to say old, sick, and broke, but it doesn't matter any longer whether you're broke. Only five alive out of the Riverside Inn now. Maybe three will get through the summer. I don't think any will get through next winter."

Driving north on Yulee, the business district, while

deserted, seemed no more battered than it had the month before, or the month before that. A few optimistic storekeepers had prudently boarded windows, split by blast on The Day or broken by looters afterwards, against water and wind. On the two principal business blocks glass had been swept from the sidewalks. Abandoned cars, stripped of wheels, batteries, radios, and spark plugs, rusted in gutters like the unburied carcasses of giant beetles.

They turned off Yulee into Augustine Road, with its broken macadam and respectable but decaying residences. They bounced along for a block and then Randy smelled Pistolville. Another block and they were in it.

There had been no garbage collections since The Day. In Pistolville each hut or house squatted in a mound of its own excretion—crushed crates and cartons, rusting tin cans, broken bottles, rotting piles of citrus rusks and pecan shells, the bones of fowl, fish and small animals. A tallow-faced, six-year-old girl, clad in a man's castoff, riddled T-shirt, crouched on the curb, emptying her bowels in the dust. She cried out shrilly and waved as the Model-A bounced past. A bearded, long-haired man burst out of a doorway and jogged down the street on bandy legs, peeling and eating a banana, turning his head as if he expected to be followed. At the corner a scrawny boy of eighteen urinated against a lamp post, not bothering to raise his eyes at the sound of the car. Buzzards, grown arrogant, roosted in the oaks and foraged in the refuse. Of mongrel dogs, cats, partihued pigs, chickens, and pigeons—all normal impediments to navigation on the streets of Pistolville—no trace remained.

Once before in his life, in Suwon, immediately after its recapture and before the Military Government people had begun to clean up, Randy had seen degradation such as this. But this was America. It was his town, settled by his forebears. He said, "We've got to do something about this."

"Yes?" Dan said. "What?"

"I don't know. Something."

"Torches and gasoline," Dan said, "except there isn't enough gasoline. Anyway, these poor devils are as well off in their own houses as they would be in the woods, or in caves. No better off, mind you. But they have shelter."

"In four months," Randy said, "we've regressed four thousand years. More, maybe. Four thousand years ago the Egyptians and Chinese were more civilized than Pistolville is right now. Not only Pistolville. Think what must be going on in those parts of the country where they don't even have fruit and pecans and catfish."

As they approached the end of Augustine Road the houses were newer and larger, constructed of concrete block or brick instead of pitch-sweating pine clapboard. Between these houses grass grew shin-high, fighting the exultant weeds for sunlight and root space. There was less filth, or at least it was concealed by greenery, and the smell was bearable. In this airier atmosphere lived the upper crust of Pistolville, including Pete and Rita Hernandez and Timucuan County's Representative in the state legislature, Porky Logan.

"How long has it been since you've seen Rita?" Dan asked.

"Not since before The Day—quite a while before."

"Does Lib know about her?"

"She knows all about it. She says Rita doesn't bother her, because Rita is part of the past, like Mayoschi's in Tokyo. You know who worries Lib? Helen. Imagine that."

They were at the Hernandez house. Dan stopped the car. He said, "I can imagine it. Lib is an extremely sensitive, perceptive woman. About some things, she has more sense than you have, Randy. And all rules are off, now."

Randy wasn't listening. Rita had stepped out of the doorway. In Hawaii Randy had seen girls of mixed Caucasian, Polynesian, and Chinese blood, hips moving as if to the pulse of island rhythm even when only crossing the street, who reminded him of Rita. She was not like a girl of Fort Repose. She was a child of the Mediterranean and Carribean, seeming alien; and yet certainly American. Her ancestors included a Spanish soldier whose caravel beached in Matanzas Inlet before the Pilgrims found their rock, and Carib Indian women, and the Minorcans who spread inland from New Smyrna in the eighteenth century. She had not gone to college but she was intelligent and quick. She had an annulled high school marriage and an abortion behind her. She no longer made such foolish errors. Her hobby was men. She sampled and enjoyed men as other women collected and enjoyed African violets, Limoges teacups, or sterling souvenir teaspoons. She was professional in her avocation, never letting a man go without some profit, not necessarily material, and never trading one man for another unless she thought she was bettering her collection.

Under any circumstances Rita was an arresting woman. Her hair was cut in straight bangs to form an ebony frame for features carved like a Malayan mask in antique ivory. She could look, and behave, like an Egyptian queen of the Eighteenth Dynasty or a Creole whore out of New Orleans. On this morning she wore aquamarine shorts and halter. Cradled easily under her right arm was a light repeating shotgun. She was smoking a cigarette and even from the road Randy could see that it was a real, manufactured filtertip and not a stubby homemade, hand-rolled with toilet paper. She called, "Hello Doctor Gunn. Come on in." Then she recognized the passenger and yelled, "Hey! Randy!"

Dan put the car keys in his pocket and said, "Better bring the whiskey and honey, Randy. I never leave stuff in the car when I make a call in Pistolville."

As he walked to the house, Randy noticed the Atlas grocery truck and a big new sedan in the Hernandez carport and a Jaguar XK-150 sports car in the driveway. A latrine had been dug behind the carport and partly shielded from the road by a crude board fence.

Rita swung open the screen door. "You'll pardon the artillery," she said. "The goons down the street are envious. When I hear a car or anything I grab a gun. They killed my dog. She was a black poodle, Randy. Her name was Poupée Vivant. That means Livin' Doll in

French. Cracked her skull with an ax handle while Pete was lying sick and I was off fetching water. I found the ax handle but not the body. The goddamn cracker scum! Ate her, I guess."

Randy thought how he would feel if someone killed and ate Graf. He was revolted. And yet, it was a matter of manners and mores. In China men for centuries had been eating dogs stuffed with rice. It happened in other meat-starved Asian countries. The Army had put him through a survival course, once, and taught him that in an emergency he could safely eat pulpy white grubs found under bark. It could happen here. If a man could eat grubs he could eat dogs. Pistolville was meat starved and, as Dan had said, the rules were off. All Randy said was, "I'm sorry, Rita."

Randy walked through the door and stopped, astonished. The two front rooms of the Hernandez place looked like show windows in a Miami auction house. He counted three silver tea services, two chests of flat silver, three television sets, and was bewildered by a display of statuary, silver candelabra, expensive leather cases, empty crystal decanters, table lighters, chinaware. Gold-framed oils and watercolors, some fairly good, plastered one wall. Table clocks and wall clocks raised their hands and swore to different times. "Great God!" Randy said. "Have you people gone into the junk business?"

Rita laughed. "It's not junk. It's my investment."

Dan said, "How's Pete, Rita?"

"I think he's a little better. He's not losing any more hair but he's still weak."

Dan was carrying his black bag. It held little except instruments now. He said, "I'll go back and see him."

Dan walked down the hall and Randy was alone with her. She offered him a cigarette. Her perfume opened the gates of memory—the movies in Orlando, the dinners and dancing at the hotel in Winter Park, the isolated motel south of Canaveral, the morning they found a secluded pocket behind the dunes and were buzzed by a light plane and how the pilot almost sideslipped into the sea banking around for a second look, and most of all, his apartment. It seemed so long ago, as if it had happened while he was in college, before Korea, but it was not so long, a year only. He said, "Thanks, Rita. First real cigarette I've had in a long, long time. You must be getting along all right."

She looked at the bottle. "You didn't bring me a present, did you, Randy?" The corners of her mouth quivered, but she did not quite smile.

He remembered the evenings he had come to this house, a bottle beside him on the seat, and they had gone tooting off together; and the evenings he had brought bottles in gift packages, discreet gratuities for her brother; and the nights in the apartment, sharing a decanter drink for drink because she loved her liquor. He realized that this is what she intended he remember. She was expert at making him feel uncomfortable. He said, "No, Rita. Trade goods. I've been in Marines Park, trying to trade for coffee."

"Don't your new women like Scotch, Randy? I hear you've got two women in your house now. Which one are you sleeping with, Randy?"

Suddenly she was a stranger, and he looked upon her as such. Examined thus, with detachment, she looked ridiculous, wearing high heels and costume jewelry with shorts and halter at this hour of the morning and in this time of troubles. Her darkling ivory skin, once so satiny, appeared dry and mottled. Her hair was dull and the luster in her eyes reflected only spiteful anger. She looked used and tired. He said, calmly, "You can take your claws out now. I don't feel them. My skin's tougher."

She licked her lips. They were puffed and brown. "You're tougher. You're not the same Randy. I guess you're growing up."

He changed the subject. "Where did you get all this stuff?" He looked around the room.

"Trading."

"I never see you in Marines Park."

"We don't go there. They come to us. They know we still hold food. Even coffee."

He knew she wanted the bottle. He knew she would

trade coffee, but he would never again trade with her, for anything. He said:

"You said this was your investment. Do you think three television sets is a good investment when there isn't any electricity?"

"I'm looking ahead, Randy. This war isn't going to last forever and when it's over I'm going to have everything I never had before and plenty besides, maybe to sell. I was only a kid after the last big war but I remember how my dad had to pay through the nose for an old jalopy. Do you know what that Jag cost me?" She laughed. "A case of beans, three bottles of ketchup, and six cans of deviled ham. For a Jag! Say, as soon as things get back to normal those three TV sets will be worth their weight in gold."

"Do you really think things are going to get back to normal?"

"Sure! They always have, haven't they? It may be a year, even two. I can wait. You look at those big new houses out on River Road. What built half of them? Wars. Profits out of wars. This time I'm going to get mine."

He saw that she believed it and it was pointless to argue with her. Still, he was intrigued. "Don't you realize that this war is different?"

She held out her left hand so that the sunlight glinted on the ring on her second finger. "It certainly is different! Look at this!"

He looked at the big stone, and into it, and a thousand blue and red lights attested to its worth and purity.

It wasn't costume jewelry, as he had surmised. It wasn't glass surrounded by green paste. It was a diamond set in emeralds. "Where did you get it?" he asked, awed, and then he looked at her crescent ear clips and saw that they too, beyond a doubt, were diamonds.

Rita held the ring out, turning her wrist. She did not answer at once. She was enjoying their reaction. "Six carats," she said. "Perfect." She slipped it from her finger and handed it to Randy.

He took it automatically but he wasn't looking at it.

He was looking at her finger. Her finger was marred by a dark, almost black circle, as if the ring were tarnished brass, or its inside sooty. But the ring was clean bright white gold.

Dan came into the room, pawing in his bag and frowning. "I don't know exactly—" he began, looked at Randy's face, and failed to finish the sentence.

Frowning, Rita inspected the dark band. "It itches," she said, and scratched. A bit of blackened skin flaked away, leaving raw flesh beneath.

"I asked where you got this, Rita," Randy said, a command.

Before she opened her mouth he guessed the answer. She said, "Porky Logan."

The ring dropped to the floor, bounced, tinkled, and came to rest on the corner of a blue silk Chinese rug.

"Say, what's the matter?" she said. "You act like it was hot!"

"I think it is hot," Randy said.

"Well, if you think Porky stole it, you're wrong. It was abandoned property. Anybody would take it."

Dan took her hand and adjusted his bifocals so he could examine the finger closely. He spoke, his voice deep, enforcing calm. "Hold still, Rita, I just want to see that finger. I think what Randy meant was that the ring has been exposed to radioactivity and is now radioactive itself. I'm afraid he's right. This looks like a burn—a radium burn. How long have you been wearing that ring?"

"Off and on, for a month I guess. I never wear it outside, only in the house." She hesitated. "But this last week, I've had it on all the time. I never noticed—"

They looked down at it, its facets blinking at them from the soft blue silk as if it were in a display window. It looked beautiful.

"Where did Porky get it, Rita?" Dan asked.

"Well, I only know what he told me. He was fishing in the Keys on The Day and of course he started right back. He's smart, Porky is. He made a big detour around Miami. Well, he was passing through Hollywood or Boca Raton or one of those Gold Coast places and it was empty and right off the main drag he saw one of those swanky little jewelry shops, you know, a branch of some Fifth Avenue store and its windows were blown out. He said stuff was lying all over, rings and pins and watches and bracelets, like popcorn out of a busted bag. So he gathered it up. Then he dumped the hooks and plugs and junk out of his fishbox and went inside and filled it up. Porky said right then he was thinking of the future. He figured that money wouldn't be worth anything but diamonds and gold were different. They never lost value no matter what happened."

"Impregnated with fallout," Dan murmured. "Suicide."

Rita's hands crept upward to her neck and Randy noticed an oval mark in the hollow of her throat, as if the skin were painted darker there. Then her hands flew to her ears. The diamond ear clips fell to the rug beside the ring. She moaned, "Oh, God!"

"What did you have to give Porky for those diamonds?" Randy asked softly.

"For the ring, hardly anything at all. For the rest of it we gave him canned meat and cigarettes and coffee and chocolate bars and stuff like that. You know how Porky ate. For Chrissakes, Doc, what are you going to do about this?" She stared at her finger.

"What else did Porky give you besides the diamonds?" Dan asked.

"All sorts of stuff. He gave us a double handful of watches just for a case of pork and beans. Pete has—" She looked down the hallway. She said, "Pete!" and led them to his room.

Pete Hernandez didn't look as bad as Bill Cullen, but he looked bad enough, his scalp scabby as with mange, face erupting, and hands swollen. He pushed himself back on his pillows, startled, as they came in.

Rita said, "Pete, take off those watches."

"Are you nuts?" Pete was wearing a gold watch pushed up absurdly on each skinny arm. Pete looked at their faces and said, "Why should I take off my watches?"

Dan leaned down and stripped them off and tossed

them on a table. The flexible gold straps left black insignia. "They're radioactive. That gold is a hot isotope of gold. They've been poisoning you. Look."

Pete looked down. "It's just dirt. It's the heat. I've been sweating."

Randy asked the question, "Where's the rest of Porky's jewelry, Pete?"

Pete looked at Rita, his dulled black eyes uncertain and appealing. He said, "They just want to get our gold and stones, Rita."

"Randy doesn't lie, Pete, and I don't think Doctor Gunn would steal anything from anybody."

Pete curled his arm to reach under his pillow.

Dan said, "Oh, good Lord," pitying him.

From under the pillow Pete brought out a plastic toilet kit.

"Open it," Dan said.

Pete unzipped it. It was packed full, watch bands twisting and curling like golden snakes.

"Is that all?" Dan asked.

"No, those are just the watches," Rita said. "Pete's been amusing himself, admiring them and winding them every day. There's more stuff in my room—a couple of necklaces and a ruby and diamond brooch and—well, all sorts of junk."

"Pete," Dan said, "throw that kit in the corner, there. Rita, don't touch anything you may have in your bedroom. There's no point in your absorbing even another fraction of a roentgen. We've got to figure out a way to get the stuff out of here and get rid of it without damaging ourselves. We'll be back."

Rita followed them to the door, whimpering. She snatched at Dan's sleeve. "What's going to happen? Am I going to die? Is my hair going to fall out?"

"You haven't absorbed nearly as much radiation as your brother," Dan said. "I don't know exactly what's going to happen because radiation sickness is so tricky."

"What about Pete? What'll I do if Pete—"

"I'm afraid," Dan said, "that Pete is slipping into leukemia."

"Blood cancer?"

"Yes. I'm afraid you'd better prepare yourself."

Rita's hand fell from Dan's arm. Randy watched her diminish, all allure, all bravado falling away, leaving her smaller and like a child. He said, quietly, "Rita, you'd better keep this, here. You'll need it." He gave her the bottle of Scotch.

As he pressed the starter Dan said, "Why did you give her the whiskey."

"I feel sorry for her." That wasn't the only reason. If he had owed her anything before, he did no longer. They were quits. They were square. "Is she going to be all right?" he asked.

"I think so, unless a malignancy develops from the burn on her finger. Improbable but possible. Yes, she should be all right so far as radiation goes. The dose she absorbed was localized. But after her brother dies she'll be alone. Then she won't be all right."

"She'll find a man," Randy said. "She always has."

Porky Logan's house stood at the end of Augustine Road, in a grove that rose up a hillside at the back of the house. It was a two-story brick, the largest house in Pistolville, so it was said. Porky's sister and niece had been caring for him, but he lived alone. His wife and two children had departed Pistolville ten years before.

They found Porky on the second floor. He was sitting up in bed, unshaven chin resting upon blotched bare chest. Between his knees was a beer case filled with jewelry. His hands were buried to the forearm in this treasure. Dan said, "Porky!"

Porky didn't raise his head. Porky was dead.

Dan stepped to the bed, pushed Porky's body back against the pillows, and pried an eyelid open. Dan said, "Let's get out of here. That's a furnace he's got in his lap."

Randy tried not to breathe going down the steps. It was not only the smell of Porky's room that hurried him.

Dan said, "We've got to keep people out of this house until we can get Porky and that hot stuff underground. How do we do it?"

"What about a sign? We could paint a sign."

They found an unopened can of yellow paint and a brush in Porky's garage. Dan used the brush on the front door. In block letters he wrote:

"DANGER! KEEP OUT! RADIATION!"

"You'd better put something else on there," Randy said. "There are a lot of people around here who still don't know what radiation means."

"Do you really think so?"

"I'm positive of it. They've never seen it, or felt it. They hear about it, but I don't think they believe it. They didn't believe it could kill them before The Day— if they thought of it at all—and I don't think they believe it now. You'd better add something they understand, like Poison."

So under "RADIATION," Dan printed, "POISON." He said, "One other. Bill Cullen."

Bigmouth Bill was as they had left him, except that he held a bottle of cheap rum in his misshapen hands, and had been hitting it. Randy hovered at the door, so he could listen but not be submerged in the odors.

Dan said, "Bill, we've found out what's making you sick. You're absorbing radiation from the jewelry Porky traded for the whiskey. Porky's jewelry is hot. It's radioactive. Where is it?"

Bill laughed wildly. He began to curse, methodically and without imagination, as Randy had heard troops curse in the MLR in Korea. The pace of his obscenities quickened, he choked, frothed, and pulled at the rum bottle. "Jewelry!" he yelled, his yellow eyeballs rolling. "Jewelry! Diamonds, emeralds, pearls, tinkly little bracelets, all hot, all radioactive. That's rich!"

"Where is it, Bill?" Dan's voice was sharper.

"Ask her. Ask the dough-faced bitch! She has 'em, has the whole bootful."

"What do you mean?"

"I've been hiding the stuff, figuring that if she got her hands on it she'd swap it all for a bottle of vino. The jewels in one boot, the rum in the other. Believe it or not, this is the last of my stock." He sucked at the bottle.

"Go on," Dan said.

"I kept the boots, these boots here—" he gestured at a pair of hunting boots—"hid under the bed. It was safe, okay. You see, my woman she never cleaned anything, especially she never cleaned under the bed. Well, when she went out for a while I thought I'd take a look at the loot. You know, it was nice to hold it in your hands and dream about what you were going to do with it when things got back to normal. But she was watching through the window. She's been trying to catch me and just a while ago she did. She walked in, grinning. I thought she was going to tell me the war was over or something. She walked in and reached under the bed and snatched the boot. All she said as she went through the door was, 'I hope you croak, you sneaky bastard. I'm going back to Apalachicola'."

Fascinated, Randy asked, "How does she expect to get to Apalachicola?"

"I keep—kept the Plymouth in the shed. It was nearly full with gas, what was in the drum I had to service the outboards. I hope she wrecks."

Dan picked up his bag. His huge shoulders sagged. His face was unhappy behind the red beard. "Do you still have that ointment I gave you?"

"Yes." Bill turned his head toward the table.

"Keep using it on your hands. It may give you relief."

"It may, but this will." Bill tilted the rum bottle and drank until he gagged.

Riding back on River Road, Randy said, "Will Cullen live?"

"I doubt it. I don't have the drugs or antibiotics or blood transfusions for him." He reached down and patted his bag. "Not much left in here, Randy. I have to make decisions, now. I have drugs only for those worth saving."

"What about the woman?"

"I don't think she'll die of radiation sickness. I don't

think she'll keep that hot gold and silver and platinum long enough. She'll either swap for booze or, being stupid, try one of the main highways."

"I think the highwaymen will get her if she's headed for Apalachicola," Randy said.

It was strange that the term highwaymen, had revived in its true and literal sense. These were not the romantic and reputedly chivalrous highwaymen of Britain's post roads in the sixteenth and seventeenth centuries. These new highwaymen were ruthless and evil men who lately had been choking the thin trickle of communications and trade between towns and villages. Mostly, according to word that filtered into Fort Repose, they operated on the main highways like the Turnpike and Routes 1, 441, 17, and 50. So they were called highwaymen.

They passed the empty McGovern place. It was already lushly overgrown. "You know," Dan said, "in a few more months the jungle will take over."

[9]

They buried Porky Logan Friday morning. It was a ticklish and exhausting procedure. Randy had to draw his gun to get it done.

First, it was necessary to obtain the cooperation of Bubba Offenhaus. That was difficult enough. Bubba's funeral parlor was locked and empty and he was no longer seen in town. Since he was Deputy Director of Civil Defense as well as undertaker, a public appearance exposed him to all sorts of requests and problems which frightened him and about which he could do nothing. So Bubba and Kitty Offenhaus could only be found in their big new house, a rare combination of modern and classic, construced largely of tinted glass between ante-bellum Greek columns.

When Randy found Bubba sitting on his terrace he looked like a balloon out of which air had been let. His trousers sagged front and rear and folds of skin drooped around his mouth. Dan explained about Porky. Bubba was unimpressed. "Let them bury him in Pistolville," he said. "Plant him in his own back yard."

"It can't be done that way," Dan said. "Porky's a menace and the jewelry is deadly. Bubba, what we've got to have is a lead-lined coffin. We'll bury his loot with him."

"You know very well I've only got one in stock," Bubba said. "As a matter of fact it's the only casket I've got left and probably the only casket in Tumucuan County. It's the de luxe model with hammered bronze handles and shield which can be suitably engraved, and reinforced bronze corners. Guaranteed for eternity and I'm damned if I'm going to give it up for Porky Logan."

"Who are you saving it for," Randy asked, "yourself?"

"I don't see any point in you becoming insulting, Randy. That casket cost me eight hundred and forty-five dollars F.O.B. and it retails for fifteen hundred plus tax. Who's going to pay for it? As a matter of fact, who's going to reimburse me for all the other caskets, and everything else, that I've contributed since The Day?"

"I'm sure the government will," Dan said, "one day."

"Do you think the government's going to restore Repose-in-Peace Park? Do you think it'll pay for all those choice plots I've handed out, free? Like fun. I suppose you want to bury Porky in Repose-in-Peace?"

"That's the general idea," Dan said.

"And you expect me to use my hearse to cart the cadaver?"

"Somebody has to do it, Bubba, and you're not only the man with the hearse but you're in Civil Defense."

Bubba groaned. The most stupid thing he had ever done was accept the Civil Defense job. At the time it had seemed quite an honor. His appointment was mentioned in the Orlando and Tampa papers, and he rated a whole page, with picture, in the *Southeast Mortician*. It was undoubtedly a bigger thing than holding office in the Lions or Chamber of Commerce. His status had increased, even with his wife. Kitty was Old Southern Family, while he had been raised in South Chicago. She had never wholly forgiven him for this, or for his profession. Secretly, he had considered Civil Defense a boondoggle, like handouts to foreign countries and spending millions on moon rockets and such. He had never imagined there would be a war. It was true that after The Day he and Kitty had been able to get supplies in San Marco that he wouldn't have been able to get if he hadn't been in Civil Defense. For one thing, he had been able to get gasoline out of the county garage. But the tanks had long been dry, all other official supplies exhausted. He said, "I've only got one hearse that will run and only a couple of gallons of gas in it. I'm saving it for an emergency."

"This is an emergency," Dan said. "You'll have to use it now."

Bubba thought of another obstacle. "It'll take eight men to tote that lead-lined casket with Porky in it even if he's lost weight like I have."

Randy spoke. "We'll get them. Plenty of strong men hanging around Marines Park."

In the park they mounted the bandstand. Randy shouted, "Hey, everybody! Come over here!" The traders drifted over, wondering.

Bubba made a little speech. Bubba was accustomed to speaking at service club luncheons and civic meetings, but this audience, although many of the faces were familiar, was not the same. It was neither attentive nor courteous. He spoke of community spirit and co-operation and togetherness. He reminded them that they had sent Porky Logan to the state legislature and he knew Porky must have been a friend to many there. Now he asked for volunteers to help bury Porky. No hands went up. A few of the traders snickered.

Bubba shrugged and looked at Dan Gunn. Dan said, "This is in your own interest. If we leave the dead unburied we're inviting an epidemic. In addition, in this case we must get rid of radioactive material that can be dangerous to anyone who finds it."

Somebody yelled, "Bubba's the undertaker, ain't he? Well, let him undertake it."

Some of the men laughed. Randy saw that they were bored and would soon turn away. It was necessary that he act. He stepped in front of Dan, lifted the flap of his holster, and drew out the .45. Holding it casually, so that it was a menace to no one in particular, and yet to each of them separately, he pulled back the hammer. His left forefinger jabbed at the faces of five men, big men. "You, Rusty, and you, Tom, and you there, you have just volunteered as pall-bearers."

They looked at him amazed. For a long time, no one had ordered them to do anything. For a long time, there had not even been a boss on a job. Nobody moved. Some of the traders carried handguns in hip pockets or holsters. Others had leaned shotguns or rifles against benches or the bandstand railing. Randy watched for a movement. He was going to shoot the first man who reached for a weapon. This was the decision he had made. Regardless of the consequences he was going to do it. Having made the decision, and being certain he would carry it out, he felt easy about it. He realized they must know this. He stepped down from the bandstand, his eyes holding his five volunteers. He said, "All right, let's get going."

The five men followed him and he holstered his pistol.

So they buried Porky Logan. With him they buried the contaminated loot in Porky's carton and out of the Hernandez house. Also into the coffin went the fire tongs with which Dan Gunn had handled the jewelry. When the grave was filled and mounded somebody said, "Hadn't there ought to be a prayer for the poor bastard?"

They all looked at Randy. Randy said, "God rest his soul." He added, knowing that it would be passed along, "And God help anybody who digs him up to get the stuff. It'll kill them like it killed Porky."

He turned and walked slowly, head down, to the car, thinking. Authority had disintegrated in Fort Repose. The Mayor, Alexander Getty, who was also chairman of the town council, was barricaded in his house, besieged by imaginary and irrational fears that the Russians had invaded and were intent on his capture, torture, and the rape of his wife and daughter. The Chief of Police was dead. The two other policemen had abandoned unpaid public duty to scramble for their families. The fire and sanitation departments, equipment immobilized, no longer existed. Bubba Offenhaus was frightened, bewildered, and incapable of either decision or action. So Randy had shoved his gun into this vacuum. He had assumed leadership and he was not sure why. It was enough trouble keeping the colony on River Road alive and well. He felt a loneliness not unfamiliar. It was like leading a platoon out of the MLR to occupy some isolated outpost. Command, whether of a platoon or a town, was a lonely state.

When they returned to River Road at noon Randy's boat shoes were stiff with caked clay of the graveyard. He was knocking them clear of clods, on the front steps, when he was attracted by movement in the foliage behind Florence Wechek's house. Alice Cooksey and Florence were standing under a tall cabbage palm, steadying a ladder. At the top of the ladder, head and shoulders hidden by fronds, was Lib. He wondered why she must be up there. He wished she would stay on the ground. She took too many chances. She could get hurt. With medical supplies dwindling—Dan had already been forced to use most of their reserve—they all had to be careful. Everyone had chores and if one was hurt it meant added burdens, including nursing, on the others. A simple fracture could be compound disaster.

Bill McGovern, Malachai, and Two-Tone Henry came around the corner of the house. Bill was wearing gray flannels raggedly cut off above the knees, tennis shoes, and nothing else. His right hand grasped a bouquet of wrenches. Grease smeared his bald head and fine white beard. He no longer looked like a Caesar, but like an unkempt Jove armed with thunderbolts. Before he could speak Randy demanded: "Bill, what's your daughter doing up that palm?"

"She won't say," Bill said. "She and Alice and Florence are cooking up some sort of a surprise for us. Maybe she's found a bird's nest. I wouldn't know."

Randy said, "What's the delegation?"

Bill said, "It's Two-Tone's idea. Two-Tone, you talk."

Two-Tone said, "Mister Randy, you know my sugar cane will be tall and sweet and Pop's corn will be up in June."

"So?"

"Corn and sugar cane means corn whiskey. I mean we can make 'shine if you says it's okay. Pop and Mister Bill here, they say it's up to you. I suggests it only on one account. We can trade 'shine."

"Naturally you wouldn't drink any, would you, Two-Tone?"

"Oh, no sir!"

Randy understood that they required something from him beyond permission. Yet if they could manufacture corn whiskey it would be like finding coffee beans. Whiskey was a negotiable money crop. In this humid climate both corn and sugar cane would deteriorate rapidly. Corn whiskey was different. The longer you kept it the more valuable it became. Furthermore, only a few bottles of bourbon and Scotch remained, and the bourbon was strictly medicinal, Dan's anesthetic. Two-Tone, the no-good genius! Cannily, all Randy said was, "If you have Preacher's permission, it's all right with me. It's Preacher's corn."

Bill said, "I've already contributed my Imperial."

"You've what?"

"Contributed the guts of my Imperial. You see, to make the still we have to have a lot of copper tubing. We have to bend condensing coils, and you have to have tubing between the boiler and condenser and so forth."

"What you're getting at," Randy said slowly, "is that you want me to contribute the gas lines out of my Bonneville."

"That's right. The lines out of my car won't give us enough length. And we have to have your lawn roller. You see, first we've got to build a mill to crush the cane. We have to get the juice and boil it down to molasses before we can make whiskey, or for that matter use it as syrup. Balaam, the mule, will walk a circle, a lever harnessed to his back to turn the roller on concrete slabs. That's the mill. That's the way they did it a couple of hundred years ago. I've seen pictures."

Randy knew it would work. He said, sadly, "Okay. Go into the garage. But I don't want to watch." It had been a beautiful car. He remembered Mark's casual prediction that it wouldn't be worth a damn to him. Mark had been wrong. Some of it was useful.

Lunch was fish, with half a lime. Orange juice, all you could drink. A square of honeycomb. Dan and Hel-

en were at the table. The others had already finished.
Helen always waited for him, Randy noticed. She was
so solicitous it was sometimes embarrassing.

Dan looked at his plate and said, "A fine, thinning diet.
If everybody in the country had been on this diet before
The Day the cardiac death rate would have been cut in
half."

"So what good would it have done them?" Randy
said. He speared his honey and munched it, rolling his
eyes. "We've got to do more trading with Jim Hickey.
We've got to find something Jim needs." Randy remembered what Jim had said about half his broods going
foul since The Day and how Jim suspected radiation
was responsible. He told Dan and Helen what Hickey
had said.

Dan stared at his plate, troubled. He cut into his
honeycomb and tasted it. "Delicious," he said, but his
mind was elsewhere. At last he looked up and spoke
gravely. "We shouldn't be surprised. Who can tell how
much cesium 137 showered down on The Day? How
much was carried into the upper atmosphere and has
been filtering down since? The geneticists warned us of
damage to future generations. Well, Hickey's bees are in
a future generation."

Helen looked scared. Randy realized that this was a
more serious matter to women than to men, although
frightening enough to anybody. She said, "Does that
mean—will it affect humans?"

"Certainly some human genetic damage can be expected," Dan said. "What will happen to the birth rate
is anybody's guess. And yet, this is only nature's way of
protecting the race. Nature is proving Darwin's law of
natural selection. The defective bee, unable to cope with
its environment, is rejected by nature before birth. I
think this will be true of man. It is said that nature is
cruel. I don't think so. Nature is just, and even merciful.
By natural selection, nature will attempt to undo what
man has done."

"You make it sound comforting," Helen said.

"Only an opinion, based on almost no evidence. In
six or seven months I'll know more. But to evaluate ev-

erything may take a thousand years. So let's not worry
about it. Right now I've got other worries, like tires.
The tires on the Model-A are smooth, Randy, and I've
got to make a couple of calls out in the country. Got
any suggestions?"

"I've been thinking of tires," Randy said. "The tires
on Florence's old Chevvy will fit the Model-A. Two of
them are almost new. Let's go over and make the
change."

It was the custom of Randy and Dan to meet in the
apartment at six each evening, listen for the clear channel station which would be heard at this hour if at all,
and, if they were tired and the rigors of the day war-
ranted, share a drink. At six on that Friday evening,
Dan had not returned from his calls, so Randy sat at his
bar alone with the little transistor portable. Life was eb-
bing from its last set of batteries. He feared the day
when it would no longer pick up even the strongest signal, or give any sound whatsoever, and the day could
not be far distant. So, what strength was left in the batteries he carefully rationed. Sam Hazzard's all-wave receiver, operating on recharged automobile batteries,
was really their only reliable source of information. He
clicked on the radio, was relieved to hear static, and
tried the Conelrad frequencies.

Immediately he heard a familiar voice, thin and grav-
elly although he turned the volume full. ". . . against
smallpox."

Randy knew he had missed the first item of news.
Then he heard:

There have been isolated reports of disorders and out-
lawry from several of the Contaminated Zones. As a result,
Mrs. Vanbruuker-Brown, Acting President, in her capacity
as Commander in Chief of the Armed Forces, has authorized all Reserve officers and National Guard officers, not
in contact with their commanders or headquarters, to take
independent action to preserve public safety in those areas
where Civil Defense has broken down or where organized
military units do not exist. These officers will act in accor-

dance with their best judgment, under the proclamation of martial law. When possible, they will wear the uniform when exercising authority. I repeat this new . . ."

The signal hummed and faded. Randy clicked off the set. Even as he began to assimiliate the significance of what he had heard he was aware that Helen was standing on the other side of the counter. In her hands she held a pair of scissors, comb, and a silver hand mirror. She was smiling. "Did you hear that?" he asked.

"Yes. Today's your haircut day, Randy. Today's Friday." Helen trimmed his hair and Bill McGovern's fringe each Friday, and barbered Dan and Ben Franklin Saturdays.

"You know I'm in the Reserve," Randy said. "I'm legal."

"What do you mean?"

"I had to pull my gun this morning to get Porky Logan buried. I had no authority. Now I do have authority, legally." His thoughts on the proclamation, at the moment, went no further.

"That's fine. Now get into a chair."

He walked into his office. Because of the swivel chair, it was also the barbershop. Helen tied a towel around his neck and began snipping, deftly and rapidly. She was some woman, he thought. Under any conditions she could keep a household running smoothly. In ten minutes it was done.

Her hand ruffled and then smoothed his hair. He could feel her breasts, round and warm, pressing against his shoulder blades. "You're getting gray hairs, Randy," she said. The timbre of her voice was deeper than usual.

"Who isn't?"

She rubbed and smoothed his temples. Her fingers kneaded the back of his neck. "Do you like that?" she whispered. "Mark loved it. When he came home, tense and worried, I always rubbed his temples and his neck like this."

Randy said, "It feels fine." He wished she wouldn't talk like that. She made him nervous. He put his hands on the arms of the chair and started to rise.

She pulled him back and whirled the chair so that he faced her. Her eyes were round. He could see beads of perspiration at the corners of her nose, and on her forehead. "You are Mark," she said. "Don't you believe me? Here, look!" She lifted the mirror from the desk and thrust it before his face.

He looked, wondering how he could gracefully escape, wondering what was wrong with her. It was true that his face, leaner and harder, looked like Mark's face now. "I do look something like him," he admitted, "but why shouldn't I? I'm his brother."

Her arms pinning him with unexpected strength, she kissed him wildly, as if her mouth could subdue and mold and change him.

His hands found her wrists and he forced her back. The mirror fell and smashed.

"Don't!" she cried. "Don't push me away! You're Mark! You can't deny it! You're Mark!"

He struggled out of the chair, clamping her wrists, trying not to injure her. He knew that she was mad and he fought to control the panic within himself. "Stop it!" he heard himself shouting. "Stop it, Helen! Stop it! I'm not Mark! I'm Randy!"

She screamed, "Mark!"

The door was ajar. Through it came Lib's voice, loud and welcome, "Randy, are you shorn? If Helen's finished, come on out. I've got something to show you."

He released Helen's wrists. She leaned against the desk, face averted, shoulders quivering, one hand stifling the sounds erupting from her mouth. He said, gently, "Please, Helen—" He touched her arm. She drew away from him. He fled into the living room.

Lib stood at the porch door, her face somber, beckoning. She said quietly, "Up to the roof, where we can talk."

Randy followed her, knowing that she must have heard and grateful for her interference. It was something he would have had to tell Lib anyway. He would have to tell Dan too. This emotional earthquake could bring down their house. It was a problem for a physician.

Up on the captain's walk, Randy lowered himself carefully into a deck chair. The canvas would rot before summer's end. His hands were shaking. "Did you hear it all?" he asked.

"Yes. All. And saw some too. Don't ever let her know."

"What's wrong with her?" It was a protest rather than a question.

Lib sat on the edge of his chair and put her hands on his hands and said, "Stop shaking, Randy. I know you're confused. It was inevitable. I knew it was coming. I'll diagnose it for you as best I can. It's a form of fantasy."

Randy was silent, wondering at her detachment and coolness.

"It is," she went on, "the sort of transference you find in dreams—the substitution in dreams of one person for another. Helen allowed herself to slip into a dream. I think she is a completely chaste person. She is, isn't she?"

"I'm sure of it, or I was."

"Yet she is a person who requires love and is used to it. For many years a man has been the greater part of her life. So she has this conflict—intense loyalty to her husband and yet need of a man to receive her abundance of love and affection. She tried to resolve the conflict irrationally. You became Mark. It was an hallucination."

"You're talking like a professional, Lib."

"I'm not a professional. I just wanted to be one. I majored in psychology. Remember?"

It was something she had told him but he had forgotten because it seemed incongruous and not in the least important. Lib looked like a girl who had majored in ballet and water-skiing at Miami rather than psychology at Sarah Lawrence. He knew that she worked for a year in a Cleveland clinic and had abandoned the job only because of her mother's illness. When she spoke of this year, which was seldom, it was with nostalgia, as some girls spoke of a year in Europe or on the stage. He suspected it must have been the most rewarding year of her life, and certainly there must have been a man, or men, in it. Randy said, "Lib, do you think she's crazy?"

"Helen's not psychotic. She's under terrible strain. She let herself go, but only for a moment. She indulged a temporary fantasy. Now it is over. Now she will be ashamed of herself. The best thing you can do is pretend it didn't happen. One day she'll mention it to you, perhaps obliquely, and apologize. Eventually she'll understand why she did it and the sense of guilt will leave her. One day, when we're better friends, I'll make her understand it. You know there is a man in the house for Helen —a perfectly fine man. I'm going to make that my special project."

Randy felt relieved. He looked out over the river, contemplating his ignorance of women and the peace of evening. On the end of the dock Ben Franklin and Peyton were fishing. It was understood that anyone, child or adult, could go fishing before breakfast or after assigned chores were done. Fishing was not only recreation but the necessary daily harvest of a crop providentially swimming at their feet. Presently the brass ship's bell on the porch sang its sharp, clean, sea note. The bell was a relic of Lieutenant Randolph Rowzee Peyton's longboats. It was the same bell that Randy's mother had used to summon Mark and him from the river to wash for dinner. There was peace and continuity in the sound of the bell. The bell announced that there was food on the table and a woman in the kitchen. So it was not only a message to the children but to Randy. Helen had pulled herself together. He watched Ben and Peyton, trailed by Graf, thread their way up through the grove. Graf still shared Randy's couch but all day he shadowed the boy. This was right. A boy needed a dog. A boy also needed a father.

When the children were close to the house Randy yelled down, "What'd you get?"

Ben held up a string of bream and speckled perch. "Sixteen," he shouted, "on worms and crickets. I got fifteen, she only got one."

Peyton danced in indignation, a slim shrill-voiced

sprite. "Who cares about fish? If I grow up I'm not going to be a fisherman!"

Helen called from the kitchen window. The children disappeared.

Randy said, "Did you ever hear a little girl say 'If I grow up' before?"

"No, I never did. It gives me the creeps."

"Not their fault," Randy said. "Ours."

"Would you want children, Randy?"

Randy considered the question. He thought of Jim Hickey's bees, and Peyton's "if," and of cow's milk you would not dare feed a baby in a contaminated zone, even if you had a cow, and of many other things.

Lib waited a long time for an answer and then she leaned across the chair and kissed him and said, "Don't try to answer now. I've got to go down and help with dinner. Don't come downstairs for a few minutes, Randy. We've whipped up a surprise."

At seven, conscious that he had not heard Dan return, Randy went downstairs. The table was set as if for a feast—a white cloth, two new candles; a salad bowl as well as plate at each place. A laden salad-boat of Haitian mahogany rode on the circular linen lagoon. Garnishing the inevitable platter of broiled fish was a necklace of mushrooms. He tasted the salad. It was delicate, varied, and wonderful. "Who invented this?" he asked. He had not tasted greens in months.

Helen had not met his eyes since he entered the dining room. She said, "Alice Cooksey. Alice found a book listing edible palms, grasses, and herbs. Lib did most of the picking."

"What all's in it?"

"Fiddlehead ferns, hearts of palm, bamboo shoots, wild onions, some of the Admiral's ornamental peppers, and the first tomatoes out of Hannah Henry's garden."

Lib said, "Wait'll you try the mushrooms. That was Helen's idea. It's funny, for the last week they've been growing all over, right in front of our eyes, and only Helen recognized them as food."

"No toadstools I hope," Randy said.

Helen smiled and for the first time looked at him directly. "Oh, no. Alice thought of that too. I've been wandering around the hammock with an illustrated book in one hand and a basket in the other."

Now that she could see he was treating the incident in his office as something that hadn't happened, she was regaining control of herself. He said, "Helen, you be careful in that hammock. And Lib, you stay out of palm trees. We don't want any snake bites or broken legs. Dan has troubles enough." He put down his fork. "Where is Dan?"

Nobody knew. Dan was usually home before six. Occasionally, he was as late as this or later when he encountered an emergency. Still, it was impossible not to worry. It was at times like this that Randy truly missed the telephone. Without communications, the simplest mechanical failure could turn into a nightmare and disaster. He finished the fish, mushrooms, and salad, but without appetite.

Randy fidgeted until eight and then said, "I'm going to see the Admiral. Maybe Dan stopped there for dinner." He knew this was unlikely, but he tried in any case to visit Sam Hazzard each evening and watch him comb the frequencies. There were other reasons. He stopped at the Wechek and Henry houses like a company commander checking his outposts. He slept uneasily unless he knew all was well around his perimeter. More compelling, Lib usually went with him. It was their opportunity to have a little time alone. It was paradoxical that they lived in the same house, ate almost every meal elbow to elbow or across the bar in his apartment, slept within twenty feet of each other, and yet they could be alone hardly at all.

Ben Franklin said, "Wait until I get the shotgun, Randy. I'll go with you. It's my night to stand guard." He raced upstairs.

Helen said, "Do you really think you ought to let him do it, Randy?"

"It'd break his heart if I didn't. I think he'll be okay.

Caleb is going to stay up with him and Malachai will be right there. Malachai will sleep with one eye open."

"Why are you letting him have your shotgun?"

"Because if something comes around the Henrys' yard I want him to hit it, not just pop away at it in the dark with a twenty-two. I've taught him how to handle the shotty. It'll be loaded with number two buck. He'll do all right."

Ben came out on the porch carrying the gun. Lib said, "Am I invited?"

Randy said, "Certainly." He turned to Bill McGovern. "If Dan shows up, give me three bells, will you?" Three strokes of the ship's bell meant come home, but it was not an emergency signal. Five bells was the panic button. The bell could be heard for a mile along the shore and across water.

Pale yellow lamplight showed in the Henrys' windows. Randy knocked and Missouri, looking almost svelte in a newly acquired waistline, opened the door. "Mister Randy. I guessed 'twas you. I want to thank you for the honey. Tasted mighty good. Will you come in and have some tea?"

"Tea!" Randy saw a kettle steaming on a brick oven in the fireplace.

"We calls it tea. I grow mints under the house and dry 'em until they powders. So we has mint tea."

"We'll skip it tonight, Mizzoo. I just came to put Ben Franklin on his stand. Caleb ready?"

Missouri's son stepped out of the shadows, teeth and eyes gleaming. Incredibly, he carried a six-foot spear.

"Let me see that," Randy said. He hefted it. It had been fashioned, he saw, from a broken garden edger, the blade ground to a narrow triangle. It was heavy, well balanced, and lethal.

"Uncle Malachai made it for me," Caleb said proudly.

"It's a wicked weapon, all right," Randy said, and returned it to the boy.

Malachai, carrying a lantern, joined them. Malachai said, "I figured that if Ben Franklin missed with the shotgun Caleb best have it for close-in defense, if it's truly a wolf, like Preacher says."

Randy was certain that whatever had stolen the Henrys' hens, and the pig, it wasn't a wolf, but he wanted to impress Ben Franklin with the seriousness of his watch. "Probably not a wolf," he said, "but it could be a cougar—a panther. My father used to hunt 'em when he was young. Plenty of panther in Timucuan County until the first boom brought so many people down. Now there aren't so many people, so there will be more panther."

They walked toward Balaam's tired barn. The mule snorted and rattled the boards in his stall. "It's only me, Balaam," Malachai said. "Balaam, quiet down!" Balaam quieted.

Randy pointed to the bench alongside the barn. "That's your stand, Ben." Bill McGovern had sat on the bench the previous night and seen nothing.

"Stand?" Ben Franklin said.

"That's what you call it in a deer hunt. When I was your age my father used to take me hunting and put me on a stand. There are a couple of things I want you to remember, Ben. Everything depends on you—and you, Caleb—keeping absolutely still. Whatever it is out there, is better equipped than you are. It can see better and hear better and smell better. All you've got on it is brains. Your only chance of getting it is to hear it before it hears or sees you." Randy looked at the sky. There were only stars. Later, there would be a quarter moon. "Chances are you'll hear it before you see it. But if you talk, or make any sound, you'll never see it at all because it'll hear you first and leave. Do you understand?"

"Yes, sir," Ben said.

"You'll get cramped and you'll get tired. So when you sit on the stand you move around all you want at first and find out just how far you can move without making any noise. You got shells in the chambers?"

"Yes, sir, and four extra in my pocket."

"You'll only need what's in the gun. If you don't get him with two you'll never get him at all. And Ben—"

"Yes, sir."

"Hold steady on it and don't miss. We want to get rid of this thing or somebody will have to sit up all night every night."

Ben said, "Randy, suppose it's a man?"

This possibility had been restless in Randy's mind from the first and he had not wanted to mention it, but since it was mentioned he gave the unavoidable answer. "Whatever it is, Ben, shoot it. And Caleb, if he misses I depend on you to stick it." He turned to Malachai. "Thanks for lighting us out. We're going on to Admiral Hazzard's house now. Good night, Malachai."

"Good night," Malachai said. "I sleep light, Mister Randy."

Lib took his hand and they walked to the river bank and down the path that led toward the single square of light announcing that Sam Hazzard was in his den. Randy chuckled, thinking of Caleb's spear. "We have just witnessed an historic event," he said.

"What do you mean?"

"North American civilization's return to the Neolithic Age."

"I don't think it's funny," Lib said. "I didn't like the way you spoke to Ben Franklin. It was brutal."

"In the Neolithic," Randy said, "a boy either grows up fast or he doesn't grow up at all."

Sam Hazzard's den was compact and crowded, like a shipmaster's cabin stocked for a long and lonely voyage. It was filled with mementos of his service, ceremonial and Samurai swords, nautical instruments, charts, maps, books on shelves and stacked in corners, bound files of the *Proceedings, The Foreign Affairs Quarterly,* and the *Annals* of the American Academy of Political and Social Science. The admiral's L-shaped desk spread along two walls. One side was preempted by the professional-looking short-wave receiver and his radio log. The radio was turned on, but when Randy and Lib entered the room all they heard was a low hum.

Sam Hazzard was not as tall as Lib and his weathered skin was drawn tautly over fine bones. In slippers and dragon-blazoned shantung robe—his implacable gray eyes shadowed and softened by the indistinct lighting and horn-rimmed glasses, cottony hair like a halo—he appeared fragile; a deception. He was tough as an antique ivory figurine which has withstood the vicissitudes of centuries, and can accept more. He said, "A place for the lady to sit." He sailed a plastic model of the carrier *Wasp*—the old *Wasp* cited by Churchill for stinging twice in the Mediterranean and then herself stung to death by torpedoes—to the far corner of the desk. "Up there," he ordered Lib, "where you can be properly admired. And you, Randy, lift those books out of that chair. Gently, if you please. Welcome aboard to both of you."

Randy said, "You haven't seen Dan Gunn, have you?"

"No. Not today. Why?"

"He hasn't come home."

"Missing, eh? That sounds ungood, Randy."

"If he comes home while we're out Helen or Bill will ring the bell. Can we hear it in here?"

"Yes indeed, so long as the window's open. It always startles me."

Randy saw that the Admiral had been working. The Admiral was writing something he called, without elaboration, "A Footnote to History." A portable typewriter squatted in the center of a ring of books. Research, Randy supposed. He recognized Durant's *Caesar and Christ,* Gibbon's *Decline and Fall,* and *Vom Kriege* by Clausewitz, indicating a footnote to ancient history. Randy said, "Any poop this evening?"

"I suppose you heard the Civil Defense broadcast."

"I caught part of it. Then my batteries quietly expired."

The Admiral gave his attention to the radio. He turned the knob changing frequencies. "I've been listening for a station in the thirty-one meter band. Claims to be in Peru. I heard it for the first time last night. It put out some pretty outlandish stuff. It doesn't seem to be on yet, so we'll try for it again later. I've just switched to five point seven megacycles. That's an Air Force frequency I can tap sometimes. You've never heard it, Randy. Interesting, but cryptic."

The speaker squealed and whined. "Somebody's transmitter is open," the Admiral interpreted. "Something's coming."

A voice boomed with shocking loudness in the small room:

"Sky Queen, Sky Queen. Do not answer. Do not answer. This is Big Rock. This is Big Rock. Applejack. Repeat, Applejack. Authentication X-Ray."

Lib spoke, excitedly, "What is it? What does it mean?"

Hazzard smiled. "I don't know. I'm not up on Air Force codes and jargon. I've heard that Sky Queen call two or three times in the past month. Sky Queen could be a bomber, or a patrol plane, or a whole wing or air division. Big Rock—whoever that is—could be telling Sky Queen—whatever she may be—any number of things. Proceed to target, orbit, continue patrol, come home all is forgiven. I can't even make an informed guess. However, I do know this. That was a good American call and so we're still in business." The smile departed. "On the other hand, it indicates that the enemy is still in business too."

"How do you figure?" Randy asked.

"That 'Do not answer' phrase. Why does Big Rock order Sky Queen to be silent? Because if Sky Queen acknowledges the call then somebody might be able to take a radio fix on her, estimate speed and course, and vector fighters—or launch ground-to-air rockets to shoot her down."

Randy considered this. "Then Sky Queen is probably stooging around over enemy territory."

"That's good deduction but we can't be certain. For all we know, Sky Queen may be hunting a sub off Daytona. It makes me wild, listening to the damn Air Force—you will please pardon me, Lib—but if the enemy is listening on this frequency it must make them wild too."

Lib asked, "What did that 'Authentication X-Ray' stand for?"

"X-Ray is simply international code for the letter X. My guess is that before every mission they change the authentication letter so that the enemy can't take over the frequency and give Sky Queen a false heading, or phony instructions."

"You know, I enjoyed hearing that," Lib said. "It gave me a nice feeling. Big Rock has a solid Midwest accent."

Sam Hazzard moved a candle so that better light fell on his dials. "Big Rock won't be back again tonight," he said. "I've never heard him more than once a night. He makes his call and that's it. I'll try the thirty-one meter band again."

In the candlelight Hazzard's hands shone with the silky, translucent patina of age and yet they were remarkably deft. They discovered a fascinating squeal. His fingers worked the band-spreader delicately as a master cracksman violating a safe and he pressed his face forward as if he expected to hear tumblers click. Very gradually, a faint voice replaced the squeal. He turned up the power. They heard, in English with an indefinite accent:

"Continuing the news to North America—

"The representative of the Argentine has informed the South American Federation that two ships with wheat have sailed for Nice, in southern France, responding to radio appeals from that city. The appeals from Nice say that several hundred thousand refugees are camped in makeshift shelter on the Côte d'Azure. Many are starving. The casino at Monaco and the Prince's palace have been converted into hospitals.

"In a Spanish-language broadcast heard here today, Radio Tokyo announced that the Big Three meeting in New Delhi has approved preliminary plans for flying desperately needed vaccines and antitoxins to uncontaminated cities in Europe, North America, and Australia."

"Big Three!" Randy said. "Who's the Big Three?"
"Sh-h!" said the Admiral. "Maybe we'll find out."
The announcer continued:

"China, where 'Save Asia First' sentiment is strong, urged that first priority for vaccine aerial shipments go to the Soviet Union's maritime provinces, where typhus is reported. India and Japan felt that the smallpox epidemic on the West Coast of the United States, Canada, and in Mexico should receive equal priority. The universal shortage of aviation gasoline will make any quick aid difficult, however . . ."

The squeal insinuated itself into the voice and subdued it. Hazzard caressed the band-spreader. "The atmospherics have been crazy ever since The Day." Abruptly he asked Randy: "Do you believe it?"

"It's weird," Randy said. "Maybe it's a Soviet bloc propaganda station pretending to be South American, set up to confuse us and start rumors. I'll admit I'm confused. I thought the Chinese were in it, on the other side."

"The Chinese never liked Russia's preoccupation with the Med," Hazzard said. "Maybe they opted out, which would be smart of them. It could be simpler. If they didn't have nuclear capability we wouldn't bother hitting them on The Day, and without nuclear weapons they wouldn't dare stick their noses into a real war. If that was it, they were lucky."

"I noticed that station quoted Tokyo? How is it you didn't hear Tokyo?"

"I've never been able to pick up any Asiatic stations. I used to get Europe fine—London, Moscow, Bonn, Berne. Africa, too, especially the Voice of America transmitter in the Tangier. Not any more. Not since The Day."

The signal cleared. They heard:

". . . but as yet the Big Three have been unable to reopen communications with Dmitri Torgatz. According to Radio Tokyo, Torgatz headed the Soviet government while the Soviet Union's capital was in Ulan Bator in Outer Mongolia. The medium-wave station operating from Ulan Bator is no longer heard."

"That doesn't sound like Soviet propaganda to me," Randy said. "Who is Dmitri Torgatz?"

The Admiral glanced up at a shelf of reference works. He selected a slender book, *Directory of Communist Leaders,* found the name, and read: "Torgatz, Dmitri; born Leningrad 1903? Married, wife's name unlisted; children unlisted; Director Leningrad Agitprop 1946–49; Candidate member Presidium 1950–53; Director waterworks, Naryan Mar, Siberia, since fall of Malenkov."

"Looks like they had a shakeup," Randy said. "Looks like they had to reach way down and find a minor league bureaucrat."

"Yes. It's surprising that Torgatz should be running Russia," the Admiral said, "until you consider that a female, last on the list of Cabinet members, is running the United States."

Randy could see that Lib wasn't listening. She was staring at the tassel of a sword resting on pegs behind his head, her lips parted, eyes unblinking. Her thoughts, he had discovered, frequently raced ahead of his or sped down dark and fascinating byways. When she concentrated thus she left the party. She murmured, "Smallpox."

Not understanding that Lib, mentally, was no longer in the room with them, Sam Hazzard inquired, "What about smallpox?"

"Oh!" Lib shook her head. "I think of smallpox as something out of the Middle Ages, like the Black Plague. It's true that every so often it cropped up, but we always slapped it down again. What happens now without vaccine? What about diphtheria and yellow fever? Will they start up again? Without penicillin and DDT, where are we? All good things came to us automatically. We were born with Silver spoons in our mouths and electric dishwashers to keep them sanitary and clean. We relaxed, didn't we? What happened to us, Admiral?"

Sam Hazzard disconnected the radio's batteries and pulled his chair around to face them. "I've been trying to find the answer." He nodded at his typewriter and

the books massed on his desk. "I've been trying to put it
down in black and white and pass it along. Up to now,
no bottom. All I've found out was where I myself—and
my fellow professionals—failed. I'll explain."

He opened a drawer and drew out a folder. "I called
this 'A Footnote to History.' You see, I was in the Pentagon when we were having the big hassles on roles and
missions and it occurred to me that I might be one of
the few still alive who knew the inside of what went on
and how the decisions were reached and I thought that
future historians might be interested. So I set it all down
factually. I set down all the arguments between the big
carrier admirals and the atomic seaplane admirals and
the ICBM generals and pentomic division generals and
heavy bomber generals and manned missile generals. I
told how we finally achieved what we thought was a
balanced establishment.

"When I finished I read it over and realized it was a
farce."

He tossed the manuscript on the desk as if he were
discarding unwanted fourth class mail.

"You see, I confused the tactical with the strategic. I
think we all did. The truth is this. Once both sides had
maximum capability in hydrogen weapons and efficient
means of delivering them there was no sane alternative
to peace.

"Every maxim of war was archaic. The rules of Clausewitz, Mahan, all of them were obsolete as the Code
Duello. War was no longer an instrument of national
policy, only an instrument for national suicide. War itself was obsolete. So my 'Footnote' deals with tactical
palavers of no real importance. We might as well have
been playing on the rug with lead soldiers."

The Admiral rose and unkinked his back. "I think
most of us sensed this truth, but we could not accept it.
You see, no matter how well we understood the truth it
was necessary that the Kremlin understand it too. It
takes two to make a peace but only one to make a war.
So all we could do, while vowing not to strike first, was
line up our lead soldiers."

"That was all you could do?" Lib asked.

"All. The answer was not in the Pentagon, or even in the White House. I'm looking elsewhere. One place, here." He tapped Gibbon. "There are odd similarities between the end of the Pax Romana and the end of the Pax Americana which inherited Pax Britannica. For instance, the prices paid for high office. When it became common to spend a million dollars to elect senators from moderately populous states, I think that should have been a warning to us. For instance, free pap for the masses. Bread and circuses. Roman spectacles and our spectaculars. Largesse from the conquering proconsuls and television giveways from the successful lipstick king. To understand the present you must know the past, yet it is only part of the answer and I will never discover it all. I have not the years."

Randy saw that the Admiral was tired. "I guess we'd better get back," he said. "Thanks for an entertaining evening."

"Next time you come over," Hazzard said, "I want you to look at my invention."

"Are you inventing something too? Everybody's inventing something."

"Yes. It's called a sailboat. It is a means of propulsion that replaces the gasoline kicker. I sacrificed my flagpole and patio awning to make it. The cutting and sewing was done by Florence Wechek and Missouri and Hannah Henry. I can now recommend them as experienced sailmakers."

"Thanks, Sam." Randy grinned. "That's a wonderful invention and will become popular. I know I'm going to get one right away, and I will use your firm of sailmakers."

They walked to the path along the river bank. Swinging at its buoy Randy saw the Admiral's compact little cruiser with covered foredeck, useless kicker removed, a slender mast arcing its tip at a multitude of stars. There were many sailboats on Florida's lakes, but Randy had seen very few in the upper reaches of the St. Johns, or on the Timucuan.

"I love the Admiral," Lib said. "I worry about him. I wonder whether he gets enough to eat."

"The Henrys see that he eats. And Missouri keeps his place neat. The Henrys love him too."

"As long as we have men like that I can't believe we're so decadent. We won't go like Rome, will we?"

He didn't answer. He swung her around to face him and circled her waist with his hands. His fingers almost met, she was so slim. He said, "I love you. I worry about you. I wonder whether I tell you enough how I love you and want you and need you and how I am diminished and afraid when you are not with me and how I am multiplied when you are here."

His arms went around her and he felt her body arch to him, molding itself against him. "There never seems to be enough time," he said, "but tonight there is time. When we get home."

She said, "Yes, Randy." They walked on, his arm around her waist. "This is a bad time for love," she said. "Oh, I don't mean tonight is a bad time, I mean the times. When you love someone, that should be what you think of most, the first thing when you wake in the morning and the last thing before you sleep at night. Before The Day that's how I thought of you. Did you know that? First in the morning, last at night."

Randy knew, without her saying it, that it must be the same for her as it was for him. At day's end a man was exhausted—physically, mentally, emotionally. Each sun heralded a new crisis and each night he bedded with old, relentless fears. He awoke thinking of food and fell onto his couch at night still hungry, his head whirling with problems unsolved and dangers unparried. The Germans, in their years of methodical madness, had discovered in their concentration camps that when a man's diet fell below fifteen hundred calories his desire and capacity for all emotions dwindled. Randy guessed that he managed to consume almost fifteen hundred calories each day in fish and fruit alone. His vigor was being expended in survival, he decided. That, and worry for the lives dependent upon him. Even now, he could not exclude worry for Dan Gunn from his mind.

The hodgepodge outlines of the Henry place loomed out of the darkness above them. They were within fifty yards of the barn and Ben Franklin was somewhere in that shadow, shotgun over his knees, enjoined to silence, alert to shoot anything that moved; and they were moving, silhouetted against the star-silvered river. He stopped and held Lib fast. "Ben!" he called. "Ben Franklin! Do not answer. Do not answer. This is Randy. We're on our way home."

They walked on.

"You know, you sounded just like that radio call on the Air Force frequency," Lib said.

"I did sound like that, didn't I?" He smiled in the darkness, snapped his fingers, and said, "I think I know now what was going on. It wasn't the way Sam thought. It was just the other way around. Big Rock was the plane, and Sky Queen the base. Big Rock had been somewhere and was coming home and was telling Sky Queen not to shoot, just like I told Ben Franklin."

"Perhaps you're right. Not that it matters to us. I've heard them up there on still nights, but they never come low enough to see. The Admiral hears them talk on the radio but they never have a word for us. Maybe they've forgotten us. Maybe they've forgotten all the contaminated zones. We're unclean. It makes me feel lonely and, well, unwanted. Isn't that silly? Does it make you feel like that?"

"They'll come back," he said. "They have to. We're still a part of the United States, aren't we?"

They came to the path that led though their grove from house to dock. "Let's go out on the dock," Lib said. "I like it out there. No sound, not even the crickets. Just the river whispering around the pilings."

"All right."

They turned left instead of right. As their feet touched the planking the ship's bell spoke. It clanged three times rapidly, then twice more. It kept on ringing. "Oh, damn it to hell!" Randy grabbed her hand and they started the run for the house, an uphill quarter mile in sand and darkness. After a hundred yards she released his hand and fell behind.

By the time he reached the back steps Randy couldn't climb them. He was wobbling and his knees had jellied, but before The Day he could not have run the distance at all. He paused, sobbing, and waited for Lib. The Model-A wasn't in the driveway or the garage. He concluded that Dan hadn't returned and something frightful had happened to Helen, Peyton, or Bill McGovern.

He was wrong. It had happened to Dan. Dan was in the dining room, a ruined hulk of man overflowing the captain's chair, arms hanging loose, legs outstretched, shirt blood-soaked, beard blood-matted. Where his right eye should have been, bulged a blue-black lump large as half an apple. His nose was twisted and enlarged, his left eye only a slit in swollen, discolored flesh. He's wrecked the car, Randy thought. He went through the windshield and his face took along the steering wheel.

Helen laid a wet dish towel over Dan's eyes. Peyton, face white and pinched, stood behind her mother with another towel. It dripped. Except for Dan's choked breathing, the dripping was for a moment the only sound in the room.

Dan spoke. The words came out slowly and thickly, each an effort of will. "Was that you, Randy, who came in?"

"It's me, Dan. Don't try to talk yet." Shock, Randy thought, and probably concussion. He turned to Helen. "We should get him into bed. We have to get him upstairs."

"I don't know if he can make it," Helen said. "We could hardly get him this far." Helen's dress and Bill McGovern's arms were blood stained.

"Bill, with your help I can get him up all right."

So, with all his weight on their shoulders, they got Dan upstairs and stretched out on the sleigh bed. Bill said, "I'm going to be sick." He left them. Helen brought clean, wet towels. Dan's body shook and quivered. His skin grew clammy. He was having a chill. Randy lifted his thick wrist and after a time located the pulse. It was faint, uneven, and rapid. This was shock, all right, and dangerous. Randy said, "Whiskey!"

Helen said, "I'll handle this, Randy. No whiskey. Blankets."

He respected Helen's judgment. In an emergency such as this, Helen functioned. This was what she was made for. He found extra blankets in the closet. She covered Dan and disappeared. She returned with a glass of fluid, held it to Dan's lips, and said, "Drink this. Drink all you can."

"What are you giving him?" Randy asked.

"Water with salt and soda. Much better than whiskey for shock."

Dan drank, gagged, and drank more. "Keep pouring this into him," Helen ordered. "I'm going to see what's in the medicine cabinet."

"Almost nothing," Randy said. "Where's his bag? Everything's in there."

"They took it; and the car."

"Who took it?"

"The highwaymen."

He should have guessed that it hadn't been an accident. Dan was a careful driver and rarely were two cars on the same road. Traffic was no longer a problem. In his concern for Dan, he did not immediately think of what this loss meant to all of them.

Helen found peroxide and bandages. This, with aspirin, was almost all that remained of their reserve medical supply. She worked on Dan's face swiftly and efficiently as a professional nurse.

Randy felt nauseated, not at the sight of Dan's injuries—he had seen worse—but in disgust at the beasts who in callous cruelty had dragged down and maimed and destroyed the human dignity of this selfless man. Yet it was nothing new. It had been like this at some point in every civilization and on every continent. There were human jackals for every human disaster. He flexed his fingers, wanting a throat in them. He walked into the other room.

Lib's head lay across her arms on the bar. She was crying. When she raised her face it was oddly twisted as when a child's face loses form in panic or unexpected pain. She said, "What are you going to do about it, Randy?"

His rage was a hard cold ball in his stomach now. When he spoke it was in a monotone, the voice of someone else. "I'm going to execute them."

"Let's get with it."

"Yes. As soon as I find out who."

At eleven Dan Gunn came out of shock, relaxed and then slept for a few minutes. He awoke announcing he was hungry. He looked no better, he was in pain, but obviously he was out of danger.

Randy was dismayed at the thought of Dan, in his condition, loading his stomach with cold bream and catfish, orange juice, and remnants of salad. What he needed, coming out of shock, was hot, nourishing bouillon or broth. On occasion, when Malachai or Caleb discovered a gopher hole and Hannah Henry converted its inhabitant to soup, or when Ben Franklin successfully stalked squirrel or rabbit, such food was available; but not on this night.

The thought of broth triggered his memory. He shouted, "The iron rations!" and ran into his office. He threw open the teak sea chest and began digging.

Lib and Helen stood behind him and watched, perplexed. Helen said, "What's wrong with you now, Randy?"

"Don't give him any food until you see what I've got!" He was sure he had tucked the foil-covered carton in the corner closest to the desk. It wasn't there. He wondered whether it was something he had dreamed, but when he concentrated it seemed very real. It had been on the day before The Day, after his talk with Malachai. In the kitchen he had collected a few nourishing odds and ends, tinned or sealed, and dubbed them iron rations, for a desperate time. Now that the time was desperate, he couldn't find them.

He found the carton in the fourth corner he probed. He lifted it out, tore at the foil, and exposed it for them to see. "I put it away for an emergency. I'd forgotten it."

Lib whispered, "It's beautiful." She examined and fondled the jars and cans.

"There's beef broth in here—lots of other stuff." He gave up the carton. "Give him everything he wants."

Dan drank the broth and chewed hard candies. Randy wanted to question him but Helen stopped it. "Tomorrow," she said, "when he's stronger." Helen and Lib were still in the bedroom when Randy stretched out on the living-room couch. Graf jumped up and nuzzled himself a bed under Randy's arm, and they slept.

Randy awoke with a gunshot echoing in his ears and Graf, whining, struggling to be free of his arm. He heard a second shot. It was from the double twenty, he was sure, and it came from the direction of the Henrys' house. He slipped on his shoes and raced down the stairs, Graf following him. He grabbed the .45 from the hall table and went through the front door. Now was the time he wished he had live flashlight batteries.

The moon was up now so it wasn't too difficult, running down the path. From the moon's height he guessed it was three or four o'clock. Through the trees he saw a lantern blinking. He hoped Ben Franklin hadn't shot the shadows.

He wasn't prepared for what he saw at the Henrys' barn.

He saw them standing there, in a ring: Malachai with a lantern in one hand and in the other the ancient single-barreled shotgun that would sometimes shoot; Ben with his gun broken, extracting the empty shells, the Admiral in pajamas, Preacher in a nightshirt, Caleb, his eyes white-rimmed, tentatively poking with his spear at a dark form on the ground.

Randy joined the circle and put his hand on Ben Franklin's shoulder. At first he thought it was a wolf. Then he knew it was the biggest German shepherd he had ever seen, its tremendous jaws open in a white snarl of death. It wore a collar. Graf, tail whipping, sniffed the dead dog, whined, and retreated.

Randy leaned over and examined the brass plate on the collar. Malachai held the lantern closer. " 'Lindy,' "

Randy read aloud. " 'Mrs. H. G. Cogswell, Rochester, New York. Hillside five one-three-seven-nine.' "

"That dog come an awful long way from home," Preacher said.

"Probably his owners were visiting down here, or on vacation," Randy guessed.

"Well," Malachai said, "I can see why we've been losin' hens and how he could take off that pig. He was a mighty big dog, mighty big! I'll get rid of him in the day, Mister Randy."

Walking home, Ben Franklin said nothing. Suddenly he stopped, handed Randy the shotgun, covered his face with his hands, and sobbed. Randy squeezed his shoulder, "Take it easy, Ben." Randy thought it was reaction after strain, excitement, and perhaps terror.

"I did exactly what you told me," the boy said. "I heard him coming. I didn't hardly breathe. I didn't pull until I knew I couldn't miss. When he kicked and I thought he was getting up I let him have the choke barrel. I wouldn't have done it if I'd known he was a dog. Randy, I thought it was a wolf!"

Randy stopped in the path and said, "Look at me, Ben."

Ben looked up, tear streaks shining in the moonlight.

"It was a wolf," Randy said. "It wasn't a dog any longer. In times like these dogs can turn into wolves. You did just right, Ben. Here, take back your gun."

The boy took the gun, tucked it under his arm, and they walked on.

[10]

Randy was having a pleasant, recurrent, Before-The-Day dream. He was awaking in a hotel in Miami Beach and a waitress in a white cap was bringing his morning coffee on a rolling table. Sometimes the waitress looked like Lib McGovern and sometimes like a girl, name forgotten, he had met in Miami. She was always a waitress in the morning, but at night she became an air-line stewardess and they dined together in a little French restaurant where he embarrassed her by eating six chocolate éclairs. She said, as always, "Your coffee, Randy darling." He could hear her saying it and he could smell the coffee. He drew up his knees and hunched his shoulders and scrunched his head deeper into the pillow so as not to disturb the dream.

She shook his shoulder and he opened his eyes, still smelling coffee, and closed them again.

He heard her say, "Damn it, Randy, if you won't wake up and drink your coffee I'll drink it myself."

He opened his eyes wide. It was Lib, without a white cap. Incredibly, she was presenting him a cup of coffee. He reached his face out and tasted it. It burned his tongue delightfully. It was no dream. He swung his feet to the floor and took the saucer and cup. He said, "How?"

"How? You did it yourself, you absent-minded monster. Don't you remember putting a jar of coffee in what you called your iron rations?"

"No."

"Well, you did. A six-ounce jar of instant. And powdered cream. And, believe it or not, a pound of lump sugar. Real sugar, in lumps. I put in two. Everybody blesses you."

Randy lifted his cup, the fog of sleep gone entirely. "How's Dan?"

"Terribly sore, and stiff, but stronger. He had two cups of coffee and two eggs and, of course, orange juice."

"Did everybody get coffee?"

"Yes. We had Florence and Alice over for break-fast—it's ten o'clock, you know—and I put some in another jar and took it over to the Henrys. The Admiral was out fishing. We'll have to give him his share later. Helen has earmarked the broth and bouillon for Dan until he's better; and the candy for the children."

"Don't forget Caleb."

"We won't."

Again, he had slept in his clothes and felt grimy. He said, "I'm going to shower," and went into the bath-room. Presently he came out, towel around his middle, and began the hopeless process of honing the hunting knife. "Did you know," he said, "that Sam Hazzard has a straight razor? He's always used one. That's why his face is so spink and unscarred and clean. After I've talked to Dan I've got to see Sam."

"Why?"

"He's a military man and I need help for a military operation."

"Can I go with you?"

"Darling, you are my right arm. Where I goeth you can go—up to a point."

She watched him while he shaved. All women, he thought, from the youngest on up, seemed fascinated by his travail and agony.

Dan was sitting up in bed, his back supported by pil-lows, his right eye and the right side of his face hidden by bandages. His left eye was purpled but not quite so swollen as before. Helen sat in a straight-backed chair close to the pillows. She had been reading to him. Of all things, she had been reading the log of Lieutenant Ran-dolph Rowzee Peyton, heaved up from the teak sea chest during last night's burrowing for iron rations.

"Well, you're alive," Randy said. "Tell me the tale. Start at the beginning. No, start before the beginning. Where had you been and where were you going?"

"If the nurse will let me have one more cup of coffee—just one—I'll talk," Dan said. He spoke clearly and without hesitation. There had been no concussion.

Each day when he completed his calls it was Dan Gunn's custom to stop at the bandstand in Marines Park. One of the bandstand pillars had become a special bulletin board on which the people of Fort Repose tacked notices summoning the doctor when there was an emergency. Yesterday, there had been such a notice. It read:

> *Dr. Gunn—*
> *This morning (Friday) two of my children became violently ill. Kathy has a temperature of 105 and is out of her head. Please come. I am sending this note by Joe Sanchez who has a horse.*
> *Herbert Sunbury.*

Sunbury, like Dan, was a native New Englander. He had sold a florist shop in Boston, six years before, to migrate to Florida and operate a nursery. He had acquired acreage, built a house, and planted cuttings and seedlings on the Timucuan six miles upstream of the Bragg house.

Dan pushed the Model-A fast up River Road. Beyond the Bragg place the road became a series of curves, following the serpentine course of the river. Dan had delivered the last two of the Sunburys' four children. He liked the Sunburys. They were cheerful, industrious, and thoughtful. He knew that unless the emergency was real and pressing Herb would not have dispatched the note.

It was real. It was typhoid. It was the typhoid that Dan had half-expected and completely dreaded for weeks, months. Typhoid was the unwelcome, evil sister of any disaster in which the water supply was destroyed

or polluted and normal disposal of human waste difficult or impossible.

Betty Sunbury said the two older children had been
headachy and feverish for several days but not until Friday morning's early hours had they become violently ill,
a rosy rash developing on their torsos. Fortunately, Dan
could do something. Aspirin and cold compresses to re-
duce the fever, terramycin, which came very close to
being a specific for typhoid, until the disease was
licked; and he had the terramycin.

He reached into his bag and brought out the bottle,
hoarded for this moment. He could have used the anti-
biotic a score of times to cure other patients of other
diseases, but he had always made do with something
else, holding this single bottle as a charm against the
evil sister. Now it would probably save the Sunbury
children. In addition, he had enough vaccine to innoculate the elder Sunburys, the four-year-old, and the babies, and just enough left for Peyton and Ben Franklin,
when he returned to the house. Correct procedure
would be to innoculate the whole town

Dan questioned the Sunburys closely. They had been
very careful. Their drinking water came from a clear,
clean spring bubbling from limestone on high ground
across the road. Even so, they boiled it. All their foods,
except citrus, they cooked.

Dan looked out at the river gliding smoothly by. He
was sure the river was the villain. "You haven't eaten
any raw fish, or shrimp, or shellfish, have you?"

"Oh, no," Herb said. "Of course not."

"What about swimming? Do you swim in the river?"

Herb looked at Betty. "We don't," Betty said. "But
Kathy and Herbert, junior, they've been swimming in
the river since March."

"That's it, I guess," Dan said. "If the germs are in the
river, it only takes one gulp."

Somewhere near the headwaters of the Timucuan, or
in the great, mysterious swamps from which slender
streams sluggishly moved toward the St. Johns, a
typhoid-carrier had lived, undetected. A hermit, perhaps, or a respectable church woman in a small truck-

farm community. When this person's sanitary facilities failed, germ-laden feces had reach the rivers. Thus Dan reconstructed it, driving back toward town on the winding road.

Dan was so absorbed in his deductions and forebodings that he failed to see the woman sitting on the edge of the road until he was almost abreast of her.

He stepped on the brakes hard and the car jarred to a stop.

The woman wore jeans and a man's shirt. Her right knee was drawn almost up to her chin and she held her ankle in both hands, her body rocking as if in pain. A swatch of metallic blond hair curtained her features. Dan's first thought was that she had turned her ankle; his second, that she could be a decoy for an ambush. Yet highwaymen rarely operated on unfrequented and therefore unprofitable roads, and had never been reported this close to Fort Repose. The woman looked up, appealingly. He could easily have switched gears and gone on, but he was a physician, and he was Dan Gunn. He turned off the engine and got out of the car.

As soon as his feet touched the macadam he sensed, from her expression, that he had stepped into a trap. Whatever her face showed, it was not pain. When her eyes shifted, and she smiled, he knew her performance had been completed.

Behind him a man spoke:

"All right, Mac, you don't have to go any further."

Dan swung around. The man who had spoken was one of three, all oddly dressed and all armed. They had materialized from behind scrub palmettos at the side of the road. The leader was squat, and wore a checked gold cap and Bermuda shorts. His arms were abnormally long and hands huge. He carried a submachine gun and handled it like a toy. His belly bulged over his waistband. He ate well. Dan said, "Look, I'm a doctor. I'm the doctor of Fort Repose. I don't have anything you want."

The second man advanced on Dan. He was hatless, dressed in a striped sport shirt, and he gripped a baseball bat with both hands. "Get that, Mick?" he said. "He don't have nothing we want! Ain't that rich?"

The third man was not a man at all but a boy with fuzz on his chin. The boy wore levis, a wide-brimmed hat, high-heeled boots, and twin holster belts slung low. He stood apart from the others, legs spread, hefting a long-barreled revolver in each hand. He looked like an immature imitation of a Western badman holding up the Wells Fargo stage, but he seemed overly excited and Dan guessed him the most volatile and dangerous of the three.

The woman, grinning, got in the car, wrestled the back seat to the floor, and found the two bottles of bourbon Dan kept hidden there. "Just like you heard, Buster," she said. "The Doc keeps a traveling bar."

"That's my anesthetic," Dan said.

Without looking at the woman, the leader said, "Just leave the liquor in the car, Rumdum. We'll take everything as is. Start walking, Doc."

Dan said, "At least let me have my bag. All the instruments and medicines I've got are in there."

The boy giggled. "How about lettin' me put him out of his misery, Mick? He's too ignorant to live."

The man with the machine gun took two steps to the side. Dan knew why. The car's gas tank was in his line of fire.

The machine gun moved. "Get goin', Doc."

Dan thought of everything that was in his bag, including the typhoid shots for Peyton and Ben Franklin. He took a step toward the car. He saw the baseball bat swinging and tried to close with the man, knowing he was foolish, knowing that he was awkward and clumsy. The bat grazed his face and he tripped and fell. As he tried to rise he saw the boy's high-heeled boot coming at his eyes and the man with the bat danced to the side, ready to swing again. His head seemed to explode. In a final split-second of consciousness he thought, I am dead.

He awoke dazed, almost totally blind, and unable to determine whether he had been shot as well as slugged and beaten. He waited to die and wanted to die. When he didn't die he sat for a long time trying to decide which way was home. It required great effort to concentrate on the simplest matter. He would have preferred to stay where he was and complete his dying. But the sight of ants wheeling excitedly around the drying blood on the road made him uneasy. If he died there the ants would be all over him and in him by the time he was found. It would be better to die at home, cleanly. The sun was setting. The Sunbury house was east of Fort Repose. Therefore, he must go west. With the orange sun as his beacon, he began to crawl. When darkness came he rested, bathed his face in ditch water and drank it, too, and tried walking. He could walk perhaps a hundred yards before the road spun up to meet him. Then he would crawl. Thus, walking and crawling, he had finally reached the Bragg steps.

When Dan finished, Randy said, "It had to come, of course. The highwaymen killed off travel on the main highways and so now they've started on the little towns and the secondary roads. But in this case, Dan, it sounds like they were laying for you personally. I think they knew you were a doctor, and you'd be going way out River Road to the Sunburys', and certainly the woman knew you kept a couple of bottles of bourbon in the car."

"All they had to do," Dan said, "was hang around Marines Park, look at the notices on the bandstand, and ask questions. I didn't know any of them, but I think I've seen one before, the youngest. I used to see him hanging around Hockstatler's drugstore before The Day."

"They didn't have a car?"

"No."

"I guess what they wanted most was transportation."

"They won't get much. We had only two or three gallons of gas left." He added, apologetically, "I'm sorry, Randy. I was careless. I shouldn't have stopped. I've lost our transport, our medicines, and my tools."

Leaning over the bed, Randy's fingers interlocked. He unconsciously squeezed until the tendons on his forearm stood out like taut wires. He said, "Don't worry about it."

"Worst of all," Dan said, "I've lost my glasses. I guess they smashed when that goon slugged me with the bat. I won't be much good without glasses."

Randy knew that Dan's vision was poor. Dan was forced to wear bifocals. He was very nearsighted. "Don't you have another pair?" he asked.

"Yes—in the bag. I always kept my spare glasses in the bag because I was afraid I might lose or break the pair I was wearing, on a call." He sat up straight in bed, his face twisted. "Randy, I may never be able to get another pair of glasses."

Randy stood up. "I've got to start working on this, Dan."

"What are you going to do?"

"Find them and kill them." He said this in a matter-of-fact manner, as if announcing that he was going downtown to have his tires checked, in the time before The Day.

Dan said, "I'm afraid you're going at this wrong, Randy. Killing highwaymen is secondary. The important thing is the typhoid in the river. If you think things are bad now, wait until we have typhoid in Fort Repose. And it's not only Fort Repose. It goes from the Timucuan into the St. Johns and downriver to Sanford, Palatka, and the other towns. If they are still there."

"All I can do about typhoid is warn people, which you have done already and which I will do again. I can't shoot a germ. I'm concerned with the highwaymen right now, this minute. Next, they'll start raiding the houses. It's as inevitable as the fact that they left the main highways and ambushed you on River Road. Typhoid is bad. So is murder and robbery and rape. I am an officer in the Reserve. I have been legally designated to keep order when normal authority breaks down. Which it certainly has here. And the first thing I must do to keep order is execute the highwaymen. That's perfectly plain. See you later, Dan."

Randy turned to Helen. "Take care of him. Feed him up," he said, a command.

Walking beside him toward the Admiral's house, Lib found it difficult to keep pace. She had never seen Randy look and speak and act like this before. She held his arm, and yet she felt he had moved away from her. He did not seem anxious to talk, confide in her, or ask her opinion, as he usually did. He had moved into man's august world of battle and violence, from which she was barred. She held tighter to his arm. She was afraid.

The admiral, freshly shaven and pink-faced, was in his den, touching whale oil to the recoil mechanism of an automatic shotgun. "I was wondering," he said to Randy, "whether you would be around here or I should come to you. How's Dan?"

"He'll be all right. We lost the car and the medicines and the last of the bourbon but we didn't lose our doctor. The most important thing we lost were his glasses. He's very nearsighted."

"You forgot something," the Admiral said, hardly looking up from his work. "We not only have lost transport but communications. We no longer have a way to recharge batteries. This battery I have now—" he nodded at the radio—"is good for perhaps another eight to ten hours. After that—" he looked up—"nothing. Silence. What do you plan to do?"

"I plan to kill them. But I don't know how to find them. I came to talk to you about it."

Lib said, "May I interrupt? Don't look at me that way, Randy. I'm not trying to interfere in your business. I just wanted to say I brought the Admiral's coffee. While you're talking, I thought I'd boil water and make a cup for him."

The Admiral said, absently, "Kettle's in the fireplace."

She went into the living room. It was silly, but sometimes the Admiral irritated her. The Admiral made her feel like a messboy.

Sam Hazzard laid the automatic sixteen gently on the desk. "Ever since I heard about it, I've been thinking," he said. "You have to go get them. They won't come to you. Not only that, they may be a hundred miles from here by now."

"I think they're right around here," Randy said. "One of the gang was a local drugstore cowboy, now toting two real guns. And they don't have enough gas to get far. I think they'll try to score a few more times before they move on. Even when they're gone, others will come. We have the problem whether it's this particular gang or another gang. I'm going to try to form a provisional company."

"Vigilantes?"

"No. A company under martial law. So far as I know I'm the only active Army Reserve officer in town so I guess it's up to me."

"Then what do you do?"

Lib came in and set a cup beside each of them. She found a clear space at the far end of the room-length desk, boosted herself up, and attempted to appear inconspicuous.

"Suppose I organized a patrol on foot? Set up roadblocks?" Randy suggested.

"The highwaymen are mobile, you're not," the Admiral said. "If they see an armed patrol, or a roadblock, they'll simply keep out of your way."

Randy said, "Well, we can't just sit here and wait for them."

"All this I've been thinking," The Admiral said. "Also I was thinking of the Q-ships we used in the first World War."

Lib started to speak but decided it would be unwise. It was Randy who said, "I remember, vaguely, reading about Q-ships but I don't remember much about it. Enlighten me, Sam."

"Q-ships were usually auxiliary schooners or wornout tramps, targets on which a German submarine captain wouldn't be likely to waste a torpedo but would prefer to sink with gunfire. Concealed a pretty hefty battery behind screens that looked like deck loads. Drill was to prowl submarine alley unescorted and helpless-looking. The sub sees her and surfaces. Sometimes the

Q-ship had a panic party that took to the boats. Best part of the act. Soon as the sub opened fire with its deck gun the Q-ship ran up the flag and unmasked the battery. Blammy! It was quite effective."

"Very ingenious. But what has it got to do with highwaymen?"

"Nothing at all, unless you can put a four-wheeled Q-ship on the roads around Fort Repose."

Randy shrugged. "We're not mobile. Plenty of cars we could use—for instance, yours, Sam—but gasoline is practically nonexistent. We might have to cruise around for days before they tackled us. I might be able to requisition a gallon or two here and there but then the word would get around and they'd be watching for us."

Lib had to speak. "Could I make a suggestion? I think Rita Hernandez and her brother must have gasoline. They're the big traders in town, aren't they?"

Randy had tried to wipe Rita out of his mind. They were even, they were quits. He wanted nothing from Rita any more. He said, "It's true that if anybody's holding gas, it's Rita."

"Not only that," Lib said, "but they have that grocery truck. Can you imagine anything more enticing to highwaymen than a grocery truck? They won't really think it's filled with groceries, of course, but psychologically it would be irresistible."

Sam Hazzard smiled with his eyes, as if light from within penetrated the opaque gray. "There you have it, Randy! Nice staff work, my girl!"

"Also," she said, "I think it would be a good idea if I drove. They'd be sure to think it was easy pickings with a woman driving."

"You will like the devil drive!" Randy said. "You will stay at home and guard the house, you and Ben Franklin." And the two men went on talking and planning, as if they already possessed the truck with full tank, and she was left out of it again. At least, she thought, if it really worked, she had contributed something.

The Admiral emphasized that whatever was done must be done quietly. Randy decided he could not go to the Hernandez house until after dark. It was not impossible that the highwaymen were holed up in Pistolville, or had contacts there. If Pistolville saw him drive off in Rita's truck, the news would be all over town within a few hours. Finally, the Admiral asked the crucial question—would Rita cooperate? Was she discreet?

"Rita wants to hold what she has," Randy said. "Rita wants to live. She is realistic."

There was one more thing he must do before he left the Admiral. He sat at the typewriter and pecked out the orders.

ORDER NO. 1—TOWN OF FORT REPOSE

1. In accordance with the proclamation of Mrs. Josephine Vanbruuker-Brown, Acting President of the United States, and the declaration of Martial Law, I am assuming command of the Town of Fort Repose and its environs.
2. All Army, Navy, and Air Force reservists and all members of the National Guard, together with any others with military experience who will volunteer, will meet at the bandstand at 1200 hours, Wednesday, 20 April. I propose to form a composite company to protect this town.

ORDER NO. 2

1. Two cases of typhoid have been diagnosed in the Sunbury family, upper River Road. It must be assumed that both the Timucuan and St. Johns are polluted.
2. All water will be boiled before drinking. Do not eat fruits or greens that have been washed in unboiled water.

ORDER NO. 3

1. Dr. Daniel Gunn, our only physician, has been beaten and robbed by highwaymen.
2. The penalty for robbery or pillage, or for harboring highwaymen, or for failure to make known information concerning their whereabouts or movements, is death by hanging.

All these orders he signed, "Randolph Rowzee Bragg, 1st. Lt. AUS (Reserve) (02658988)."

Lib reading over his shoulder, said, "Why wait until Wednesday to form your company?"

"I want the highwaymen to think that they have plenty of time," Randy said. "I want them to laugh at us."

There were a number of ways by which Randy could have traveled the three miles to Marines Park, and then the two additional miles to the Hernandez house on the outer fringe of Pistolville. The Admiral had offered to take him as far as the town dock in his outboard cruiser, now converted to sail. But Sam Hazzard had not as yet added additional keel to the boat, so it would sideslip badly on a tack. Sam could get him to Marines Park all right, but on the return trip might be unable to make headway against current and wind and be left stranded. Randy could have borrowed Alice Cooksey's bicycle, but decided that this might make him conspicuous in Pistolville. He could have ridden Balaam, the mule, but if he succeeded in persuading Rita to let him have the truck and gasoline, how would Balaam get home? Balaam didn't fit in a panel truck. Besides, he was not sure that Balaam should ever be risked away from the Henrys' fields and barn. The only mule in Timucuan County was beyond price. In the end, he decided to walk.

He set out after dark. Lib escorted him as far as the bend in the road. She had tacked his notices firmly to a square of plywood which he was to nail to the bandstand pillar. Thus, she had explained, they would not be lost or overlooked among the offers to trade fishhooks or lighter flints, and the pleas for kerosene or kettles. Across the top of the board she had printed, "OFFICIAL BULLETINS."

Randy wore stained dungarees, old brown fishing sneakers, and a floppy black hat borrowed from Two-Tone. His pistol was concealed in a deep pocket. When walking Pistolville at night, he wanted to look as if he belonged there.

When he told Lib it was time to turn back, she kissed him. "How long will it take you, darling?" she asked.

"Depends on whether I get the truck. Counting the stop at the park to nail up the orders, I should get there in less than two hours. After that, I don't know. Depends on Rita."

"If you're not home by midnight," she said, "I'll come after you. With a shotgun." She sounded half-serious. In the past few weeks she had been more tender to him, embarrassingly solicitous of his safety, more jealous of his time. She was possessive, which was natural. They were lovers, when there was time, and place and privacy, and respite from fatigue and hunger and the dangers and responsibilities of the day.

He walked on alone under the oak arch excluding starlight, secure in night's black velvet cloak yet walking silently, eyes, ears, and even nose alert. So he had learned, in the dark hammocks as a boy hunting game, in the dark mountains as a man hunting man. Before The Day, except in hunting or in war, a five- or ten-mile walk would have been unthinkable. Now it was routine for all of them except Dan and after Dan got out of bed it would become routine for him too. But all their shoes were wearing out. In another month or two Ben Franklin and Peyton would be without shoes entirely. Not only were the children walking (or running) everywhere but their feet inconsiderately continued to grow, straining canvas and leather. Randy told himself that he must discover whether Eli Blaustein still held shoes. He knew what Blaustein wanted—meat.

Marines Park was empty. As he nailed up his order board an animal scuttled out from under the bandstand. At first he thought it a possum but when he caught its silhouette against the starlit river he saw it was an armadillo.

Walking through the business section, he wondered whether armadillos were good eating. Before The Day he had heard someone say that there were several hundred thousand armadillos in Florida. This was strange, because before the first boom there had been no armadillos at all. Randy's father had related the story. Some real estate promoter on the East Coast had imported two from Texas for a roadside zoo. Knowing nothing of the habits of armadillos, the real estate man had penned them behind chicken wire. When darkness fell, the armadillos instantly burrowed out, and within a few years armadillos were undermining golf greens and dumping over citrus trees from St. Augustine to Palm Beach. They had spread everywhere, having no natural enemies in the state except automobiles. Since the automobile had been all but exterminated by the hydrogen bomb, the armadillo population was certain to multiply. Soon there would be more armadillos than people in Florida.

It was Saturday night, but in the business blocks of Yulee and St. Johns no light showed nor did he see a human being. In the residential area perhaps half the houses showed a light, but rarely from more than one room. He had not seen a moving vehicle since leaving home, and not until he reached the pine shanties and patchwork bungalows of Pistolville did he see a person. These people were shadows, swiftly fading behind a half-opened door or bobbing from house to house. It was night, and Fort Repose was in fear.

He was relieved when he saw lights in the Hernandez house. Anything could have happened since he and Dan had stopped there. Pete could have died and Rita could have decamped; or she could have been killed, the house pillaged, and everything she was holding, including the truck and gasoline, stolen.

He knocked on the door.

"Who is it?" Rita's voice said. He knew she would have the shotgun up and ready.

"Randy."

She opened the door. She was holding a shotgun, as he guessed. She stared at his costume. "Come in. Looking for a handout?"

"In a sense, yes."

"What happened? Your two women run you off?"

As she laid down the gun the burn still showed on her ring finger. He said, "How's Pete?"

"Weaker. How's Doctor Gunn?"

"You heard about it, then?"

"Sure. I hear all the bad news in a hurry nowadays. We call it lip radio."

The word had come to town, Randy guessed, via Alice Cooksey, earlier in the day. Just as Alice brought the town news to River Road, so each day she carried the news from River Road to town. Once spoken in the library, the news would spread through Fort Repose, street to street and house to house. He said, "You know Doctor Gunn lost his bag with all his instruments and what drugs he had left, and his glasses. So, if we can, we have to get those highwaymen and that's why I came to you, Rita."

"They're not Pistolville people," she said. "These Pistolville crackers hardly have got gumption enough to rob each other. Now I heard them described and one of them—the young one with two guns—was probably Leroy Settle, a punk who lived on the other side of town. His mother still lives there, I think. Maybe if you stake out his house you'll get a shot at him."

"I don't want him in particular," Randy said. "I want them all. I want them and everybody like them." And he told her what his plan was, exactly, and why he must have the grocery truck and the gasoline, if she had any. He knew he must trust her entirely or not at all.

She listened him out and said nothing.

"If you are left alone here, Rita," he said, "With all the canned food and other stuff you've got, you're bound to become a target. When they've cleaned out what's on the roads, they'll start on the houses."

"I'm way ahead of you." Her eyes met his steadily. She was evaluating him, and all the chances, all the odds. She made her decision. "I think you can get away with it, Randy."

"You're holding gas, then?"

"Certainly I'm holding gas. Fifteen gallons under the back steps. You can have it, and the truck. Anything you don't use I expect back."

He rose. "What're you going to tell people when they see your truck is gone?"

"I'm going to tell them it was stolen. I'm going to tell them it was loaded with choice trade goods and that while I was in the bedroom, attending to Pete, somebody jimmied the ignition and stole it. And to make it sound good I'm going to let off a blast with this gun when you whip out of the driveway. The news will get around fast, don't worry. It'll get to the highwaymen and they'll be looking for the truck. That should help, shouldn't it?"

"It should make it perfect."

"Go out the back way. Load the cans in the back of the truck, quietly. There's enough gas in the tank to take you out River Road. I'll salute you when you hit the street."

He said, "You're a smart girl, Rita."

"Am I?" She held out her left hand to show the black circle left by the radioactive diamond ring. "I've got a wedding band. I was married to an H-bomb. Will it ever go away, Randy?"

"Sure," he said, hoping it would. "Dan will look at it again when he's better."

He walked through the hallway and kitchen and out into the darkness. He found the three five-gallon cans under the back steps, opened the truck's rear doors, and silently loaded the gasoline. He got in and stepped on the starter. The engine turned over, protesting. Rita had been careless, he guessed, and had forgotten to fill the battery with distilled water, for it was close to dead. He tried again and the engine caught. He nursed the choke until it ran smoothly, backed out of the Hernandez carport, turned sharply in the yard, shifted gears, and roared out on the street. He glimpsed Rita's silhouette in the doorway, the gun rising to her shoulder, and for an awful instant thought she was aiming at him. Red flame leaped out of the muzzle. At the first corner he cut away from Augustine Road and followed rutted dirt streets until he was clear of Pistolville. He saw no other cars, in motion, on the way home.

It was past eleven when he drove the truck into the garage and closed the doors so no casual passerby or visitor would see it. The lights were out in Florence's house and in his own house only a single light burned, in his office window. That would be Lib, waiting up for him. He had urged the women to get to bed at their usual hour or earlier, for they planned to go to the Easter sunrise services in Marines Park.

This was good. It was good that they should all be there, so that no one would guess of unusual activity out on River Road. From a less practical standpoint he felt good about it too. He was, as a matter of fact, surprised at their anticipation and enthusiasm. Many things had happened in the past few days and yet their conversation always come back to the Easter services. People hadn't been like that before The Day. He could not imagine any of them voluntarily getting up before dawn and then walking three miles on empty stomachs to watch the sun come up, sing hymns, and listen to sermons however short. He wished he could walk with them. He couldn't. It was necessary that he remain there to complete his plans with Sam Hazzard and also to work on the truck. Walking toward the house, he wondered at this change in people and concluded that man was a naturally gregarious creature and they were all starved for companionship and the sight of new faces. Marines Park would be their church, their theater, their assembly hall. Man absorbed strength from the touch of his neighbor's elbow. It was these reasons, perhaps, that accounted for the success of the old-time Chautauquas. It could be that and something more— the discovery that faith had not died under the bombs and missiles.

She wasn't upstairs. She was waiting in the gloom of the porch. She said, "I saw you drive it in. It's beautiful. Did you get the gas to go with it?"

"Total of seventeen gallons including what's in the tank. We can cruise for a day or two if we take it easy. Are you tired, darling?"

"Not too."

"If you're going to be up at five with the others you really ought to be in bed."

"I've been waiting for you, Randy. I worry. I'm not tired, really."

They walked through the grove down to the dock.

The river whispered, the quarter-moon showed its

profile, the stars moved. She lay on her back, head resting on her locked fingers, looking up at the stars.

His eyes measured her—long, slender, curved as if for flight, skin coppery, hair silvered by the night. "You're a beautiful possession," he said. "I wish we had a place of our own so I could keep you. I wish we had just one room to ourselves. I wish we were married."

Instantly she said, "I accept."

"I'm not sure how we'd go about it. Last I heard the courthouse in San Marco wasn't operating. For a while it was an emergency shelter like our school. I don't know what they use it for now but certainly not for issuing marriage licenses. And the county clerk has disappeared. I heard in the park that he took his family and started for an uncontaminated zone in Georgia where he used to live."

Without moving her head she said, "Randy, under martial law, can't you make your own rules?"

"I hadn't thought about it. I suppose so."

"Well, make one."

"You're serious, aren't you?"

"I certainly am. It may be an old-fashioned, Before-The-Day attitude but if I'm going to have children I'd like to be married."

"Children! Are you going to have a baby?" Thought of the difficulties, dangers, and complexities of having a baby, under their present circumstances, appalled him.

"I don't know. I can't say that I am, but then again I can't say that I'm not, can I? I would like to marry you tomorrow before you go off chasing highwaymen." She turned on her side, to face him. "It isn't really convention. It is only that I love you very much, and that if anything happened—I don't have any bad premonitions, dear, but you and I know that a bad thing could happen—well, if anything happened I would want the child to have your name. You'd want that too, wouldn't you?"

"Yes," Randy said, "I would want that very much. I'm not going to put the truck on the road until late in the afternoon—that's when the highwaymen took Dan—so there'll be time."

"That's nice," she said. "It'll be nice to marry on Easter Sunday."

He took her hands and drew her up and held her. Over her shoulder he saw a pair of green eyes and a dark snout sliding downstream past the edge of the dock. It was spring and the gators were out of their holes. He had heard somewhere that the Seminoles ate gator meat. Cut their tails into steaks. It was a source of meat that should be investigated. He knew he shouldn't be thinking about food at this time but he was hungry again.

[11]

Elizabeth McGovern and Randolph Bragg were married at noon that Easter Sunday. The bride wore the same white silk dress she had worn to the sunrise service in Marines Park. She was unsteady on high heels, for she had not worn heels since The Day.

The groom wore his Class A uniform with the bold patch of the First Cavalry Division on his arm and the ribbons of the Korean War and Bronze Star on his chest, along with the blue badge of the combat infantryman. He wore the uniform not because of the wedding but because it was required in the radioed orders to reservists assuming active duty, such as ambushing and killing highwaymen, which he presently intended to do.

The bride was given away by her father, W. Foxworth McGovern, the retired Cleveland manufacturer. Bill McGovern, who had been helping Malachai cut gun ports in the thin steel sides and rear doors of the grocery truck, wore greasy dungarees. A chisel had slipped and one of his hands was bleeding.

The best man was Doctor Daniel Gunn. He was clad in a tentsized, striped bathrobe. Grinning through his red beard, his head bandaged, a square gauze patch covering his right eye, he looked like a turbaned Mediterranean pirate.

Among the guests was Rear Admiral Samuel P. Hazzard (USN, retired) who wore khaki shorts, a khaki hunting vest bulging with buckshot shells, and during the ceremony held his gold-braided cap across his stomach.

The matron-of-honor was Mrs. Helen Bragg, the pre-

261

sumed widow of Colonel Mark Bragg. She furnished the wedding ring, stripping it from her own finger.

The ceremony was held in the high-ceilinged parlor of the Bragg house. The marriage was performed by the Reverend Clarence Henry, pastor emeritus of the Afro-Repose Baptist Church.

Randy was certain it was perfectly legal. It was performed under his Order No. 4, written that morning in Sam Hazzard's house.

Malachai and Bill McGovern had been working on the truck, and Randy was breakfasting with Dan Gunn, when the women and children returned from Marines Park. The services had been wonderful, they said, but the news they brought was terrible. During the night highwaymen had raided the isolated home of Jim Hickey, the beekeeper, on the Pasco Creek Road. They had killed Jim and his wife. The two children had walked to Fort Repose and found their aunt's home. Whether it was the same band that had beaten Dan Gunn was uncertain. The Hickey children were inarticulate and hysterical with fear and shock.

Randy, raging for immediate retaliation, had raced to the Admiral's house with the news. The Admiral's experience in meeting the unpredictable and brutish pranks of war had saved them from premature or imprudent action. "Wasn't this sort of thing exactly what we expected?" Sam Hazzard asked.

"I suppose so, but dammit—"

"I don't think we should change our plans by so much as a minute. If we put out with the truck now we'll just burn fuel for nothing. These people operate like beasts, Randy. Having gorged themselves in the night they sleep through the mornings, perhaps through the whole day."

Randy, recognizing the sense of this, had calmed himself. They had talked of the wedding, and the legal problems attending martial law, and the Admiral had helped him in framing Order No. 4. It read:

Until county offices resume operations and normal communications are reestablished between this town and the

Timucuan County seat, the following regulations will govern marriages and births in Fort Repose.

1. Marriages can be performed by any ordained minister. Marriage licenses and health certificates are waived.

2. Marriage certificates will be issued by the presiding minister, and will be valid when signed by the contracting parties, the minister, and two witnesses.

3. So that a permanent record may be preserved, a copy of the certificate will be left at the Fort Repose Library. I designate Librarian Alice Cooksey custodian of these records. I designate Miss Florence Wechek her deputy.

4. Birth records, signed by the attending physician or midwife, or by the mother and any witnesses if medical attention is unavailable, will be deposited in the same manner.

One copy of this order is to be kept with the records in the library. This order is retroactive to The Day, so that any births or marriages that have occurred since The Day may be properly recorded.

Randy signed Order No. 4 and said, "Well, when the rules are off you make your own."

"This is a good one," Sam Hazzard said. "I wonder what they're doing elsewhere?"

"Elsewhere?"

"There must be hundreds of towns in the same fix we're in—local authority collapsed or inoperative, communications out. I fancy that elsewhere they're not doing so good."

"How could they be worse?" Randy was thinking of what had happened to Dan Gunn and the Hickeys.

"They could be," the Admiral said, positively.

Randy had gone to see Preacher next. "Preacher," he said, "you're an ordained minister, aren't you?"

"I sure am," Preacher said. "I am not only ordained but in my church I can ordain people."

"Would you mind marrying Miss McGovern and me? We don't have a regular courthouse license, naturally, but I have fixed it up to make it legal under martial law."

"Miss McGovern told me you was going to wed, Mister Randy. I will be happy to marry you. I don't need papers. I've joined maybe a thousand pairs in my life. Some had papers, some didn't. Some stuck, some didn't. The papers didn't make the difference. It's the people, not the papers."

So they were married, in a room filled with flowers of the season and furniture of less bitter centuries and people of all ages.

Randy produced the certificate and when Preacher signed it he signed "Rev. Clarence Henry," and Randy realized that this was the first time he had ever known Preacher's full name although Preacher had always been there.

Randy had found a large-scale county map in his desk and they had planned their movement as carefully as a Q-ship captain plotting his course through submarine alley. There were four roads that led out from Fort Repose. River Road stretched east along the Timucuan until it swung into a main highway to the beaches. The Pasco Creek Road ran north, the San Marco Road west, from the bridge across the St. Johns. A narrow, substandard road followed the St. Johns toward its headwaters.

The map, with two crosses to mark where the highwaymen had stopped Dan Gunn and killed the Hickeys, lay on the garage floor. They bent over it, Randy tracing the route they would take. The highwaymen could be anywhere. They could be one band, or two, or more. They could be gone entirely. It was all guesswork, and yet it was necessary to plan the route so as to cover the most territory using the least amount of gas, for when the truck's tank was empty, that would be all. There was no reserve, not anywhere. They would take River Road first because it was closest. After twelve miles a little-used lateral led toward Pasco Creek and they would go almost to Pasco Creek and then cut into the road for Fort Repose. Thus, by using the clay or washboard laterals, they could avoid retracing the same highway and save a few miles.

On his hands and knees, his seagoing cap pushed back on his pink head, the Admiral murmured, " 'Give me a fast ship for I intend to go in harm's way'—Paul Jones. Remember, Randy, this should be a very slow ship. The slower we go the less gas we use and the more chance they have of spotting us."

Randy was going to drive. Malachai, Sam Hazzard, and Bill McGovern were to be concealed in the body of the truck. Randy said, "I don't like to drive slow but I can. I think about twenty miles an hour is right. Anything slower would look suspicious."

He checked the weapons. They were taking everything that might be handy—the automatic sixteen for the Admiral and the double twenty for Bill McGovern. Malachai would have the carbine. The big Krag, long as a Kentucky squirrel rifle and as unwieldy, would be in reserve. From Dan's description of how the highwaymen had acted, Randy guessed that the fire fight, when it came, would be close in, and the shotguns of greater value than the rifles. He himself, alone behind the wheel, would have only the .45 automatic on the seat beside him. That, and the hunting knife which was almost, but not quite, razor sharp, in a sheath at his belt.

Randy walked around the truck for a final look. He thought he was doing something that was familiar and then he remembered that he had seen aircraft commanders do this before takeoff. He examined the tires. They were good. The battery water had been replenished and the battery run up. Malachai and Bill had done a good job on the gun ports, fairing them into the big, painted letters, "AJAX SUPER-MARKET." On each side, one port in the "J" and one in the "M." Camouflage. The holes cut into the rear doors, under the tiny glass windows, were more conspicuous. Randy went outside and returned with a handful of mud. He spread it on the edges of the ports, erasing the glint of freshly cut metal.

It was four o'clock, the time to sortie. "You know your positions," he said. "Sam, you have the starboard side. Bill takes the port. Malachai, the stern. If I see your fire can't be effective from inside I'll yell, 'Out!' and everybody gets out fast while I cover you."

Then, at the last second, there was a change.

Malachai suggested it. "Mister Randy, I want to say something. I don't think you ought to drive. I think I ought to drive."

Randy was furious, but he held his voice down. "Let's not get everything screwed up now. Get in, Malachai."

Malachai made no move. "Sir, that uniform. It don't go with the truck."

"They won't see it until they stop us," Randy said. "Then it'll be too late. Anyway, all sorts of people are wearing all sorts of clothes. I'll bet you'd see highwaymen in uniforms if they got their hands on them."

"That ain't all, sir," Malachai said. "It's your face. It's white. They're more likely to tackle a black face than a white face. They see my face they say, 'Huh, here's something soft and probably with no gun.' So they relax. Maybe it gives us that extra second, Mister Randy."

Randy hesitated. He had confidence in Malachai's driving and in his judgment and courage. But it was the driver who would have to do the talking, if there was any talking, and who would have to keep his hands off the pistol. That would be the hardest thing.

The Admiral spoke, very carefully. "Now Randy, I'm not trying to outrank you. You're the Captain. You're in command and it's your decision. But I think Malachai is right. Dungarees and a black face are better bait than a uniform and a white face."

Randy said, "Okay. You're right. You drive, Malachai. You take the pistol up front. Keep it out of sight. There is only one thing to remember. When they stop us they'll all be watching you. They don't know we're here. They'll be watching you and they'll kill you if you go for your gun. So leave your gun alone until we start shooting."

Malachai grinned and said, "Yes, sir," and they got in and departed. Looking through the glass in the rear door, Randy saw his wife and Helen and Dan on the porch. They were waving. Peyton was there too but she was not waving. She had her face buried in her mother's dress.

They drove east on River Road. After a few miles Randy told Malachai to look for signs of the place where Dan Gunn had been decoyed and beaten. They found a sign. Since there was no longer any care of the roads, the grass had grown high on the shoulders and in one place it was trampled. In a ditch, nearby, they discovered slivers of broken glass. Then they found the twisted and empty frame of Dan's glasses. The frame was useless and yet Randy picked it up and shoved it in a pocket. A lawyer's gesture, he thought. Evidence.

They drove on, past the Sunbury home. Randy was tempted to order a stop to inquire about the children's typhoid. Dan would want to know. He did not stop. The Sunburys were good people and he trusted them, but the truck was a secret, a military secret, and it was senseless to expose it.

River Road was clear. Nothing moved on River Road. They took the lateral north. Even though Malachai avoided the worst potholes and drove with exasperating deliberation, it was rough riding. It shook up Bill McGovern and Sam Hazzard. They were older and they would tire.

Near Pasco Creek they passed a group of inhabited shacks. Approaching them, Malachai called back, "People!"

Randy turned and looked over Malachai's shoulder. He could see, from behind the front seat, but not be seen. He saw two children scurry indoors and at another place a bearded man crouched behind a woodpile, training a gun on the truck. He made no hostile move, but the muzzle tracked them. It was obvious that few people traveled this road and those who did were not welcome.

Randy was relieved when they turned into the better road toward Fort Repose. They were all stiff by then, for it was impossible to stand upright in the panel truck. The Admiral and Bill could sit cross-legged on the floor and view the landscape through their ports, but Randy had to half-crouch to see through the rear windows. When the truck reached higher ground, where the road was straight and they could see anything approach for nearly a mile, he told Malachai to stop. "We'll take ten," he said.

He threw open the back doors and got out, groaning, feeling permanently warped. He walked, waving his arms and flexing his knees. Bill McGovern shuffled down the road, humpbacked. The Admiral tried to stretch, and a joint or tendon cracked audibly. He cursed. Malachai grinned.

"Now I see why you wanted to drive!" Randy said. He looked both ways. Nothing was coming. He went back to the truck and found the thermos Lib had given him. He opened it, expecting water. It was sweetened black coffee. "Look!" he said. "Look what Lib—my wife did for us!" He knew it was the last of the jar.

There was a cup for each, but they decided to take only half a cup then, saving the rest for the tag end of evening when they might need it more.

They got back into the truck and continued the patrol, past the Hickey house, empty, door open, windows wantonly smashed. Randy noticed that the beekeeper's car was gone. Jim Hickey, with such valuable trading goods as honey and beeswax, must have been holding gasoline. In the past month anyone who had it would have traded gas for honey. The objective of the highwaymen was probably the car and the gas, Randy deduced, rather than honey. This conclusion disheartened him. The highwaymen might be hundreds of miles from Fort Repose now.

Nearing Fort Repose—they must avoid being seen in the town—they turned off on a winding, high-crowned clay road that ran two miles to an antique covered bridge across the St. Johns. Once across the river they would turn south and shortly thereafter hit the road to San Marco.

Rattling over the clay washboard, it seemed hardly worth while to keep a watch from the back, and yet Randy did. Suddenly he saw that they were being followed. He had seen no car on the Pasco Creek Road before making the turn. They had passed no car on the clay lateral, nor any houses either. The car was simply there, following them at a respectable distance, making no effort to catch them and yet not dropping back. He recalled an abandoned citrus packing shed at the turn. It must have been concealed there. Randy called so that Malachai could clearly hear, "We've got company—about three hundred yards back."

He strained his eyes through the dirty little rear windows. It was difficult to make them focus, like trying to train a gun from a bouncing jeep, and it was almost dusk. It was a late model light gray hardtop or sedan and Jim Hickey had owned such a car but all makes looked pretty much alike and it seemed half of them were either light gray or off-white. He called to Malachai, "Speed up a little. See what happens."

Malachai increased their speed to forty or forty-five. The car behind maintained its distance, exactly, as if it were tied to them. This proved nothing. This would be standard operating procedure for an honest citizen following a strange truck on a lonely, unfrequented road. He wouldn't want to get too close, but he was probably in a hurry to get home before dark. So if the truck sped up, he would too. "Drop back to twenty," Randy ordered.

The truck slowed. So did the car. Again, this proved nothing except caution.

Randy turned to Sam Hazzard and Bill McGovern. "This fellow behind us is either an innocent bystander or he's herding us."

"Herding us?" Bill said.

"Herding us into the gun of some pal up front." They hit a smoother strip of road and Randy could see two men in the car. He thought the back was empty but he couldn't be sure. "Two of them. Both men."

They rode on, silently. This was entirely different from a patrol in war when you went out in fear and despite your fear, hoping you would find no trouble. His only fear was that they might miss them, exhaust their gas in futile cruising, and lose their one best chance to wipe them out. This was a personal matter and a matter of survival. It was like having a nest of coral snakes under the house. You had to go in after them and kill them or certainly one day they would kill a child or your dog. In a matter such as this, the importance of your own life diminished. So he prayed that the men behind were highwaymen.

In a minute or two he knew that they were, because the opposite end of the narrow, covered bridge was blocked. They were being herded into a cul-de-sac and the tactical situation was changed and their plan useless. There would be no field of fire from the side ports of the truck. The fight would have to be made entirely from front and rear. He said, "Keep going." They had to drive right into it. If they stopped short of the bridge and jumped out to make their fight at a distance then the highwaymen could shoot and run. They had to get in close.

Malachai kept going.

"Sam, you and Bill take the ones in back," Randy said. "I'll help Malachai in front. Forget the sides."

The Admiral and Bill crawled to the rear. Randy crouched behind Malachai's back. He checked the carbine. It was ready. He shifted an extra clip to his shirt pocket where it would be handiest.

The block at the opposite end of the bridge was their Model-A, its boxy profile unmistakable. A man waited at each bumper. You could ram the car but you could not ram the men so this tactic would do no good. Randy recognized them from Dan's description. The one with gorilla arms and the submachine gun stood at the front. The gun was a Thompson. The man with the bat was on the other side. He carried a holstered pistol too, but from the way he hefted the bat, like a hitter eager to step to the plate, the bat was his weapon. Four men, then, instead of three. And no woman. Understandable. The personnel of these bands probably changed from day to day. "Right up to them," he told Malachai. "Close."

The wheels hit the first planks of the bridge and Malachai slowed.

Randy saw the muzzle of the Thompson rise. This was the one he had to get. He pushed the butt of the carbine into Bill McGovern's ribs. He said, "Let them come right up to you. Let 'em come right in with us if they want. We've got troubles up front."

Bill nodded. The rhythmic timpani beat of tires on planks stopped. They were twenty feet from the Model-A. The man with the bat advanced toward the left side of the truck. The Tommy gunner stayed where he was. In his light Randy doubted that they could see anything in the truck body but he did not stir. He was immobile as a sack. He whispered, "Make the son of a bitch with the gun come to us. Make him move, make him come."

The man with the bat was three feet from Malachai and five feet from the carbine's muzzle. If he looked into the truck cab Randy would have to shoot him and in that case the Tommy gunner might get them all. There was nothing more Randy could say or do. He could not even whisper. It was all up to Malachai now.

The man whacked his bat viciously against the door. "What you got in there, boy?"

"I ain't got nuthin, boss," Malachai whined. From the set of his right shoulder Randy knew Malachai had his right hand on the .45, but he was acting dumb and talking dumb, which was the way to do.

The Tommy gunner moved a step closer and two steps right so he could observe Malachai. He said, "Come on, Casey. Get that dinge outta there!"

The man with the bat said, "Step down, you black bastard!"

Randy knew that the man couldn't use the bat while Malachai stayed in the truck and he prayed Malachai would wait him out. He watched the gunner. *Please, God, make him take one more step so I won't have to try through the windshield.* A shot through the windshield was almost certain to miss because of light refraction or bullet deflection. It would be foolhardy and desperate and he would not do it.

The gunner said, "Drag him out or blow him out. I don't care which."

Malachai cringed and cried, "Please, boss!" The fear in his voice was real.

The man with the bat put his hand on the door handle. At the instant he turned it, Malachai uncoiled, hurling himself through the door and on him, pistol clubbed.

The gunner took two quick steps and the Thompson jerked and spoke. The gunner's thick middle was in Randy's sights and he squeezed the trigger, and again, and again before the Thompson's muzzle came down and the gunner folded and began to fall. When he was on his face he still twitched and held the gun and tried to swing it up and Randy shot him again, carefully, through the head.

He had not even heard the shotguns but when Randy crawled over into the front seat and got out, looking for another target, the battle was over. Close behind the truck two figures lay, their arms and legs twisted in death's awkward signature. The Admiral stood over the man who had held the bat, his shotgun a foot from his head. Malachai was curled up as if in sleep, his head against the left front tire. It had lasted not more than seven seconds.

Malachai choked and groaned and Randy dropped to his knees beside him and straightened him and lifted his head. Malachai choked again and Randy turned Malachai's head so the blood could run out of his mouth and not down his windpipe. He tore open Malachai's shirt. There was a hole large as a dime just under the solar plexus. In this round well, dark blood rose and ebbed rhythmically, a small, ominous tide.

The Admiral said, "Shall I get rid of this scum?"

Randy said, "Just a minute." He picked up the bat and forced himself to think ahead. First, Malachai. Get Malachai home in a hurry so Dan could do something if there was anything to be done. Dan didn't have his tools, or much eyesight. He might make do with one eye if he had the tools these men had stolen. Randy ran to the Model-A. It was empty. The doctor's bag wasn't there.

He walked back to the truck where Sam Hazzard stood over their captive. One side of the man's face was scraped raw. Malachai's plunge had carried the long-jawed, twisted-mouth face along the bridge planking. "Where's the doctor's bag?"

The man said nothing. Randy saw his right hand moving. He still had a holstered weapon. Randy tapped him on the nose with the bat. "Keep your hand still." The Admiral leaned over, unbuckled the holster, and took the weapon. A .38 police special. "Talk," Randy said.

The man said, "I don't know nuthin'."

Randy tapped his face with the bat, harder. The man screamed. Randy said, "Where's the black bag?"

The man said, "She took it. Rumdum took it."

"Where is she?"

"I don't know. She goofed off with somebody last night—maybe it was this morning—I don't know—goofed off with some bastard with a bottle."

Randy called, "Bill! Where's Bill?"

Bill McGovern was on the other side of the truck. He said, "I'm here, Randy."

"Bill, go look in that car and see if you can find Dan's bag. And be sure those two back there are good and dead."

Malachai choked again. Randy tried to ease him over on his side but he began to bleed more from the stomach wound so he had to let him be.

Sam Hazzard said, "I don't think this one's doing us any good. He's just holding us up. I think we should convoke a military tribunal right now and pass sentence. I vote he be executed."

"So do I," Randy said, "but I want him to hang. If he makes any trouble let him have it, Sam, but I'd like to have him alive."

Bill came back with a cardboard carton. "Nothing in that car, except this. A little food in here. A few cans of sardines and corned beef hash and a box of matches. A couple of boxes of ammunition. That's all. Not a sign of Dan's bag. And the sedan is finished. It was in our line of fire and it looks like a sieve with all that buckshot through it. There's gasoline all over the road."

Randy started the Model-A and looked at the fuel gauge. It showed almost empty. He backed it away from the bridge entrance, put the key in his pocket, and left it. He said, "We'll lift Malachai into the truck and

get going. First, I'll collect their weapons and ammo."
He was thinking ahead. There would be other highwaymen and this was armament for his company.

"What about these?" Bill asked, pointing his shotgun
at the bodies.

"Leave them." He looked up. The buzzards already
attended. "I'll come back tomorrow or we'll send somebody. Whatever they leave—" he watched the black
birds wheeling and swooping—"we'll give to the river."

One of the highwaymen trailing them had been Leroy
Settle, the drugstore cowboy. When Randy examined
his two guns he was surprised to find that they were
only .22 caliber, lightweight replicas, except in bore, of
the big frontier .45's. His companion's pistol apparently
had gone into the river, for it wasn't on the bridge although he had a pocketful of ammunition.

Then Randy leaned over the leader. He saw that his
shots had all been good, the three in the belly making a
neat pattern, diagonal ticktacktoe. When he picked up
the Thompson the dead man's arm astonishingly rose
with it, clinging as if his fingers were glued to the stock.
Randy jerked it free and saw that it was glue, of a sort.
The man's hands were smeared with honey.

It was after dark when Randy wheeled up to the
front steps of the house. As he cut the engine he heard
Graf barking. All the downstairs windows showed light.
Lib burst out of the door and ran down the steps, saw
him at the wheel, and was there with her arms and lips
when he got out.

Preacher Henry appeared, and Two-Tone, Florence
Wechek and Alice Cooksey, Hannah and Missouri, the
children. Dan Gunn came out, robe flapping, carrying a
lantern. They had all been waiting.

The Admiral and Bill were in back with the prisoner
and Malachai. Bill stepped out, holding a pistol, and
then the man with the bat, called Casey, prodded by
Sam Hazzard's shotgun. Sam climbed down and that
left Malachai. Malachai had been unconscious after the
first mile. Until they reached Fort Repose, the road had
been very bad.

Randy said, "Killed three, grabbed this one. They got Malachai through the middle. Look at him, Dan. Is he still with us, Sam?"

The Admiral said, "He was a minute ago. Barely."

Randy said, "Ben Franklin, get some clothesline."

"We going to hang him right now?" Ben asked, not casually but still as if he expected it.

"No. We'll tie him."

Dan crawled into the truck. He held up the lantern, shook his head in exasperation, and then tore the patch away from his right eye. The eye was still swollen but not entirely shut and any assistance to his left eye was helpful. He crawled out and said, "He's in shock and shouldn't be moved and ought to have a transfusion. But we have to move him if I'm to do anything at all. On what?"

There was a discarded door in the toolhouse. They moved him on that.

They laid Malachai on the billiard table in the game-room and then massed lamps and candles so that Dan would have light.

Dan said, "I have to go into him. Massive internal hemorrhage. I've got to tie it off or there's no chance at all. How? With what?" He leaped on the edge of the table, swaying not in fatigue or weakness but in agony of frustration. He cried, "Oh, God!"

Dan stopped swaying. "A knife, Randy?"

"My hunting knife, the one I shave with? It's sharp as a razor, almost."

"No, Too big, too thick. How about steak knives?"

"Sure, steak knives."

The short-bladed steak knives even looked like lancets. The Judge and Randy's mother had bought the set in Denmark on their summer in Europe in 'fifty-four. They were the finest and sharpest steak knives Randy had ever used. He found them in the silver chest and called, "How many?"

"Two will do."

From the dining room Helen called, "I've put on water to boil—a big pot." The dinner fire had been going and Helen had piled on fat wood so it roared and Dan would soon have the means of sterilizing his instruments.

Randy put them into the pot to boil. After that, at Dan's direction he put in his fine-nosed fishing pliers. Florence Wechek ran across the road for darning needles. Lib found metal hair clips that would clamp an artery. Randy's six-pound nylon line off the spinning reel would have to do for sutures. There was enough soap to cleanse Dan's hands.

Dan went into the dining room, fretting, waiting for the pot and his instruments to boil. It was hopeless, he knew. In spite of everything they might do sepsis was almost inevitable, but now it was the shock and the hemorrhage he couldn't lick. He wondered whether it would be possible to rig up a saline solution transfusion. They had the ingredients, salt and water and fire; and somewhere, certainly, rubber tubing. He would not give up Malachai. He wanted to save Malachai, capable, quiet, and strong, more than he had ever wanted to save anybody in his years as a physician. So many people died for nothing. Malachai was dying for something.

In the gameroom Helen was at work, quick and competent. She had found their last bottle of Scotch, except what might remain in Randy's decanter upstairs, and was cleansing the wound with it. Randy and Lib stood beside her. The pool of blood in the round hole ebbed and did not rise again.

The water was boiling in the big iron pot when Randy walked into the dining room and touched Dan's shoulder. "I'm sorry," he said. "I'm afraid it's all over."

In a dark corner of the room where she thought she would be out of the way and not a bother, Hannah Henry had been sitting in an old scarred maple rocker. The rocker began to move in slow cadence, and she moaned in this cadence for the dead, arms folded over her empty breasts as if holding a baby except that where the baby had been there was nothing.

Dan Gunn went into the gameroom and saw that Randy was correct, that Malachai was gone. His shoulders felt heavy. He was aware that his head throbbed and eyes burned. There was nothing more to do except empty the makeshift sterilizer with its ridiculous make-shift tools. He did this in the kitchen sink. Yet when he saw the knives and the pliers and the hair clips steaming he realized they were not really so ridiculous. If he was very careful and skillful, he could make do with such tools. They had not and probably could not have saved Malachai. They might save someone else. A century ago the tools had been no better and the knowledge in-finitely less. Out of death, life; an immutable truth. Hel-en was at his side. He said, "Thanks, Helen, for the try. You're the best unregistered nurse in the world."

"I'm sorry it was for nothing."

"Maybe it wasn't for nothing. I'll just keep these and try to add to them. I wonder if we could find a small bag somewhere? Any little traveling bag would do."

"I have one. A train case."

"We'll start here, then, and build another kit." His eyes hurt. Who in Fort Repose could build him another pair of glasses, or give him new eyes?

At nine o'clock that night Randy's knees began to quiver and his brain refused further work and begged to quit, a reaction, he knew, to the fight on the bridge and what had gone before and after, and lack of sleep. It was his wedding night. He had been married at noon that same day, which seemed incredible. Noon was a life ago.

But now that he was married, he thought it only right that he and Lib have a room to themselves and the pri-vacy accorded a married couple. All the bedroom space was taken and he hated to evict anyone. After all, they were all his guests. Yet since it was inevitable that beds and rooms be shifted around, the victim would have to be Ben Franklin, since Ben was the junior male. Ben would have to give up his room and take the couch in Randy's apartment and Mr. and Mrs. Randolph Bragg would move into Ben's room.

He was sitting on his couch, trying to still his quiver-ing legs, face in his hands, thinking of this. Lib sat be-hind the bar drinking a warm limeade. She was thinking of the problem also but was reluctant to mention it, feeling that it was the husband's duty and she should allow him to bring it up.

Her father came in, a thin and wan Caesar in his sandals and white robe. Bill McGovern had been standing guard over the trussed prisoner, wondering the while that he had killed a man that day and felt no guilt at the time or after. It was like stepping on a roach. He had just been relieved by Two-Tone Henry, who had left his house of mourning to assume the duty. Bill asked for Dan. Randy lifted his head and told him that Dan, exhausted by being too long on his feet, slept. "Well, I'll tell you, then, but I don't suppose it will do any good tonight."

He spoke directly to his daughter. "I didn't know what to give you for a wedding present, Elizabeth. There's a good deal of real estate in Cleveland but I don't suppose it'll ever be worth much now. There are bonds and stock certificates in our safe deposit vault right here in Fort Repose, and the cash—well, the Confederate money in Randy's chest is just as good. You can have the house and property down the road, if you want it, but I don't think anybody can ever live there unless electricity comes back. So I thought, what can I give Lib and Randy? I talked it over this morning with Dan. He made a suggestion and we decided to give you a present jointly, from the best man and the father of the bride."

Bill looked from one to the other and saw they were interested. "We are jointly making you a present of this whole apartment. Dan is going to move in with me."

Lib said, "That's perfectly wonderful, Father!"

Bill said, hesitantly, "Only, if Dan's asleep I don't think we ought to disturb him, do you?"

"No, not tonight," Lib said. She kissed her father, and she kissed her husband, and she went across the hall to her old room. Randy fell across the couch and slept. Presently Graf jumped up beside him and snuggled under his arm.

At noon Monday the man with the bat was hung from a girder supporting the bandstand roof in Marines

Park. All the regular traders and a number of strangers were in the park. Randy ordered that the corpse not be cut down until sunset. He wanted the strangers to be impressed and spread the word beyond Fort Repose.

While he had not planned it, on this day he accepted the first enlistments in what came to be known as Bragg's Troop, although in orders he called it the Fort Repose Provisional Company. Seven men volunteered that day, including Fletcher Kennedy, who had been an Air Force fighter pilot, and Link Haslip, a West Point cadet who had been home on Christmas leave on The Day. He created them provisional lieutenants of infantry. The other five were even younger—boys who had finished six months of Reserve training after high school or had been in the National Guard.

After the execution, Randy posted the notices he had typed earlier and brought to the park in his uniform pocket. The first read:

On 17 April the following highwaymen were killed on the covered bridge: Mickey Cahane, of Las Vegas and Boca Raton, a gambler and racketeer; Arch Fleggert, Miami, occupation unknown; Leroy Settle, Fort Repose.

On 18 April Thomas "Casey" Killinger, also of Las Vegas, and the fourth member of the band which murdered Mr. and Mrs. James Hickey and robbed and assaulted Dr. Daniel Gunn, was hung on this spot.

The second notice was shorter:

On 17 April Technical Sergeant Malachai Henry (USAF, reserve) died of a wound received on the covered bridge while defending Fort Repose.

[12]

Early in May a tube in the Admiral's radio flared and died, cutting off the voice of the world outside. While these communications had always been sketchy, and the information meager and confusing, the fact that they were gone entirely was a blow to everyone. The Admiral's short-wave receiver had been their only reliable source of news. It was also a fount of hope. Each night that reception was good some of them had gathered in the Admiral's den and listened while he conned the wave lengths, hoping for news of peace, victory, succor, reconstruction. While they never heard such news, they could always wait for the next night with hope.

After consulting with the Admiral and the Henrys, Randy posted a notice on his official bulletin board in Marines Park. He asked a replacement for the tube and offered handsome payment—a pig and two chickens or a five-year file of old magazines. A proper tube never came in. Before The Day the Admiral had been forced to order replacement tubes directly from the factory in New Jersey, so he had not been optimistic.

Even had they been able to acquire a new tube, the radio could not have operated long, for the automobile batteries were depleted and it was in May that gasoline vanished entirely.

In June Preacher Henry's corn crop ripened, the sweet yams swelled in the ground, and the first stalks of Two-Tone's sugar cane fell to the machete. June was the month of plenty, the month in which they ate corn pone and hoe cake with molasses. In June they all fleshed out.

It was in June, also, that they ran their first batch of mash through the still built by Bill McGovern and Two-Tone. It was an event. After pine knots blazed for three hours under a fifty-gallon drum, liquid began to drip from the spout terminating an intricate arrangement of copper tubing, coils, and condensers. Two-Tone caught these first drops in a cup and handed it to Randy. Randy sniffed the colorless stuff. It smelled horrible. When it had cooled a bit he tasted it. His eyes watered and his stomach begged him not to swallow. He managed to get a little down. It was horrid. "It's wonderful!" he gasped, and quickly passed the cup on.

After all the men had taken a swallow, and properly praised Two-Tone's inventive initiative and Bill's mechanical acumen, Randy said, "Of course it's still a little raw. With aging, it'll be smoother."

"It ought to be aged in the wood," Bill said. "Where will we get a keg?"

"It'll be a cinch," Randy said. "Anybody who has a keg will trade it for a couple of quarts after it's aged."

But for Dan Gunn, the corn whiskey was immediately useful. While he would not dare use it for anesthesia, he estimated its alcohol content as high. It would be an excellent bug repellent, liniment, and pre-operative skin antiseptic.

One day in July, Alice Cooksey brought home four books on hypnotism, and presented them to Dan Gunn. "If you can learn hypnotism," she suggested, "you might use it as anesthesia."

Dan knew a number of doctors, and dentists too, who commonly practiced hypnotism. It had always seemed to him an inefficient and time-consuming substitute for ether and morphine but now he grasped at the idea as if Alice had offered him a specific for cancer.

Every night Helen read to him. She insisted on doing his reading, thus saving his eyes. They no longer had candles or kerosene but their lamps and lanterns burned furnace oil extracted from the underground tanks with a bilge pump. It was true that furnace oil smoked, and stank, and produced yellow and inefficient light. But it was light.

Soon Dan hypnotized Helen. He then hypnotized or attempted hypnosis on everyone in River Road. He couldn't hypnotize the Admiral at all. He succeeded in partially hypnotizing Randy, with poor results, including grogginess and a headache. Randy attempted to co-operate but he could not erase everything else from his mind.

The children were excellent subjects. Dan hypnotized them again and again until he had only to speak a few sentences, in the jargon of the hypnotist, snap his fingers, and they would fall into malleable trance. Randy worried about this until Dan explained.

"I've been training the children to be quick subjects, because in an emergency, they have their own built-in supply of ether."

"And if you're not around?"

"Helen is studying hypnotism too." He was thoughtful. "She's becoming quite expert. You know, Helen could have been a doctor. Helen isn't happy unless she's caring for someone. She takes care of me."

A week later Ben Franklin developed a stomachache which forced him to draw up his right knee when he tried to lie down. The ache was always there and at intervals it became sharp pain enveloping him in waves. Dan decided Ben's pain was not from eating too many bananas. It was impossible to take a blood count but the boy had a slight fever and Dan knew he had to go into him.

Dan operated on the billiard table in the gameroom, after putting Ben into deep trance. Dan used the steak knives, darning needles, hair curlers, and nylon line, all properly sterilized, and removed an appendix distended and near to bursting.

In five days Ben was up and active. After that Randy, somewhat in awe, referred to Dan as "our witch doctor."

In August they used the last of the corn, squeezed the last of the late oranges, the Valencias, and plucked the last overripe but deliciously sweet grapefruit from the trees. In August they ran out of salt, armadillos destroyed the yam crop, and the fish stopped biting. That terribly hot August was the month of disaster.

The end of the corn and exhaustion of the citrus crop had been inevitable. Armadillos in the yams was bad luck, but bearable. But without fish and salt their survival was in doubt.

Randy had carefully rationed salt since he was shocked, in July, to discover how few pounds were left. Salt was a vital commodity, not just white grains you shook on eggs. Dan used saline solutions for half a dozen purposes. The children used salt to brush their teeth. Without salt, the slaughter of the Henry pigs would have been a terrible waste. They planned to tan one hide to cut badly needed moccasins, and without salt this was impossible.

As soon as they were out of salt it seemed that almost everything required salt, most of all the human body. Day after day the porch thermometer stood at ninety-five or over and every day all of them had manual labor to do, and miles to walk. They sweated rivers. They sweated their salt away, and they grew weak, and they grew ill. And all of Fort Repose grew weak and ill for there was no salt anywhere.

In July Randy had gone to Rita Hernandez and she had traded five pounds of salt to him for three large bass, a bushel of Valencias, and four buckshot shells. She had traded not so much for these things, Randy believed, but because he had helped her arrange decent burial for Pete, and provided the pallbearers to carry him to Repose-in-Peace Park. Since July, he had been unable to trade for salt anywhere. In Marines Park, a pound of salt would be worth five pounds of coffee, if anyone had coffee. You could not even buy salt with corn liquor, potent if only slightly aged.

In August the traders in Marines Park dragged themselves about like zombies, for want of salt. And for the first time in his life Randy felt a weird uneasiness and craving that became almost madness when he rubbed the perspiration from his face and then tasted salt on his fingers. Now he understood the craving of animals for salt, understood why a cougar and a deer would share the same salt lick in the enforced truce of salt starvation.

But even more important than salt was fish, for the fish of the river was their staple, like seal to the Eskimo. It had been so simple, until August. Their bamboo set poles, butts lodged in metal or wooden holders on the ends and sides of their docks, each night usually provided enough fish for the following day. In the morning someone would stroll down to the dock and haul up whatever had hooked itself in the hours of darkness. If the night's automatic catch was lean, or if extra fish were needed for trading, someone was granted leave from regular chores to fish in the morning, or at dusk when the feeding bass struck savagely. Their poles grew in clumps, they had line aplenty, hooks enough to last for years (fishing had been the pre-Day hobby of Bill McGovern and Sam Hazzard as well as Randy) and every kind of bait—worms, crickets, grasshoppers, tadpoles, minnows, shiners—for anyone capable of using a shovel, throw net, or simply his hands.

Randy had more than a hundred plugs and spoons and perhaps half as many flies and bass bugs. He had bought them knowing well that most lures are designed to catch fishermen rather than fish. Still, on occasion the bass would go wild for artificials and in the spring the specks and bream would snap up small flies and tiny spoons. So fish had never been a problem, until they stopped biting.

When they stopped they stopped all at once and all together. Even with his circular shrimp net, wading barefoot in the shallows, Lib beside him hopefully carrying a bucket, Randy could not net a shiner, bream, cat, or even mudfish. Randy considered himself a good fisherman and yet he admitted he didn't understand why fish bit or why they didn't. August had never been a good month for black bass, true, but this August was strange. Only during thunderstorms was there a ripple on the river. A molten sun rose, grew white hot, and sank red and molten, and the river was unearthly still and oily, agitated no more than Florence's aquarium. Even at crack of dawn or final light, no fish jumped or swirled. It was bad. And it was eerie and frightening.

In the third week of August when they were all weak and half-sick Randy spoke his fears to Dan. It was evening. Randy and Lib had just come from the hammock. For an hour they had crouched together under a great oak waiting for the little gray squirrels to feed. They had been utterly quiet and the squirrels had been noisy and Randy had blasted two of them out of the tree with his double twenty, a shameful use of irreplaceable ammunition for very little meat. Yet two squirrels was enough to give meat flavor to a stew that night. What they would have for breakfast, if anything, nobody knew. They found Dan in Randy's office, with Helen trimming his hair. Randy told them about the two squirrels and then he said, "Dan, I've been thinking about the fish. I've never seen fishing this bad before. Could anything big and permanent have happened? Could radiation have wiped them out, or anything?"

Dan scratched at his beard and Helen brushed his hand down and said, "Sit still."

Dan said, "Fish. Let me think about fish. I doubt that anything happened to the fish. If the river had been poisoned by fallout right after The Day the dead fish would have come to the surface. The river would have been blanketed with fish. That didn't happen then and it hasn't happened since. No, I doubt that there has been a holocaust of fish."

"It worries me," Randy said.

"Salt worries me more. Salt doesn't grow or breed or spawn. You either have it or you don't."

Helen swung the swivel chair. Dan was facing the teak chest. Suddenly he lifted himself out of the chair, flung himself on his knees, opened the chest and began to dig into it. "The diary!" he shouted. "Where's the diary?"

"It's there. Why?"

"There's salt in the diary! Remember when Helen

was reading it to me after I was slugged by the highwaymen? There was something about salt in it. Remember, Helen?"

Randy had not looked into the log of Lieutenant Randolph Rowzee Peyton for years, but now it was coming back to him, and he did remember. Lieutenant Peyton's Marines had also lacked and needed salt, and somehow obtained it. He dropped on his knees beside Dan and quickly found the log. He skimmed through the pages. Lieutenant Peyton, as he recalled it, had run out of salt in the second year. He found an entry, dated August 19, 1839:

"The supply boat from Cow's Ford being much overdue, and my command lacking salt and suffering greatly from the heat, on 6 August I dispatched my loyal Creek guide, Billy Longnose, down the St. Johns (sometimes called River May) to discover the cause of delay. Today he returned with the information that our supply boat, beating its way upstream, had put into dock at Mandarin (a town named to honor the oriental nation from which it imported its orange trees). By ill luck, on that night the Seminoles raided Mandarin, putting to death a number of its inhabitants and burning the houses. The master of the supply boat, a civilian, and his crew, consisting of a white man and two Slaves, escaped to the woods and later reached St. Augustine. However, the boat was pillaged and then burned.

All other privations my men can endure except lack of water and lack of salt."

The next entry was dated August 21. Randy read it aloud:

"Billy Longnose today brought to the Fort a Seminole, a very dirty and shifty-eyed buck calling himself Kyukan, who offered to guide me to a place where there is sufficient salt to fill this Fort ten times over. So he says. In payment he demanded one gallon of rum. While it is unlawful to sell spirits to the Seminoles, nothing is said about giving them drink. Accordingly, I offered the buck a half-gallon jug, and he agreed."

Randy turned the page and said, "Here it is. Twenty-three April":

"This day I returned to Fort Repose in the second boat, bringing twelve large sacks of salt. It was true. I could have filled the Fort ten times over.

"The place is near the headwaters of the Timucuan, some twenty-two nautical miles, I should judge, up that tributary. It is called by an Indian word meaning Blue Crab Pool. The pool itself is crystal clear, like the Silver Springs. I thought it surrounded by a white beach, but then discovered that what I thought sand was pure salt. It was quite unbelievable. In this pool there were blue crabs, such as are found only in the ocean, yet the pool is many miles inland, and two hundred miles from the mouth of the St. John, or May."

Randy closed the log, grinned, and said, "I've heard of Blue Crab Run but I've never been there. My father used to go there when he was a boy, for crab feasts. He never mentioned salt. I guess salt didn't impress my father. It was always in the kitchen. He had plenty."

The next morning the Fort Repose fleet set sail, five boats commanded by an admiral whose last sea command had also been five ships—a super-carrier, two cruisers, and two destroyers.

By August most of the boats in Fort Repose had been fitted with sails cut from awnings, draperies, or even nylon sheets for the lighter outboards, and with keels or sideboards, and hand-carved rudders. For the expedition up the Timucuan, Sam Hazzard chose boats of exceptional capacity and stability. Randy's light Fiberglas boat wasn't suitable, so Randy went along as the Admiral's crew. With the south wind blowing hot and steady, they planned to reach Blue Crab Pool before night and be back in Fort Repose by noon the next day, for their speed would double on their return voyage downstream.

Their five boats crewed thirteen men, all well armed. It would be the first night Randy had spent away from Lib since their marriage, and she seemed somewhat distressed by this. But Randy had no fear for her safety, or for the safety of Fort Repose. His company now numbered thirty men. It controlled the rivers and the roads. Knowing this, highwaymen shunned Fort Repose. The phrase "deterrent force" had been popular before The Day and effective so long as that force had been unmistakably superior. Randy's company was certainly the most efficient force in Central Florida, and he intended to keep it so.

Sitting at the tiller, gold-encrusted cap pushed back on his head, the wind singing through the stays, the Admiral seemed to have sloughed off a decade. "You know," he said, "when I was at the Academy they still insisted that we learn sail before steam. They used to stick us in catboats and make us whip back and forth on the Severn and learn knots and rigs and spars. I thought it was silly. I still do, but it is fun."

They reached a curve of the river and Randy watched the captain's walk on his roof disappear behind the cypress and palms. It was fun, he thought, and it was quiet. In a sailboat a man could think. He thought about the fish, and what had happened to them, for his stomach was empty.

Peyton Bragg was bored, disgusted, and angry. She had helped Ben Franklin plan the hunt. She had even walked to town with Ben and helped him locate the books in the library that told about armadillos. The armadillo, they had learned, was a nocturnal beast that curled up deep underground in daylight hours. In the night he burrowed like a mole just under the surface, locating and eating tender roots and tubers, in this case the Henrys' yams. The exciting thing they learned was that in his native Central America the armadillo was considered a delicacy. The armadillo was food.

Then, when it came time for the hunt, Ben had refused to take her along. A girl couldn't stay out all night in the woods, Ben said. It was too dangerous for a girl. She would have presented her case to Randy for judgment, but Randy was gone with the Admiral, and her mother agreed with Ben.

So Ben had gone off that evening with Caleb and

Graf. It was Ben's contention that Graf was the key to armadillo hunting, and so it had proved. In Germany the dachshund was originally bred as a badger hound, which meant that he could dig like mad and would fearlessly and tenaciously pursue any animal underground.

Ben had been armed with a machete and his .22 rifle, but it was Caleb's spear that had been the effective weapon against armadillos. They had gone to the yam patch in the moonlight. The whole patch was plowed with armadillo runs. Ben introduced Graf to an opening and Graf, sniffing and understanding at once, had wormed his way into the earth. Presently there came an awful snarling and growling from a corner of the patch. Locating the armadillo from Graf's sounds, Caleb prodded it with his spear, and the armadillo burst out. This eruption so surprised Ben that he shot it. The others, he decapitated with the machete.

In the morning, five armadillos had been laid out in the Henrys' barn. Two-Tone and Preacher cleaned them, and Peyton had eaten armadillo for breakfast. She would have choked on it, except that it was tender and delicious and she was starving. Ben Franklin was credited with discovering a new source of food, and was a hero. Peyton was only a girl, fit for sewing, pot washing, and making beds.

Peyton threw herself on the bed and stared at the ceiling. She wanted to be noticed and praised. She wanted to be a hero. She recently had been talking to Lib about psychology, a fascinating subject. She had even read one of Lib's books. "I'm rejected," she told herself aloud.

If she wanted to be a hero the best way was to catch some fish. She set her mind to the problem, why won't the fish bite? She had heard the Admiral say that the best fisherman on the river was Preacher Henry and yet she knew that Randy hadn't talked to Preacher about the no-fish. If anybody could help, Preacher could. She got up, smoothed the bed, and sneaked down the back stairs. This was her day to sweep upstairs. She would finish when she got back.

Peyton found Preacher in the cool of his front porch,

rocking. Preacher was getting very old. He didn't do much of anything any more except rock. Preacher was the oldest person Peyton had ever seen. Now that he had grown a white beard, he looked like a dark prophet out of the Bible. Peyton said, "Preacher, can you tell me something?"

Preacher was startled. He hadn't seen her slip up on him, and her voice had broken his dream. He started to rise and then sank back into the chair. "Sure, Peyton," he said. "What do you want to know?"

"Why don't the fish bite?"

Preacher chuckled. "They do bite. They bite whenever they eat."

"Come on, Preacher. Tell me how I can catch some fish."

"To catch fish, you got to think like a fish. Can you think like a fish, little girl?"

Peyton felt injured, being called a little girl, but she was a child of dignity, and it was with dignity that she answered. "No, I can't. But I know that you can. You must, because you're a great fisherman."

Preacher nodded in agreement. "I was a great fisherman. Now I feel too poorly to fish. Nobody thinks of me any more as a great fisherman. They only think of me as an old man of no use to anyone. You are the first one to ask, 'Why don't the fish bite?' So I'll tell you."

Peyton waited.

"If it was very hot, like now, the hottest I ever remember, and you was a fish, what would you do?"

"I don't know," Peyton said. "I know what I do. I take showers, three or four a day. Outside with nothing on."

Preacher nodded. "The fish, he wants to stay cool too. He don't hang around the shore there—" his arm swept to indicate the river banks—"he goes out into the middle. The water close to the shore, it's hot. You put your hand in it, it feels like soup. But out in the middle of the river, way down deep, it's nice and cool. Down there the fish feels lively and hungry and he eats and when he eats he bites."

"Bass?"

"Yes. Big bass, 'way down deep."

"How would I get them? Nobody's been able to net any bass bait—no shiners."

"That's the trouble," Preacher said. "The little fish he gets hot too and so he's out there in the middle deep, being chased by the big fish like always."

Peyton thought of something. "Would a bass bite a goldfish?"

Preacher looked at her suspiciously. "He sure would! He'd take a goldfish in a second if one was offered! But it against the law to fish with goldfish. But if I did have goldfish, and if it weren't against the law, and if I did fish out in the deep channel, then I wouldn't use a bobber. I'd just put a little weight next my hook so that goldfish would sink right down where the big bass lie."

Peyton said, "Thank you, Preacher," and skipped away, not wishing to incriminate him further, if it really was true that goldfish were illegal. She went home, found a bucket on the back porch, and then walked across River Road for a talk with Florence Wechek. She and Florence were good friends and often had long talks, but about simple subjects, such as mending.

Florence wasn't home—she was probably in town helping Alice at the library—but the goldfish were. She watched them swimming dreamily, ignoring her in their useless complacency. "In with you," she said, and dumped fish and water into the pail. She borrowed Ben Franklin's rod and reel and made for the dock. She was forbidden to go out in Randy's boat alone, but since she was already involved in one criminal act, she might as well risk another.

At noon Randy had not returned and Elizabeth McGovern Bragg climbed to the captain's walk where she could be alone with her fears and anxiety. Her father and Dan Gunn had walked to town that morning. With some volunteers from Bragg's Troop, they had begun to clean up and repair the clinic. So there was no man in the house and she was afraid for her husband. He had told her there would be no danger but in this new life the dangers were deadly and unpredictable. She kept her face turned steadily to the east, where the Admiral's striped-awning sail should appear at the first bend of the Timucuan.

She told herself that she was silly, that Randy and the others, if they found the place at all, might tarry there for hours. They would undoubtedly feast on crab, and she couldn't blame them. They might find it difficult to load the salt. Anything could delay them.

From the grass behind the kitchen Helen called up, "Lib!"

She leaned over the rail. "Yes?"

"Is Peyton up there with you?"

"No. I haven't seen her."

"Is she out on the dock?"

Lib looked out at the dock and saw that Randy's boat was missing. Before she told Helen this she scanned the river. It was nowhere in sight; Randy had sailed in the Admiral's cruiser, and the boat should be there.

At five that evening the Fort Repose fleet sighted Randy's house. There was no doubt that it had been a triumphant voyage. The five boats were deep with salt, the thirteen men were filled with boiled crabs, lavishly seasoned, so they were all stronger and felt better, and in every boat there were buckets and washtubs filled with live crabs.

The Admiral ran his boat alongside Randy's dock and turned into the wind. "You unload what salt you want here," Sam Hazzard said, "and that washtubful of crabs, and I'll sail back with the Henrys' share, and mine."

Randy unloaded. He had expected that Lib would be down at the dock to greet him, or certainly watching from the captain's walk. Coming home with such rich cargo, he was chagrined. He lifted the washtub to the dock and then two fat sacks of salt. Fifty pounds, at least, he thought. It would last for months and when it was gone there was an unlimited supply waiting on the shores of Blue Crab Pool. He said, "So long, Sam. See you tonight."

The Admiral pushed away from the dock and Randy

picked up the washtub, deliberately spilled some of the water that had kept the crabs alive, and walked to the house.

The kitchen was empty except for four very large black bass in the sink. He lifted the largest. An eleven-pounder, he judged. It was the biggest bass he had seen in a year. It was unbelievable.

There was a plate on the kitchen table heaped with roasted meat. It looked like lamb. He tasted it. It didn't taste like lamb. It didn't taste like anything he had ever tasted before, but it tasted wonderful. He thought of the crabs, and their value dwindled to hors d'ouevres.

It was then he heard the first sobs, from upstairs, he thought, and then a different voice weeping hysterically somewhere else in the house. In fear, he ran through the dining room.

Three women were in the living room. They were all crying, Lib silently, Florence and Helen loudly. Lib saw him and ran into his arms and wiped her tears on his shirt. "What's happened?" he demanded.

"I thought you'd never come home," Lib said. "I was afraid and there's so much trouble."

"What? Who's hurt?"

"Nobody but Peyton. She's upstairs, crying. Helen spanked her and sent her to bed."

"Why?"

"She went fishing."

"Did Peyton catch those big bass?"

"Yes."

"And Helen spanked her for it?"

"Not that. Helen spanked her because she took out your boat and drifted downstream. We didn't know what had happened to her until she rowed home an hour ago. She said she couldn't make it sail right."

Randy looked at Helen. "And what's wrong with you?"

"I'm upset. Anybody'd be upset if they had to spank their child."

Florence wailed and her head fell on her arms.

"What's wrong with her?"

"Somebody or something came in and ate her gold-fish."

Florence raised her head. "I think it must have been Sir Percy. I'm sure of it. I did love that cat and now look how he behaves." She wept again.

Randy said, "Isn't anybody going to ask me whether I got salt?"

"Did you get salt?" Lib asked.

"Yes. Fifty pounds of it. And if you women want it, you'll take the wheelbarrow down to the dock and lug it up."

He went into the kitchen to clean the beautiful bass and put the crabs in the big pot. It was all ridiculous and stupid. The more he learned about women the more there was to learn except that he had learned this: they needed a man around.

Then he found a tattered goldfish in the gullet of the eleven-pounder. He examined it carefully, smiled, and dropped it into the sink. He would not mention it. There was enough trouble and confusion among all these women already.

So ended the hunger of August. In the fourth week the heat broke and the fish began to bite again.

In September school began. It was impractical to re-open the Fort Repose schoolhouse—it was unheated and there was no water. Randy decided that the responsibility for teaching must rest temporarily with the parents. The regular teachers were scattered or gone and there was no way of paying them. The textbooks were still in the schoolhouse, for anyone who needed them.

Judge Bragg's library became the schoolroom in the Bragg household, with Lib and Helen dividing the teaching. When Caleb Henry arrived to attend classes with Peyton and Ben Franklin, Randy was a little surprised. He saw that Peyton and Ben expected it, and then he recalled that in Omaha—and indeed in two thirds of America's cities—white and Negro children had sat side by side for many years without fuss or trouble.

In October the new crop of early oranges began to ripen. The juice tasted tart and refreshing after months without it.

In October, armadillos began to grow scarce in the Fort Repose area, but the Henrys' flock of chickens had increased and the sow again farrowed. Also, ducks arrived in enormous numbers from the North—more than Randy ever before had seen. Wild turkeys, which before The Day had been hunted almost to extermination in Timucuan County, suddenly were common. Randy fashioned himself a turkey call, and shot one or two every week. Quail roamed the groves, fields and yards in great coveys. He did not use his shells on such trifling game. But Two-Tone knew how to fashion snares, and taught the boys, so there was usually quail for breakfast along with eggs.

One evening near the end of the month Dan Gunn returned from his clinic, smiling and whistling. "Randy," he said, "I have just delivered my first post-Day baby! A boy, about eight pounds, bright and healthy!"

"So what's so wonderful about delivering a baby?" Randy said. "Was the mother under hypnosis?"

"Yes. But that's not what was wonderful." Dan's smile disappeared. "You see, this was the first live baby, full term. I had two other pregnancies that ended prematurely. Nature's way of protecting the race, I think, although you can't reach any statistical conclusion on the basis of three pregnancies. Anyway, now we know that there's going to be a human race, don't we?"

"I'd never really thought there might not be."

"I had," Dan said quietly.

In November a tall pine, split by lightning during the summer, dropped its brown needles and died and Randy and Bill felled it with a two-man saw and ax. It was arduous work and neither of them knew the technique. It was at times like this that Randy missed and thought of Malachai. Nevertheless they got the job done and trimmed the thick branches. The wood was valuable, for another winter was coming.

Randy went to bed early that night, exhausted. He woke suddenly with a queer sound in his ears, like music, almost. He looked at his watch. It was a bit after midnight. Lib slept quietly beside him. He was frightened. He nudged her. She lifted her head and her eyes opened. "Sweetheart," he said, "do you hear anything?"

"Go to sleep," she said, and her head fell back on the pillow. It bounced up again. "Yes," she said, "I do hear something. It sounds like music. Of course it can't be music but that's what it sounds like."

"I'm relieved," Randy said. "I thought it was in my head." He listened intently. "I could swear that it sounds like 'In the Mood.' If I didn't know better I could swear it was that great Glenn Miller recording."

She kicked him. "Get up! Get up!"

He flung himself out of bed and opened the door to the upstairs living room, lit by a lamp on the bar, turned low. It was necessary to keep fire in the house for they no longer had matches, flints, or lighter fluid. Randy thought, it must be the transistor radio, started up again, but at the same time he knew this was impossible because he long ago had thrown away the dead batteries. Nevertheless he picked up the radio and listened. It was silent yet the music persisted.

"It's coming from the hall," Lib said.

They opened the door into the hallway. The rhythm was louder but the hall was empty. Randy saw a crack of light under Peyton's door. "Peyton's room!" he said.

He put his hand on the door handle but decided it would be gentlemanly to knock first. After all, Peyton was twelve now. He knocked.

The music stopped abruptly. Peyton said, in a small, frightened voice, "Come in."

Peyton's room was illuminated by a lamp Randy had never seen before. Peyton didn't have a lamp of her own. On Peyton's desk was an old-fashioned, hand-crank phonograph with flaring horn. Stacked beside it were albums of records.

Randy said, softly, "Put it on again, Peyton."

Peyton stopped plucking at the front of her pajamas, hand-me-downs from Ben Franklin, just as Ben's pajamas were hand-me-downs from Randy, so fast did children grow. She started the record, from the beginning. Hearing it, Randy realized how much he had missed music, how music seasoned his civilization. In the Henry house Missouri often sang, but in the Bragg house hardly anyone could carry a tune, or even hum.

Over the rhythm, Lib whispered, "Where did you get it, Peyton? Where did it come from?"

"The attic. I went up the little ladder in the back hall. Mother will be furious. She told me never to go up there because the rungs were cracked and I might fall."

"Your mother was up in the attic a few months ago. She didn't see anything."

"I know. I was crawling around behind the big trunk and there was a door, a board door that looked like part of the wall. I opened it and there was another room, smaller."

Randy said, "Why did you do it, Peyton?"

"I don't know. I was lonely and there wasn't anything else to do and I'd never been up there. You know how it is. When you've never been some place, you want to go."

Randy opened one of the albums. "Old seventy-eights," he said, his voice almost reverent. "Classic jazz. Listen to this. By Tommy Dorsey—'Come Rain or Shine,' 'Stardust,' 'Chicago.' Carmen Cavallaro's 'Stormy Weather.' Also 'Body and Soul.' Artie Shaw's 'Back Bay Shuffle.' All the best by the best. I guess—I'm certain this must have been Father's collection. I've never seen this machine before, but I remember the records."

"In the Mood" ended. Randy said, "Turn it over, Peyton. No. Put on this one."

"You're not angry, Randy?" Peyton said.

"Angry! I should say not!"

"I found some other stuff in there too."

"Like what?"

"Well, there's an old-time sewing machine—the kind you work with your feet. There are some big kerosene lamps, the kind that hang. This one on the desk I found up there, too. All I had when I went up was a little stub candle. Then there's an old pot-bellied stove and a lot of iron pipe. Oh, and lots of other junk. I left it because I wanted to try the record player. The only other thing I brought down I brought for you and Dan, Randy. It's there on the bed."

Randy picked up the black leather case. It looked familiar. He had seen it before. He opened it and saw the two matched straight-edge razors that had belonged to his father.

He leaned over and kissed the top of Peyton's head. "Don't worry about what your mother will say," he told her. "I'll handle everything for you. If I had medals to give, I would pin one on you, Peyton, right now."

In this manner, Peyton became a heroine.

[13]

One morning in November, when Randy was breakfasting early and alone, Dan Gunn came downstairs smooth-shaven, his jaw looking oddly pallid in contrast to brown forehead, nose, cheekbones, and neck. "Good morning," Randy said. "You swore you'd never shave again! Why?"

"Well," Dan said lamely, "I had the razor and it seemed a shame not to use it after Peyton gave it to me. Then there was the soap." Within the past few weeks, bars of homemade soap had appeared in Marines Park, produced by Mrs. Estes, who had been senior teller at the bank, and two former co-workers. Everyone agreed that it would be a prosperous and rewarding business.

"The truth, Dan!" Randy said.

"Helen asked me to do it. She said she was getting tired of trimming it."

"Oh, that's different. You'd better be home in time for dinner tonight. John Garcia just made another run up to Blue Crab Pool and he's dropping off a washtub of crabs here. In exchange for one quart of lightning."

Dan said, "I'm very fond of Helen. I don't know what I'd do without her."

"Why do anything without her?"

"Randy, I want to marry her."

Randy rose from the table, bowed, and said, "I give you my blessing!"

"It isn't funny."

"Marriage is rarely funny."

"She won't marry me."

"Then why did you shave off your beard?"

"Damn it, Randy, I love her. And she loves me. She admitted it. She wants to marry me. But she won't. She

thinks there's a chance Mark's still alive. She's afraid
that if we married then Mark would turn up alive and
there'd be one of those awful messes we've all heard
about or read about. Like when men were reported dead
in the Philippines or Korea and they turned up after the
war in an enemy prison camp. They came home and
found their wives happily married to someone else.
Sometimes there were children. It's always a mess."

"It's happened," Randy said, "but in this case I don't
think there's a chance. Want me to talk to her?"

Dan rubbed his face where his beard had been. "I
feel naked. No, Randy, thanks. I don't think Helen
would want it discussed. Not yet, anyway. She just has
this feeling, and I'm afraid she'll have to empty it herself."

It was in this month that the first low-flying plane
frightened and exhilarated them.

At irregular times planes had been reported before,
but always jets, flying very high, usually no more than a
silver splinter in the sky, or contrail, in day, and only
sound at night.

But in the second week in November a big four-
engined transport roared over Fort Repose at a thousand feet. It bore Air Force markings. In Marines Park
everyone screamed and waved. It did not even waggle
its wings, but went on, south. Dan Gunn, who was in
town, saw it directly overhead. Randy heard and saw it
from River Road. The Admiral, who was out on the
river in his flagship, was able to observe it through binoculars.

That night Randy and Lib and Dan and Helen went
to Sam Hazzard's house to hear his opinion. "I noticed
two cylinders slung under the wing," he said. "Not extra
gas tanks. I think they might be air traps. I think they
might be taking radiation samples."

A week later the same plane, or one like it, came
over again. This time it circled Fort Repose, and a
stream of what appeared to be confetti, at the distance,
fell from its belly and drifted down on the river banks
and in the town.

Randy was in Marines Park, at the time, discussing an alarm system with officers of his company. Church bells had been used in England during the second World War, and there were bells in the Catholic and Episcopal churches. It was possible to evolve a code by which his troopers could understand the type and location of the emergency. The plane came over and everyone yelled, as before, as if they could hear up there. Then the leaflets fluttered down. They read:

DO NOT BE ALARMED

This leaflet comes from a United States Air Force plane conducting atmospheric surveys of the Contaminated Zones.

At a future date a more precise survey will be undertaken by helicopters.

Should a helicopter land in or near your community do not interfere with the activities of personnel aboard. Lend them your cooperation if requested.

This activity is an essential preliminary to bringing relief to the Contaminated Zones.

In a sense, it was disappointing. But it was something. It was something you could put your hands on, that you could feel, that had come from the outside. It was proof that the government of the United States still functioned. It was also useful as toilet paper. Next day, ten leaflets would buy an egg, and fifty a chicken. It was paper, and it was money.

In December the helicopter came. It made a fearful racket, wind-milling over Fort Repose. At various open spaces, including Marines Park, it hovered low and dropped a long wire from its belly, a small cylinder on the end of the wire actually touching the earth. It was like a gigantic bug dipping for honey.

It came up the Timucuan and circled the Bragg house.

The children were down at the dock; Helen and Lib were in the house; Randy was visiting with Sam Hazzard.

It circled four times. The two women ran up to the captain's walk. They had the best view. They waved their arms and then Helen took off her pink apron and waved that.

Inside the helicopter they saw faces and the pilot opened a window and waved back. Then it went away, up the Timucuan.

In five minutes Randy, the Admiral, and the children, all out of breath, were at the house.

Helen was weeping. "He waved!" she said. "He waved at us! Nobody else, us! I'm sure he came just to see us!"

"Now let's not get too excited," Randy said. "It may be that he was just looking for people—not anyone in particular—and saw the kids out on the dock and then circled the house to encourage us and give us heart."

Helen wiped her face with her apron. She said, "Oh, I wish he'd come back. Please, God, send him back!"

At that moment, they heard it coming back.

The children ran up to the roof. Randy went outside and sat on the porch steps. He was still out of breath and he wasn't going to run upstairs. If the damn helicopter wanted to see him it would have to come here. He couldn't go to it. Sam Hazzard sat down beside him.

Randy watched for it. From the sound he knew it was circling again. It came low over the trees and hovered over the lawn. Everything else was overgrown and choked with weeds and sprouting saplings but this single stretch between house and road Randy kept in lawn. It was one of Ben Franklin's chores to mow once a week, and it was a link between the house and the time before The Day, like shaving.

It hovered there and slowly lowered. Randy said, "It's coming in!" He rose to receive it.

Its wheels touched the ground, its engines cut off, and its rotors drooped and slowed. Peyton ran down the steps and Randy grabbed her. "Don't go out there until the rotors stop!" he ordered. "Cut your head off!"

Now that it was down, the helicopter looked ungainly and enormous. There were five men in it.

The rotors stopped.

They waited in stillness so complete that they heard the creak of hinges as the hatch opened. A metal ladder fell from its side and two men climbed down. Plastic helmets covered their heads and they were encased in silver, translucent plastic suits, oxygen tanks strapped to their backs. Like divers, Randy thought, or maybe Spacemen. Peyton and Ben Franklin had run out on the lawn. Now they shrank back. One of the men, laughing silently inside his helmet, held up his hand in a gesture, "Wait!"

The two men carried machines that looked like miniature vacuum cleaners, a cylindrical nozzle in one hand, an oblong black box in the other. They allowed these nozzles to sniff at grass and earth. "Geiger counters," Sam Hazzard said. "Maybe we're hot."

One of the men approached them, hesitated, and selected Randy. He bent over and allowed the nozzle to sniff Randy's last pair of boat shoes, big toe protruding through the canvas, soles reinforced with possum hide. The nozzle investigated the tattered shorts, the belt, and finally Randy's hair. At each point, the head in the helmet glanced at a dial in the box. It was very efficient.

The man swept off his helmet, slammed his hand on Randy's shoulder as if in congratulations, and called back to the helicopter, "Okay, Colonel. The terrain's clear and they're clears. You can come down."

His back toward them, a man climbed down. He wore a blue, zippered Air Force flight suit with the eagles of a full colonel on his shoulders.

When he turned and stepped forward, Randy did not immediately recognize him, he was so changed.

It was not until the man held out his hand, and spoke, that Randy saw it was Paul Hart, who had been a light colonel, sandy-haired instead of gray, his face cheery and freckled instead of lined and aged, when he saw him last. Randy could think of nothing to say except, "Come on in, Paul, and bring your people. We're just about to sit down for lunch."

Lib cried, "The quail!" and dashed into the house, letting the screen door bang.

"My wife," Randy said. "It's her lunch day."

"Your wife? Congratulations. My wife—I'll save it for later."

Randy saw that the men with the Geiger counters had stripped off their plastic suits. "You'll all have a drink before lunch?" he suggested, thinking that this had been the proper thing to say, long ago, and would still be proper and expected.

"Why, I'd be delighted!" Paul said. "I haven't had a drink since—" he asked a question: "You people haven't saved your liquor all this time, have you?"

"Oh, no. This stuff is new. Well, it's aged a bit. In a charcoal keg. We think it's very good."

He led them up to his apartment and mixed sours with the corn whiskey and fat, ripe limes. Then there were the introductions. There was a Captain Bayliss, the pilot, a Lieutenant Smith, chief radiologist, and the two sergeant technicians. They all considered the sour very good and Paul said, "It's impossible to find anything to drink, even in Denver. Not even beer. Shortage of grains, you know. Nobody would dare make his own whiskey in the clear zones. He'd go to jail. The older people say it's worse than prohibition."

There were a thousand questions Randy wanted to ask but at that moment he only had time for one because Lib called from downstairs. Lunch was ready. The men all wore brassards with the letters D.C. on the right arms. "What's that?" Randy asked, touching Paul's brassard. "District of Columbia?"

"Oh, no," Paul said. "There isn't any District of Columbia. Denver's the capital. That stands for Decontamination Command. It's the biggest command, nowadays, and really the only one that counts. I was seconded to the D.C. last spring. I put in for a C.Z. right away and asked for Florida and Florida was the C.Z. I got."

Paul Hart thought the soup was wonderful and said he had never tasted anything exactly like it before and Randy replied that he wasn't surprised. They always kept the big soup pot simmering on the fire and everything went into it. "This particular soup," he explained, "is sort of a combination. Armadillo, gopher, and turkey carcass."

Lib brought a dozen quail, and more were broiling, and placed pitchers of orange juice in front of them and they all drank it greedily. Captain Bayliss kept mumbling that he felt they were imposing, and that there were K-rations in the helicopter and that he actually expected to find C.Z. people all starving, because certainly most of them were in other parts of the country. He also kept on eating.

"How does it happen," Randy asked Hart, "that you found us?"

Hart said, "You haven't heard anything from my wife, Martha, have you?"

Randy shook his head, no, apprehending Paul's tragedy.

"Of course that's why I asked for duty in this C.Z. I wanted to find out what happened to Martha and the children." He looked up. "It was just a year ago, wasn't it, that I met you at McCoy Operations? Wasn't it on the day before H-Day?"

"H-Day? We just call it The Day."

"Hell Day or Hydrogen Day or The Day, it's the same thing."

"Yes. That was the last time I saw you."

"It was also the last day I saw Martha except to kiss her goodbye the next morning. Post-strike we went on to Kenya, in Africa. When I got back to this country I learned right away, of course, that McCoy received one. But it wasn't until I flew over Orlando last week that I gave up hope. I suppose you know what happened to Orlando."

Randy said, "Oh, no! Nobody's been that far off!"

"It's as if no man was ever there. Even the shapes of the lakes have changed and there are a couple of lakes that weren't there before. Find my wife? I couldn't even tell where my house stood. I think they must've dropped a five-megaton missile on McCoy and another on Orlando municipal. Nothing stands. Everything is burned and still hot. It's the damn C-14 that does it."

"C-14?"

"Radioactive carbon. It's half-life is more than five thousand years. That and U-238 and cobalt and stron-

tium is what makes rebuilding impractical in the T.D.—
the totally destroyed—cities. You have to start somewhere else, here for instance. Did you know that you
are living in the center of the largest clear area in the
whole C.Z.?"

"No, I didn't, but I'm glad to find out."

Helen had been waiting, tensely, to ask the question
that she must ask, yet knowing the answer before she
asked it; for had there been any other answer Paul
would have told her before now. She said, "Paul, nothing about Mark, I suppose?"

"I'm sorry, Helen. Nothing. There were a few survivors from Omaha but Mark wasn't one of them. After
all, it was a primary target with SAC Headquarters, Offutt Field—itself an important base—and the biggest
rail complex between Chicago and the Coast all
grouped together. I don't think we'll ever find out exactly what happened."

Helen nodded. "At least I know for sure. That's important—to know." No tears, Randy thought. He
glanced at the children. Ben Franklin stood firm, chin
outthrust, taut facial muscles containing his emotions.
But Peyton, eyes lowered, slipped away into the other
room.

Then for a long time Hart and the lieutenant radiologist questioned Randy and Sam Hazzard about the way
things had gone in Fort Repose, taking notes and showing remarkable interest in details of how the emergencies were met. "Of course we need everything," Randy
said, "but the town could get along fine if only we had
electricity because if they had power then they'd have
water. They wouldn't have to boil it or haul it from
springs, as they do now."

"It'll be a long time—a very long time," Hart said.
"Even major cities that weren't touched—cities in the
clear zones lost their electricity a month or so after H-
Day and don't have it back yet. The only towns which
have had uninterrupted power were those served by hy-
droelectric plants, provided the plants were undamaged
and the aqueducts intact. There aren't many."

"What about the other towns in the clear zones?" Randy asked. He noted how quickly you picked up the jargon of the post-Day age. It was like entering a totally new environment, like joining the Army.

"To have light," Paul said, "you either have to have water power or fuel. Most cities had supplies for a month or so. After that, darkness. Some of our big oil fields are still burning. The coal regions of Pennsylvania and West Virginia were saturated with fallout. But the transport problem is what really cripples us. Think what happened to the pipe lines, the railroads, the ports. Our big hope is atomic power. Thank goodness we still have a big stockpile of nuclear fuel."

The radiologist and the two technical sergeants excused themselves. They were going to the river to bottle water samples.

Randy said that if the river was hot they'd all be hot because ever since The Day they'd been living on the bounty of the river.

Hart said that apparently the river was going to be all right, and this was hopeful. "If we're going to get this C.Z. on the road back, I think I'd like to start in this area. Of course you understand, Randy, that before we can be of much help to the C.Z.'s we have to get the clear country in decent shape." He shook his head. "Some of our scientists think it will take a thousand years to restore a saturated C.Z., like Florida or New Jersey, to anything close to normal, even scratching the T.D. cities."

He talked of the cities that remained, and of the shortages, and the epidemics, and how fortunate they had been to live in Fort Repose. In the following year the government was going to take a census, including the contaminated zones if possible. "There's no use kidding ourselves," he went on. "We're a second class power now. Tertiary would be more accurate. I doubt if we have the population of France—or rather, a population as large as France used to have." He talked of farm areas out of production for an indefinite period, and how the South American nations had begun lend-lease

shipments to the northern continent, and how Thailand
and Indonesia were contributing rice. Eventually, it was
hoped that Venezuelan oil would alleviate the transport
fuel shortage, although he doubted that in his lifetime
he would again see gasoline for sale to private citizens.

They listened, their eyes marbled as if in shock.

The technicians returned from the river. Paul Hart
looked at his watch and said they would have to take
off. It was necessary that they drop into a small field
near Brunswick, Georgia, before dark. It was presently
his headquarters but in a few years he planned to re-
habilitate Patrick Air Force Base, on Cape Canaveral,
and transfer there. The enemy had overlooked Patrick,
perhaps deliberately since it was a test not an operational base, perhaps because the missile designed for it
had gone elsewhere. They would never know. Hart was
thoughtful for a moment. Then he spoke to Randy:

"You know, you and all your clear people can come
out if you want. Of course you'll have to have a physical and be officially cleared and processed but I doubt
that you'd have any trouble. I'll be back here in a week.
We're short on choppers but I could bring you out, two
or three at a time."

This was Randy's town and these were his people and
he knew he would not leave them. Yet it was not right
that he make this decision alone. He looked at Lib without finding it necessary to speak. She knowing what was
in his mind, simply smiled and winked. He said, "I
guess I'll stay, Paul."

"And the others?"

Randy wished Dan was with them and yet he was
confident he could speak for Dan. "We have our doctor
here, Dan Gunn. If it wasn't for Dan I don't think any
of us could have made it. He saved this town and I'm
sure he wouldn't want to leave now." He turned to Hel-
en. "Would he?"

Helen said quietly, "I wouldn't and he wouldn't."

"But there's one thing you have to do, Paul. Bring
supplies for our doctor."

"What's he need?"

"Everything. Everything that a hospital needs. But most of all he needs a new pair of glasses."

"I could requisition those for him, I think, if I had his prescription."

Helen said, "I know where it is. Don't you leave, Paul! Don't you dare!" She left the room and ran upstairs.

"What about you, Admiral Hazzard?" Paul asked. "What about the children? What about the two women who live across the road—the librarian and the telegraph gal?"

Sam Hazzard laughed. "Colonel, I have a fleet under my command. If the Navy Department will give me a fleet, I'll go with you. Not otherwise."

"We don't have any fleets," Paul Hart said. "All we've got left, really, are nuclear submarines. The subs saved us, I guess. The subs and the solid fuel rockets and some of the airborne missiles."

Lib said, "Alice Cooksey and Florence Wechek are in town but they were talking about the possibility of going out only a few nights ago. They'll both want to stay. You see, they're terribly busy. They've never worked so hard or accomplished so much in their whole lives. And I don't know what Fort Repose would do without them. They're practically our whole education system, and they keep all the records."

"Isn't anybody going?" Hart asked.

Ben Franklin said, "Not me!"

Peyton, who had quietly returned to the conference, said, "Me either."

Helen came downstairs with the prescription for Dan's glasses. They all walked out to the porch and Randy went out with Paul to the helicopter. They shook hands.

Randy said, "Paul, there's one thing more. Who won the war?"

Paul put his fists on his hips and his eyes narrowed. "You're kidding! You mean you really don't know?"

"No. I don't know. Nobody knows. Nobody's told us."

"We won it. We really clobbered 'em!" Hart's eyes lowered and his arms drooped. He said, "Not that it matters."

The engine started and Randy turned away to face the thousand-year night.

SPECIAL OFFER: If you enjoyed this book and would like to have our catalog of over 1,400 other Bantam titles, just send your name and address and 25¢ (to help defray postage and handling costs) to: Catalog Department, Bantam Books, Inc., 414 East Golf Rd., Des Plaines, Ill. 60016.

OUT OF THIS WORLD!

That's the only way to describe Bantam's great series of science-fiction classics. These space-age thrillers are filled with terror, fancy and adventure and written by America's most renowned writers of science fiction. Welcome to outer space and have a good trip!

☐	FANTASTIC VOYAGE by Isaac Asimov	2477	$1.25
☐	STAR TREK: THE NEW VOYAGES by Culbreath & Marshak	2719	$1.75
☐	THE MYSTERIOUS ISLAND by Jules Verne	2872	$1.25
☐	ALAS, BABYLON by Pat Frank	2923	$1.75
☐	A CANTICLE FOR LEBOWITZ by Walter Miller, Jr.	2973	$1.75
☐	RAGA SIX by Frank Lauria	7249	$1.25
☐	THE MARTIAN CHRONICLES by Ray Bradbury	7900	$1.25
☐	HELLSTROM'S HIVE by Frank Herbert	8276	$1.50
☐	HIERO'S JOURNEY by Sterling Lanier	8534	$1.25
☐	DHALGREN by Samuel R. Delany	8554	$1.95
☐	20,000 LEAGUES UNDER THE SEA by Jules Verne	8569	95¢
☐	STAR TREK XI by James Blish	8717	$1.75
☐	THE DAY OF THE DRONES by A. M. Lightner	10057	$1.25
☐	THE TOMBS OF ATUAN by Ursula LeGuin	10132	$1.75

Buy them at your local bookstore or use this handy coupon for ordering:

Bantam Books, Inc., Dept. SF, 414 East Golf Road, Des Plaines, Ill. 60016

Please send me the books I have checked above. I am enclosing $_____
(please add 35¢ to cover postage and handling). Send check or money order—
no cash or C.O.D.'s please.

Mr/Mrs/Miss_____

Address_____

City_____ State/Zip_____

SF—8/76

Please allow three weeks for delivery. This offer expires 8/77.

Bantam Book Catalog

It lists over a thousand money-saving best-sellers originally priced from $3.75 to $15.00 —bestsellers that are yours now for as little as 60¢ to $2.95!

The catalog gives you a great opportunity to build your own private library at huge savings!

So don't delay any longer—send us your name and address and 25¢ (to help defray postage and handling costs).

BANTAM BOOKS, INC.
Dept. FC, 414 East Golf Road, Des Plaines, Ill. 60016

Mr./Mrs./Miss_____
(please print)

Address_____

City_____State_____Zip_____

Do you know someone who enjoys books? Just give us their names and addresses and we'll send them a catalog too!

Mr./Mrs./Miss_____

Address_____

City_____State_____Zip_____

Mr./Mrs./Miss_____

Address_____

City_____State_____Zip_____

FC—7/76